David Murray is a part time autho
first novel. His second, Prosperity
Publishing next year. He is curren
stories.

D1589319

Special thanks go to the following without whose help this novel
may not have happened: Paula Lingard for all the initial proofing
and ideas; Matt Harrison and Tina Crockett for publishing advice;
Julie Cutts for the design work and motivation to get me to publish
it; and Hambros Bank for the inspiration. Thanks to all those who
read the novel and gave feedback. A final thanks to Charles
Fremuth, my school English teacher, who changed my world.

Enjoy the read -

David Murray

Fiddles Retreat 21/5/04

Please let me know your
thoughts on david.murray
@ bbc.co.uk.

First published in Great Britain by Boris Publishing 2002

A CIP catalogue record for this book is available from the British Library.

ISBN 0-9543344-0-X

Printed in England by Antony Rowe Limited

Boris Publishing
56 St Andrews Wharf
Shad Thames
London SE1 2YN

www.borispublishing.com

The Naked Bank

by David Murray

Boris Publishing

For Mum and Dad

The Naked Bank

September

As the tube trains rumbled, their packed and antiquated frames struggling towards the City, a sleek limo slumbered, cruising across town, no faster than the underground but a good deal more profound. In its reclining, black leather backseat rode James Carter, a man with ideas above his station, an upstart, a time bomb to blast the establishment from its bunker. His companion Giles Bonnier, slept in the corner, worn out by corporate exertions, chasing Carter's rainbow. As he snored, Carter jawed, gently talking to his wife, Caroline, then mother of his children but not his confidant. To her he was a successful business man, father, and childhood sweetheart. Away from home, he was something more sinister. If she was his Hillary Rodham, then work was his Monica Lewinsky. His secrets belonged Bonnier, his Eleanor Roosevelt. Plenty of advice but no sex.

"The trip went well, darling. It looks like matters will be tied up today. I've booked the jet for tomorrow...yes...yes..you can tell the kids we're going to Disneyland....I love you too...See you tonight."

Bonnier's snoring grew louder as they hit a pothole, bouncing his head back against the seat. Carter nudged him.

"Wake up, Giles, we're almost there." At this hour of the morning he needed a break from the man's tonsils.

Bonnier came to, smacking his lips.

"I was having a great dream."

Carter was not interested in Bonnier's fantasies, long bored of his boorishness.

"I'm sure you were. We'll be at Gilbert's soon. Why don't you shave and make yourself look a bit respectable."

David Murray

Bonnier pulled the mirror in front of him and examined his stubble, both hands pulling on his face. Reaching into his bag, easily stowed in the vast backseat area, he pulled out his electric razor. Carter stared out the window, immaculately turned out, an ironed white handkerchief poking from the breast pocket of his tailored suit. As the limo pulled up, Bonnier combed his hair, and with a prompt, straightened his tie.

"How do I look?" he asked.

"Beautiful, simply beautiful."

Bonnier laughed for Carter was the boss.

The driver opened the door and they both hopped out, Bonnier tugging an oversized briefcase, Carter a small satchel.

"Thanks driver," said Carter forgetting the man's name. "Take the baggage back to the office. We'll pick it up later. Then go home. I'll call if we need you."

"Very good, Mr Carter."

"Come on Giles, snap to it."

Bonnier eyes were closing before being jolted open. "Sorry, I didn't get much sleep last night."

"What you do in hotel rooms isn't my concern. Drink more coffee or something."

Through the unimposing glass doors, after observing the usual security formalities, they were greeted by Byron Black. He led them upstairs, deep into the heart of Gilbert, Wilkins & Horsefly, a City firm of solicitors of impeccable character - they had never been caught. Black was the brightest star.

"My secretary's not in yet, so I'm afraid there's no coffee. She shouldn't be long. Please come in."

They followed him into his office, sitting down around sofas. Bonnier wondered how long the coffee would take as he forced himself to concentrate. The walls were covered with photographs of yachts, several featuring Black's windswept cheeks. A large desk dominated the room, lacking the usual piles of paper that lawyers enjoy having around them. A tidy in-tray and a family photo gave the impression the man was on holiday. Perhaps he worked elsewhere. Tidiness was a foreign concept to Bonnier's cluttered mind. He lit a cigarette, oblivious to a prominent 'no smoking' sign. Black said nothing. These men were his biggest clients.

The Naked Bank

Carter spoke. "We have a meeting at three with Forrest to agree the deal..."

Black nodded.

"...Before then, I thought it would be useful to set things in motion for Bluebird."

"Bluebird?" asked Black, wary of acting prematurely.

"It's the code word for the CRA. Our next target."

"The whole thing?" Black was incredulous. "Its massive." His legal mind whirled. "Technically very difficult."

Carter tolerated Black's spontaneous advice. Months of planning meant he knew the potential pitfalls, knew the deal was possible. Would be done. And would make him millions, hundreds of millions, billions, a lot of dosh. "Thank you Byron, but I am aware of the difficulties. Giles."

Bonnier drifted back from high seas adventure. The long ash from his cigarette dropped to the sofa, making a small mark before he thoughtfully brushed it onto the Persian rug. Slapping the butt between his lips, Bonnier opened his crammed pilot case and tugged out a chewed looking folder from the middle of the crush. After a quick press against his chest to straighten it, he passed the document across the sofa divide to a remarkably placid Black, who secretly vowed for the hundredth time never again to allow this man in his office.

"Thank you," he said as he took the file and opened it on his lap.

"That contains our initial thoughts and research," said Bonnier, his cigarette hanging on his every word. "It lists all the information we will need and notes its expected source. You'll see there are a number of legal papers you can get started on."

"But we're flat out on Dedalus," protested Black.

"You're a large firm, find someone. Why do you think I pay you so much?" Carter stood to leave as he spoke. "You'll also see a structure I've devised for the operation. I'd be most grateful, if its not too much trouble, for you to set up the companies as outlined. Think up your own names, just make sure they're unrelated."

Black started to read the front page of Carter's jottings.

"Good," said Carter. "We're off to breakfast. See you at three."

David Murray

"Yes, see you at three," Black replied. There was a lot of work. Christine would be busy.

*****

Fergus felt a strong desire to kiss the woman standing next to him. He glanced at her features, radiant as the morning light brightened. Chosen by the gods, she was perfect. Perfect for his new lease of life. For this morning he was reborn, a superman. An investment banker. An open door to explore the mysteries of serious money.

Perception can alter a man. To Janet he was unchanged as he kissed her in bed, the usual routine. As her sleepy lips touched his, it was different. He felt dynamic, she lay snoozing. His was a new look, a new feel, a new uniform, proudly displayed on that platform for the first time. A pale, chalk stripped, navy suit, tailored, he had been reliably informed, somewhere close to Saville Row. Regulation mock army tie, a combination of blue and red diagonal stripes. A Thomas Pink striped shirt the final piece in this clashing montage.

As he stepped onto the Northern Line train, cosmetically his image seemed in the bag. As the stranger lightly jumped ahead of him, he gave thanks to destiny. She would be his Mistress of the Universe, there beside him as he strove towards the summit of achievement. A mother for his children, a diplomat for his superiors, an entertainer for his colleagues. As Janet dozed, he chose.

Confidence is fleeting. His superficial dominance disappeared as his new leather soles slipped on the carriage step, propelling him head first into the waiting bosom of the woman of his dreams. Betrayed by destiny, he embraced her. Well endowed in more ways than one, she possessed a strength of purpose carefully honed in the corporate gym. Many months of sacrificing lunch to the greater morality of step aerobics allowed her to stand firm in the face of this unexpected morning rush.

"Excuse me," he muffled to no reply.

Fergus hastily stepped backwards, inadvertently colliding with the inert passengers following behind.

"Sorry," cried another woman as he cracked the back of her

6

The Naked Bank

shins.

She moved back setting off a chain reaction. Carnage ensued as bodies bounced. One polite unfortunate was even forced straight back onto the platform, just as the doors closed. His stare at Fergus through the departing window was one of shock rather than anger.

Fergus managed to ricochet into a empty seat, much to the amusement of the woman, his cover of credibility blown. With communication on the tube strictly forbidden, a slight smirk was sufficiently damming before being hidden behind a pristine FT.

Without the comfort of his own pink paper, there was nothing to prevent his eyes making accidental contact with other passengers. Rather than cause social *faux pas*, he checked his finely polished black brogues for scuff marks. In the general melee he had felt a shoe heel on his toes and his suspicions were confirmed when he saw a slight mark on the tip of his new left shoe. Ordinarily, Fergus would have made a mental note to give the shoe a quick buff once he arrived at work. Being an unordinary day, he preferred to make a fool of himself.

In lifting his left leg, and then rubbing it behind his right, he managed to convey the impression of a man uneasy with his pants. Worse, the woman of his dreams, only pretending to read her FT, witnessed this ongoing contortion act. Who was the idiot? After a few rubs, quite by accident, Fergus caught her glance before it quickly returned to its safe haven behind an article on the single currency. While not a particularly robust defence, it served its purpose.

Fergus returned to the task of innocuously doing nothing. Fiddling with his cufflinks filled some time. As did reading the tube advertisements, and pretending to be interested. Had he not always wanted to own his own portable office air conditioning unit? Until now he hadn't realised how affordable they were.

As his eye lingered on the photograph of the first auto-flush water closet, displayed in the new Lottery funded London Museum of Plumbing, his gaze uncomfortably dropped once more to take in the woman opposite. From a more relaxed distance of several feet, he observed her features while pretending to read the front page of her raised paper.

David Murray

Here was a City woman who knew her style. Low heeled shoes spoke volumes about her confidence in her ability. No need to be artificially raised, I'm as tall as the next man. A blue tailored suit was set off by Hermes scarf and the pre-requisite string of cheap pearls. She wore a skirt rather than trousers, revealing, apart from an elegant leg, that she was not American. The skirt was short, but not unprofessionally so. Blue tights confirmed she was a Sloane, by far the most common sub-group of women in the City. It was Fergus's wish to duplicate the male of the species, the Putney Lad. Her lack of flirting gave cause to question the success of his strategy.

The train stopped at Moorgate and she rose. Her hair was brown and bobbed, her make up understated. Her nose was cute, not too small, turned slightly up to indicate a superior social position. Her neck blushed ever so slightly as she felt prying eyes. Straightening her skirt, she picked up her briefcase and alighted, all so much without a glimpse at her soul mate. Fergus was in love, his eyes following her trail as she walked slowly towards the exit, escorted by a hundred others, all herded towards the surface. Then he remembered Janet.

*****

Christine Edgerley tossed the newspaper in the bin next to a bent bouquet, a gift from yesterday's unwanted admirer. She couldn't recall his name, the card was unopened.

Her office was small and compact, piled with files, drafts, books, periodicals and the odd Cosmopolitan. She stepped her way to her desk, avoiding the fragile towers of paper, mostly sorted by client. Mostly.

She drank yesterday's coffee. Cold, but she drank it all the same. Breakfast appeared from her briefcase, a croissant, and was carefully laid out on a napkin amidst the mess. The pile to her left was her in-tray to be completed today, the pile to her right needed clearing before the Three O'clock. The thought was enough to induce a headache, the remedy being a bottle of paracetemol stored in her top drawer. Her cup was empty. More coffee required.

Retracing her path out of her room, she passed to the kitchen on the far side of the floor. Her office was tucked by the

The Naked Bank

stairs. Less likely to be bothered by colleagues with little else to do but chat. Someone had to finish all the work around here.

The kitchen was pokier than might be expected for such a prestigious law firm. A basin, a kettle, a pint of milk and assortment of instant coffee granules, both in a jar and on the counter, a Tupperware container of budget tea bags, a mangy bag of sugar and the remnants of yesterday's spillage. A machine for making filter coffee stood idly by, no one having bothered to buy ground coffee for several months. She preferred instant anyway, both the taste and the quickness.

Once made, she popped pills before scanning the empty department. No life following last night's office party. The place would fill by lunch, in time for traditional hair of the dog remedies. By then her right hand pile would be half cleared.

It was always difficult summoning up enough energy to work in the morning. She had left the office at midnight, missing the party which was a relief. her latest admirer was there and she found office flings so messy. She preferred the silence of the mostly dark office, illuminated by only the odd night owl. If no-name really wanted to impress he could take some of her work. Until then she was happy with her fountain pen and the occasional conversation with Byron.

The caffeine from the coffee began to kick in, jump starting her brain. Byron was in, his door closed. Who was with him at this hour?

Returning to her office she ate breakfast while contemplating this question. She worked exclusively for the senior partner who normally told her everything. This was no internal meeting. Not after last night's drinks. So what was he up to?

Leaving her door open to hear Byron open his, she pulled the first document from the top of the pile, sighing when she remembered it had finally driven her to leave last night. Delving into the middle pages she resumed her painful progress.

It wasn't long before she heard voices. In the corridor that is. The meeting over, she crept to her doorway without revealing herself. The mysterious guests were Carter and Bonnier. Her clients. So why wasn't she invited?

They were bound to take the lift rather than her stairs She

listened from her spot without risk of detection. There was not even small talk, Bonnier in no mood to chat, Carter despising irrelevant conversation. The lift pinged and they were gone.

Nonchalantly she strolled to Byron's office. Keep cool she kept repeating to herself.

"Byron, was that James Carter I just saw?"

There was no point denying it. "Yes, I didn't realise you were in."

"Why didn't you tell me they were coming?" She could be disrespectful when tired.

"It was nothing. I didn't want to bring you in early. You need your sleep."

"Thanks, but I think I can decide that. What did they want?"

"A few more requests. I'll inform you when I'm ready," he said re-enforcing his authority.

"I'd appreciate it." Christine's manner was corporate happy while inside she fumed.

"Oh, and Christine," Black said as a matter of fact. "I appreciate all your help. We all do. I'd like you to have this."

He handed her an envelope from his inside jacket pocket.

"What is it?" she said sharply in no mood to be palmed off.

"Just my way of saying thanks. Go and buy something pretty."

She opened it and found Selfridges vouchers. Many Selfridges vouchers. Five hundred pounds worth. She was speechless.

"Thanks again. I'll see you at three," said Byron.

Christine ran along like a good little girl. Her reward a shopping trip. What century did the man live in? She was livid at his assumptions, livid at being sidelined from the meeting, just plain livid. Yet despite everything she felt pleased with his recognition. Nothing wrong with an unexpected gift, she thought as she tossed the empty envelope in the bin, the vouchers safely in her handbag.

*****

The entrance to the Bank was either a disappointment or a

statement of restraint. There were no fountains, no marble pillars. No atrium swirling high into the stratosphere. There were no second rate Renaissance paintings displaying the Bank's wealth. No deep piled carpet to welcome fee-paying clients. There was no complicated electronic tagging system allowing employees to pass the security guards with a knowing assurance. Instead a rather bland entryway lead to a bank of faceless lifts. A security desk was placed out of the way as an afterthought. This building had won no architectural awards. Prince Charles had not criticised its lego-like style for clashing with the busy ring road that swept past its revolving door. Apart from those who worked there, very few even recognised its presence.

Fergus did not mind this lack of grandeur. His previous firm threw up fountains and bathed in fine marble. Such extravagance almost bankrupt the company, keeping his salary below his own self-inflated worth. To Fergus the Bank's modesty was a clear indicator it was here to make money, nothing else. Money for itself, and more importantly, for its staff.

With a self confidence born of optimism, Fergus swung through the revolving door and strode to the security desk.

"I'm here to see Jennifer Bu Gerrie."

"Good morning, Fergus," Ms Bu Gerrie shouted in a matronly tone before the door was even half open. It was not until she was half way through, "Did you have any trouble finding us?" that he secured a first glimpse of the Corporate Finance Personnel Director. Designer Frump. Neither attractive nor unattractive, neither overweight nor underweight, neither tall nor short, her hemline was neither up nor down. Her hair was as non-descript as her skirt. She was the ideal personnel officer - inconspicuous.

"No trouble at all," said Fergus. "With all the interviews I feel like an old timer already."

"Of course you do."

Miss Bu Gerrie's words were clipped, rapid and struggled to keep up with her thoughts. He also suspected she was slightly deaf.

There was a pause, during which Bu Gerrie seemed to weigh up her options, starring at the coffee pot as if perplexingly

11

familiar.

"Shall I be mother?" she finally said.

There was no objection.

Miss Bu Gerrie served treacle coffee for Fergus. Tea for herself.

"I'm glad you finally made it," Miss Bu Gerrie said after taking a delicate sparrow sip.

Fergus was unsure of her meaning and so remained silent. Miss Bu Gerrie was awkward, a peacock twitching with indecision.

"I have a Confidentiality Agreement for you to sign, our version of the Official Secrets Act."

A joke. She paused for applause.

Miss Bu Gerrie thrust a handful of paper at Fergus as she continued,

"Once you have signed it, we can allow you into the department."

Fergus looked up for a moment, and if he had worn glasses would have quizzically peered over their top. He then continued reading, to ensuring he was not about to enter some sort of Faustian pact. Miss Bu Gerrie was no Mephistopheles. But they say the devil's a lot subtler these days. A personnel department would be the ideal base to wreak havoc on the world.

A quick scan of the fifteen page document and Fergus signed at the spot indicated by Miss Bu Gerrie's bony finger.

"There's one other thing..."

Miss Bu Gerrie let her sentence hang in the air.

"Yes," prompted Fergus.

"The small matter of your....reference."

"Yes," sunk Fergus.

"Well, we've not......received it yet. I'm sure its just an oversight and we're not really concerned about it," she said playing her position of power for all it was worth, her tongue lightly clicking between phrases, "but we do need it - otherwise you just never know..."

Again she allowed her cadence to trail expectantly.

"I'll chase it up."

"That would be super." she said as she clasped her hands in anticipation.

The Naked Bank

The department was separated from the reception area by a pair of frosted glass doors.

"Your team's over there."

Miss Bu Gerrie pointed her finger across a large space resembling an airport lounge both in terms of openness, overcrowding and random placing of people and objects. There were numerous desks, grouped together, each containing diligent bodies surrounded by mounds of paper. Paper not just piled on the desk, but on the floor, on shelves and even on top of each computer terminal. Paper poked out of draws, filled bins and spilt out of half open briefcases. Even the closed briefcases seemed to bulge grandly with their contents, no doubt, of paper. Paper churned from printers, fed through faxes and spewed forth from high powered copying machines. It was everywhere, impossible to avoid, and clearly illustrated how hard the department was working. The disorder impressed Fergus. To his tidy accounting mind he felt certain it represented creativity.

Those not buried underneath their produce, hurried forth, not running yet walking far faster than natural. Their whole demeanour was one of industry. No time for trivia, I have papers to read, to write, to post, to shred, to copy and to file. They criss-crossed each other, too busy to pass the time of day. Up and down the office, to the printer, to the copier, to the fax machine, and most importantly to the coffee machine. Maintain that buzz.

Fergus walked slowly and carefully as Miss Bu Gerrie guided him across the floor of the department. He stepped over each piece of paper littering the carpet, stepped clear of every through coming executive, and genuinely felt overwhelmed. Miss Bu Gerrie, however, was unfazed as she slowly steered him towards the centre of the maelstrom, bobbing her head to the important, ignoring the drones.

And then there it was. The oasis amidst the blur, an empty desk. Well, not quite empty. It suffered from overflow, for what is an empty surface if not for attracting paper. As Fergus looked as his space, Miss Bu Gerrie introduced his new lord and master.

"John, may I introduce you to Fergus McKay. Fergus, this is John Snead." Bu Gerrie stumbled, struggling to pluck the names from her mental address book.

Snead rose and shook Fergus's hand vigorously, so much so that it ached for several hours afterwards. Snead was tall, athletic, with a full head of neatly trimmed jet black hair. His suit was smart, very English, and dark grey. His shirt white, his tie spotted. The contrast with Fergus's own garb could not have been greater.

"Great to have you on board, Fergus. We've been looking forward to your arrival for some time now." Snead spoke with Etonian grace.

"Really?" was all Fergus could muster, perplexed.

*****

"So you can see, the valuation we could achieve through a trade sale would not be substantially greater than the offer on the table."

Claire loved the limelight. The eyes of the room were upon her. She continued.

"It seems a good deal."

"Thanks Claire," responded Forrest, "That's excellent."

Claire Snow felt a swell of pride as her boss praised her in front of the client. Working flat out for the past week, she barely remembered the last time she had enjoyed a full night's sleep. Adrenaline kept her going, the buzz of the deal, the lure of the bonus and the satisfaction of a job well done. She felt proud to be working for such an established institution as the Bank and welcomed the opportunity to be involved with such prestigious and entrepreneurial clients.

Across the table sat James Carter, her most important client during her short, but upwardly mobile, career. Carter was a genius, a financial arbitrageur. A man who bought and sold companies to make money. He was not interested in the long-term merits of a company, only its trading potential. He made a lot of money. The Bank a healthy fee.

It was Claire's work that earned that fee. Sure, Hayden Forrest had won the business, but all the graft in preparing the documentation was Claire's. As was a possible promotion.

Up until this point James Carter remained silent. He had

14

listened to both Snow and Forrest present their case. His mind was made up the moment he entered the room.

"I agree - the offer's too good to pass up. We'll take the cash and use it for our next little venture."

The lure of further fees prompted Forrest to ask,

"What do you have in mind James?"

"Given the success of buying Dedalus out of CRA, we'll be examining other opportunities in the same area. Its premature to discuss, but I'm sure it will generate substantial fees for you guys. You've done well. You've both done well."

Both Forrest and Snow recognised this double edged compliment, the offer of large future fees an indication the Bank would have to accept a modest fee for the current assignment. No matter, Forrest felt the subject had to be raised.

"Speaking of fees," he began, then paused to gauge the feeling in the room. As there was no reaction, he continued, "we need to finalise the amount for Dedalus."

"What do you have in mind?" asked Carter, placing the initiative on Forrest to open the negotiation.

"Well, although its been a straight forward transaction, there's been a substantial time cost..."

"Yes, get on with it," Carter interrupted, not in the mood for all this positioning. He knew exactly how much effort the Bank had injected into the process. Not a lot. He brought them the deal.

"Five hundred thousand pounds?" nervously ventured the bank director. He hated discussing money.

"What do you think, Giles?"

Next to Carter sat Giles Bonnier, his assistant and holder of the purse strings. Carter rarely deferred to Bonnier and it surprised his audience.

Bonnier had been a high flyer at one of the large US investment banks before joining Carter and his amazing gravy train.

"I think that seems reasonable."

Forrest was relieved. Bonnier's approval meant they were sure to get the fee. Claire was more than happy. She had managed to generate five hundred thousand pounds with two weeks work. Even if she did nothing else for the rest of the year, her bonus already looked healthy.

"I disagree," said Carter, leaning back in his chair and placing his hands behind his head.

The words were greeted with a sharp intake of breath around the table. Split second calculations re-evaluating bonuses.

"It's important both sides recognise our relationship. We want to use the Bank on our next deal. Fifteen times the size of this one..."

Fifteen times! The selling price for Dedalus was £100 million. That meant...riches.

"...I think a gesture will help cement that relationship."

Here came the let down. Claire nervously shuffled in her chair trying desperately not to show her disappointment.

"I'll give you a million."

Forrest managed to keep a straight face. After all he was experienced in such matters, although even he could never recall such a gesture. Claire broke into a broad grin then forced her lips over her teeth. It wasn't professional to demonstrate greed in front of a client.

"That's very generous," was all Forrest could muster.

"Not at all. A down payment. I'll expect your full co-operation."

"Naturally."

"Good. Accept the offer. Giles'll sign all the paperwork. Byron will handle the contracts. Its past four and I have to go. Its been a pleasure."

And then the roadshow moved on. Carter, Bonnier, Black, a lawyer from Gilbert, Wilkins and Horsefly, and his female associate, whose name Claire had not quite caught, all collectively stood and left the room.

Normally Forrest would have shown his clients out but today it would have ruined Carter's sense of drama. And Carter very much enjoyed his demonstrations of power. In his absence, Forrest and Claire broke into broad grins and for the first time Claire felt like hugging her portly boss. But she didn't.

*****

16

The Naked Bank

*****

Same meeting, but to new boy Fergus a different perspective. This was Room One, where the big meetings took place. There was space for twenty around the large board table. It hosted seven, clustered at one end.

The participants had been introduced, a kind touch given his lowly status. What he did not realise, until later, was that to the outside world he was a mergers and acquisitions executive, an authority on the subject. That was what the client paid for.

There were two distinct sides to the table. On Fergus's side sat the Bank men. Fergus was at the end of the row with Claire Snow his immediate neighbour. Claire was a member of his team. He was impressed by the quality of her input to the meeting and the attentiveness given her by the other side. She was clearly very good.

To Claire's left sat Hayden Forrest, a Director of the Bank and regarded by many as a big hitter. A small man, with a client

17

David Murray

Forrest was large in stature. Completely bald, a small moustache dominated his upper lip, seemingly quivering whenever he became excited. His clothes were neat and unremarkable save for a slightly bulging waistcoat. Forrest was relatively new to the department, headhunted to help originate new business. The chairs to Forrest's left were empty.

Facing Fergus sat the client, James Carter and his entourage. Carter was neither skinny nor plump, his face possessing no feature of note. Average eyebrows guarded an average nose which overhung an unremarkable mouth. His chin could not be described as rugged and lacked a Spartican dimple, but neither did it resemble hundreds of years of aristocratic in-breeding. His hair, however, was immense. Wild and floppy, his black locks swept over his forehead giving him the corporate presence which comes with all good mops. Most of the time the hair was stationary while its owner trained his eyes upon the speaker. Only when he spoke, which he tended to do with exaggerated mannerisms, did his hair burst fully into life, bouncing back and forward like an untamed beast. More than sufficient to give a crucial concentration advantage when intensely negotiating. For no matter how hard Fergus attempted to listen to the words, it was always the hair that triumphed.

Carter was flanked by Giles Bonnier, a man who resembled a corporate hitman, and Byron Black, a lawyer, and didn't he know it, exuding all the smooth charm of a man who has seen it all before, and wasn't flustered the first time. He spoke slowly, choosing each word with the care that comes from charging four hundred pounds an hour. Or five pounds a word. But what value each word represented. So carefully formed they meant something to everyone, no matter how contrary their point of view. The words placated, soothed and convinced, so much so it was only after he was long gone that his audience realised he had said nothing at all.

Finally there was Christine Edgerley. As soon as he laid eyes upon her, Fergus realised they had met before. It took several minutes of rummaging his mind before it struck him with the impact of an amorous ferret up an overly tight trouser leg. She was the woman of his dreams. And she stared at him with a disbelieving sneer of superiority that made his stomach sink. He was the bag man, she was the heavyweight lawyer. He was nothing, and didn't she just know it.

*****

Christine was uncomfortable. She found herself crammed in the back of the black taxicab with nowhere to put her legs. Being the junior, it was her role to sit on the cramped swing seat behind the driver. Her boss took the other, more spacious, swing seat, whilst James Carter sat opposite him in comfort. Giles sat across from Christine in the other proper seat, and while he was of average build, his legs occupied the bulk of the available space.

Christine tried to avoid rubbing against his trousers, but in drawing in her own legs she only succeeded in raising them, along with her knees, and thus her short skirt, adding to her embarrassment. She was perched with a bulging briefcase on her lap, reducing any manoeverabilty, including being able to lower her skirt. Giles made no attempt to make the scene any easier, staring quite openly at her squeamishness. He was the client and she just had to lump it. Besides, she could hardly interrupt his phone conversation, only making it more galling that he stared while casually conversing to an important business contact on his mobile.

"...so are we in the same ballpark here, Bob..."

As soon as the group had jumped in the taxi the three mobile phones ambushed her. James had of course led the way and probably did have an important call to make. He was important.

"...come on Joe, it's a slam dunk deal..."

Giles quickly followed giving him the opportunity to ogle her. Feeling left out, Byron also pulled his phone from his briefcase and called the office.

"Hi Fiona, its me....Any messages...I'm in the taxi...Are you sure there're no messages....I'll be there in ten minutes....Ok, bye."

Christine had her own phone but thought twice about retrieving it. Buried at the bottom of her briefcase she dreaded to think what she might reveal to Giles attempting to fish it out. So she stayed still. At least as still as she could given Giles's twitching foot forcing her constantly to slightly readjust her position.

She hated not being taken seriously. She hated being the bag carrier. To her friends she was a high profile lawyer, always able

19

to earnestly discuss her latest exploits. Her achievements always seemed so worthy in the telling. In the doing they were mundane, even humiliating. One day she would sit in the big seat. One day she would eye up some fresh faced graduate opposite, her toes up his trouser leg. In the meantime it was essential to maintain that aura of competence, and try not to contemplate the greasy pole.

*****

Giles leaned back in the taxi only to find his legs restricted by Byron's sidekick sitting opposite. As he chatted to Bob Brady on the phone, one of Mr Carter's many business associates, he stared at the female lawyer. She seemed most uncomfortable, a real case of ants in her pants. What might it be like for that ant, he wondered before his thoughts moved on, fascinated by her jumpy movements, feeling almost sorry for the difficult position she clearly found herself in. The eye naturally wanders when the brain is engaged in telephone conversation. Giles's eye initially worked its way up and down the lawyer's body with no more than a passing interest in her appearance. Her blouse was half untucked from her skirt, which in itself was desperately trying to contract into the sartorial equivalent of the foetal position. Her case snagged her tights. While she squirmed, he watched the run slowly ascend, picking up a head of steam. A polite man would have averted his gaze. Giles was not polite.

Bob Brady continued his monologue and Giles's gaze shifted to Byron Black. The man was a bundle of nervous energy, but unlike his colleague, experience taught him to channel it. Instead of fidgeting, he sat quite still, with the exception of his head darting to and fro as if fearful the Old Bill were chasing him in connection with a criminal drafting error.

Black wore grey, lifted by a stripe as strong as the opinions he offered. His shoes were well polished, his suit well creased, his white shirt well starched. All to be expected from a man with such a nose for detail. His long, angular beak gave him an almost hawk like manner, his jumpy head movements reinforcing the image. Giles lost interest in the legal bird of prey and returned to the woman whose name he had forgotten.

The Naked Bank

She appeared fit, probably worked out. His thoughts stared at his own stomach, bulging over the edge of once carefully tailored trousers. He must get in shape. Opportunity was restricted by the tireless rounds of breakfasts, lunches and dinners his business required. A diet for the New Year, perhaps. There was no point during the run-up to Christmas. Besides it would be miserable.

The thought of fitness was stressful and he pulled out a packet of Marlboro with his free hand. The sign said "No Smoking." A good fifteen minutes since his last fag, the tension was rising. Brady waited for a Giles to continue the conversation, wondering why it was so one sided. Still holding the mobile, Giles relaxed as he flicked a cigarette from its packet. Not the cardboard imitations available in the UK but the genuine American soft pack. They were flown in by a business associate who knew how to appeal to Giles's weakness. Once back-flipped into the corner of his mouth, a gold lighter went to work on the cigarette, igniting the tobacco with a single finger movement. Swiss precision. Giles pulled the window down and took a drag, aware of the woman's disbelief at his willingness to break the rules. Anti-smoking fascist. He shrugged at her, thinking she should relax and forget about her precious law school principles. No longer relevant, dear, no longer relevant.

"Hey, mate. Would you mind putting that fag out."

The blast from the cabby was as inevitable as it was sharp.

"Why's that," he returned playfully, taking another puff.

"Can't you read the bloody sign?"

The woman's satisfied features read, *"I told you so."*

"Sorry. Didn't notice. How about a tenner tip to compensate."

Giles took another drag with no intention of putting out the cigarette. The driver turned back to the traffic, only partially satisfied, muttering something about fat cats.

Everyone and everything has its price. That price was less than twenty pounds, the value Giles currently placed on a good smoke.

Carter paid no attention to Giles. He was used to these little foibles and accepted them as part of the package. His man was a good investment.

It was not Black's place to question the client.

David Murray

The woman continued to stare. So uptight. Clearly needs a good shag.

"Stop the cab," yelled Carter suddenly.

The cab pulled over after a few yards.

"Here OK mate?" the driver questioned.

"Fine. We're getting out here Giles," stated Carter before leaping out and striding down the street with purpose, phone conversation on-going. Giles gathered his case.

"Ring me later and we'll discuss the next steps," he said to Black.

"About five?"

"Yes, but no later. I've got a flight to catch."

Giles hopped onto the pavement, struggling to escape the cab as he dragged his over hanging belly and over flowing pilot case in one hand, and half finished cigarette in the other. Just as he turned to shut the door he again noticed the woman's stare of disbelief.

"Oh, and bye the way, darling," he said for no reason other than he could, "You've got a run in your tights."

With that he slammed the door and turned to follow his rapidly disappearing boss, having forgotten the insult as if having dealt with an annoying insect. If he had cared, he might have notice her expression was more than black.

*****

Another meeting, another profession, another building.

Lara Waters was biting her tongue. Perhaps twenty minutes ago Hogg Midgely and floozy had purposely strolled into her audit room. Hogg adopted a regal air, expecting her to perform the role of sycophantic courtier. Lara's assistant, William Hudson, had taken this unexpected audience with the Partner as reason to duck out and make the coffee. A traditional function of a junior, without doubt, but his willingness to leave the room, and clear sloth in returning, made her blood boil almost as much as Hogg's boorish behaviour. She was alone with a Neanderthal, Middle Aged "Lad", adorned with fawning floozy.

Hogg was sitting on her chair, leaning back on the chair

22

The Naked Bank

against the wall, his shoeless feet splayed on her desk. Leafing through the files, he coughed, hacked and frequently scratched his balls. His suit was crumpled, his crotch well worn.

Every time Hogg didn't understand Lara's written comments, he launched a question at her, propelled like a fart from between his buttocks. The obvious explained, he would re-bury his head in the papers, thinking she could not see him picking his nose. The file presented no barrier to her view of his feet, cased in holed socks, reeking like an extra mature Albanian goat's cheese. If a person's smell is indicative of their health, Hogg was clearly at death's door. A few days of decomposition would offer pungent relief.

During this interrogation, Fifi Flynn sat quietly on the other side of the small room, avoiding the occasional glare of Lara and seeking eye contact with Hogg whenever his head surfaced. It was common knowledge that Fifi, a new graduate, was sleeping with Hogg. What was so amazing was the openness of their affair. Hogg asked for Fifi to be assigned to all his jobs and then proceeded to use her as a very personal assistant.

"So what does this sentence mean?" asked Hogg wafting the words across the room.

"Which sentence do you mean - I can't see the file," said Lara trying to retain her composure. She sat on a wonky chair directly in front of the big man, forced to sit straight or else topple over backwards.

"This one about salary levels not being properly approved."

Lara remembered the page, which was fortunate given Hogg's reluctance to share her own work with her.

"It seems Mr Rodgers pays himself more than approved by the remuneration committee."

"So." His gut wobbled as he spoke, his elongated nose hairs quivered.

"Well, strictly speaking it falls foul of the Cadbury Code."

"Oh, I see."

Hogg scratched his balls as he pondered the problem.

"You don't expect me to put this in the accounts do you?"

Lara remained silent for there was no satisfactory answer. It was his job to tell her.

David Murray

"I don't think there's any need to get heavy about this. I'll have a quiet word with Rodgers and sort it out. Don't you think?"

Lara stayed quiet.

"Don't you think?"

Hogg sought comfort for his tendency towards client collaboration.

"Well, actually, I think it should be discussed at the audit committee," said Lara as forcefully as possible without risking eternal banishment.

"Do you?" he asked as if the thought had never crossed his mind, which it probably had not. "I think you'd better leave it to me."

Lara was about to make a career limiting statement when Hudson arrived, saving her from Hogg's legendary temper.

"Anyone for coffee?"

Lara glared. Fifi grinned. Hogg scratched.

"Sounds great," Hogg said with a cough. "Mine's black."

Hudson looked dumbfounded. All the coffees were white.

Hogg was known to explode when a junior brought him the wrong sandwich. Lara feared for the boy. But it was half past five and Hogg was keen to get out of the office.

"Oh don't worry, lad," he said not knowing Hudson's name. Rubbing his hands, which made a pleasant change for them, he continued with enthusiasm, "Let's go to the pub." His drawn out hack discouraged any dissent.

"Sounds good to me," replied Hudson before realising how much work there was to do.

Lara was unamused by Hudson's lack of commitment. A second's contemplation, however, and the option became preferable to being cooped up with the big man. Even if they did fall behind schedule. At least in the pub she could have a drink and leave.

"I can't come," said Fifi, the first words she had uttered. "I've got my aerobics class tonight...Sorry."

Hogg was dumbstruck for a second. Without the wall he would have fallen off his chair. Then he optimistically leapt to his feet, tossing the over complicated file on the desk. One of the advantages of being intellectually challenged is the ability always to look on the bright side.

The Naked Bank

"Bad luck. I guess it's just the three of us then."

"I guess," said Lara.

*****

The winebar was beginning to bulge with the usual office escapees for this time of day. And those with reason to drink themselves silly. Fergus was with his team officially celebrating the Carter deal. Unofficially it was an excuse for a departmental piss up. Fergus could hardly complain about the wasps latching on to the honey of success. He had attended only one meeting. His first day and already he was quaffing champagne, discussing big deals and generally acting important. It was a pleasure to abuse another's Corporate Amex card.

"Here's to success," toasted John Snead standing bolt upright at around six foot five. The clock read five past six.

"Big bonuses," cried an unknown scruffy looking youngster.

The others laughed and downed another glass of bubbly. There were perhaps ten standing around the raised table at Buttons Bar. The table strained under enough empty bottles to hold an impromptu game of ten-pin bowling. As Snead began to refill everyone's glasses, it was clear the aim was to open a second lane.

With the exception of Snead, the others resembled a rabble. While his perfect head of hair stood above the general melee, each strand behaving as part of the greater whole, jackets and ties were gradually being discarded about the room with little concern for their condition. The strands of lesser mortals' quiffs had long renounced any loyalty to team play.

The volume of debate intensified, and Fergus, unsure of his standing in the midst of the fracas, found himself with Claire in a relatively quiet corner.

"How have you enjoyed your first day?" she asked genuinely, a trait generally reserved for outside office hours.

These were the first friendly words she, or anyone else, had uttered to him today, and came as a relief.

"Oh, it was great. The whole place's a bit overwhelming but," he gushed a gesture towards the drinking gang, "I think I'll get used to it."

25

First day enthusiasm. Naiveté. Claire laughed. Not a laugh of derision, more a laugh of sympathy.

"You don't honestly think we behave like this all the time?"

Work hard. Play hard. Yuppie excess.

"Uh, well, I suppose I had."

"You couldn't be further from the truth. We're letting our hair down because it's the first time we've been let out in weeks. Normally we work well into the night. I'm surprised you weren't told at the interview."

"Oh, I was. And I know I've got to work hard. I guess...," Fergus did not want to dig a hole for himself. He was keen. He wanted to work. But the end goal was the trappings of success. "...How long have you been at the Bank, Claire?"

Hardly a subtle change of subject.

"Only a couple of years. I'm an accountant, like you." More than he needed to know.

"Really."

"Yeh, most of us have professional qualifications. Most are accountants."

This lifted Fergus. He was no different.

"What, even them?" he said pointing at the others who were beginning to sing. He didn't recognise the tune.

"Some of them. John's a career banker. Joined eight years ago out of college. He rowed for Oxford you know," Claire said this with a hint of pride in her Alma Mater. "With the exception of Sean, the others have all joined in the last year from accounting firms."

Fergus assumed Sean was the Irish lad leading the chorus of what sounded like 'Danny Boy', his undone shirt hanging over his trousers.

"He joined from another bank," she continued. "He's very good at his job...but a bit of a lad."

Fergus looked at Claire, searching for any trace of sarcasm. There was none, so he followed her now distracted gaze towards the others, forming a ring around Sean, applauding as he finished his song. Flamboyantly bowing, he lifted a full bottle of champagne and attempted to down it.

"Down in one, down in one, down in one..." sang the others egging him on even though it was evident he required no encouragement. Half of the champagne went down the front of his shirt. No matter, when he placed the empty bottle back on the table a wild round of applause followed. Claire smiled and politely clapped. Fergus realised she was probably the only sober member of the group.

Sean swaggered to the side, picking out one of three women who were part of the circle.

"Come on Charlotte. It's your turn."

"I can't," she pleaded, "It's too much."

"Call yourself a banker," he taunted, his eyes glazing as the champagne took effect, his legs performing an uncontrolled wobble.

Charlotte looked around the room for help, worry surfacing above her mask of fun. There was only encouragement.

"Don't you think we should help her?" Fergus asked Claire.

"Be my guest. Just remember, he's a strong lad."

Fergus studied Sean and saw what she meant. While perhaps five foot nine, Sean was very stocky. A rugby player, he guessed, judging by his physique and tolerance to booze.

Dutch courage is an amazing thing and gallant Fergus decided to save the damsel in distress. She matched Sean's height. Unlike him her blouse was still tucked in and she was in control of her senses. More to the point, she had looks to die for, precisely the risk Fergus ran by intervening.

"We haven't met. I'm Fergus," he offered to Charlotte.

"Pleased to meet you, Fergus," she said taking his hand with a slight curtsey.

"Fuck off Fergy," said Sean. "Charlotte's at the plate."

"Come on Charlotte, show us your style," shouted Loud Woman, for want of another name, considerably more pissed than her target.

Sentiment was obviously against rescue. Suddenly antagonising his new peers no longer held such heroic attractions. Fergus began to back out of the expectant ring which had now formed around the two of them. Then Charlotte made her bid for freedom. In the jungle, the fittest survive.

"I'll go after Fergus," she said seizing her opportunity. Danger.

"What do you say Fergy?" said Sean loudly, grabbing both

his arms. "Ready to volunteer." And then in a whisper, "You'll drink the bottle either way."

Champagne Man brought forward a bottle. Fergus did not know his name and had no desire to be introduced by having champagne poured down his gullet. But there was no escape from Sean's vice-like grip.

"OK, I'll do it." How ill could he get?

"That's the spirit."

Taking the bottle he braced himself.

"Hurry up then."

Fergus' mind was ready to go, his hand unwilling.

"Need some help," said Sean kindly.

"No thanks."

Fergus took a deep breath, and forgetting to remove his jacket and tie, lifted the bottle to his lips, and poured. After a second he choked, spilling at least a glass down his front.

"Breathe through your nose," helpfully offered Sean.

Again the bottle went to the mouth and this time the fizz flowed down his throat with remarkable ease. He even began to enjoy it, oblivious to the slop that drenched his new clothes. Breaking them in. And then there was no more, and he placed the bottle on the table with the dizzy satisfaction that accompanies a successful alcoholic dare.

The cheers were muffled by the growing sogginess he felt in his head, the stirrings he felt in his stomach.

"Excuse me," began his acceptance speech as he rushed for the toilet, not knowing where he was going or for that matter where he was. All the time his world span faster and faster. The next thing he knew his face was down the toilet watching vintage vomit splashing around the bowl like a Technicolor roulette wheel.

By the time the toilet's revolutions slowed, there was nothing left. No champagne. No lunchtime sandwich, a sandwich he had eaten on his own, at his desk. His breathing returned to normal and sense gradually pervaded the chaotic realm of instant intoxication. He looked at his new suit and tie? Saveable? Who could tell. He was kneeling on the floor and took a moment to stand. A moment in drunk time was five minutes. Without showing his face his kudos would be lost.

The Naked Bank

Collecting himself, he staggered, bashed, bumped, spilt and apologised his way back to the party. Joining the circle he recognised a tipsy Charlotte, the centre of attention, without her blouse. Next to her was Sean who seemed to be missing his shirt.

"What happened?" asked Fergus although it sounded more like, "Wha haened."

He stood next to Claire who clearly had not yet been 'Dom'-ed, her exterior immaculately unamused.

"She spilled champagne over herself and Sean offered to clean her blouse."

Of course, that made sense. Fergus wanted to ask another question, if he could. No, instead he watched and waited for his head to clear. The next day he recalled some of the following.

The circle began to chant,

"Get them off, get them off, get them off."

By this time other people in the winebar were joining the crowd curious to see what was happening. Charlotte undid Sean's trousers to much cheering and then pulled them down around his ankles. He wore Tasmanian Devil boxer shorts.

"All off, all off, all off."

As Charlotte's hands reached for his shorts, for the first time Sean looked uncomfortable. No need to be extreme. He brushed her hands aside and moved around behind her, unzipping her skirt before yanking it to the ground. And there they stood, unsure of themselves amidst the baying throng. He defending his remaining pride, his fingers offering his shorts some protection, and she suddenly aware of her unladylike pose. Sean reached forward for her bra, egged on by both the males and females in the crowd. Except Claire, who left at this point, disgusted. A good move if she had not bumped into Ian Carpenter, her boss, as he came in.

"Leaving early Claire? I thought I'd come along and congratulate the team." he said before taking an interest in the chanting crowd.

"Yes. I've one or two things to tidy up tonight. I'll be back later."

This answer satisfied Carpenter who respected Claire for her diligence. "I'll see you later then. And well done."

He moved forward, John Snead managing to intercept him.

Snead was not too drunk and with quick thinking took the departmental boss towards the bar.

"Would you mind putting your Amex behind the bar?" was all he could say.

"What's wrong with yours?" said Carpenter looking back as he was moved away from the crowd.

"Uh, its over its limit."

This was not a particularly bright thing to say. It duly grabbed the attention of Carpenter who wondered how much Snead had spent given Amex cards theoretically have no credit limit. Meanwhile, Champagne Man and Loud Woman led the courting couple off the floor and quickly out the side door, each clutching several pieces of clothing. Sean tripped over his trousers. By then he was outside, his clatter shared only with empty beer barrels. And the semi-conscious form of Charlotte, head in a rubbish bin.

*****

Hogg Midgely held court at the bar, the space around him a symptom of Fifi's aerobic absence and Hudson's prolonged spell in the toilets. Lara strove to prevent Hogg from openly discussing sensitive client information. That meant stringing him along while he expounded on another of his pet interests.

"Did you see that program on Channel 4 last night?" he asked.

"Brookside?" Lara replied knowing categorically it was not.

"No," he said with an alcohol induced whine. "The one about lesbians in the police."

"I must have missed it," she said with a sigh. He was sure to make up for her oversight.

"It was great. Apparently one in two policewomen is a lesbian. Too much convent education if you ask me."

Lara kept her mouth tightly shut. She had attended a Catholic girls school, doubtless falling within Hogg's lesbo spectrum.

"They reckon one in five women is a lesbian."

"Really." Where was Hudson? He was sure to have buggered off.

The Naked Bank

"What do you think about that?"

She ignored the question.

"Another lager please," asked Hogg of the barmaid, "and another water for the little lady."

Lara hoped a fresh beer would change the subject. She was mistaken.

As the barmaid bent to pick up a bottle of water the inevitable comment came.

"Do you think she's a lesbian?"

"I've no idea."

"I thought you girls could tell. I can spot a poof straight away."

Again his words were not worthy of comment.

"You're not a lesbian are you?" came the inevitable.

"I don't see what that has to do with anything," retorted an angry Lara.

"Sorry," said Hogg taken aback. "Do you have a boyfriend then?"

Lara did not appreciate the connotation so she lied.

"Yes, I do."

"Really - what does he do."

"He's a policeman." Seemed a good idea.

"Hah - no wonder he's going out with you then. He works with a bunch of lesbians."

Groan.

"What's he like, then," said Hogg placing his hand on her back, remarkably close to her bottom, having read in FHM that this turned women on. His lager breath smoothly blended with a cocktail of pickled onion, garlic and baloney.

Lara took a step back.

"I'll only be a moment - I have to powder my nose."

"Take all the time you need, dear." Hogg liked to be polite with the ladies. Part of his natural charm.

Escaping to the sanctuary of the ladies, she realised how much water she had drunk. The cubicle next door contained someone being violently ill, giving Lara the choice of suffering this soundtrack or quickly returning to face the creature from the pit.

Washing her hands and checking her face, she stepped out

into the atmosphere of a cockfight, which was one way of describing what she saw next. She was about to sneak out when Hogg caught sight of her, a miracle in itself considering the action playing out in front of him. He was part of the cheering circle as he motioned Lara to join him. As the evening progressed she had noticed the antics of the merchant bankers whose actions she found contemptible. At least Hogg was a harmless lech. The bankers were obscene.

Unable to leave, she joined Hogg in time to see a semi-naked man remove the bra of a woman dressed only in her underwear. Placing the cups on his head he giggled.

"Take a look at those," Hogg spat in her ear.

"I've got to go," Lara replied. "Excuse me, I'll see you in the morning."

"How do you like your eggs," he said as he slapped her on the rear.

"You bastard," she shouted loud enough for even the ring combatants to briefly restrain themselves.

Lara turned and stormed towards the door around the same time as the circle began breaking up. As she pushed out into the fresh air it was clear Hogg was following.

"Lara, wait," he cried. "How about coming back to my place for a night-cap."

"I think not!"

"Why's that - it'll be good for your career."

Lara looked at the man in disgust.

"And if I don't."

"Well, your performance needs improving..."

Lara had worked at the accounting firm, SNZS, for ten years to reach her current grade and would do practically anything to make partner. This was the exception. Hogg was a powerful man. She loathed him, desperately wanting this nightmare to end. Looking around she saw a man leaning against a lamp post. He was still dressed and so worth a try.

"Excuse me," she said to Hogg, amazed at her coolness, "That's a friend of mine who will take me home."

She walked away from the Partner to the stranger.

"Bet she's a lesbian," muttered Hogg as he leant against the outside wall and inhaled cool air, already scanning the pavement for

The Naked Bank

his next rejection.

"Sir, would you mind helping me out," she said to the man. It was only when he turned that she saw the state of his suit. It was soaked with alcohol. But she could still feel Hogg's eyes. There was no choice.

"Would you mind taking me home?"

The man grinned.

"I'd be delighted," he attempted to say and somehow amidst the drunken slur Lara understood.

"Taxi," he cried appealing to the night air with raised arm, briefly releasing the lamp post before remembering why he was clutching it in the first place. "Taxi," he repeated with considerably less volume.

Lara waved at an on-coming black cab.

"Where to, love?"

"Islington, please."

"Is he coming with you?"

Lara looked at the man, at Hogg, and then back at the man. He was in a sorry state but something told her she could trust him.

"Yes, he is."

"It's thirty quid if he throws up, love."

"Fine," she said bundling him into the cab. "You're in no condition to get home. You can sleep on my couch."

"OK," he said with childlike innocence. "What's for tea?"

Lara remained silent as he fell asleep, his head resting on her shoulder. Hogg's words had hurt her and this strange man offered her comfort. Goodness knows why.

"Why is it the only men I go out with are comatose?" she said to herself.

He snored, and Lara, who had never done anything spontaneous in her life, rethought her offer. Rummaging through his pockets, fearful that he might interpret it as a pass, she found his wallet, and fortunately his name and address.

"Driver - make that Finchley, then Islington."

The journey was short and uneventful. The man burped a few times but was never in danger of throwing up, although the smell of his suit seemed to indicate the act was not foreign.

"Wait here," Lara said to the driver as she helped the man

up the steps to his flat. He leaned on her shoulder, his soaking jacket rubbing against her designer suit. What was she doing with this man? She was tempted to leave him on the front step. But Lara was a kindly woman, and he had saved her from Hogg. First she rang the door bell. No point in bumping into flat mates or jealous girlfriends. No answer. Seemed safe enough. She had already found his keys, and after a brief moment of fiddling with the lock, the door opened.

"Toilet," he said, pulling her towards the bathroom.

"You're going to have to do this on your own," said an unamused Lara.

The next thing she knew he had fallen into the empty bath.

"I'm not dirty," was all he could say.

"I wouldn't bet on it," she said softy and went to find a blanket.

Returning, she heard him trying to climb out of the bath. As she entered the room he gave up. It was futile. He was stranded for the night, unable to summon up the strength to lift himself out of his predicament. Lara took his shoes off. They were new, expensive, and splattered. She thought about undressing him and then thought twice. He was asleep again as she placed a pillow under his head and a blanket on top of him. Then he woke and tried to remove his jacket.

"It'll get creased," he said.

Lara knew better than to argue and helped him out of it. He would not succeed on his own.

"Goodnight," he said as he slid back into place.

"Goodnight," she replied, "You'll be sore in the morning." He did not reply.

Taking the sodden jacket, she hung it on the door handle, before returning to the waiting taxi. On the way home her thoughts were of Hogg, and what he might do to her career. Thought about how to rid herself of the over bearing oaf who threatened the natural order of her life. How much did a hitman cost anyway these days?

Fergus thought of nothing. It had been a busy day.

*****

It was eleven o'clock and Christine was still at work. The

last document from her left hand pile was still being drafted. It was likely to take all night.

"Goodnight," said Byron popping his head in through the door to her office.

"Oh, are you off?" she asked as she raised her head.

"Got to or the wife will kill me. You'll be OK won't you."

"Sure," she said with a willing smile.

"Thanks. I remember your hard work, you know. I wish all our staff were as diligent as you."

"Thanks, Byron. Thanks for the vouchers. I'll buy something attractive for you," she flirted.

Their eyes met for a moment.

"Anyway," he said, "I'd better be off. I'll see you tomorrow."

"Bye," said Christine returning to the document.

Byron left and shut the door behind him.

"Was it me, or does he fancy me?" Christine asked herself. She shook her head and then laughed. The thought of an affair with her boss was strangely appealing. It was nice to be noticed.

*****

The plane touched down at nine o'clock. Milan airport was insane as usual. Disembarking, the passengers were loaded onto a bus. What was the point of having a business class ticket if he then had to wait for all the pleb class passengers to get on before he could clear customs. First on, last off meant by the time he cleared customs there were only a few saddoes behind him. Those who didn't take their luggage in the cabin. Giles carried a large case. It had been too big for the overhead locker and in the end one of the stewardesses had stuck it in the galley. Better than in the hold.

Emerging from the arrival gate, Giles recognised his driver as the man with the large 'Mister Bonnier' sign. The man relieved him of the case and set off to the car without a word. Franco was used to dealing with foreign guests, most of whom could not speak Italian, so why try and converse. Giles preferred it. He was tired and still had an important task to complete before he could retire for the night.

David Murray

The car was a large, black Cadillac, parked in front of the main airport exit. Illegally parked, none of the traffic police made any effort to move it on. More than their jobs were worth. They knew who owned the limo. The case went in the trunk, large enough for several bodies. Giles went in the back. The seats were black and swallowed him with their comfort. He wanted to fall asleep. It was not wise, alertness was essential for his next meeting.

Speeding along the motorway, they quickly entered town. After bypassing some non-descript suburbs, the car moved more slowly along the glamour packed streets of Milan. Some of the most expensive shops in the world lined the streets. Some of the most glamorous people in the world walked those streets. Giles did not notice. He did notice the car pulling up outside a large gateway, the entrance to a villa.

A doorman opened the car door, the driver handed Giles his case. The gate closed behind Giles, the last visitor for the day. The only visitor of the day. They entered a large courtyard, with a simple fountain in its centre. The roof sloped down towards the centre of the quadrangle revealing red clay tiles. The guest was led to the far side and climbed a large sweeping staircase winding its way into the building. Giles was deposited in a large room and allowed to admire the walls.

Whereas earlier in the day, the Bank's paintings had looked cheap and third rate, the walls and ceiling of this room were covered with hand painted murals. It was magnificent.

"Coffee, sir," asked a small, aged man in a white coat.

"Yes please, it's been a long flight."

The man smiled giving the impression that he would listen to whatever Giles wanted to say. Listen, not understand.

A few minutes later he returned with a tray bearing a small coffee urn, a tiny cup, sachets of sugar and a glass of water. Expresso. Giles hated expresso. To explain this to the waiter was pointless.

"Thank you," he said, sipping the treacle substance with a grimace.

The man made himself scarce. Giles leaned back and enjoyed the angels.

The Naked Bank

An hour later he was called into the adjoining office. If the last room was amazing, this room was staggering. Dripping with wealth. The floor was mosaic, the curtains silk and the walls once again hand painted. At one end of this vast room sat an antique desk, and behind the desk, Mr Vittori. A chair awaited Giles who sat when bade.

Immediately a man, who until then was admiring the view from the huge rectangular windows, stood behind Giles.

"I am Mr Vittori's interpreter. He prefers to speak Italian and I understand you only speak English."

The man subtly flung these words as an insult.

"That's correct." Giles would take whatever was thrown at him.

"Mr Vittori is pleased that you are here and hopes you had a good trip." Vittori had not spoken.

The man spoke with a soft Italian accent. Before Giles could answer, he continued.

"Mr Vittori wonders if you have the cash." Telepathy again.

"I do - it's in the case." Giles patted his suitcase.

"Mr Vittori is very pleased with the return on his money. May he have his money now please."

Giles looked at Vittori who was studying him in considered silence, with the interest of a collector. Vittori's light grey suit was understated in the way only expensive clothes can be. His tie was hand painted with a matching handkerchief neatly placed in the jacket top pocket. His hair was silver and while he looked as if he ate well, his image incorporated the extra pounds with ease. Vittori was perhaps fifty, and patient. He waited for Giles to open the case in front of him. It was full of crisp fifty pound notes. Satisfied, Vittori nodded and Giles closed the case, leaving it on the desk.

"Mr Vittori looks forward to participating in your next venture. When do you start?"

"Uh, it should be underway by Christmas. We have a few, how should I put this, arrangements to make. I'll give you more details next month."

The interpreter was not repeating Giles' words. It was clear his master understood. More perplexing, Vittori still said nothing. The interpreter continued.

David Murray

"We await your report with interest. If you need any help with your *arrangements* please let Mr Vittori know. If you will excuse him, he is tired and will now retire for the evening. The footman will show you to your room. Would you like your usual companion for the evening?"

The man made the offer as if it were nothing more than an after dinner mint.

"No, thank you. I appreciate the offer, believe me I do, but it's late and I'm very tired."

"As you wish."

"But I'd love some milk, and cookies?" No point asking for coffee.

"I'll see what I can do."

Giles was shown out of the office and round the building to the guest wing. His room was cosy, lacking the earlier grandeur. There was a bed and a bathroom. Enough. Closing his eyes he thought of the next deal. It was dodgy but then how can anyone make serious money by being honest?

A knock.

"Come in," he stirred, remembering their was no lock on the door.

"Hello," said a deep voiced, well muscled man in a posing pouch, "I'm Cookie."

Clearly something had been lost in translation.

The Naked Bank

December 21st

On a dark December day, a motorway service station is a far
from a perfect location to conduct business. The road was slushy as
James Carter pulled his Jaguar into the car park. The miserable
weather meant spaces close to the cafeteria were at a premium.
Braving the sleet without an overcoat, he half ran to the large glass
plated doors marking the beginning of the services within. Pulling
his unbuttoned suit jacket around his chest did little to ease the cold.
Once inside, the rise in temperature was barely noticeable.

Carter ventured past the flashing lights of arcade games, the
queue for overpriced soggy sandwiches, and the lack of queue to use
the 'design your own business card' machine. He recalled from
somewhere that the company which manufactured the machines was
in financial trouble. His mind then moved on to the prospect of a
piping hot coffee and sticky bun.

Finding a table to himself was more difficult than he would
have thought, considering he was in the middle of nowhere. His
lukewarm coffee slopped around the tray with the verve of a Chinese
'woman' swimmer overdosed on testosterone. At least the bun was
sticky, resembling the aforementioned swimmer's face. Soggy,
spotty, but nonetheless sticky. With time to kill he opened his copy
of the December issue of Mergers Monthly.

Ian Carpenter, the Rolls Royce of Bankers
by Sophie Cotton-Wood, Mergers Monthly

Ian Carpenter's office reflects his desire for success above all
else. With the exception of photographs of his wife and
children, it seems to lack activity of any sort. There is no paper

41

on the desk, the bookshelves are neatly ordered and the two leather sofas that frame the room give the impression of being unused. There must be some truth in the old wife's tail about a tidy desk reflecting a tidy mind.

When Carpenter was appointed head of the Bank's corporate finance department, there was much scepticism about his suitability for the role. While he had a great deal of success at London Bank, it was more for his role in executing deals than generating business or running a department. Many said that such was the state of the Bank, Carpenter was the only man who would accept the job. How he has proved his critics wrong. Turning the Bank's blue blood image on its head, he has adopted a policy of actively touting for business, in stark contrast to the previous unwritten policy of waiting for a relation of the Board to walk in the door bearing gifts. Even though the rest of the City abandoned such practices with their bowler hats, it has taken until now for the Bank to change its image. And with some results. Three years ago, the Bank lay twenty seventh in the mergers monthly league table. This year it is eighth, second behind only London Bank in the list of UK independent banks. Carpenter believes there is further to go. "This year we aim to be the top independent bank as well as break into the top five overall. I don't think that is an unreasonable ambition."

A team man, when asked how much of this success is down to him, Carpenter replies with modesty, "I do very little really except create the right atmosphere for people to strive in. If you get that right and hire talented people, I like to let them get on with it. My job is easy really."

With the current problems surrounding rest of the Bank, how easy is it for Carpenter to maintain the right atmosphere? A people business can always lose its people. "Sure, there is some risk. But this is a risky business. I think the Bank is on the right track and in any case, Sir Wig is quite content to let us get on with what we do best and I am happy to let him do what he does best." While many wonder what exactly Sir Wig does do best, there is no doubt that Ian Carpenter is held in high regard throughout the City, and with good reason.

Carter was about to turn the page when a man sat down opposite him.

"Is this seat taken?"

Carter looked up to see who dared to invade his privacy. Only in England can someone get uptight about not having four seats to themselves.

"Not at all."

The man took the seat diagonally opposite Carter. He was fairly nondescript. He placed his tray on the table in front of him and his briefcase by his feet. His well behaved coffee remained in its cup

Carter looked around. There was no interest in two total strangers striking a conversation over coffee in an anonymous service station.

"You have the goods?"

"Yes."

"Good."

Carter reached into his jacket pocket and pulled out a chunky brown envelope which he held under the table. The stranger grasped it before placing it inside his raincoat.

"The usual arrangement you'll find. I have included a list of further requirements."

"More!" said the stranger in a raised tone before remembering where he was. "What do you mean more? I thought this was the last request," he frantically whispered.

"You'll be more than adequately compensated. Besides you wouldn't want Mr Whittle finding out, now would you?"

"You..," the stranger did not finish what he thought.

"You do still want to work for me after the deal, don't you."

"Yes. You know I do."

"Then pull with the team," implored Carter. "Same time next week?"

"It's not much time. They're beginning to get suspicious."

"Well make sure you don't get caught then. I'll see you in exactly one week's time."

"Yes," mumbled the resigned stranger.

"Good."

Carter stood without touching his coffee. He wasn't thirsty.

"There's a bun there if you're hungry."

Picking up the stranger's briefcase, he walked slowly back to his Jag. Once inside its still warm interior, he allowed himself a sigh of relief. Why did he bother with all this subterfuge? Silly question, really.

*****

A whiff of the 100% proof coffee would have been enough to jolt most people bolt upright. For the corporate financiers slowly filing into the conference room it was no more than a gentle nudge towards their monthly departmental meeting. Many had worked most of the night, many worked most nights, viewing Ian Carpenter's 8.30am call to arms as a chance to gain a valuable hours kip. For others, whose preference was dining out in the evening over chewing a Mars Bar in front of a computer screen, it was a chance to verify the weeks of rumour and gossip seeded in the pubs, winebars and restaurants of the City. These people were known by the troops as the 'overheads'. They did not pull their weight, generally did not surface until ten o'clock in the morning, yet contrived to gain most credit for successful deals. If a deal 'cratered', they were nowhere to be seen. It was in these meetings they shined. When it mattered, while their rivals dozed. When there was an audience.

As the staff slowly filed into the conference room, Ian Carpenter sat quietly at the raised podium, observing their body language. His was an important speech. The Bank's results were not good, severely limiting the size of this year's bonus pool. His job to raise morale while at the same time dampening expectations.

He stood. At perhaps six foot one, his action called the room immediately to silence. Expectancy.

"Good morning, ladies and gentleman, and thanks for coming today."

The front row was filled with directors, no one else having the temerity to sit there. An empty space was reserved for Douglas Montgomery, who would arrive late to show how busy and important he was. Carpenter was an external appointment for the Head of

The Naked Bank

Department job two and a half years ago. Montgomery, the internal favourite, never forgave him for upsetting the natural flow of the Bank. You do your time and you move up. It was precisely this attitude Carpenter was attempting to address. Change or die.

"To begin with I'll quickly run through the department's results and how they fit into the Bank's figures as announced yesterday. I'll then look at our prospects for next year, including our agreed budget, and then say a word or two on bonuses."

The room shuffled at these final words. Then Montgomery walked in.

"Sorry I'm late."

Claire sat in the third row. She greatly admired his energy and honesty. Impressive at his job. Claire was a 'child of Ian'. He had recruited her along with half the department. Forging corporate finance in his own image. The old guard did not like it, seeing their own cohorts gradually cleansed. He was an anathema to everything they held dear. Carpenter, more than half way through his speech, was just warming up.

"...we live in the real world. I'm sure you've all read the press over the last few days. The Bank is under pressure. The competition is fiercer than ever. We're told it's the era of the global bank. Perhaps it is, but as you all know this presents us with great opportunities. An independent corporate finance house can offer the client independent advice. Time and time again I am told by our clients that this is what they need. They don't want a one stop shop, a featureless financing conglomerate. We thrive by being different. We thrive by being innovative. To thrive in the future is going to require greater effort from each and every one of you. There will be tears. I expect as much. I demand as much. But in return there will be reward.

"This year's bonus structure rewards effort. The better your results, the better your bonus. Some of you won't like it. Some of you will. But remember. We are in this for the long term. The ride may be bumpy. I'm here for the duration and I want people by my side who feel the same. This is our great opportunity. We can and will be the best. And I've never felt more confident in the team around me. Together we will succeed."

45

David Murray

As Ian sat down Claire felt uplifted and almost began to applaud before realising there was a deathly hush. The bonuses would be low. The 'overheads' were unhappy. 'We have payments to make on our Porsches.' Claire felt confident.

"Are there any questions?" asked Carpenter after a moment to collect himself from his 'fight them on the beaches' exertion.

Stillness descended. There was always a lull, no one wanting to draw attention by asking the first question, especially if controversial. There were many thoughts in audience land. To raise them was to be singled out. Those with nothing to prove asked the questions. Those with nothing they could prove.

"Ian," began Wilfred Kite, the Assistant Director in charge of Administration, "one thing I'm sure we're all curious to know is what next year's pipeline of business is looking like."

A suitably neutral question from Kite whose manner resembled a constipated Captain Peacock. No one respected the man who was particularly anal, spending his life snooping around peoples' desk in the hope of uncovering incriminating evidence. Quite what, who could say. Any document left on a desk, and in many cases locked away in the desk, would fall prey to Kite's prying eyes. Apart from seeking to uncover non-existent conspiracies, it was unclear precisely what the man did.

"I'm glad you asked that," replied Carpenter suitably primed. "There are a number of medium sized deals that should come to fruition over the coming months. Of course, they won't all succeed, but I am confident in at least two which will generate fees in the order of two million pounds each. Then there is Project Bluebird. I can't really say much about this at the moment as it's highly confidential. However, if successful the fees will greatly boost the bonus pool, not to mention raising the bank a whole flight up the M&A league table. It will demonstrate all the Bank's innovative qualities and provide a deal flow for a good year or two after as businesses are sold off. Hopefully I can tell you more about it next month."

"Any other questions....no, well then why don't we get back and do some work." Carpenter did not want any controversial questions. "I'll see you all at the Christmas party tonight."

The Naked Bank

Carpenter walked out the side door, the cue for Claire to stand and breathe.

"I hope you feel suitably impressed now," said Snead lacking sincerity. He stood directly behind her, a career Bank man, and card carrying member of the old guard.

*****

Bank under attack for poor results
by Josh Walker, Staff Writer

Once one of the finest institutions in the City, the Bank has now fallen well and truly behind its main competitors. As other independent merchant banks are picked off one by one by foreign predators, analysts are guessing how long it will be before an approach is made to the Bank. Many now wonder after yesterday's results whether anyone will bother. Last year's much heralded restructuring, if anything, seems to have increased overheads. Pre-tax profit is down 10% year on year.

Minority shareholder Walter Greenhalgh again criticised the Bank yesterday saying, "Today's results indicate more than ever that the top management should be sacked and the Bank broken up to realise shareholder value." Greenhalgh bought 3% of the Bank last month making his much quoted comment about the Bank's top executives being "more concerned about their cigars than their shareholders." To date the Bank has refused to meet Greenhalgh whose abrasive style contrasts with the Board's blue chip pretensions. One leading analyst stated Greenhalgh does not get involved unless he thinks he can win. Sooner or later Bank Supremo Sir Wig Forthwright will have to talk to Greenhalgh and other disgruntled investors. Yesterday Sir Wig stated that the Bank's main shareholder, the medium sized Banco Republica, stood firmly behind the management's restructuring plans. Banco Republica, based in Milan, bought its 25% strategic stake a year ago.

*****

David Murray

The gents at the Bank was nothing special. Blue tiles for the boys. Four cubicles, three urinals. Unlike some of the American banks, the cubicles were not equipped with Reuters screens printing out the latest announcements, bad news accelerating the flow of shit. Good news producing constipated whoops. No, the gentleman's sanctuary is his toilet. In the Bank only the rustling of newspapers, usually The Sun which was too embarrassing to read in public view, could be heard upon entering the gents. Fergus had chosen his moment well when he entered. He was alone.

Standing at the left urinal he contemplated his world, enormously changed after three months in the Bank. The deal was exciting but Janet did not appreciate his long hours. Did not appreciate, who was he kidding. Loathed his hours. He was under pressure to get home early. He was under pressure to work late. He was tired but no longer cared for his health. The buzz of the deal was the only thing that mattered.

As both his mind and aim wandered, he was brought back to earth with a slap. The slap of two hands on the urinal wall. The smell of distinguished cigar smoke. Turning his head ever so slightly, he recognised the Fat Controller, known to many as Jonathan Gross. Once a star corporate financier, he now lived upstairs, exploiting a faded reputation. The size of his bonus was impressive.

The sound of heavy splashing told him the centre urinal was now fully occupied. This man was a Big Swinging Dick and had no qualms demonstrating his prowess. Puffing on his oversized cigar, he pushed his hands against the wall and groaned a pleasure of relief. Fergus was ready to go. Zipping himself up he studied the problem of how to slip past the big man. He was trapped.

Gross felt Fergus's unease and took another puff.

"I don't think I know you," he voiced with a boom.

"I'm Fergus McKay. We haven't met."

"Pleased to meet you," said Gross as he removed his right hand from the wall and reached across his body to offer it to Fergus. Naturally Fergus shook it without considering the hygienic consequences. Career consequences were the only consideration. The Fat Controller returned the hand to its resting place, his direction remaining impressively true throughout.

The Naked Bank

"Excuse me," said Fergus as he squeezed past trying desperately not push the man forward. Hands washed, with special care, he left before the human fire hose was exhausted.

*****

Byron was behaving differently. Christine could not fathom why but was in no doubt about the subtle change. Normally a routine meeting was held in one of the many anonymous legal meeting rooms, replete with dusty, leather backed tomes. Unread for fifteen years they imparted necessary gravitas. The fusty atmosphere gave the client value for money, or at least a belief he was not being over charged. No wonder lawyers cost so much having to wade through impenetrable libraries to form opinion. In reality, they used the latest CD Roms and online research tools, the volumes of obscure legal precedents remaining untouched, their very dustiness proof of the pudding.

Today they sat in Byron's own office, a touch reflecting a degree of personality. Rule One: Don't let the clients get to know you. Rule Two: Don't flirt with your colleagues. At least one of these rules was under threat.

The sofa was low and soft, part of the daily conspiracy to make Christine's life uncomfortable. Her suits were designed for straight backed chairs and solid meeting tables. Working around a coffee table was all very well for a man but to adjust her short skirt every time she moved back or forward was a distraction both for her and the male banker opposite. Claire on the other settee had a longer skirt, trying to impress Byron with her authority rather than her cellulite.

Byron wore a red tie, red braces and red socks. Most out of character. He leaned back on the sofa without apparent care. Christine scribbled while he relaxed, balancing the pad on her knees while he casually crossed his legs. His right arm gestured while his left reached along the back of the sofa. It almost fell behind Christine's head making her far more self conscious than the furtive glances of the pip-squeak Fergus sitting in front of her. What was wrong with Byron?

49

David Murray

Claire was performing well. She looked around Christine's age which irked the lawyer who played second fiddle whilst this woman was in control. Christine looked her up and down with some satisfaction at her lack of style. A crumpled tan suit showed she did not have much of a dress sense. But it did not detract from Claire's assurance. Byron did not notice such things.

"Thanks for your update on the documentation. It was most useful. It sounds as if things are progressing well." said Claire. "The main reason we are here, however, is to discuss another matter."

Christine could have sworn Byron moved slightly forward in his seat after these words. If there is one thing lawyers hate it is unpredictability. It is impossible to prepare for. She felt his arm tense behind her head.

"And what might that be?" he asked with the calmness of a man not quite at one with his surroundings. To the discerning eye, Black's beak-like tendencies began to re-emerge.

Claire paused to gather her thoughts.

"The Bank has in its possession a number of documents. These documents have come from the CRA."

She stopped to study Black's reaction. If he was aware of the papers, he gave nothing away, his features only revealing their usual twitch. Christine kept her head down avoiding eye contact. This was a relief. There was something about the woman which made Claire uncomfortable.

"They've been passed to us by a person from within the company without the knowledge of his or her employer."

Claire gave the impression of not wanting to reveal any more than Black needed to know. In reality she had no idea of the mole's identity.

Christine suspected the identity of the mole. The man had been foolish enough to leave a message for Black, Christine having answered her boss's phone one evening when she was alone in the office. She had never confronted Black with her intelligence, waiting in vain for him to confide in her. Now she dwelt on the name, revelling in her one-upmanship, playfully doodling it on her pad.

The Naked Bank

Robert Parsons. She carelessly circled the 'o's in his name as she listened to the speaker.

Fergus watched her doodling, unable to see the pad. He studied her mannerisms. Half cocked head. Twirling of a curl. Concentration on the trivia of a pen stroke. Why did this woman hold him in such contempt? Experience had yet to teach him some people naturally dislike others. It was in the genes. In the City, if there was no obvious reason to like someone, it was far easier to dislike them. It made the anti-social need to stab them in the back so much easier.

Claire continued.

"It may be necessary to use these documents as part of the bid. As you know, the CRA is a very secretive organisation. It's hard to get any meaningful data out of them."

"So it's necessary to, how should I say it...borrow some?" interrupted Black.

Claire remained on message.

"Quite. The information is invaluable. It is, however, confidential. Now it's my understanding that 'information sharing' is normal practice in contested take-overs. Given the potential controversy of our venture, the Bank is keen to ensure we do nothing illegal. Nothing that can be thrown at us when the going gets tough."

"I understand."

"We'd like to know your views on the legality."

Black said nothing.

"Of the use of the documents?" added Claire.

He pondered. He mulled. His giant legal brain started earning its fee. Externally, nothing changed save the placement of both hands on his chin in contemplation.

"And whether we can pass them on to other institutions?"

"Yes, I understand," said Black. "I'll come back to you shortly with my views."

"Do you have an initial opinion?" asked Claire with little respect for legal decorum.

David Murray

Christine looked up from her pad. Fergus jumped as Christine caught his eye. The crows in the tree outside the office window scattered. A church bell tolled. Three blocks away a black cat was run over.

"Young lady. This is a complicated matter on which I must seek detailed counsel. It is not a matter upon which I can toss out a hunch. It requires many hours of research. Many, many hours."

Claire looked down.

"But, if you were to ask me casually over a glass of fine Bordeaux, I might be able to explain the layman's view."

Was this an insult or an invitation? She took the latter.

"I'd be happy to buy you lunch and we can discuss it further."

Now if there are any words guaranteed to sweeten a lawyer's heart more than those, they are buried deep within the realms of precedent. The very realms into which it was Christine's lot to delve.

"I know a nice little bistro. In fact by co-incidence I've a table booked for two. Shall we go?"

"Yes."

Claire was taken aback at the speed at which this ultra conservative lawyer moved when more than precedent was at stake. Still, he seemed harmless enough.

Claire and Byron left quickly and Fergus now found himself alone with Christine.

"Shall we have lunch too?" he ventured.

"Err, I'd better get on with this research. Perhaps some other time?"

A rebuttal rather than a raincheck.

"OK," said Fergus misreading the signals.

"I'll show you out."

Fergus stood with ease. Christine struggled to find purchase of the slick leather, the deepness of the sofa conspiring with the single mindedness of her heels to hold her in place.

"Let me help you up," said Fergus offering his hand.

52

The Naked Bank

While she abhorred accepting help, especially someone like Fergus's, it was better than further floundering. She took his outstretched hand with trepidation.

The ease with which Fergus yanked her out of the seat surprised him. Christine jumped forward, cracking the top of her head on the underside of his jaw before both fell back onto the coffee table with a crash. Fergus lay stunned for a moment, Christine on top of him, failing to see the funny side.

It was even more difficult for her to rise this time, enveloped as they were by the smashed pieces of furniture. Somehow she gathered herself, and with little concern for Fergus, pushed up, kneeing him in several spots, none vital. She stood and brushed herself down, trying to remove the splinters from her suit.

"Will you help me up?"

Christine extended her hand and pulled him up easily.

"Ouch," she suddenly exclaimed, as she caught a splinter in her finger.

"Let me see."

"It's OK."

"No let me look. I'm a trained medic," he lied, having learnt the first lesson of Investment Banking - overstate your qualifications with confidence.

Seeing she was unable to refuse, she offered her hand, so to speak.

"That's a nasty one."

"What is it?" she asked with sudden concern.

"Unless this is removed immediately it could be dangerous," he wildly exaggerated.

"Really. Should I go to hospital?" said a worried Christine.

"No. Don't worry. You'd better sit down for a moment, though."

So then Fergus found himself next to Christine on the couch, still with her finger in his hand.

"This may hurt."

He squeezed the finger with his nails.

"Ow," she said pulling her hand back.

"Sorry."

"I'll get the nurse to look at it."

"No need," said Fergus.

Fergus held the small splinter in the palm of his hand.

"Is that it?"

"'fraid so."

"Thanks," she smiled.

Fergus smiled back.

"Shall we try again," he asked as he stood and extended his hand.

"Yes please," she laughed.

With a gentler pull she was on her feet.

"Fergus," she said. "Thanks."

"Don't mention it. We'll have that lunch sometime?"

"Perhaps."

Promising. He then remembered the carnage.

"What about the table?"

"I'll sort it out with Byron's PA. Let's hope they have a long lunch."

They laughed.

"You dropped your pad."

Fergus reached down to pick it up.

"No!" said Christine sharply as she grabbed it off him.

Her manner turned to ice.

"You'd better go."

"OK," said a confused Fergus.

"This way out."

As she showed him to the door his head spun with questions. For a start, who was Robert Parsons?

*****

It was a trendy winebar. The type with polished wooden floors, pink walls framing obscure multi-coloured sketches, pine tables and a black curved bar, lined with stools higher than practically comfortable. The waitresses were young, mostly antipodean, whose tailored green aprons almost complimented their black Doc Martens, their accents clashing with the decor. The music was low key, playing last year's latest thing, slightly out of touch with today's youth. The food was well decorated on over-sized, hand

The Naked Bank

painted plates, accompanied by over-sized cutlery. House mineral water failed to fill over-sized glasses. Fresh bread rolls spilled crumbs across the bare tables and the well starched over-sized white napkins stretched across designer legs. Everything here cost just a little too much.

The place was full to bursting, in a civilised City sort of way. Not the overcrowding of a West End pub on Cup Final day, but the polite standing room only revelry of Wednesday lunch. The girls sat on the high stools and played the men like a hand of gin rummy, collecting the best bank balances while discarding the unwanted. The men clustered around, vying with each other for the attention of the blondest, the wittiest, and the most sophisticated.

Byron sat at his usual table, handily situated in the corner to give him the maximum vantage point. He was able to look out at the trendy young professional wannabes with their short skirts and carefree laughter. Sometimes he dwelt on those days early in his career when lunch was more important than clients. When thoughts of the evening's frolics preoccupied him. Other times he forgot his passing years and joined the game, the size of his wallet usually ensuring an easy conquest of some attractive, young impressionable who usually dumped him by the weekend, allowing him to return to his wife in the country with a clear conscience.

Today he sat with Claire, pleased with her presence, which made him feel both desirable, and less conspicuous in a venue brimming with people half his age.

Byron ordered the best champagne, since he was not paying. Claire sat opposite and studied the man who visibly relaxed after a glass of bubbly.

"So Claire, do you have a boyfriend?"

Claire was keen to keep the conversation on business.

"How's your wife?" she said hoping he was not divorced.

"Away," replied Black momentarily downcast. "She doesn't like the city?"

"But you live in Chelsea?"

"Yes, we have a town house there."

At that moment, one of Byron's past 'friends' noticed him and took the opportunity to re-introduce herself. Walking over to the table, Felicity Farquharson, loudly announced herself to Byron,

Claire and the rest of the winebar with the penetrating cadence taught at the finest Swiss finishing schools.

"Oh, Poppsie, how are you?"

She was tanned, her shoulder length blond hair straining to wander across her face despite being restrained by a velvet black head band. Her suit was Chanel. Her scarf was Hermes. Her nose was by Doctor Hanif Hussain of Harley Street.

Byron was stunned for a moment by this sight, before politely standing to greet her.

"Hi Flick."

She kissed him with the abandon of the Gallic, two pecks for either cheek, each accompanied by the requisite 'Mmwoi'. Her bright lipstick left Byron a faint impression.

"Where have you been poppsie? I've missed you terribly."

"I've been busy," said a blushing Byron, all too aware the eyes of the crowd were upon him. "This is Claire Snow."

"Claire, its lovely to meet you." Felicity glanced in her direction before continuing to ignore her. "What are you doing tonight, dear?"

"I have to work, I'm very busy at the moment. I'll call you."

"You'd better, or I'll sue." Felicity left, her sopranic laughter tailing off with her departure back to a small gathering of well to dos by the bar.

"Who was that?" asked Claire.

"Oh, a friend. She's not as bad as she seems," said Byron reminiscing.

"Poppsie?"

"Her little joke....she thinks I'm her little popsical."

"You have lipstick on your cheeks."

Byron removed his handkerchief from the top pocket of his jacket and nervously wiped the offending area.

"You've missed a bit..." said Claire pointing but not touching.

"Thanks, Christine would not be impressed."

"And that matters?" asked Claire stirring the waters.

"Sure. Christine works for me...and her opinion matters."

Claire thought it best to press no further. As a barmaid deposited two plates of up-market sausages and mash on the table, she took the opportunity of Byron's distraction to rapidly change the subject.

"So Byron," said Claire, "off the record, of course, what is your view on the documents?"

"What?" said Black absent mindedly.

"Do you think they are legal?"

After being softened up by Felicity Farquharson's lipstick, Byron's professional mask had slipped.

"Oh, yes."

"Really?" asked Claire.

Byron registered his lapse. There was no harm in expounding. He might impress the young lady.

"Yes, it's highly unlikely I may write in my opinion that the documents are not legal."

"Not - so they are not stolen?"

"No, technically not. You see you cannot steal information, only the paper its printed on. Its an ancient legal loophole. The government is trying to introduce legislation to correct this view, but it is not top of their priority list. In the meantime, as long as the documents are photocopies, they are not illegal."

"Isn't that a bit odd?"

"Some people think the law in totality is odd. The law is the law, and the law says the documents are not stolen."

"I see," said Claire thinking the law, in this case, was an ass.

*****

Icarus Shares one to watch
Investor's Weekly

Readers will recall this magazine tipping Icarus in September when they stood at 23p a share. In an amazing burst, the shares have now climbed to £15.70. This climb is purely based on speculation. James Carter, the founder of Icarus, is renowned for his deal doing ability and this share is a punt on his future abilities. The market believes there is a take-over in the air and is driving the shares ever higher. When this magazine tipped them they seemed a good bet. The shares may well go higher but unless Carter pulls a rabbit out of the hat, will surely eventually fall. Sell.

*****

.

The Thames was once a thriving river port with hundreds of ships daily making their way to and from the warehouses along its banks. If Hayden had been prone to considering history, he might have marvelled at the transformation of one such warehouse from a spice store to an elite block of flats and restaurants. Only fifty years ago, the spot where he sat was occupied by a crane. One hundred years ago the place was buzzing with the activity of locum dock workers, breaking their backs to ensure the well off received their cardamom and ginger. These same temporary employees now wore white jackets, occasionally wiping the crumbs from starched table cloths, politely changing the ashtrays at opportune moments.

The restaurant was Tous Nos Plats Sont Garnis, one of the more fashionable establishments in town. So fashionable that when Giles Bonnier requested a table outside, by the river, in the middle of December, the maitre'd did not bat either of his exquisitely manicured eyebrows. A table was set, complete with cosy overhead electric heater. Seated with a view of Tower Bridge, the temperature resembled summer so long as they didn't stray more than a few feet. They were alone and that was what mattered.

The meal was excellent. Overpriced, but on corporate expenses who cared. Restaurants were not chosen by price, taste the only discerning factor. Taste of clientele, taste of decor, and the quality of the wine list. Sometimes even the food counted. Giles and Forrest were progressing their way through the cellar, finishing with a couple of glasses of vintage tawny port. Set off against the stilton it gave the occasion a festive feel.

"Going away for Christmas?" asked Giles.

"Yes. We're taking the kids to see Amanda's parents in the Cotswolds. They enjoy it over there. What about yourself?"

"I'll probably go skiing. James has said I can use the jet so I'll leave it to the last minute. Did I tell you my wife ran off with a younger man?"

"No, I can't say you did," Forrest said quite taken aback.

"Yes. Not quite the milkman. Her dancing instructor. She used to take the damn classes every day. So she said. With hindsight probably not."

"I'm sorry to hear it."

"Don't worry. I suppose it was coming. I spend all my time running around the world. No time for family. I imagine that's why James employs me - gives him time to spend at home."

"Do you have any kids?"

"No, I'm gay," he said for effect.

"Shit Giles, I mean great, I think. Great."

There was a pause for a few minutes while both men pretended to savour their port. They had the deal in common. They both lived for the deal.

"You've done very well for us this year," said Giles.

Out of the blue.

"Thanks - I try my best."

"I know. James appreciates your efforts."

"That's good to know."

"What's more, he wants to make sure you stay part of the team."

"You know I am..."

"You see, Forrest, soon its going to get tough. I know the going always is tough in complicated deals, you don't need to tell me. But this time it'll will be worse. We're up against a difficult opponent. There's a lot riding on this deal. A lot. We can't afford to have divided loyalties."

"I'm not sure I follow you."

"Your loyalty must be with us, not with the Bank."

Forrest let this sink in. They both took another sip.

"My loyalty is with you as a client. You're my top client. But the Bank pays me."

"So predictable," said Giles wanting to sneer. "James thought you would say that. That's why he wants to give you this."

Bonnier passed a thin white envelope across the table.

"What is it?"

"It's a down payment for services rendered. You must remember there are people with a lot of money invested in us. People who do not like to lose. They back winners and they pay very well. Far more than the peanuts you earn working your balls off at the Bank. We want you on the team."

"To join you? What about my role at the Bank?"

"We want you to do both. The Bank is where we need you. But your loyalty with us. Think about it. But remember, once you accept there is no going back."

"I see." He didn't understand the veiled threat.

They finished their port in silence.

"I must go," said Giles. "It's your bill today."

Forrest stood and they shook hands.

"I'll see you soon."

"Yes, " replied Giles. "And remember, we are relying on you to keep driving the process forward. Navigate the obstacles. I'll call you tomorrow."

"Speak to you then."

Giles walked off down the river. Forrest watched him framed by the bridge. He waited until Giles turned the corner, disappearing from sight. Picking up the envelope, he turned it over, sliding his finger under the flap. It contained a Bank statement. United Swiss Bank account number 1493058204. The sum in the account was £500,000. No problem picking up the bill then.

*****

Jonathan Gross's office resembled his name. It was situated on the seventh floor, impressive enough in itself. His desk was

carved oak. Enormous. The carpet was plush blue. Very deep pile.
An extensive drinks cabinet sat to one side, framed by shelves
bearing momentoes of deals past. Tombstones. Plastic blocks issued
as trophies for successful deals. Sort of a bankers' Oscar ceremony.

Sitting at his desk, he puffed on a thick cigar, smoke
flooding the air. When Ian Carpenter, Forrest Hayden and Claire
Snow entered his den, the pollution made it difficult to locate the
man. The chairs in front of them were a good indication of where to
sit. And wait to be addressed.

"What can I do for you?" said the unseen Wizard of Oz.

Claire nervously clicked her heels and wished to go home.

"I'd like to discuss one of the deals we're doing. Project
Bluebird," said Carpenter. "I've brought Forrest and Claire along
with me since they're closest to the client."

The big man nodded through the smoke at them. He had
met them both before. He said nothing.

"Are you familiar with Bluebird?"

"Somewhat," said Gross. "Why don't you refresh my
memory."

The Fat Controller had forgotten. Responsible for the entire
bank, he couldn't remember such trivia for long.

"We've been appointed advisors to Icarus, a quoted vehicle
controlled by James Carter. Carter was our client in the Dedalus
deal."

Gross nodded again. Forrest's eyes were running, a
combination of the smoke and the port. At least Claire had relaxed
into her hard backed antique chair, her lunch time champagne
helping to nullify the stiffness of the wood. Carpenter continued.

"Icarus has identified a target company, the Consolidated
Rescue Association, or CRA. Dedalus was the publishing interest of
the CRA before bought by Carter."

"Making a significant profit, if I recall."

"You recall rightly." Nothing wrong with surreptitious
brown nosing. "Now Carter has identified the whole CRA as a
break-up opportunity. It's a venerable old institution which has
outlived its day. It has a complicated structure, but basically is a
Motor Rescue service owned by its members - three million of them.
Because it operates regionally, there are also regional associations

which have an enhanced vote. Both associations and members have to accept a price if we are to do a deal."

"And why is it worth buying a mutual rescue association?"

"It's no longer just that, more like a conglomerate. It has banking, insurance, driving schools, retail outlets and more. Because of its structure, the sum of its parts are worth far more than the assets recognised on the balance sheet."

"So Carter intends to bribe the members to sell their company?"

"It's no different to the building society sales," said Carpenter defensively.

"I didn't say anything was wrong with it. Sounds like a good, but complicated, way to make a great deal of cash. Where are we in the process?"

"We are progressing with confidential, off the record, enquiries with the appropriate regulatory authorities. Neither the Bank of England nor the DTI have identified any insurmountable hurdles. We can expect to get clearance from them before the bid is launched. John Snead has done a good job."

"Snead's a good man." Gross and Snead went to the same Oxford College.

"We have established a price for the deal and need to secure funding for two billion pounds."

"If you need my help here, I'm always available." Two billion was a big enough number to grab Gross's long-term attention back from his fine cigars and lunches.

"We have secured some documents under the table from a source within the CRA. A source very close to Board level. It gives us detailed financials and forecasts, as well as membership lists. We plan to send the numbers to the Banks we approach for financing. At the moment we are awaiting legal clearance, but it is our understanding there are no illegalities. That's right, isn't it Claire?"

"Yes, Ian. In fact..."

"The old can't steal information, only paper trick," Gross interrupted. "I've seen that one a few times. Thought it had gone out of fashion with insider trading."

"We then need to finalise the offer document and get it out to the members."

The Naked Bank

"How up to date is the list?"

"As of last week."

"Presumably it will be several weeks before the bid is announced. Won't it be out of date by then?"

"Sure. We have a source who will update it when necessary."

"Good. You seem well in control. Carter's a good egg. You must bring him in for lunch one day. I'll bring Sir Wig along."

The seal of approval.

"I'll arrange it immediately."

"My diary's looking pretty full at the moment. Seasonal goodwill and all that. I expect it'll have to wait until middle of January. What's your timetable on this one?"

"We hope to launch in mid January."

"Well, sounds like you have your work cut out for you. Keep me informed."

A deep drag on the cigar was their signal to leave. The three retraced their steps through the fog. Gross puffed and contemplated the size of the Bluebird tombstone.

*****

Notice to All Staff

You will probably have read in the press that Walter Greenhalgh has just increased his stake in the Bank to 5% and is making various noises about breaking us up. It is possible for this kind of irresponsible nonsense to cause distress to some of you who do not fully understand the position. Let me clarify.

This man is a professional corporate raider who makes his money by breaking up stable companies and selling the parts for profit. He has no feeling for the integrity of the organisation or its staff. He has approached the Bank to negotiate but we have rebuffed him. Our main shareholder, Banco Republica, stands firmly behind us and agrees with our policy of non-dialogue.

Greenhalgh will attempt to make as much noise as possible in the media in a bid to carry more weight over the Bank than he possesses. Jonathan Gross and myself will be meeting all our main shareholders to explain the position. The Bank's restructuring is well underway and will begin to bear fruit shortly. The Bank's value will rise accordingly. Mr Greenhalgh knows this and is hoping to make a quick buck.

Do not believe everything you read in the press. There will be no sell off. The Bank stands one hundred per cent. behind its staff.

Yours

Sir Wig Forthwright

*****

Robert Parsons stood silently in his secretary's office. There was no one about. He closed the outer door. Susan filed all his documents in three stainless steel filing cabinets. He carefully opened the first drawer, making as little noise as possible. His boss's office was just down the corridor and he would wonder why Parsons, a perennial nine to five man, was working late the week before Christmas.

Parsons was the operations manager of CRA. His entire career with one company, a once grand institution now in a mess, a mess only he could sort out. An injection of fresh blood was needed, the kind Mr Carter possessed in abundance. Parsons would take his rightful place at the top of the company. Not for long the dead end job in which he currently found himself. Not for long skulking around motorway service stations.

Carefully fingering his way through the documents, he occasionally pulled one, setting it on a pile building up on the floor. He worked quickly, his fingers still nimble at flicking through the files, a throwback to his old days as a filing clerk. Steadily working his way through nine drawers, he built a pile a least a foot high.

The Naked Bank

Pulling the documents was the easy part. Opening the outer door of the office, he looked up and down the corridor. No one. The photocopy room was about ten yards down the hall. Navigating those ten yards was the riskiest part of his task. Picking up half the files, he closed the door behind and walked towards the photocopier. Each step an eternity as he felt the thin carpet beneath his feet struggling to sound the alarm. *Stop Thief!*

As he reached the room, he began to wonder if he had the building to himself. Upon entering, it was clear the machine was still hot. Someone else was here. Were they finished, or set to return with another batch of copying?

He placed the first sheet on the glass and pressed the green button. A gentle hum was followed by the click of the copy. The results of his first effort slid out the side of the machine. One down. Why did it have to be so noisy? Suspending his fear, he quickly found that the act of placing, pressing, removing, over and over again, took his mind off the danger. Absorbing himself, the job was quickly completed. When he glanced at his watch he noticed fifteen minutes had passed.

Gathering the copies and the originals, he retraced his steps to the office with a little more confidence. The door closed behind him, the copies went into a deep desk draw. It took forever to replace the originals back in the filing cabinet. He could afford no mistakes. Susan's inquisitive mind would be attracted by any error.

His watch read half past six. Another fifteen minutes gone. The entire exercise had consumed forty minutes and there was still the second half of the pile to complete. Again he journeyed down the corridor, by now feeling a little more relaxed. There was no one here or he would have heard them by now.

The photocopier was conserving its power. The wait was excruciating as it powered up again, making a variety of noises in an attempt to sound the alarm. It felt as if the entire building was conspiring against him. When finally the copier clicked into action, he returned to his previous routine.

Place, press, remove.
Place, press, remove.
Place, press, jam.

David Murray

JAM!!!

Parson's nightmare.

The machine flashed at him a cartoon of a jam in section 3 of the machine. He had no idea. He considered leaving immediately. In fact he was just gathering the papers when a horrible thought struck him. The jammed copy will be of the document. Who ever clears the machine in the morning will discover the incriminating evidence. Panic. Papers down. On knees he opened all the parts that opened. Door 1, Door 2. Where the hell was Door 3? Not at the back, or the side. There were numerous levers that he opened. Still nothing. How could a piece of paper disappear so effectively into such a small machine? Perhaps it was a mistake. He closed everything back up and pressed the start button again.

JAM. The machine goaded him.

Knees again. Doors open. Fuck fuck fuck.
There you are you little sod.
Yank, rip, pull out the little pieces.
Slam the door.
"Please wait while the copier warms up," it taunted at him.
Pace, pace.
Finally.
Place, press, remove

And he was off again, able to sink back to routine. Apart from his stressful diversion, the pages moved smoothly from the pile on his left to the pile on his right. Relaxing into the job, he was ten pages away from total success when the machine jammed again.

"You little bugger," he yelled, followed by "Shit" in a whisper as he realised he had broken his own code of silence. He sank to his knees and once again pulled open the front copier door.

"Need any help?"

Parsons leapt. No more than a couple of inches, but sufficient to hit his head on the top edge of the open flap. Turning with trepidation he looked at his assailant. It was Jean, Fred Whittle's secretary.

The Naked Bank

"What are you doing here?" he asked.

"I work here, remember."

"No, why haven't you gone home yet?" He tried to sound caring.

"Oh, Mr Whittle has a presentation that needs to be done tonight so I'm working late. I can use the overtime."

"Fred's here as well?" asked Parsons with little enthusiasm.

"Oh, no. He's gone home. Once I'm done I'll fax the stuff to him at home."

Only one to kill.

"Are you sure I can't help. I'm quite good at getting out of jams," she joked not realising how close to the truth she was.

Without waiting for an answer, Jean kneeled by Robert, pulling back the correct lever and removing the jammed paper.

"I'd better take that," he said as he took it from her. "Top secret, need to know, secret squirrel stuff."

"Really."

"Yes. If you read it I'll have to kill you."

She thought he was joking and laughed.

"You are always so serious, Robert."

There was a history here. Both Robert and Jean were married, neither particularly happily. A fling at last year's office party continued for several months before Jean called it all off. Robert had been devastated. That was before Carter came into his life. Now Jean was an inconvenience.

"Can I help with your copying? It'll be much quicker."

"I'm almost done," he said apologetically. "Don't you think you'd better finish that thing for Whittle?"

"It doesn't matter. The old fool won't read it until tomorrow, assuming he manages to turn his fax machine on this time."

"Thanks for the offer Jean, but I'm almost done and I must get home. Myra's expecting me."

The mention of Parson's wife prompted Jean to stand.

"I'll see you at the office party tomorrow," she flirted mischievously as she left the room.

Parsons felt his old attraction to the woman rekindle. Putting thoughts of mistletoe to one side, he quickly finished his work and returned to the office. Replacing everything took longer than expected. Two pilot cases sufficed for the copies. He locked the cabinets and set out for the door.

The lift took so long to arrive he placed the cases on the floor while he waited. They were very heavy. A single ping signalled its arrival.

"Hold the lift."

He could feel the sweat gathering under his armpits as the tension and the cases weighed heavily on his frame.

"Hello, Jean," he said with resignation.

"Hi, you look busy. What's in the bags?"

Thinking on his feet was never Parson's forte.

"Just some old stuff from my desk. Thought I'd make space for the New Year."

"Not leaving us are you?" she joked.

"Certainly not," he said with far more than a hint of seriousness.

He would have to kill her.

"Like a lift. You look like you need one."

Parsons did have a car but it was permanently under repair. Jean knew that. This evening was no different. Act naturally.

"That would be great. Thanks Jean."

"My pleasure."

They reached the ground floor and walked past the security guard with a wave. With hindsight Jean helped his cover. How could he be stealing with the boss's secretary in toe. No doubt they would generate abnormal gossip tomorrow, but at least it gave him a cover for having worked late. His luck was changing.

Crossing the road, Jean's car was parked on a meter.

"I'll open the boot for those bags."

She clicked the boot of her Mondeo.

"Let me help you."

"No, I can manage." Which he could, just.

The car started immediately despite the unseasonably cold weather.

"Where to?" he asked expectantly.

Jean drove off in silence, unsure. Parson's knew any office gossip would be good for his cover. As long as she didn't open the cases what was the harm? As long as she helped him steal the documents, he did not care.

As she moved down the road, her Mondeo was followed by an empty taxi cab. Someone else apparently did care.

*****

Snow fall in December is nothing unusual except when from inside a marquee. Flakes floated down, released to mark the start of the disco. Dinner was over and an army of under-aged waitresses struggled to clear the debris of plates and empty bottles. Josh Walker stood by the port-a-cabin toilet, at the edge of the giant big top, observing the evening's events. As guests stood for the first number, he turned on the tape recorder inside his dinner jacket pocket, and moved forward to join the fray.

Dancing Queen is the only track guaranteed to launch an evening's dancing with success. It cleared the table of all but the most serious bankers. Even Claire leapt to her feet, released from her inhibitions by an evening of champagne, gin and tonic, and wine, both red and white. Tomorrow her head would be dreadful. Tonight she was determined to enjoy herself. Unlike some, her bonus had been more than expected, she was here to have fun. It was Christmas.

Her dinner dress was uncharacteristically short, low cut and sexy. Her heels were high. Tonight she felt good and was looking for compliments.

The floor was full of women, most of them secretaries resembling professional clubbers. Sequinned mini skirts and black boots distinguished them from their more sober female bosses. The men flocked around like moths, attracted by figure hugging outfits and the chance of a no strings fling. Claire felt old as she danced away from the centre of the honey pot. There were some excellent dancers on show making her movements seem even more awkward. None of the office hunks showed the least bit of interest in her. John Snead was more interested in Wendy from public relations, a Sloane dressed in spangley straps. It would be hard to wear any less without being arrested for indecency. Bitch. Claire jiggled to herself as the two of them performed a passable imitation of dirty dancing, the lambada and the birdy song all wrapped up as one.

Then the seemingly impossible happened.

"Mind if I join you," shouted a man Claire did not recognise.

"Not at all," she replied to the smartly dressed stranger whose tie was straight and whose shirt lacked any red wine stains.

He smiled as the music changed to an anonymous dance track, totally beyond Claire's rhythmic comprehension. She started to leave the floor when he clasped her hand.

"Don't go. Please don't go," he crooned with a passable singing voice.

"I can't dance to this," she pleaded as the floor began to empty around her.

"Relax and I'll show you."

He seemed so assured, making Claire wonder why she had never met him before. It was normal for the Christmas party to exclude partners so he could not be spoken for by one of her office rivals. He must work in the Bank. Perhaps he was new.

Boy could he move. His body moved sweetly to the music, almost guiding hers as if attached to puppet strings. Her confidence rose, her own limbs began to flow. They spun, jived and rocked to the track before moving seamlessly into the next, and the next, and the next, oblivious to the room, and its gawking inhabitants. She was the centre of attention, and did not realise. Which was why she was so good.

As the DJ switched to Jive Bunny, it was time to take a rest. Out of breath she grinned at her partner, who pulled her tight in a hug.

"Let's make them jealous," he whispered.

Only then did Claire see the incredulous audience. Her initial urge was to pull away, to save her dignity. His grip overcame this instinct and a deeper inclination won her over. She held him, a slightly odd feeling given the less than romantic music. Odd, but wonderful. Locking arms, he led her from the crowd to a cleared table in a dimly lit corner.

"Did you enjoy that?" he asked no longer needing to shout.

"It was brilliant. Where did you learn to dance like that?"

70

The Naked Bank

"Mis-spent youth, I expect."

He laughed and she joined him.

"What's your name. I don't think we've met."

"I'm Josh, from Project Finance. We met on a course once, though I can't for the life of me remember which one."

"I'm Claire. I can't remember you, but then I do tend to get absorbed in courses."

"You seemed very intense at the time. Nothing a little dancing can't cure."

"I'm an intense person," she said seriously.

"So it seems."

"What's that supposed to mean?"

"Relax. No offence was intended." Josh smiled, changing the subject. "What are you doing for Christmas?"

"I'm going home, to my parents in Kent. Should be good fun. I haven't ridden my horse for months. Too busy working."

"I know the feeling. I must've worked the last ten weekends. It'll be good to have a break."

"What are your plans?" asked Claire not just making small talk.

"None really. Both my parents died last year in a car crash. I'll probably check into a nice hotel and treat myself."

"That's awful. Don't you have anywhere else to go?"

"No. I split from my girlfriend last month. I never saw her. Working all the time. I think she gave up on me becoming a decent human being."

"You are decent."

"You don't know me," said Josh.

"Maybe not, but I can tell these things," Claire lied. She had been engaged to her ex-boyfriend who dumped her after he met a woman with a larger inheritance. And larger primary features.

"Well, Claire, I would say that you're a good judge of character."

More laughter. Hand holding. Thoughts of kissing. Was this guy real or a dream? She was wide awake.

Earlier Claire had fallen asleep in the taxi to the party, dreaming of receiving her bonus letter from Ian in the toilet. He passed it to her under the side of the cubicle, written on toilet paper.

Knickers round her ankles, when his head popped through the gap and asked, *Do you have anything to say?*, she felt uncomfortable. Unsure of her place. Snead was tap dancing on the washbasin, his head shaved, singing 'I'm the long haired lover from Liverpool.' It was surreal, and scary. Scary for Claire who never questioned anything at the Bank. The Bank that had just given her fifty thousand pounds.

"Penny for your thoughts."

"What."

"You just went blank," said Josh, "I wondered what you were thinking."

"You don't want to know. Work."

"You'd be surprised. I'm probably working on the same deal as you, on the finance side."

"Really, you're involved in Bluebird."

"Yeah, have been for several months."

"I didn't know. But then I'm usually the last person to know."

"How's it going. The bid must be in the air," asked Josh.

"Not for a while yet. There's a lot to do on the financing. I'd have thought you knew that."

"Sure, my bit's quite specialised though. It's the mezzanine debt."

"Oh. Complicated structure is it?"

"Very. I'd like to see the target's faces when it is launched."

"Yes, Whittle'll be furious."

"I expect he will. He deserves it the silly old fool." Josh chuckled.

"I've never met him," said Claire as the alcohol shifted up a notch. "Listen, why don't you come down to my house on Boxing Day. Got to be more fun than a hotel."

"Why, that's very generous.."

"But?" demanded Claire who had never been this spontaneous in her life.

"Deal."

They shook on it and Josh pecked her on the cheek. They looked into each others eyes and their lips moved close and kissed

The Naked Bank

deeply. Passionately. With alcohol pickled tongues, mixing each other's drinks. Then Josh pulled back.

"Would you like a drink to toast Christmas?" asked Josh.

"I'd thought you'd never ask," said Claire disappointed the kiss was over.

"I'll be right back."

Josh stood and wandered into the crowd towards the bar.

*****

The evening was bitter as Christine hurried along the Kings Road. Snow flurries permeated the cold air, nipping at her cheeks. A thick, black, woollen single breasted coat offered some protection, as did her leather gloves. It was her feet that were freezing. Fashionable suede court shoes looked good in an office, but were impractical when trudging through icy slush. Not even the bright and creative shop window displays could take her mind off numb toes. How long before frost bite set in? Then amputation. And would it stop at her feet? She had read about gangrene. Her whole leg might be removed. All because of her devotion to the cause. Why was it Christmas? It was impossible to get a cab. She had been forced to take the tube to Sloane Square, sitting po-faced amidst the revellers, before setting out on her arctic expedition.

It couldn't be much further. Her briefcase occasionally tried to take off in the wind but was generally well behaved. It carried a document for Byron to sign. His opinion on the legality of 'borrowed' papers. Christine had spent the entire day trawling through precedents, drafting and re-drafting so that now she carried the perfect letter. Her goal to impress Byron. That was why she took it round in person. It was easily couriered but that could be done by a secretary. This was the personal touch. She wanted to see his house. And him.

Round the bend and she entered Palmerston Street, a semi-exclusive road lined with high class terrace houses. Nothing special elsewhere in the country, but situated in Chelsea worth over two million pounds a pop. Byron lived at number 12 in a row of identical white houses with black doors and brass knockers. There was a bell which she pressed. It was ten o'clock.

David Murray

A hall light flicked on before she heard the security chain being slid across the door. Two keys unlocked the door, which then slid open several inches.

"Who is it?" asked Byron's familiar voice.

"It's Christine."

"Hang on a sec."

The door closed again for an instant and she heard the removal of the chain. As the door fully opened, the light flooded out across the dimly lit street. In particular it illuminated Christine's sorry state.

"Christine. What are you doing here at this hour? You'd better come in."

"I've brought something for you to sign," she said as she crossed the portal.

There was a mat on which she wiped her shoes to little effect. They were unlikely to recover. She had bought them with Byron's vouchers.

"Christine. You shouldn't be out in weather like this. Look at you."

"It's not that bad," she said feebly.

"Come into the lounge. There's a fire to warm you up a bit. Can I take your coat."

"Thanks, but I'll hang onto it for a while."

The floor was black and white tiles and her heels clicked as she walked behind the padding of Black's felt slippers. He was dressed in cords and some form of green smoking jacket. She hadn't thought such garb still existed.

The lounge was not large, but there was room for three sofas all positioned around an ornate open fireplace. The fire was low. No need to be fed at this hour.

Christine sat shivering as close to the fireplace as she could get while clinging to her remaining dignity..

"I'll put another log on the fire," said Black.

"Don't go to any bother for me."

"It's no trouble."

Black disappeared out of the room for a moment, reappearing with a bundle of wood which he popped on the fire, temporarily dousing the flames.

74

The Naked Bank

"So tell me again why you are here?" he asked.

"I have a letter for you to sign for the Bank on the legality of their documents."

"Couldn't it have waited until tomorrow?"

"I suppose. But I thought it was important."

"Your enthusiasm is commendable. I must say it seems a lot of effort to save a few hours."

Christine thought of her wet feet.

"But I appreciate it," said Black sensing the sensitivity of the situation. "You'd better give me the letter then."

"Oh right," said Christine clutching her briefcase to her chest. "Here you go," she continued after rescuing the letter and handing it over.

"Thanks."

Black pulled out his reading glasses and balanced them on the end of his nose as he studied the page. He looked most serene, in his element. Christine still felt wretched. It was stupid to have come. She was cold. Her shoes were ruined. There was still the trip home.

After several minutes of careful study, Black reached the end of the letter. Looking up at his expectant assistant, he again lowered his gaze and re-read the piece. Thoroughness was a virtue. It did not pay to make even a grammatical error which could be manipulated at a later date by an aggressive brief. Christine studied his face as he read. She admired his calmness, believing she understood him as well as anyone. She was happy because he was not twitching. He liked it.

"Very good," said Black confirming her intuition. "I can sign it without amendment."

He pulled an expensive Mont Blanc fountain pen from within his jacket, and leaning on the low coffee table that separated the three sofas, placed his signature on the bottom of the letter. 'Byron Black' he wrote in smooth, elegant pen strokes, practised over the course of his distinguished career. After waving the paper to dry the ink, he returned the paper to Christine.

"Thanks."

Once it was safely placed in the case, she stood to go.

"Where are you going?"

"I'd better get back. Its late."

"You must at least stay for a brandy. I can't let you go out until you've warmed up a bit."

"Oh," she said with a flutter.

"Sit down and I'll get you a drink. Have you eaten tonight?"

The question triggered hunger. Christine often worked late, skipping her evening meal.

"No, but I'm not hungry," she lied not wishing to be any more trouble.

"Nonsense. You really should look after yourself more. Why don't you order some food in when you're working late?"

"It takes too much time," she protested. "I'd rather finish quickly and get home."

"On your own?" Black knew she was a workaholic.

"Yes."

Black paused, his hawk mind ticked.

"So it's even more important you look after yourself. No one else will."

Black poured a large brandy from a crystal decanter on a side table.

"Sorry about the tumbler," he said as she took the crystal glass, "Drink this and I'll see what's in the kitchen. The wife and kids have gone to the country for Christmas and I'm not very good at shopping but she's bound to have left something interesting."

Christine took a sip of the brandy which immediately warmed her soul. She felt pathetic. Here she was receiving emergency medical care for no more than a journey across London. She did feel tired, the last few weeks' work taking their toll, and looked forward to a few days off. Byron was so kind. Placing the glass on the floor, she soon fell asleep in front of the resurgent fire.

*****

The tent party moved towards its conclusion. The casino was packing up, the jugglers, musician and acrobats were all nowhere to be seen. Staff patiently waited on the fringes for the music to finish and the clearing to begin. It was half past twelve and the energy of early in the evening was now replaced by the dull recognition of hangovers future.

Fergus was the new boy on the block, and although he had enjoyed himself, he still found many in the department unapproachable. Arrogant in their aloofness. Taunting him over his lack of prestige. Not that he was paranoid, or anything. Perhaps they just didn't like him.

Fergus danced the night away with half familiar faces, awkwardly joining groups of dancers without partners, where outward exhibitions of fun were mandatory and eye contact not recommended. To the outsider the half crazed jigging, to a beat far slower and variable than any song played, looked peculiar. It resembled a collective swaying, the massed behaviour of a previously unheard of religious cult. Dancing around handbags without the bag. Saturday Night Fever it was not.

With a nudge from his manager, the DJ switched out of bland pop mode in a bid to wrap up. 'New York New York' was his answer which had the desired effect of increasing the swaying tempo in one final downhill belt to the finish. The people who up until now had been content to watch others, acting cool with a drink and a smoke, leapt in unison to join the fray. It was now or never, the floor was busy enough to hide any embarrassed jerks.

The exception was Claire who remained seated in the corner. Fergus noticed this, his dulled eyes forever scanning the room for something on which to latch, giving him that bored look that is so vital when performing the office dance. He took the excuse to go and talk.

"Hi."

"Hi," she replied.

"Are you feeling OK?" he asked.

"I'm all right."

"It's just sitting on your own made me start to wonder."

"Thanks...thanks."

"Do you want a coffee?"

"I didn't think they did them here."

"No - not here. There's a bar we can get one. Get out of here."

David Murray

Claire was fed up and the idea of escaping the tent far outweighed the prospect of being seen leaving with her junior.

"Sounds good. Lead on."

Claire wobbled a little as she stood. Fergus, far from being sober himself, offered an arm to steady her.

"Do you have a coat?"

"Yes."

The coats were handed over and Fergus draped Claire's around her shoulders.

"Come on," he said, "We'll get a cab before the others."

They exited the noise walking into a wall of cold silence. The tingling silence which follows an evening of music, laughter and smoke. The air was clear and still. The night pitch black. No taxis either, which given the time of year, was not unexpected.

"Let's walk," said a rejuvenated Claire, "It'll clear my head."

"I'm happy if you are." His lungs coughed the party atmosphere out into the night air.

"That's a lovely thing to say, Fergus."

"Is it?" asked a puzzled chaperone.

"So many people only care about themselves. My entire life seems to be about looking after number one. The Bank's about trying to make as much money as possible from other people's misfortune. For every penny we make, someone else loses. Have you ever thought of that?"

"No."

"And men. They're only in it for one thing. And then you get over the hill and it's too late and they're chasing the next generation of young things. And when someone really nice comes along, who seems really caring, he buggers off leaving you looking like an idiot with a smug grin on your face because you feel so shit but don't dare to admit to your heartless colleagues that you have a soul."

They walked in silence for a while.

"If it's any consolation, I don't think you're over the hill," said Fergus latching onto the one part of her conversation he followed.

"You don't? Your a sweetie Fergus."

The Naked Bank

"I think you're very attractive."

"No need to push it."

"Seriously."

"If I didn't know better I'd think you were trying to chat me up."

"Maybe I am."

"Don't be silly. You have a girlfriend. You're as good as married."

"I doubt it."

"What do you mean?" asked Claire putting her own self pity aside for a moment.

"Things aren't going so well. I think she's going to leave me. I hardly see her anymore. She's really nice, I love her, but lately we just seem to be growing apart. She has her job in theatre and can't understand the point of my job. She has to understand. Can't just accept that it's a job for the sake of being work. Everything has to have meaning for Janet. Things don't just exist."

"How profound."

"Do you think I belong in banking?"

"As much as I do."

"But you're so assured. You know what you're doing while I just muddle along. No one gives me any responsibility. The only clients I see are the lawyers who seem to despise me."

"I wouldn't worry about Christine. She hates everyone except Byron."

"How do you know?"

"I just do. Look, you'll do fine. You just need a bit of confidence. Half the job's an act. Bravado. The clients believe anything you tell them. They are paying a fortune for your advice. The more they pay, the better the advice. That's the way of the world. Otherwise they'd look silly."

"The Emperor has no clothes," said Fergus.

"Sorry."

"You know, the story of the Emperor with no clothes. Everyone buys into how wonderful his costly suit is when he's naked."

"I see what you mean. Life's like that I guess."

They walked on listening to the breeze in the trees, the way
lit by park lamps. The old gas lamps now converted to electricity.

"Fergus."

"Yes."

"Are you happy?"

"I suppose."

"I'm depressed."

They stopped and Fergus turned Claire to look her in the
face.

"You've just had too much to drink."

"That's true but I'm still depressed."

"Care to tell Uncle Fergus about it?"

Claire thought about it, straightening her story.

"There was a bloke in the tent. I'd never met him before. He
was wonderful. If it's possible to sweep someone off their feet, he did
it to me. I invited him to my parent's for Christmas."

"So what's the problem?"

"He ran away."

"What?"

"He went to get me a drink and never came back. I scared
him away. I'm useless."

"Don't say that. You're not."

"You're so sweet. Will you get me a cab? I think I'm going
to throw up."

*****

Claire and Fergus arrived at her flat at three in the
morning. Taxi-less, they had walked. Although about five miles, it
had seemingly flown by in their inebriated state. To Fergus, walking
along in his tuxedo, with a beautiful woman on his arm, he felt like
the man who broke the Bank at Monte Carlo. Time entered a
different dimension, the alcoholic dimension where it speeds up.
There are many different types of time. There is Friday afternoon
time, visiting in-laws time or jogging time, where each second is
protracted, re-lived several times before passing. Then there is drunk
time, lunch time and sleep time where whole hours simply
disappear. One day someone will incorporate this truism into

physics. Otherwise any theory of relativity is incomplete. Until then, Fergus and Claire had to content themselves with the speed of their trek across London.

As they turned into Claire's street, Fergus started to speculate on the worth of the houses. This was Chelsea. How could Claire afford to live here? Her house was huge, certainly not acquired on the sort of salary she earned.

"Come up," she said as they stopped on the lower step.

"I'm not sure I should," responded a hesitant Fergus.

"Don't be silly, you live miles away."

"Look, there's a taxi over there. Maybe he'll give me a lift."

"His light's not on, he's waiting for someone. Come in. I won't bite."

"OK, if you promise." Why did he say that?

Claire unlocked the black front door. The hall was large.

"Are you coming to bed?"

"Is that a trick question?"

"No, not with me. You're in the spare room - it's too late too try and get you home."

"Oh, fine."

Claire led him up the stairs.

"There are towels in the bathroom. Make yourself at home. I'm next door if you need anything."

Claire left him and he heard her own door close as he sat on the King sized bed, incapable of working out whether she was being suggestive or not. Removing his jacket, tie and shoes he determined to find out. Creeping out his door, he listened at hers. Nothing. He slowly opened the door to see her draped on her back across the bed. Still fully clothed.

He moved forward.

"Fergus," came her voice, "Go to bed."

He stopped.

"See you in the morning?"

"Yes."

He turned and left. At least it was better than a bathtub.

*****

David Murray

The man sat in his cab watching the man and woman stagger past. He heard their conversation as she opened the door and went inside. He saw the light turn on in the house next door, and remain on. He was patient and sat pulling his sheepskin coat around him. It was cold and he lit a cigarette. Taking a puff he tossed the matchbook on the dashboard. 'Tous Nos Plats Sont Garnis'. He took another puff and settled in for a short night.

Icarus to bid for CRA
by Josh Walker, staff writer

City sources yesterday revealed that Icarus, the listed shell company, is preparing to make a bid for CRA, the rescue services mutual. In recent weeks, Icarus's shares have soared on speculation that a bid was imminent, although until now no target company has been publicly identified. It is believed that the Bank is advising Icarus on its strategy in what is likely to be a heavily contested bid. James Carter, the Chief Executive of Icarus, recently made a profit of £90 million when he bought and sold CRA's publishing business within the space of eighteen months. The CRA as a whole would be an even juicier proposition containing assets ranging from banking and insurance to shops and driving schools. Its performance has been criticised for several years by analysts who find Fred Whittle's management unsuitable for such a diverse range of assets. This poor performance has put the company 'in play' although its antiquated membership structure could provide it with its most valuable defence against a predator. Both the regional membership companies and the individual rescue members have to vote in favour of any proposals, the true test of their feeling of discontent.

The Naked Bank

January

Daily Herald, January 12
CRA appoint bid defence advisor
by Josh Walker, Staff writer

Under pressure CRA yesterday took the dramatic step of formally appointing United Swiss Bank as its advisor. There has been growing speculation, particularly in this column, that Icarus PLC is poised to make a bid for the troubled mutual. Most commentators believe that any such move would be extremely difficult. The CRA's actions, however, indicate its belief a hostile take-over is possible. Icarus was unavailable for comment.

Taking charge of operations for USB will be Nicola Macintosh, the legendary corporate wheeler dealer. Macintosh made her name successfully defending the Wellington Group against attack from Richardson Croft. Since then she has become one of the City's most sought after advisors, her tactics regarded as both innovative and controversial. For reasons of libel, this correspondent cannot detail rumours except to say that her legendary toughness has resulted in the nickname "Mac the Knife."

What is not in issue is the seriousness with which the CRA views its position judging by the recruitment of Macintosh. It is sure to be a fascinating battle.

Icarus's shares rose yesterday to a new high of pounds 23.

*****

"What do you propose?"

David Murray

Fred Whittle paced the room in front of his mahogany desk. Seated on his sofa was a large woman, her feet resting upon cushions.

"That's a very good question and one which I'll need some time to think over."

This was not the decisive action Whittle wanted from Nicola Macintosh.

"I hope we'll do something soon?" he asked with expectation.

Macintosh sensed his unease, so evident it could not be overlooked even by her bludgeoning style.

"Naturally. It will be used for maximum embarrassment."

"Embarrassment? Shouldn't we go to the police?"

"The police? No," Mac's slight Mancunian accent emphasised the disdain evident in her voice. "Now why would we want to do that?"

"To put him in jail?" suggested Whittle. "Isn't that where crooks belong?"

He still had a lot to learn. Mac despaired at his woolly liberal appearance. Reads the Guardian. Open toed sandals with socks in the summer. Tweed jackets a size too small. A beard. The man wouldn't last five seconds in a bank. He was dependent on her.

"Sure. But first you've got to prove he's a crook. In the City that's much harder than it sounds. Too much of a grey area between right and wrong. And supposing you do prove it, a trial defeats the point."

"You're kidding."

"No. Think about it. If Bonnier is charged, there'll be a restriction on reporting. Far better to spread half-truths through the press. In the short term it's more damaging. And take-overs are all about the short term."

"You intend to leak this to the press?"

"You bet," said Mac. "There're a few journalists I trust."

"What do they get in return?"

"Nothing - this is a scoop. They print it, they please their bosses, and they please me. Pleasing me means another juicy story somewhere down the line."

The Naked Bank

The City played its own game, foreign to Whittle. Mac revelled in these Machiavellian manoeuvres. She stood, her dress falling into place just below the knee, cleverly complimenting her size. She wore her hair in a bob, little makeup, and only the requisite pearls were a sure give-away of her profession. Whittle was in awe of the power of this woman. She exuded confidence, her booming voice more Margaret Thatcher meets Rob Roy than Tony Blair meets Maid Marion.

"Who will you call?"

"Don't ask. The less you know the better. Leave it to me."

"How can you be so sure?"

Mac looked at her man in disbelief. "I've never lost. And I don't intend to break the habit now."

Whittle wished he possessed such self belief. The CRA's finances were not improving and the members were restless. His job was on the line. His company was on the line.

*****

Business breakfasts were nothing new for Josh Walker. At the paper they were common place, snacking on cold croissants washed down with concentrated black coffee and watery orange juice. Often he met a contact at a greasy caff' or a motorway Happy Eater to enjoy a slightly more sedate cooked breakfast. Sausage, eggs and beans, complete with production line tea and complimentary copy of the Sun.

The woman seated opposite had a totally different perspective to the start of the day. Reared on three in the morning snacks accompanying outgoing documentation from the printers, her career quickly progressed to British Airways Executive Lounge coffee followed by the 7.30am altitude stodge that passes for business class breakfast. As her star ascended so did the quality of her morning meal. Champagne and caviar were a splendid way to pass the time on Concorde, racing to finalise trans-Atlantic deals just in time for a weekend's shopping in Manhattan. Today was a compromise between luxury, functionality and confidentiality. She was sure none of her rivals would be seen in this middle of the road hotel.

David Murray

"Sorry I'm late," Mac said feeling nothing of the kind. She was always late. To be on time meant having to wait herself. "I hope the restaurant's to your taste. I didn't want to go anywhere too obvious. I'm told its not too bad."

Walker looked at the starched white waiters, swingable chandeliers and plush tourist clientele, and personally found no flaw.

"Don't worry, I just got here myself," he lied having arrived an hour ago.

Mac knew that, having watched him from her car while she made phone calls. He had read his newspaper cover to cover, twice, drunk four cups of coffee, read and re-read his notes and then stared out the window at the sun coming up over the river. Quite cool considering the magnitude of the story she was about to give him.

Researching Walker had been easy. Two years out of a post-grad journalism course he secured a place on the Daily Herald, as a trainee, and had excelled ever since. Placed on the City desk he had penned a number of scoops including breaking the news of the potential Icarus take-over of CRA. It seemed only fair to reward him for that story. Leaking the take-over had proved he was independent of the Icarus camp. Soon he would belong to her.

"Have you ordered?" asked Mac.

"No, just coffee."

"Good," she said rubbing her hands. Breakfast was her favourite meal of the day, with the possible exception of lunch, and dinner. Afternoon tea ran a close second. Still, she earned her enormous appetite.

Without looking at the menu she called the waiter over.

"Double cooked breakfast with black coffee, white toast, fried eggs, no black pudding."

The waiter was just about to remind the woman that his establishment did not serve black pudding when her stare reminded him of his place.

"Thank you madam."

The waiter made a mental note. This was a dining room above the banalities of writing orders down. A quick move to the side was in the best tradition of restaurant ephemeral.

"Just a minute," Mac said, "You've forgotten my friend here."

The Naked Bank

Both the waiter and Walker swapped looks of confusion. The waiter, being experienced in such matters, realised the situation before Josh and attempted to smooth it.

"A Double Cooked for madam, and for you sir?"

"The same please." Josh looked to Mac for confirmation which she gave with a nod.

"In single?" asked the waiter with a sneer.

"Yes thanks."

"My pleasure," replied the waiter as he spirited away.

Sensing Walker's discomfort, Mac broke the ice.

"I do enjoy a good nosh."

"So I see."

"You know breakfast is the most important meal of the day. So important I always have two. I like to think I do twice as much as other people." Without a pause Mac moved onto her agenda. "I have some information for you which may be of interest."

Josh looked over the rim of his raised cup of coffee.

"You no doubt recall Icarus, and your story about CRA?" she continued.

"I assume that's why we're here."

"Given that I'm advising CRA, you're right to make that assumption. What you may not know is the background to Icarus."

Josh was very aware of the background to Icarus. He could smell a story and had spent the past week digging out whatever he could lay his hands on. Nevertheless, he was very interested in what Mac had to say.

"You may know some of this but indulge me," she said. The main player in Icarus is James Carter. As you know, before Icarus he was involved in buying the publishing business of CRA, renamed it Dedalus, and sold it last year for a substantial profit. What you may not know is that the value of Dedalus was heavily dependent on the contracts in place with CRA. A lot of the books Dedalus published used the CRA brand name and relied on CRA copyrighted material. While Dedalus is the largest map publisher in the country, the map rights were owned by CRA. Makes sense given that CRA is a rescue service and the books were a spin off, albeit a lucrative one.

"Six months before Carter sold Dedalus he did a deal with CRA to secure a long lease on the rights to the maps. One hundred years, which on the stockmarket is as good as perpetuity. CRA got what it thought was a good price..."

"Which was?" asked Josh.

"It wasn't disclosed. But it was believed to be a good deal. Only when the company was sold did CRA realise they'd been fleeced. They sold all publishing rights to the maps, including electronic. That means internet, CD ROM, even in GPS."

"GPS?"

"Global Satellite Positioning. Navigation systems use satellites to identify their position on, you guessed it, a map. Eventually every car will have a navigation system. The map rights are worth a fortune. There is enormous potential here that passed the management of CRA by."

"That doesn't surprise me. So they made a bad deal."

"Yes they did. The question is what was the motivation behind such a deal?"

Josh shrugged.

"It was negotiated on behalf of Dedalus by Giles Bonnier. Heard of him?"

"James Carter's right hand man. So what."

"Relax. I'll get to the point." Mac was used to interruptions. It was punishment for her superior intellect. "The interesting thing is disclosed in the latest set of Dedalus accounts."

"But they haven't been published yet. I checked."

"That's where I have the advantage. Let's just say my network's better than yours."

Josh said nothing, but was impressed. Accounts were highly confidential before they were published. Private companies like Dedalus merely had to file their accounts with Companies House ten months after their year end. Dedalus had another three months before that was necessary and it was unlikely any information would be disclosed early.

"Anyway, this is what I've got," continued Mac tossing a package across the table. "It seems Bonnier's been a naughty boy."

*****

"Welcome, it's good to have you on board."

The Naked Bank

Lara was still breathless from a climb up ten flights of stairs as the man in front of her extended his hand.

"I'm John Greggor," he said crushing her fingers. "You'll be working for me over the next two years."

She had no relish for introductions. "It's good to finally meet," she said without much conviction.

"I've been expecting you for some time now. I wondered if you were ever going to come," said Greggor half joking.

"Me too," said Lara not joking at all.

"Has Phil given you the tour?"

"Oh yes, he's been most thorough." Lara looked at her sprightly guide who had whisked her around the Bank of England offices as if it were an Olympic event. Phil was eighteen, six foot four, and lithe of limb. Lara felt over the hill at thirty one, a self professed office potato. She assumed Phil worked for Greggor, his incessant chatter giving away of nothing importance and little of interest. Another Fifi was Lara's instant pigeon-holing of the girl. An unfortunate appraisal, but understandable given her recent experience with Hogg Midgely.

"I've got a couple of meetings to attend. Let's meet for lunch and I'll brief you on what's happening at the moment."

"OK."

"In the meantime, Phil can show you your office and let you settle in."

Lara had no time to answer before Greggor disappeared inside what she assumed was his office. No manners.

"Cool," squeaked the towering Phil. "Your office is this way."

Presumption would have guided Lara to one of the offices adjacent to the open area in which she stood. Practice indicated otherwise as Phil guided her down a never ending corridor. As they progressed, first the carpeting disappeared, then the paint work and finally the central heating.

"Here you are," said Phil as he pushed open a fraying door. "Home for the next few years."

Lara's face fell as she looked inside at her assigned dump. It was large. That was about the only positive description she could come up with. Thin carpet, peeling paint, missing ceiling tiles and what appeared to a dripping puddle in the middle of the floor. The room bore more than a passing resemblance to a multi-story car park.

"Terrific."

"Don't worry. It's not as bad as it seems. I'll help you tidy the place up." Phil was more than willing.

"I'm not sure its worth redemption. Isn't there an office a bit closer to the boss?"

"Believe me, you're better off here."

"Why? Is it tough working for him?" Lara was apprehensive of the answer.

"I wouldn't know personally. So far I've worked in the typing pool. But I've heard loads of stories. The girls do like to gossip. I might be the only bloke but I do fit in. From today, Miss Waters, or can I call you Lara, I'm working for you," he said enthusiastically.

"Lara."

"I'm the best secretary here."

"I'm sure you are." Lara had to give him high marks for chutzpah.

"I have ordered the decorators for this afternoon and IT will install your system on Thursday. At the moment it's in my office."

"Your office?"

"Yes, I thought you might want to share with me until yours is sorted out."

"Thanks. But why wasn't this sorted out before I arrived?"

"Don't look at me. I was only assigned to you this morning."

"Uh, ha." So far Greggor had scored 'nul points'.

"Would you like a coffee?" asked Phil desperate to make a good impression and avoid being returned to the typing pool.

"Thanks, I'd love one." Lara's features softened.

"My office is next door."

"I'll be there is a minute. I'd like to look around first."

"Fine. It's on the right."

And then he was gone.

There was an old desk in the centre of the room. Lara went over and brushed off some of the dust. The wood was old, possessing

The Naked Bank

a lovely grain. A bit of restoration and it would be grand. She sat on the cleared spot and surveyed her kingdom. Two chairs, a filing cabinet and a framed poster celebrating the Queen's Silver Jubilee.

This could not be real. A long holiday over Christmas with her parents in Cheltenham had failed to produce any enthusiasm for a secondment forced upon her by Hogg. Several resignation letters were drafted and binned. She was unable to throw her career away just because of Hogg's jealousy for her ability, his contempt and his crude sexual advances. If she had known about these working conditions she would not have come back. She gave herself a week. And then the headhunters. A week. She did not know her role, her boss, although she could guess what he was like, or even the location of the ladies toilet. And she had a boy for a secretary. Another drip from the ceiling hit the puddle with a splash. Hogg's revenge.

*****

David Murray

The Day Times, January 12
Battle of the Bankers
by Sophie Cotton-Wood

There is no such thing as friendly contemporaries in the high flying world of mergers and acquisitions. A case in point is the relationship between USB's Nicola Macintosh and the Bank's Hayden Forrest. Both spent their formative years together at USB, quickly rising up the greasy pole. In fact, at one point both worked together on the same transaction team. As they developed at an unhealthy rate, it quickly became apparent that there was not room for the two of them within the same institution. Macintosh distinguished herself during the legendary Wellington defence, establishing a power base within the investment bank. Forrest, in true City tradition, offered his services to the highest bidder.

New head of corporate finance at the Bank, Ian Carpenter, saw the opportunity to pounce for Forrest offering him a lucrative package as Head of Development. Life has been tough, though, at the Bank. Forrest has brought in small deals, but his only significant achievement has been the sale of Dedalus, the former CRA publishing business. He is now believed to be involved in advising Icarus plc in their bid for CRA, the City's worst kept secret. Icarus's chief executive, James Carter, is known for his flamboyance, his style fitting well with Forrest's. Carter was formally a client of USB before jumping ship with Forrest. City sources suggest that Carter was pushed by USB, allegedly "difficult to get a handle on" and "flies by the seat of his pants." Read into that what you will.

Of course, the CRA recently appointed USB and Macintosh as advisors. Sit back and enjoy the battle as the two protagonists go head to head for the first time. Sources are confident of a CRA victory, Forrest and the young Carter believed to be too lightweight to pull off this complex deal. One thing is for certain. 'Mac the Knife' is back in town and out for blood. Both the Bank and Forrest better beware.

*****

The restaurant was small and intimate. Italian with red and white table cloths. Wine endless. Bread readily on hand. Buzzing

The Naked Bank

waiters polite but difficult to ignore as they moved around the enclosed space with full and empty plates balanced on both arms. Pouring wine. Shaking their heads as they poured fashionable fizzy water while Italy's finest red went untouched. Salad and pasta a plenty, three courses a rarity.

"No, I'm sorry. I've got to work tonight," said Fergus.

"But you promised. It's Jean's birthday tonight."

"I'm sorry. It's important."

"It's always important."

Fergus stared at Janet, his girlfriend in name only, their relationship like two ships following the same star, occasionally bumping into each other in the dark. Things had gone from bad to worse since he began his role as Supreme Banker. Janet was a theatre manager and worked in the evenings, not arriving home until late. That meant her evenings off and weekends were the only time they could meet, in theory. They lived in the same house. But not at the same time. Fergus could be required to work the evening or weekend without notice. Janet thought he ignored her. And to a point she was right.

"You know how I feel about you."

"Do I?" she replied as the waiter delivered a plate of pasta, temporarily plunging the already disjointed conversation into silence.

"What's that supposed to mean?"

"It means I never see you."

They had been through it all before. Jean was Janet's best friend and she was upset he would miss the party.

"It's not all my fault. You're out most evenings at work."

"At least you know when I'm around. These days I never know about you. Can't you at least get the weekend off."

"You know I can't."

They ate in silence. Janet finished half her plate, pushing it to one side. She took her full wine glass and knocked it back. Poured another and did the same.

"Well you'd better decide what's more important, your job or me. If you don't come to the party, I'll leave. I promise, I will."

Fergus was speechless. Things were bad. But that bad?

Janet stood and walked out, which given the proximity of the tables, was not easy.

"Excuse me, excuse me, excuse me.."

Fergus looked on as she slowly left.

Greggor was late. Lara was alone, watching the argument raging on the other side of the restaurant. It was far enough away she could not fully catch it, close enough that its resonance was obvious, its action distracting. The man was Fergus. The man she had left in a bathtub. Drunken man. Immediately, all kinds of questions leapt into her head, obstructed only by buzzing waiters anxious for her to order, eat and move on. Who was he? Where had he been? What was he doing here?

The woman he was with made her apologetic trip towards the door. Lara was tempted to go over to say hello. Reintroduce herself. Unfortunately Greggor chose that moment to enter the crowded eatery, brushing Janet on his way in, exchanging wordy smiles of apology.

Pushing past the densely packed chairs, he reached the table and sat, clearly out of breath and flustered by the inconvenience of his lunch obligation.

"Look, Lara, I'm sorry I'm late, something's come up. We're going to have to have this conversation some other time. You understand, don't you?"

"Yes," was all she could say.

"Look, I don't want to spoil your lunch so why don't you order whatever you want and claim it back on expenses. I'll catch you later. I've got to dash. Ciao."

And with that he slowly departed.

The waiter buzzed back, disappointed she would occupy the prime table on her own. She ordered a salad and looked back across the room to see Fergus had gone.

*****

"I've got something you might be interested in seeing."

Jonathan Gross strode into Carpenter's office, a trail of smoke marking the route, a regular banking steam train. Carpenter

The Naked Bank

stood behind his desk pondering the motive for this rare and unexpected venture onto the lower floors.

"Get Forrest in here," Gross called to Carpenter's secretary. The office was a gold fish bowl, looking out onto the open plan floor, observing the paper industry of the department. Gross's arrival always raised heads. Usually smelt before being heard, he preferred to speak in low tones to safeguard confidentiality. Everything he said could be used by an enemy against the Bank, such was its immense importance.

His cigars, however, lacked such a discreet touch. Large, long and pungently sweet, they dominated the office, leaving an aromatic afterlife of several minutes. The office itself was a no smoking zone. No smoking for the workers. No smoking for Carpenter. Only the top brass openly lit up, chiefly Gross and Sir Wig. It was never ascertained if anyone had informed them of the policy or whether they chose to ignore it. Department folklore told of a young graduate who took time from his photocopying to remind Gross of his obligations. The only trace of the lad the next day was a second hand bin bag and an old pair of unpolished shoes. The subject was never raised again. The shoes were rumoured to now adorn Max, the Tower Hill beggar.

Today was no normal day in the history of the Bank. Not only did Gross raise his voice as he stormed into Carpenter's office, but he slammed the door behind him. If he had wanted to do a better job in attracting attention to the piece of paper he was waving at Carpenter, it would have challenged even his great strategic mind. When Hayden Forrest scurried into the office without so much as a knock, the mystery deepened. Was Carpenter being sacked? The paper was certainly not peace in our time. Had Carpenter reminded Gross of the no smoking policy? All eyes fixed on the goldfish bowl. Not obviously, but as each pile of paper was shifted from one side of the desk to the other, a quick glance kept the worker in the picture. That afternoon more paper than usual circulated around the office. Less work than usual was conducted.

"Have you seen this?" repeated Gross as Forrest entered the room knowing damn well he had not.

"No," he replied wondering what it was and how he could have missed it.

Carpenter, himself still in the dark, gestured to Forrest to sit.

Gross began his speech, thrusting his belly forward to its full magnificence. "I have a friend who works at the Daily Herald. He owes me a favour. This is a copy of an article that's going into tomorrow's first edition, out on the streets tonight at around eleven. Gentlemen, I suggest you examine it and then explain it to me."

Gross slapped the paper down on the desk and stood back to allow the other two space to read it.

Daily Herald, January 13
Strange Affairs at Dedalus
by Josh Walker, Staff Writer

Where is the line between business and corruption drawn? In the world of high finance, is there a difference between right and wrong? Is there really a common good or is it every man for himself?

These are some of the questions that are bound to be asked upon reading the latest set of accounts for Dedalus, the former publishing arms of CRA. Sources close to events reveal that these accounts include a note stating that "Giles Bonnier, a director of Dedalus, received a lump sum payment of £4 million relating to work performed securing the publishing rights to CRA's map business." Six months before the sale of Dedalus to Capscan International for £100 million, Bonnier and his master, James Carter, bought the rights to the CRA maps for an undisclosed amount. It is now widely recognised that the CRA received a 'bum deal' failing to recognise the future electronic value of these rights. Good negotiating on the part of Dedalus, it would seem.

Further investigations at the CRA have revealed that Giles Bonnier only spent two days on the negotiations. This begs the question, what did he do which justified such a fee? The money was transferred off shore where it disappeared. Was all this money intended for Bonnier, or did some of it work its way back to the UK? There is no accusation that any CRA staff received bribes of any kind. But as Icarus, Carter's new vehicle, launches its expected bid for the rest of the CRA, the question needs to be asked whether Icarus are legitimate enough to own such important assets?

The Naked Bank

There was no reason for either Carpenter or Forrest to have seen the unpublished accounts of Dedalus. Forrest was loathe to admit this, leaving his boss to face Gross.

"I don't know whether this is true or not. It could just be newspaper speculation."

Gross was unconvinced. "My source at the Herald tells me the story's substantiated. They wouldn't have printed it otherwise. Their lawyers have crawled all over it."

"I'm not saying it isn't true, just that we don't know it's false." Carpenter was a civil servant in a past life.

"Then I suggest you find out. I'd have thought this sort of thing is covered in our standard client due diligence. What do we do these days before we take on new clients? Isn't any kind of digging done at all?"

Far more than in your day, mused Carpenter. When Gross ran the department, any man who could pass the port correctly was good enough.

Forrest felt obliged to speak. "We'll find out. I'm sure there's nothing in it."

"I hope you're right." Gross sat down for the first time since entering the room. After a long drag on his cigar, he calmed down, his voice dropping to its normal decibel range. "How is the rest of the exercise going?"

This was Forrest's baby. "Very well, Jonathan. The documentation is almost there and we've managed to secure an up to date membership list. As soon as the bids announced we'll have the papers in the post. We'll offer the members about £1000 a person. I doubt if they'll turn that down. A bit like the building society windfalls. Take the money and run."

"How did you get the membership list, or shouldn't I ask?"

"From our usual source inside the CRA."

"You're sure its legal?"

"Oh yes, we have advice from Gilbert, Wilkins and Horsefly on file. Everything seems in order."

"What about a second opinion?"

"Well, that would be tricky."

"Why?" asked Gross.

David Murray

"First of all, we want to keep this business as close to our chest as possible. Its already in the press and the we certainly don't want it generally known where we are getting our information." Gross took another puff as Forrest paused and then continued. "Secondly, what if we get different advice. Then we would be in a pickle. We have all the documents. Do we give them back? It would kill the deal and be most embarrassing for the Bank. Far safer to keep the advice we have, which we can fall back on if needed."

"Let me be the judge of what is far safer, Mr Forrest."

Gross normally addressed people by their surname, but never with Mister. Carpenter was intimidated. Forrest noted the comment without fully appreciating its ramifications.

"How's the debt raising going?" asked Gross after a series of puffs, the air quality in the enclosed office was fast taking on third world health and safety ramifications.

"Not bad," began Forrest, "We've had a number of set backs recently although we are confident there are willing takers lining up."

"What does that mean? Will you get the debt?"

"Yes, almost certainly. I am going to Milan this evening to talk to a number of Italian banks who appear keen. The Japanese, Yamora, are willing to help out. The UK banks, on the other hand, have not been helpful."

"Have you shown them the documents?"

"Yes, all interested banks have seen the sale plans, and the forecasts for the businesses. Even those not interested have remarked on the ingenuity of the deal."

"Its a shame they don't put their money where their mouth is then." Gross drew on the cigar. "And the buyers are still in place?"

"Yes. If we sell the Retail, Insurance and Banking businesses we'll recoup most of the outlay, leaving the residual motor rescue business bought for a song."

"Good. You'd better get cracking on the debt side. When does the bid go live?"

"Assuming all goes well, this Friday."

"Don't leave it any later. The press are on to us and I don't like their tone. One more thing. Is this a deal we want to do? I am placing a lot of reliance on you two here." Gross looked at Carpenter and Forrest in turn, searching for indecision.

Forrest felt Carpenter about to speak and jumped in ahead.

"This is exactly the deal this bank needs to pull itself back into the premier league where it belongs. There are a few risks, but this game is all about risks. This is a deal for a serious player."

Carpenter was beginning to have some reservations but decided now was not the time to voice them. He believed in backing his troops, and Forrest was the best. He felt annoyed Gross was raising the question at this late stage.

Gross, conversely, was drinking in his memories of when the Bank was number one in the UK mergers and acquisitions table. That was where he belonged. The Bank was still great and its vision was right. So what if the global banks were trying to muscle in. Independence was the key. The Bank did not need change to succeed. Its philosophy was right, it just needed the best people to succeed. Like the good old days.

"I agree. Let's get this thing on the road."

Debate over.

*****

Claire was not one of those gym junkies occasionally featured on television documentaries or in the society pages of middle-brow newspapers. She worked out to stay reasonably fit. She worked out to keep her shape, control her cellulite, and most importantly escape the office for an hour. Exercise helped the day go faster. It helped her stay alert in the dangerous afternoon hours when the morning caffeine buzz has faded and the mind would really rather do anything other than concentrate. Exercise relaxed her and improved her work performance. If she could steal an edge on her colleagues, she would.

Claire was not alone in this assessment of the gym. The Bank's corporate membership allowed staff to use the facilities at a reduced rate. For mere mortals, the Gym cost an astronomical amount each month, not to mention the joining fee which required a second mortgage. To the City elite, the joining fee was waived, and a much reduced monthly fee deducted from their wages. Gym costs became a nominal health tax. And once paid, it made sense to use the place.

It was mid-afternoon, Claire's preferred time. Her colleagues mostly came during the lunch time rush. In the afternoon she had the pick of the machines. The best views of the people. For what is a gym if not a place to hate those with better bodies and laugh at those with worse.

Currently she enjoyed, if that is an appropriate term, the step machine, a mind numbingly boring contraption of rolling stairs. Keep walking or fall off. Good for the bum and thighs. Apparently.

A personal stereo blocked out the worst of the banal techno-funk piped throughout the Gym. She preferred something more sedate and today settled for a Mozart piano concerto. As piano and orchestra intermingled, she placed one foot ahead of the next, developing a routine, unbroken for half an hour. It would take three visits to the Gym to climb Everest. That thought tickled interest for a few seconds before her mind returned to numbness. Emptiness crowded out her daily trauma.

The step machines were raised at the back of the Gym and she duly studied the other punters at work. Today was fuller than most afternoons. January was always the busiest month as people tried adhering to New Year's resolutions. By February they broke, returning to the more satisfying lifestyle of fatty lunches, boozy evenings and stagnant weekends recovering from the excesses of the week.

The crowd today were no exception, tilting at windmills. New colourful leotards adorned female figures of jogging and jiggling flesh. Worn over lycra cycling shorts, the most popular colours were pink, for the exhibitionists, and black for those quietly confident in their bodies. Baggy grey T-shirts and shorts revealed a lot about their owner's bodies through default. In this place, well toned figures were flaunted. Pristine white designer trainers were worn by all, none having trodden outside the anti-septic environment of the health club. The Gym was not a fashion statement it was a fashion reality.

For the men, tight fitting vests huffed over rowing machines, blowing air like an asthmatic sperm whale. Toes were touched with bended knees by the corporate bellies, futilely

The Naked Bank

attempting to work off last night's drinking games. The athletes sauntered around as if they owned the joint, too good to exert themselves in anything other than drinking isotonic lucosade and mopping the imaginary sweat from their brows. The gay weightlifters staggered, their thighs too thick to walk with any composure, their shorts bulging with thoughts of one another.

Claire recognised Felicity Farquharson, sat on a bike next to a friend, slowly turning the pedals as she chatted. Felicity, the woman from the winebar. She wore a purple leotard over white lyrca leggings, with the pre-requisite pink and white Air Nikes. Her friend matched Felicity almost exactly, her leotard only slightly darker, her tan slightly lighter, and her nose not so tucked. Their conversation was burning more calories than their cycling. Too much sweat and their blond hair colour might run.

Claire's eye moved on until it met another familiar face. Josh. He wore a grey running vest and exceptionally tight fitting black shorts. Claire immediately remembered the man's attractions. Having been swept of her feet, she now regretted every moment. The man had pumped her for information on the Icarus deal and then published it. She had not seen him again until now. Dumped like a sack of potatoes. Probably thought she looked like one. He hadn't even wanted cheap, no frills sex, so she had spent the festive period alone, dwelling on cosy Christmas's past. Annoying memories became anger. She'd be sacked if anyone ever found out. She quickened her pace and almost went over the top. Not a good idea on a Stair Master.

He looked around as she averted her gaze. He was the last person she wished to meet in such a vulnerable position. Despite her anger she thought first how sweaty she must look, never her best with a beetroot face. A glance back and he had vanished. Now on the machine to her right? Dare she look. Eyes straight ahead. Finish soon. Escape.

From the left, a hand lifted her headphones mixing Mozart with muzak. She turned and he was there, smiling, unrepentant. She almost lost her balance and was forced to re-position her body to prevent toppling in an undignified heap. He whispered, his breathe brushing her ear,

David Murray

"I must talk to you. Please meet me in the bar. Please. It is important."

She looked around and he was gone, once more blending into the surroundings. An apparition. An adrenaline induced hallucination.

Claire finished early, leaving her summit attempt for another day. Quickly showering, she determined to meet him, to hear his excuses. To hear him grovel. As she marched purposefully to the changing room exit, she stopped. What was she doing? Ignore him and leave. Or contemplate revenge. Humiliation. Break him and his oversized balls. That meant seeing him.

The bar was nothing special for such an exclusive club. A few stools, a few sofas. More a place to chill out and drink expensive fruit juice, graze on grass and watch MTV. Felicity sat on a stool and smoothed her short skirt, mirroring the image of her friend in clothes and manner. They continued to talk without pause in extremely loud and penetrating voices, laughing occasionally for effect.

Josh sat on a sofa reading a newspaper. She would have preferred a stool to sitting next to him. More formal. So she stood, in front of him, above him.

"What do you want?"

He looked up.

"Aren't you pleased to see me?" His grin was cheeky.

"Get to the point. I'm a busy person. I have a flight to catch."

Grin became serious. "Please sit down. I must tell you something and I don't want to shout it across the room."

Confidentiality was something with which Claire was comfortable. She sat, edging towards the arm rather than the centre of the sofa.

Josh spoke quickly and fluently. "I am not looking for any information or confirmation from you, you must understand that. I'm sorry the last time we met that I had to hurt you. I went to the party to do a job and got carried away with myself. That was why I left without saying goodbye. It would have hurt me too much and I might not have written the story. It's my job to get scoops and so I

104

make no apologies for my behaviour. I'm only sorry it had to be you. I enjoyed your company more than you can believe."

Claire made no comment although her features slightly softened.

He continued. "I would not have come back into your life unless I cared."

"Spare me, please."

"No, let me finish. Tomorrow there will be an article written in the Herald, by me, that in effect says Giles Bonnier is a crook. Now there was a lot of information we could not publish for legal reasons but believe me, both him and James Carter are crooks and you'd better watch out. Be careful - these guys are in for a fall and they will take you with them. I have my doubts about Hayden Forrest as well."

Claire was paying Josh more attention. "How do you know this? What have they done?"

"Read tomorrow's article and this support," he said handing her a brown envelope, "and then ask yourself whether you are on the right side. Don't show this to Forrest whatever you do. These guys are hard and would kill you if it suited their ends. Don't ask where I got the info from. Let's just say it's a reliable source."

Claire did not know what to say. The man who had courted and then used her now expected her to betray the faith of her colleagues. Colleagues who had no idea she was the source of the original leak. "Thanks," was all she could muster. "Thanks."

Josh put his hand on her shoulder and she did not object.

"Call me if you need anything. And I mean, anything. I promise I won't use you again."

He stood leaving his card on the table in front of her.

Claire picked it up without looking and slid it into the envelope. She studied the blank cover as time stood still - until Felicity's hilarious guffaws brought her consciousness back to the bar. Then she left, taking the unread envelope with her, unsure why she still trusted the rat.

*****

"I'll be back by eight."

David Murray

Fergus replaced the handset with relief. With Forrest and Claire off to Milan this evening he felt able to slip out of the office and attend the party.

It was six o'clock now giving him plenty of time to get home early and surprise Janet. Looking around there was no sign of Snead, probably still at a Bank of England meeting, sifting through various regulations. It was necessary to get the Bank of England's permission for the acquisition of CRA's finance division. Advance consent would speed things up and allow Icarus to quickly sell it on to Cameron Bank of Canada, the pre-arranged buyer. Snead would be some time yet so now was ideal to make a break.

The Bank had an empty desk policy. In principle, each employee had to clear their desk before they went home every night. In practice, they did nothing of the sort, at least in Corporate Finance. An empty desk was a unproductive one. Far better to leave a mess. As well as creating the impression of industry, in the evening it was difficult to tell if someone was in a meeting or had gone home. One of the most important factors in generating a healthy bonus was the desire to work long hours. Even when at home, it was important the powers that be didn't realise. Ian Carpenter generally walked around the department between 8.00pm and 9.00pm which had become the unofficial leaving time. Some nights as he walked from one end of the floor towards his office at the other, people could be seen literally bailing out behind his back. The end of his walk generated a ripple of exodus, turning to a wave when he finally left the building shortly afterwards.

Fergus made his move. He left his briefcase behind - in hand would make his flight too obvious. It was cold outside which meant taking his suit jacket. While during the summer the jacket on the back of the chair trick came in handy, in the winter it risked hypothermia. Walk to the door, glance over the shoulder, grab coat and umbrella.

"Skiving off early today McKay." Sean grinned while he shook his head. It was not a question but a statement.

Fergus mumbled something about his girlfriend being ill and scurried out the door. Why did he feel so guilty about leaving at 6.00pm?

The Naked Bank

He waited by the lifts, praying Ian Carpenter would not walk past. He was just going out to get some sweets. No, just going out to move his car. That was it. Many drove to work and parked at an empty building site car park. It closed at 6.30pm resulting in a mass rush to move cars onto free meters before returning for the evening. The directors parked in the NCP. They had more money and didn't need to park for as long. No chance of bumping into them this evening, they were long gone. Promotion meant a high salary and a life of long lunches, cricket, rugby and the occasional foray into the office just to remind minions of your existence. Sitting on hard won reputations.

"Goodnight lad." Dave the messenger sat behind the desk. He knew everything that went on from how late people worked to who slept with whom. The whole department was videoed every night and then viewed first thing each morning. "Go and enjoy yourself tonight. You've been working far too hard."

"Thanks. Have a good evening too."

"I doubt that, son, I doubt that. It'll be a late one for me."

The lift door opened and Fergus stepped inside. "Goodnight," he said to the loyal messenger. Twenty years at the Bank without a complaint, people like him were the backbone of the institution. Sometimes they even gave the man a cigar for Christmas.

Bidding goodnight to the security guard on the door, Fergus stepped out into the street. It was raining heavily and he thanked his good fortune for remembering his brolly. To return for one would surely arouse suspicion.

It was not a cold night and despite the rain Fergus was in the mood to walk. He rarely exercised these days never managing to use his gym membership. Always too much to do. He used to enjoy walking and as he stretched his limbs he once again grew accustomed to their use, taking the opportunity to kick an imaginary can along the street.

He enjoyed his job at the Bank even though it wasn't quite what he had expected. Far more drafting of documents and routine administration than imagined when lured by the glamour. However, he was in the middle of a headline grabbing deal which would make his reputation. He was lucky to get such a chance so early on. In many ways, he suspected that was why the department felt so impersonal. Apart from those he worked with, it was difficult to talk to his colleagues. Were they jealous of the deal? Most were from public school and Oxbridge. His was a middle class upbringing without the trappings of wealth the others almost took for granted. While he aped their dress and even some of their mannerisms, there was a limit how far he would go to be accepted. He had his own identity to protect, a fine balancing act. When the deal was a success they would accept him. Everyone was friends with the deal doers.

Claire was lovely, guiding him through these first few months of confusion. There were a few others. Charlotte was very nice although the rumours of her and Sean were probably true. Snead was quite a character. Fergus was unsure precisely what he did all day, but he appeared very efficient at it. Very dapper. A true blue.

With a couple of notable exceptions, the Bank people were generally very good at their jobs. Ian Carpenter was a revelation, able to grasp a detailed brief and run with it during a meeting as if having spent the past fortnight immersed in its minutiae. Hayden Forrest was very sure of himself and was on the verge of greatness. The verge of becoming a living City deity, another Fat Controller.

The deal was exciting though sometimes he wished he could be more at its heart. His involvement in the documentation, which although initially complex, became less challenging as each successive draft was produced and checked. It was Forrest who pulled all the strings and was the centre of everything, the ring master and perhaps the only person with a total perspective on events. Even Carpenter appeared heavily reliant on Forrest's knowledge and organisation. Claire worked for Forrest and Fergus worked for Claire. She kept Fergus informed with all he needed to know and little else. In a corporate finance department, knowledge is power, and as a result each rung on the ladder understood more of the strategy than the previous. Neither Carpenter nor Gross were on the ladder. More like on the roof.

Fergus drop kicked the can further down the street, his thoughts jumping with each imaginary bounce.

Janet.

Why couldn't she understand his job, a defining moment in his career and she was not there for him. They had gone out for over two years now. He met her at a party of a university friend. He and she were different but in many ways alike. At the time she had been a struggling actress working in a pizza restaurant, her career waiting for its big break. She had enjoyed bit-parts on The Bill, Eastenders and Coronation Street but nothing more than the lady walking her dog in the park, or the shop assistant yelling, "He went that-a-way." The odd fringe play granted audiences of tens rather than the hundreds or millions she craved.

Fergus introduced her to another friend of his whose father owned one of the smaller West End theatres in London. They hit it off and Janet was offered the post of theatre manager, grander than it sounds. She enjoyed the job which was hard and rewarding. Deep down, though, Fergus felt she still hankered to be in front of an audience rather than behind the scenes. She probably blamed him for getting her the job in the first place, her first admission to herself she was no longer destined for stardom. He was blamed for most things these days.

Tonight was his last chance and he was not hopeful.

With a clatter the can rolled into the gutter announcing Fergus's arrival at Moorgate station. It was 6.40pm. Forty minutes had disappeared into a cloud of memory and a fair length walk.

He joined the throngs descending into the bowels of the earth. Why had he chosen Moorgate as his destination? Perhaps the seed was sewn back in September. It was an off-chance, one of those curious co-incidences that forever arise and are regarded as a fluke. Or as fate. Was it fate that led Fergus to the platform? Was it fate that he found himself quite by chance standing next to Christine Edgerley? Was it fate that Christine had also left early having suffered a particularly bad day and would have opened up to the first familiar face she came across?

"Hello," said Fergus.

And Christine smiled as if he were a long lost loved one.

Fergus's arm held the carriage pole at an unnatural angle. It was a long time since he had travelled during rush hour and the tube train was packed. The only advantage of working long hours was missing the daily sardine impersonation otherwise known as commuting.

David Murray

Christine was shorter than him and had managed to wedge herself between his body and the carriage door. He felt both awkward and aroused as he was squashed almost full-on into her by the people behind. She talked openly, as if it were a common occurrence to have a passing acquaintance invade her intimate personal space.

"I can't believe what a shit day it's been," she said for fifth time.

"Tell me," replied Fergus fighting over the din of the public address apologising for unrecognised timetable delays.

"Why is it that I always get dumped with all the shit assignments. It's like I'm Miss fucking rubbish dump."

"You mean Bluebird?" said an astonished Fergus unused to hearing such language from a legal professional.

"No, that's OK. In fact, its quite interesting although I'm beginning to get really pissed off with all the drafting changes. It's everything else. The partners always seem to dump the urgent stuff on me."

"Perhaps that's a compliment."

"It is. I know it is. My reward for being reliable and hard working is to get more thrown at me. The men in the office have much less to do and always seem to disappear off to the pub. Even if I wanted to go, none of them ever ask me....Oh, I'm fed up of all this shit."

The last words were spoken in relative silence and boomed across a listening audience amused by the sentiments expressed. Chatter in the evening, particularly amusing chatter, was tolerated by London's battered commuter classes. It livened up the trip and saved the public from reading the parts of their newspaper too boring for the morning. Of course they also bought the London Chronicle, the evening paper, but that took about five minutes to read, assuming there was a decent football story.

Christine suddenly became aware of her listeners.

"Don't you have any of your own problems," she said in a raised voice. Eyes glanced down at incomplete Chronicle crosswords amidst the sound of cackles.

"Anyway," she continued in a lowered voice, "I've been in this business for six years now and I just want someone to appreciate me. Is that too much to ask?"

The Naked Bank

"No, I don't think it is. Doesn't Byron appreciate you?"

"Ha, Byron. Now there's a story. No matter what I do, he doesn't seem to notice me. I've practically thrown myself at the man without a dent in his upright demeanour. I've got a crush on a guy who barely acknowledges my existence except when there's more work to be done."

"Byron?" said Fergus loudly before whispering. "Byron? Doesn't he have a wife and kids." Christine's outburst began to make sense.

"Sure. But he doesn't love them or he'd spend more time with them. If I had a happy family I wouldn't spend all my time at work."

"So why do you spend all your time at work?" A reasonable question.

"I want success. There's no point if you're not the best. It's all or nothing for me."

Silence and small talk filled the rest of the trip, the train eventually reaching Finchley Central, where they disembarked. It was pouring with rain and Fergus opened his umbrella, an act appreciated by Christine.

"I always seem to lose my brollies."

"Where do you live. I'll walk you home."

Christine was going to protest but the umbrella swayed the vote.

"It's five minutes. Palmer Street."

It was difficult to shelter both he and Christine without wrapping his arm around her, pulling her tight. Fergus compromised, moving closer while offering her the greater portion of the umbrella, sacrificing his coat to the elements. The trip was short and puddled.

In Finchley the residential streets mirror each other. Roads of leafy semi-detached houses stretching into lamp lit darkness. A couple of turns and they entered Palmer Street. Number 22.

"Do you own this on your own?"

"No, I rent the ground floor. Can't afford to buy I'm afraid."

Fergus found this astonishing. She inserted her front door key while he sheltered her.

"Would you like to come in for a coffee. You've been very kind."

"I'd love to, but I've got to get..."

"Oh God," cried Christine. "I've been burgled."

The door swung open. Christine switched on the hall light to witness a minor tremor. Belongings were strewn across the carpet.

"Wait here," said Christine as she ventured bravely in.

Fergus was hardly a man of action, and as she disappeared into the living room, he decided to guard the door. In case the burglar made a dash for it. His rear guard thankfully proved pointless for after a quick search it was evident the intruder had long gone.

"Oh bloody, bloody, shit, fuck, buggeration," she screamed.

For a mild mannered society girl, Christine had language to grace a minor Tarrantino flick.

"I can stay for a while if you want," offered Fergus.

"Please."

Fate smiled cruelly.

*****

When Claire arrived at the Forum Hotel she was quickly whisked off to the conference facilities before she could even inspect her room. The luxurious trappings of the foyer, marble everywhere, a fountain and a legion of praetorian footmen, were surpassed once inside the conference room lined with its velvet curtains, mosaic floor, and Italian Renaissance masterpieces. More a museum of fine art than a business facility. Despite the rush, Claire could not fail to be impressed at the majesty of the cherubs and angels looking down on her with heavenly tranquillity. For a split second she shared that peace.

"Let's get set up. The first of the banks will be here in ten minutes." Forrest called the shots.

Rush. Their plane had been delayed. Their limousine hit rush hour. Forrest was nervous. Bonnier smoked half a pack during a forty minute crawl through traffic. The pressure was intense. If the deal was to proceed as planned the debt financing had to be in place.

The Naked Bank

Their presentation was good. They knew it was good. But so far no one had taken its juicy bait.

"Lets get ready to rumble," said Forrest for the third time, a passing imitation of a white Don King without the electric hair or charisma. The roadies finished assembling the set. Nothing extravagant. The Bank's backdrop around a projection screen. A desk draped with the Bank's banner had room for the three to sit, a podium to the side equipped with laser pointer gave the speaker prominence. It was designed for City presentations. Within the sterilised offices of London institutions it almost worked, a cosy around the table chat probably being more effective. Here, it was the royal Blue of the Bank's colours that almost worked. The stand, however, was tacky.

Bonnier sat on an antique chair polluting the atmosphere with his fag. "That looks shit guys."

"I know - let's give it our best shot." Forrest was group cheerleader. Only in America.

The first two presentations were over and Claire was not confident of their success. The sober Italian bankers listened quietly lacking enthusiasm. Perhaps they conducted their business in that way. A polite couple of questions were hardly the probing of serious intent.

"Let's change the set-up. Its too impersonal. I hate the set." Bonnier had returned to his seat by the window, looking out across the Milanese rooftops. "Get a table and we can present from there."

Forrest and Claire looked at each other. They had thirty minutes. Forrest barked the orders as the roadies dismantled the set in record time. From nowhere a table appeared, a majestic 18th Century oak table was bound to impress.

"I'm going to freshen up," said Forrest in the middle of the mayhem. "Claire, you set up the PC."

The presentation was driven by Forrest's portable PC. As Forrest spoke, it was Claire's job to press the mouse on his cue, thus changing the slides. Like most directors, Forrest enjoyed showing off technology but was uncomfortable using it. His hypocrisy gave Claire a role, for which she was grateful. Bonnier was there to answer questions. And bark orders.

David Murray

Setting up the PC was easy. She plugged its port into the projector, now positioned on the table. She sat on the right, Forrest in the centre with Bonnier on the left. The Republica Bank personnel would sit around the table.

She booted the PC. There was ten minutes. Plenty of time. Clicking on the mouse she entered Powerpoint, the graphics presentation package. There were three files in the Icarus directory. Earlier, Forrest himself had retrieved the presentation so she was unsure which to enter.

"Start from the top," she muttered.

The first file was password protected. No problem. She knew Forrest's password and typed in 'wolves', the nickname of his favourite football team, Wolverhampton Wanderers. She was in. A quick glance indicated it was the wrong file, an old version of the presentation. File two was also protected and she quickly determined was the correct presentation. She set it up, ready to run. Sitting back in her chair, there were still a few minutes and her curiosity was intense. What was the third file? Better check in case she had mixed up the presentations. She was sure she hadn't, but was thorough.

This time 'wolves' did not work.

"That's strange," she muttered.

Forrest was not the most imaginative man when it came to passwords. She knew he sometimes used 'wolverines.' She tried it and opened the document. Not a presentation, more a chart. A corporate structure showing Icarus linked with several Trust Companies. There was Republica Bank. There was a Russian bank, all connected with dotted lines. It didn't make any sense. Then the words of Josh went through her head. *Bonnier's a crook. It wouldn't surprise me if Forrest was in on it too.* In on what? She stared at the chart wondering if there was a connection.

"Everything OK?" asked Forrest from behind her.

Claire almost wet herself.

"Yes, just about there," she struggled, as she fumbled to click the file shut.

"That's not the presentation."

Claire went cold, her mouse hand unresponsive as she tried to close the PC icon.

The Naked Bank

Forrest put his hand on her shoulder as he looked at the screen. She hit the correct button just in time, switching windows to his presentation.

"What was that I saw?" he asked slightly suspiciously.

"The presentation. What else would it be?"

Forrest looked at the screen unsure of his ground.

"Ready to go?" asked Bonnier as he stubbed his cigarette out.

Forrest looked up and removed his hand. "Yes. Ready to kick ass."

Claire breathed a little easier.

Forrest's regurgitated presentation passed her by.

"....two hundred basis points above LIBOR...re-financing in three months..."

What did the chart mean? What did the Russians and the Italians have to do with Icarus?

"...mezannine debt...sale of assets realising debt within two years..."

If there was a link with Republica Bank, why are we presenting to them? As the leading shareholder in the Bank, wasn't there a conflict of interest? Why was the normally cool Bonnier so nervous, shifting in his seat like a baby with a soiled nappy.

"...arrangement fees...great opportunity to make money..."

The Republica bank men looked no different from the others. Reacted no different.

"...forecasts...inside information on the company..."

They asked no questions.

"You can count on our support, Giles. You know you can count on our support."

Forrest's grin made even the cherubs look miserable. "Champagne everyone."

Pops corked, but Claire was unable to celebrate. Having worked so hard, she felt deflated, her energy sapped, her morale dented by unsubstantiated allegation. Betrayed, but unsure by whom or by what. Unswerving loyalty questioned.

David Murray

"A toast," said Forrest as he raised his glass, "To success and to hard work."

Bonnier raised his glass as did Claire. A sip was all she fancied. She forced herself to drink the entire glass.

"Feeling all right, Claire?" asked Bonnier.

"Yes, I'm fine," she lied suddenly feeling the urge to flee the room.

"You don't seem very happy."

"I'm just a bit tired. I think I'll skip the celebrations and have an early night."

"Claire - you're the life and soul of the party. It won't be the same without you." Forrest suddenly seemed to care.

"Sorry. I guess I've overdone it lately. Suddenly it all seems a bit of an anti-climax. The relief of getting the debt I suppose." She was not sure if that was a lie or not. Her thoughts were jumbled and she longed for the solitude to sort them.

"Thanks for your hard work today, Claire," said Bonnier genuinely. How could he be a crook? "I guess it's just you and me tonight Hayden."

*****

Fergus sat on the rug surveying the damage around him. The furniture was tipped over, some of it smashed. Books were all over the floor, papers everywhere. It was total chaos. As if someone's intention was to cause maximum damage. The police had been and gone. *Nothing valuable was missing so it was not serious. Let us know if you find anything gone. Lock not forced. Old boyfriend returned did he? Think who might harbour a grudge and we'll look into it.* Sod all use.

"Could you take these," said Christine as she handed him two cups of tea. She sat down opposite him sitting cross-legged. "Thanks," she said as he passed one back. "Thanks for staying. I don't think I could have coped with this on my own."

"Well, you did say you were having a bad day."

"No I didn't. I said I was having a shit day. You stub your toe on a bad day. You catch a cold or, I don't know, run out of sugar. When your house's turned over it's a shit day."

The Naked Bank

"Understood."

"Good, you're not as dim as you look."

"I'm not?" said Fergus unsure if she was serious.

She was. "Don't take it so seriously. I do tell the occasional joke you know."

"Really?" Fergus sounded incredulous.

Christine playfully whacked him in the arm. "Shut up."

"Ow. That hurt."

"I'm sorry," she said attracted by his feebleness, reaching over to rub his wound. "I always overreact."

"No you don't," replied Fergus sweetly, Christine inches from his face.

"I intimidate you, don't I?"

"No, not at all." He voice quivered.

"Don't lie," she warned. "It's one of my great strengths, playing to people's weaknesses. Do you think I'm too earnest?"

"I can't say I've noticed. I think you're probably a very nice person."

"I am too earnest," she said not listening as she continued to run her fingers along his arm. "Everyone tells me. I just take my job too seriously. Always looking for weaknesses. The importance of being earnest."

"Oscar Wilde?"

"Yes, I know."

Supping of tea.

"Do you remember when we first met?" ventured Fergus.

"Some ghastly meeting I expect. You'll probably tell me I completely ignored you."

"That was the first time we officially met. We first met on the tube."

"Did we?"

"I bumped into you on my first day at the Bank. I was a nervous wreck. I definitely fancied you."

"Did you? I don't remember. When was this?"

"September 14th."

"No. No, I don't remember... Don't look so upset. You can't expect me to remember every bloke that eyes me up on the tube."

"Sorry I mentioned it."

"No, I'm sorry. I didn't mean to put you down. It's just the number of blokes that stare at my legs on the tube. You'd think they'd never seen a woman before. They keep their heads behind their papers and think I can't see them peeking underneath. And those are the normal blokes. Its disgusting sometimes. And as for the Japanese men..."

"You do have attractive legs," said Fergus feeling able to look at them as they lay next to him, wanting to touch them.

"I know. I like to show them off. But that doesn't mean men have to stare." She spoke as a matter of fact, now stroking his chest.

Fergus said averted his gaze while enjoying the way she soothed his imaginary pain. And then he remembered Janet and changed the subject. He was enjoying this too much.

"Why do you rent a flat in Finchley? I would have thought a girl, I mean a woman, of your means would own a flat in Kensington or Putney or somewhere like that."

"You think I'm a Sloane Ranger?"

"Well, yes."

"I'll take that as a compliment." She pulled away, giving him no choice but to nod in agreement. "I'm nothing of the sort. Just a victim. I come from a poor background. Dad went bankrupt when I was young. We struggled throughout my childhood. My mother left us when I was eleven. Ran off with some Australian surfer to Perth. She cleaned out the joint account. Dad was up to his neck in debt. Most of my salary helps pay that off, plus my law school debts. After I buy my Sloaney clothes, there's not much left. I'm just an imitation clone."

"Sloane."

"Yes, Sloane. Freudian slip."

"And that's why you work so hard."

"I guess. Plus, I like it."

"Even when it's shit?"

"Even when it's shit." she repeated. "Would you like some more tea?"

"No thanks, I'll help you tidy up a bit and then I'd better be going."

"Why don't you stay for dinner. Assuming they haven't raided the freezer as well. You could tidy while I cook."

The Naked Bank

"I'd love to, but my girlfriend will kill me. She'll probably kill me anyway."

"Why's that. Keep leaving the toilet seat up?"

"No, I think she's going to leave me. If I'm not back by eight o'clock."

"What's the time?"

"Eight thirty."

"Oh, shit, I'm sorry. I've put my foot in it again."

"Don't worry. It's probably for the best. She can't cope with my hours."

"Tell me about it. All my recent boyfriends have lasted less than a week. Can't cope with me not being there to tuck 'em in at bedtime. You'd better go then. As you don't need to tuck me in. I appreciate you staying as long as you have."

"If it's all right, I'd like to tuck you in. I'll only return to an empty house.."

"Great," said Christine enthusiastically. "How do you like your eggs?"

Blank look from Fergus.

"Joke, Fergus. Joke. Why don't you clean up in here and I'll see what food I've got." Christine talked as she moved into the kitchen next door. Rat-a-tat-tat. "It will have to be Marks & Sparks ready meals. There should be a bottle of plonk in there somewhere. Put the books back on the shelves. Any order you want. I was bored with the room so just put things where you want. How about a Chinese banquet? Usually quite good."

By the time the microwave pinged for the final time, Fergus had just begun to place some books on the shelves. The furniture was the correct way up, a coffee table placed for dinner.

The food was pleasant, the wine awful.

'Cheap taste in plonk, I suppose,' he thought. "Tarty," he said when asked, "just how I like it." His thoughts had fully shifted from Janet to Christine.

They finished the food and sat back, side by side on the settee, half contented.

"Thanks for being here," said Christine.

"It's been a pleasure. Where else can I eat and drink so well."

"Don't be a smart arse...What do you think of my arse then?"

"Sorry?" The conversation seemed to have taken a galactic u-turn.

"You said you thought I had attractive legs. What about my arse?"

"Err, well...I can't..."

"What do you think?" said Christine pulling her skirt over her waist. "Don't you have an opinion."

"Very pleasant." said an overly polite Fergus.

"You can do better than that surely."

Fergus was beginning to enjoy this.

"Well, I like the way your attractive leg curves it way up to your bottom."

"My bottom?"

"Your gorgeous arse."

"Tell me more," said Christine purring as she began unbuttoning her blouse.

"I love the sheen of your stocking. I love the contrast between its black top and the white of your flesh. I want to lick your thighs"

"Look but do not touch. Tell me more."

"I love your lacy bra, the way it holds your bosom. I'd love to hold and knead those tits."

"OK." said Christine as she knelt and offered them to his gentle squeezes, as if exploring a new fruit. He flipped her bra down to fully expose them.

"Lovely."

"Now my thighs"

Fergus groaned as he ran his hands upwards along her shapely pins, slowly, moving from her stockings to their laced tops to the forbidden flesh beyond.

Teasing him, she caught his hands and replaced them on her breasts.

"Now big boy, what do you have to offer me?" she said unzipping his trousers. "I'm glad to see you're excited." She slowly

120

The Naked Bank

unbuttoned his shirt. "Not bad," was her verdict of his chest. This woman was gorgeous. Off came the trousers, yanked to the floor. "Nice legs too," she said running her hands up and down them. Was she taking the piss? He didn't care. Grabbing his tie, she yanked him forward into a long open mouthed kiss. "The bedroom's this way," she said pulling him behind her.

"That's an expensive tie," was all he could say.

*****

Claire sat on her bed watching television in a language she could not understand. The game show required little translation. Contestants jumped up and down winning cheesy prizes with no sign of stripping housewives.

Her mind raced, she was not tired. It was early morning and there was only one thing to do. She had to get a copy of the file. It was stupid. It was dangerous. If she was caught she could not guess the consequences, the very least being instant dismissal. Somehow she had to know. She had to know if all her effort, all her pride in her work, all her desire to please at all costs, was sadly misplaced. Was she the betrayer or the betrayed? She could not continue unsure which way up her world existed.

The room was part of a three bedroom suite, inter-connected with a large living area, complete with balcony overlooking the old city. Each bedroom had its own external door as well as a lockable door onto the central area. Bonnier and Forrest had finished boozing in the communal area about an hour ago. They should be asleep by now. It was time.

The computer was in Forrest's room. Her first problem was to gain access as he kept the door locked.

"Housekeeping," replied the voice on the phone.

"I have some laundry for tomorrow. Could someone come and pick it up now, before I go to sleep."

"Certainly madam."

One of the advantages of a five star hotel.

"Could they knock quietly. I don't want to wake my colleagues in the adjoining suite."

"Of course, madam."

Five minutes later came the quiet rap.

Claire opened the door to a young Italian bell boy. Perfect.
"Please come in."

He stepped in a little hesitantly. It was late and this woman
was alone. There were stories of women propositioning the staff.
Leaping on them in time honoured Italian romanticism. In England
they called it lust. The bellboy hoped for some English lust. He could
use the extra spending money.

Claire recognised his hesitancy.

"Don't worry, I won't bite. Have a seat."

"I've come for the laundry madam."

"Of course you have."

Claire rummaged around in her suit bag and retrieved a
blouse. Clean. No matter.

"Here you are."

"Thank you madam."

He did not move.

"I have a small favour to ask of you," she said.

He smiled. "Of course, madam."

"I need to borrow your pass key."

The smile faded. "I can't do that. The hotel will fire me."

"No one will know. My colleague has left something in his
room which I need to retrieve. Come back in an hour and I'll return
the key."

"Why don't I open the room for you?"

Claire was prepared for this question. "It's a very delicate
matter. I'm sure you understand. I want to surprise him. A little love
game, no?" The words reached deep into the lad's compromised
soul. She reached into her handbag and pulled out a 50,000 lire note,
about twenty pounds she thought. "I'd be very grateful."

The bellboy looked at the note, far less than he hoped to
earn.

"Sorry."

He turned to go.

"Wait. Do you take travellers cheques?"

"Of course, and all major credit cards."

Claire took out a fifty pound travellers cheque and signed it.
"Will this help?"

The Naked Bank

The bell boy took the cheque. "One hour?"

"One hour. And knock lightly please."

"Naturally," he said The money told him not to ask questions.

Once gone, Claire slowly unlocked her own adjoining door. The living area was dark. She listened and heard nothing. Removing her shoes, she quietly padded across the lush carpet towards Forrest's door. The only sound was the gentle rustling of her slip. So loud. Approaching the door, she suddenly realised in the dark she would be unable to see inside his room. She could hardly make out the door. A small lamp slightly brightened the room. Sliding the key card into the lock, she heard the click and pulled the door ajar as quietly as possible. It slid effortlessly over the carpet.

There was light inside the room. She listened, then looked through the crack she opened. A candle burned inside the room. Putting her head round the door, she was unprepared for what lay inside.

Forrest, at least she assumed it was he, lay naked spread-eagled on the bed. His wrists and ankles were bound to the four corners. He was blindfolded and gagged. His well endowed penis pointed north. Bloody hell, she thought. What to do?

A moment and she decided to press forward. He was hardly in a position to notice, and if he did, what could he do?

Inching into the room she saw his head slightly stir, as if hearing a noise. There were lipstick smears all over his body, particularly in the genital area. A big swinging dick, eh, she rused. Glancing away from the entertainment, she saw his PC in its case on a side table. Tip-toeing over she picked it up, knocking an ashtray to the floor.

Forrest moaned as Claire's heartbeat pounded. Her whole body throbbed. His blindfolded head stared straight at her. She froze, telling herself there was no way he could tell it was her. His head rolled back upright, her blood resuming its circulation.

There was a noise from the bathroom. Only now she noticed the light from under its door. The toilet flushed. Forrest moaned again, head swinging to the left, confused. She leapt for the adjoining door as the bathroom door opened. Quietly Claire shut it behind her, allowing her to peep back at the person who walked into

David Murray

Forrest's bedroom. PVC jump-suit. Big hair. High heeled boots. Tough to tell if it was a man or a woman.

Leaving the door slightly ajar, she returned to her room and quickly unzipped the case. Booting and opening the file took no time. She downloaded everything onto a disk. No more than a glance at the offending diagram before closing the machine down, the whole process taking no more than five minutes. There was still the problem of returning the machine. Before the bell boy returned. But what of Forrest's guest?

Had to be a prostitute. Claire took another travellers cheque and put it in the waist of her skirt. A tight fit. For once she was happy about her Christmas indulgences. Tight. Too much pasta. Back to Forrest's door, she again looked in. The woman, for indeed it was a woman, was on top of him in a contorted manner which Claire found unimaginable. Hers was a sheltered life. There was no time for shock, amusement or indeed, education. She opened the door and crept, this time on her hands and knees, to the table where she replaced the PC.

The woman naturally heard and looked at her with disinterest while she thrashed her blindfolded client. The whore had a magnetic charm that called Claire to her. A vampiric hypnosis which beckoned Claire to her doom, or would have done if not dismissed with a shake of the head. The sight of Forrest was enough to break any spell. Instead she took out the cheque, and, finding a pen, counter-signed it. She raised her finger to her lips and walked to the bed, her toes tingling with both fear and anticipation. Slowly she reached out and handed the cheque to the woman. The whore's hand, the free one, lingered on Claire's as she took the cheque. Mouthing a sloppy kiss, she deposited the paper within the vault of her bosom. Sensing the repulsion in her new found friend, she turned away, allowing Claire to escape those emphatic eyes.

Claire left in a hurry, shutting the door behind her. If she had looked back, she might have noticed the cigarette glow emanating from the balcony.

*****

The Naked Bank

CRA House
12 Brooks Road
Birmingham

Sir Wig Forthright
Chairman
The Bank
42 Tower Rise
London

13 January

Dear Sir Wig

It was with much disappointment that I read in the press of the imminent bid by Icarus plc for CRA. Given that you, in your capacity as Chairman of the Bank, are advising Icarus, I thought it appropriate to inform you of events. I can only assume that you are not in full possession of the facts or else you would have withdrawn your advice to the afore mentioned company.

CRA is one of the oldest and most respected mutual companies in the country. It has a long tradition of support for the poorer members of society through cheap loans, insurance and breakdown cover. Many people, particularly in rural areas of the country, would never have bought a car or farm vehicle if it was not for CRA. We aid people the big banks abandon. CRA is the last resort for many of the disadvantaged members of society.

A bid for CRA by Icarus is a pure money making opportunity taking no account of the social damage a break-up will cause. When viewed in a cold commercial light, the CRA should not exist. Without its mission it has no point. Taking it over can only be described as an act of wanton vandalism.

As a traditional merchant bank, your reputation is built on honesty. You, of all people, must recognise the value of reputation over commerciality. Think again over advising Icarus, the very antithesis of the Bank's values. James Carter is a young upstart seeking to make a quick buck. Yours is an institution of long standing relationships built on solid foundations. I appeal

125

David Murray

to your common decency to put an end to this charade to protect not just our reputation, but your own as well.

I look forward to your response.

Kind regards

Yours sincerely

Frederick H Whittle

The Naked Bank

January

The Bank
42 Tower Rise
London EC13 7JK

Frederick Whittle
Chairman
CRA
CRA House
12 Brooks Road
Birmingham

14 January

Dear Mr Whittle

Thank you for the concerns raised in your letter of 13 January. I always welcome opinion from differing sources and am happy to respond to your points. I was, however, disappointed that you chose to leak your letter to the national press. This would suggest your motivation was more than just concern.

You would not expect me to comment on any particular rumour that has been circulated in the national press. However, as for your attack on James Carter, I can only say he is a highly valued client of the Bank. We have the utmost confidence in his suitability. As you alluded in your letter, the Bank is very careful with whom we form a relationship.

David Murray

I also recognise the esteem in which the CRA is held and the good and valued work your organisation performs. I wish you every luck in continuing that work in the future and hope your financial fortunes improve.

Ever yours

Wig

*****

There's nothing like the smell of double cooked breakfast in the morning. Especially when the setting is the exclusive Henry Club. Situated in St James, it is one of the more elitist London gentlemen's clubs. In fact it is one of the few remaining bastions of male chauvinism. A jacket and tie must be worn at all times, and although wives and mistresses are permitted in the front door, there are many areas from which they are forbidden. Any show of the female form might induce a fit in some of the more fossilised remains who passed as members.

What was not widely publicised, for to do so would cause an outcry of both internal outrage and external applause, was Mac's membership. A gentleman's club had its uses discussing business in a place acceptable to the social circles in which Mac moved. Dinner at Henry's a guaranteed business winner. But how? While no one would dispute it is Mac that wears the trousers, but there is no escaping biological fact. The answer is simple. The reason so many of these clubs are still exclusively male is because women are not desperate enough to join. Unsurprising given the clubs' deep-seated Victorian roots.

For Mac, however, gaining membership was just another challenge. A push upwards on the glass ceiling. She met the Chairman of the club, and after an amicable, though forceful, meeting the club announced it would be delighted for her to become a full member. Though the club would deny any suggestion vigorously, the mention of action in the European Court of Justice may have swayed the Chairman's decision. Sex equality is one of

The Naked Bank

those pesky human rights adopted by Europe meddlers, intent on destroying the British way of life.

Mac's membership was conditional on her not entering any of the male changing or toilet facilities, and it not being publicised. If word escaped there would be no end of trouble from other female 'agitators'. Mac was quite happy with this arrangement since it placed her at the top of her gender tree. Sisterhood was nothing when it came to superiority.

She now sat in the club dining room, renowned for its fine food, in particular its breakfast. For members, who often stayed overnight, breakfast was the foundation upon which the day was built. For Mac it was one of many. Today she wore a jacket, trousers and tie out of respect for the rules of the institution. Opposite her sat the Right Honourable Doug Youngblood, MP for Barnsley North, Chair*man* of the influential Trade and Industry Sub-Committee. Sports jacket and working man's club tie was his uniform.

"How's your father these days?" he asked.

"Very well, thanks. I'm not sure if he's taken to retirement yet. Deep down he still wishes he was leading marches against the government."

"Yeah, I can understand that. Those days are long gone now. We are the government."

"Are you?" mocked Mac. "I realise your party's in power. But the same people who fought alongside my father?"

"That's a good question and far too complicated to answer over breakfast."

"Dodged like a true politician."

"Things change Nicola. The responsibilities are much greater in power."

"You don't need to convince me. I'm not my father. I'm the capitalist sell-out, remember."

"How could I forget in a bloody place like this? So how much do they pay you these days? More than the entire flipping cabinet, I dare say."

"They're underpaid."

"Perhaps you're overpaid."

"Perhaps," said Mac not wanting to debate it. She had enough arguments with her father, on the odd occasion she talked to him.

Breakfast arrived anonymously.

"At least you haven't lost your working class appetite," he joked.

"You can say that again. Tuck in."

Mac took a large forkful of bacon and egg, and chewed. She talked as she ate.

"You're wondering why I invited you along today?"

"It had crossed my mind. You're not someone to act without a reason."

"You know me too well," she swallowed. "How close are you to the CRA?"

"As close as most Labour supporters, I suppose. We greatly respect their work. They were after all a rival party before the war. Did a lot of social good. You know there's still a pact never to stand opposing candidates against each other?"

"No, can't say I did. I didn't know they were political."

"Not any more. I don't think even they know what they're for these days. Then I guess we don't either. Who knows, they may decide to break our pact. Stand as true socialists."

"That would be interesting."

"Highly inconvenient if you ask me."

Mac seized the opening. "How would you like it if they pledged to stay out of politics for a fixed period?"

"What do you mean?"

"Well, right now the CRA needs friends. The Labour Party's its biggest ally."

"Go on."

"No doubt you've read the press about the potential take-over of the CRA by the break-up merchants. Horrible money grabbing types. You know the kind. The CRA have appointed me to help them."

"Can't say I'm surprised. You're very good at your job. It's good to see you returning to your roots. Though I'm sure they're paying you exceptionally well"

The Naked Bank

"I haven't thought about it. Its a job. Roots or not." Mac wished she hadn't said that as she saw Youngblood flinch. "But now I'm glad I working for a worthy cause." A good touch. "In any case, the CRA need your help."

"So it's that serious?"

"Yes it is."

"What can I do?" Youngblood always welcomed a social battle. Especially if there was the potential for good publicity.

"I would be grateful if you could organise an Early Day motion supporting the CRA against aggressors and pledging the support of the government for the CRA."

"I'm not sure I can do that, and even if I could, parliamentary time is precious. It won't be immediate."

Mac had expected this response. The request was a softener for what she really wanted.

"How about a letter of support for the CRA signed by as many MPs as you can get?"

"Now that I can do. I don't think you'll have a problem getting support. Would you like to draft the letter?"

"I have one here." Mac pulled an envelope from her jacket pocket.

"Surprise me." He took the letter and jacket pocketed it. "Would you like me to get the signatures or do you have them as well?"

"No, that's where I need your help. I'd be very grateful..."

"Usual arrangements for reimbursing expenses?"

"Of course," said Mac.

"It may cost a bit to get the time of some people. MPs are very busy people."

"I understand. Make sure you account for your own time as well. My budget is generous. Very generous"

"You can count on it."

Mac smiled. Buying MPs was cheap at the price.

*****

David Murray

Josh Walker
Staff Writer, Daily Herald
Phone: 0171 667 3452   Fax: 0171 667 1234

Claire looked at the card and dialled the number on her mobile phone. The hotel phone was too risky. The number would be itemised on her bill. An expenses bill Forrest would approve.

"Good morning, Daily Herald," answered the receptionist with the detachment that takes years of practice.

"Good morning. Josh Walker please."

"One moment please."

A knock at the door. "Claire. Are you ready. We'll miss the flight."

Claire looked at her packed bag and picked up her coat. "Just a minute."

As the phone rang, she walked into the bathroom and shut the door. Less chance of being heard through two doors. The phone kept ringing.

"Come on, come on..." she muttered.

"Hurry up," shouted an impatient Forrest.

The phone still rang unanswered. Finally it was picked up. "Herald."

"Hello, can I speak to Josh."

"Err, he's not in yet. Can I take a message?"

"Hurry up," said Forrest.

"No I'll call back." It was 7.30am in Milan. 6.30 am in London. No wonder he wasn't in yet.

"Coming," she shouted, flushing the toilet, grabbing her bags and opening the door.

The trip to the airport was quiet. Giles smoked and Forrest dozed. Claire thought of the previous night, constantly reminding herself the bizarre does happen as she tried not to let her disgust at Forrest show. The atmosphere in the car was surprisingly tense given they had just secured the debt for the deal. Was it her imagination? She could not relax. Last night's short sleep had been punctuated by dreams. Dreams of cigarettes entwined with ropes.

The Naked Bank

She was blindfolded, couldn't see, at one point waking in a cold sweat. The dreams were still vivid.

Arriving at the airport, they quickly checked in. There's not a great deal to see at Milan airport, so ten minutes before boarding they sat on the plastic seats that pass for comfort at the world's airports, and read yesterday's newspapers. Claire excused herself to visit the ladies.

There was a woman mopping the floor as she entered. No one else. Claire entered the cubicle by the far wall, shut the door and sat on the toilet lid. Pressing the re-dial button on her phone she wondered whether the world had descended into a comedy of subterfuge.

"Good morning, Daily Herald."

"Josh Walker," she whispered.

"I'm sorry, could you repeat that."

"Josh Walker," Claire said louder, aware of the sound of her voice.

"One moment please."

Ringing

"Come on Josh, be an early bird."

It was around 7.15am in the UK.

"Hello, Josh Walker's phone." Different person, not Josh.

"Is Josh there please?"

"I don't think he's come in yet. Can I take a message?"

"No thanks.."

"Hang on a sec, he's just coming in. I'll put him on."

It was refreshing to be put through to Josh without numerous questions about name, firm, what the call concerns, only to be told he was in a meeting. Story of her unimportant life.

"Hello." It was Josh.

"It's Claire, I can't speak for long. I have something I need to give you a.s.a.p."

"OK. Where are you?"

"Milan airport. The ladies."

"Well, I'm afraid I can't help you there."

"Josh, this is serious," she whispered loudly. "My plane arrives at Heathrow at 9.45. Meet me and be discreet. I have a disk for you. I'm travelling with some people you know."

"Bonnier?"

"Good guess."

"I'll be there. I'll make contact with you."

"Got to go. Bye."

"Good luck," said Josh as she hung up.

Leaving the lavatory she received a strange look from the cleaner. 'You English are all mad' was the general gist.

Everyone was settled on the place when the newspapers came around. English newspapers including the Daily Herald. Forrest knew what to expect having seen the leaked story yesterday. Claire had seen the story in the package supplied by Josh. Giles was in the dark.

"What the fuck...?" he exclaimed upon seeing the article on the front page of the business section. His reaction provided a much needed outbreak of early morning merriment among the other passengers.

"Have you seen this?" he asked Forrest, sitting next to him. Claire was fortunately situated several rows back, not important enough to sit with the big boys.

"Yes," was all he could say not wanting to reveal his advanced notice. He had forgotten to tell Bonnier in the rush yesterday evening. After the presentation there were other things on his mind.

"Shit, where did they get this from?"

"It's true?"

"Yes, it's true. It's all above board." People were looking at him, the photo in the newspaper, and back at him. They had a genuine business celebrity on board and pricked their ears accordingly. "We'll discuss it later."

Bonnier agreed. Claire read Cosmo and an article on how to reduce stress in your life while carrying evidence which might relate to an organised crime ring, stolen from your sexually perverted boss sitting three rows in front of you. She was also a nervous flier.

Heathrow was a zoo as always. Leaving the plane was an Olympic event. Not just a race to passport control, customs and taxis.

The Naked Bank

A test of strength in retrieving items from overhead while being jostled from behind, bashed and bruised.

Needless to say, Forrest and Bonnier were prime movers in the disembarkment routine, somehow squirming to the front door, ready to leap when it opened. Forrest had a kind word or two to say to the bored stewardess. Rather be flying long haul, having to make do with the business cattle flight.

"Thank you for flying Rip-off Air."

Claire saw no need to push forward as her colleagues disappeared into the bowels of the airport. So much for manners she thought, actually pleased they had left her behind. She moved forward in small steps, the briefcase of the man behind constantly bashing her calf. She could cope. She would not hit him. She would not hit him. Damn him. As the jam cleared she accidentally swished her case backwards catching him in the groin.

"Sorry," she said as she moved forward leaving him groping for his briefcase on the floor like a blind man who has mislaid his marbles.

She walked calmly. Josh could not contact her until through customs. There was a good chance Forrest and Bonnier would not wait for her until the taxi rank, giving her white knight every opportunity to meet her alone.

Passport a formality. Pity non-EU nationals forced to queue. Customs. What customs as she walked through the non-manned Blue Zone. The relative serenity of the complex was broken as she entered the throbbing arrival hall. People jostled to hug, kiss and quarrel as they were met. A whole army of chauffeurs held up boards with names of corporate bigwigs. She ignored them seeing Forrest and Bonnier waiting for her at the oasis that was the rental car stand. Bonnier even waved. Perhaps hallucinating after the plane's magic mushroom breakfast. She waved back and felt a fool.

"Miss Snow?" asked a chauffeur next to her.

Surprised, she turned to see Josh wearing a grey suit, tie, peaked cap and the most ridiculous false beard this side of her local pub's Osama Bin Laden impersonation evening.

"Josh?" she asked.

"Don't give me your info - we're being watched. Can you put it inside a paper and leave it by the exit?"

"Yes."

"Then go."

Claire reached her colleagues.

"What was that all about?" asked Forrest. Bonnier conversed with his tobacco fix.

"Mistaken identity. The man virtually propositioned me. Can't be too careful these days."

"No," said Bonnier examining his stained fingers. Claire assumed he was reflecting on the newspaper article.

"Let's get a cab," said Forrest.

The rank was just outside the exit. As she walked, Claire pulled the disk from her handbag and slipped it into her paper, managing to cling to her suit bag. Trailing the other two by a few steps allowed the act to go unnoticed. She dropped the paper by the revolving door. A glance back saw Josh completing the transfer by picking up the paper and stuffing it inside his jacket. She hoped the trip to the City would be quick.

*****

Fergus woke alone and reached for the light switch that wasn't there. No, not at home. It was very dark, and as he climbed out of bed he fell over his shoes. This prompted him to crawl until reaching what he guessed was the door, and a switch. And there was light.

It was Christine's room, still a mess from last night's break in. Clothes all over the floor, a few of which belonged to him. Opening the curtains it was daylight. They were thick and heavy. Dust swirled in the sun's early morning rays. It was 9am and he was late. Did she really own a Bob the Builder clock?

Rummaging around on the floor he found enough of his own clothes to dress. The room led to the living room where he found the rest of his things. And a note. *Dear Fergus, Had to run. Enjoyed last night. Let yourself out. C.* Still a little groggy, he did not dwell on its succinctness. Home for a shower and a clean shirt.

He was nervous as he turned the key in the latch. The walk to his flat had reminded him of Janet's ultimatum. There would be a row. Entering, it was soon evident that there would not be. Her clothes were gone. She was gone. There was no note. No mess.

It was eleven o'clock when Fergus entered the Bank. As he stood waiting for the lift, Claire walked in.

"Good morning Fergus, a bit late aren't we?"

"I could say the same."

"My excuse is I've just got back from Italy, popped home to get some clothes for tonight, dumped my stuff, and I'm still here by eleven. Not too shabby. How about you?"

They entered the lift.

"I had an affair and my girlfriend dumped me."

Claire felt like asking more but already felt guilty for scoring a cheap point. There were other more pressing matters.

"We've got the debt."

"Fantastic - so we can rock'n'roll?" Fergus had quickly realised that the more extreme the cliché, the more respect he gained.

"You bet. I'm afraid it will be an all-nighter." The lift door opened.

"Hence the change of clothes." Fergus was relieved he had taken the time to shower and change.

"We're going to launch tomorrow."

Fergus suddenly felt exhilaration tinged with first night nerves. Gunpowder lurking within his blood, ready to blow apart his charade of quiet competence. They entered the department, and immediately smelt the cigar smoke in the air.

"Claire," said Hayden Forrest, "Would you be so good as to step into room 4. There's something we need to discuss."

*****

Josh sat with his notes spread out in front of him. He was at home, his flat in Clapham. It was closer to Heathrow than the office at Canary Wharf. The contents of the disk were intriguing. What could be so important to make Miss Claire Sensible, cool banker extraordinaire, turn into a gibbering wreck. A femme fatale. A Mary Astor without the devil, a Lauren Baccal without the pout. A woman to make him drop everything for the type of chase that for a journalist usually ends in frustration.

He was wary as he popped the disk into his laptop, quickly virus checking it. Force of habit. No booby traps just a collection of files, all compatible with Microsoft Office. Some were Word, some Powerpoint. The soft scratching of the printer accompanied his reading of each document, only distracted by the need to add more paper.

An hour later the pile was an inch high. On top sat the document Claire had originally stumbled across. A structure diagram, linking a number of companies, the names joined by both plain and dotted lines. The distinction was unclear. He guessed they represented shareholdings, with the dotted lines indicating indirect relationships. There in the middle of the corporate maze sat Icarus plc, a spider linked to its web. But what did it mean?

Brewing a pot of coffee, Josh decided to think. If he studied the diagram for long enough he might find an answer. His research on Icarus was to hand. Brain power was needed. A puzzle box which when solved would flick open its lid, revealing the prize which gave Claire such excitement. Or was she just suspicious? He could not call her at the Bank. Phone conversations were recorded and besides, it might place her in a difficult position if Forrest were standing nearby. He had to think. This was his chance. Be a banker. Think like a banker. Staring at the piece of paper, he resolved to re-read the files, re-read his notes and piece it all together. He enjoyed a mystery. First he poured the coffee.

*****

Claire followed Forrest into the meeting room with trepidation. Did he know? Was she finished? She wished she had a photograph to use as a bargaining chip. Who would believe her word against his?

The room was not empty. There was Jonathan Gross, Ian Carpenter, James Carter and Giles Bonnier all sitting around the table. Behind them rain lashed the window, so strong the view of the Tower of London had vanished behind the downpour.

The Naked Bank

She took her place by Forrest. There were only two available seats giving her no choice where to sit.

The meeting belonged to Carpenter.

"Thank you all for coming. I think the purpose of this meeting is obvious. In light of today's newspaper revelations, none of which we were aware of when we took Icarus on as a client, I think it's important to clear up any potential misunderstanding."

"Not that we think you have done anything wrong," smoothed Gross offering the clients complimentary Cuban cigars. The Bank owned the troubled manufacturer, purchased to prevent any disruption to Sir Wig's supply.

Carpenter bridled at the interruption which watered the firm line he was trying to take. "I have received several phone calls this morning from journalists asking if the Bank cares to comment on this article or on the letter published by Whittle yesterday. If we are to be effective in advising Icarus we need everything on the table. And that means any other snippets of information which may come to light in the future. If there's anything to be found, Nicola Macintosh will find it."

Carpenter looked at Carter, who looked at Forrest as if to say, 'who is this man? Why is he bothering me?' Carter was not easily flustered by an upstart banker.

"I appreciate your concerns Ian, and would like to lay them to rest, if I can."

Carpenter indicated the stage was his. Bonnier leaned back in his chair and lit up, puffing complimentary cigar smoke into the room. Gross had never stopped.

Carter continued in his most reasonable tone, "The so called allegations printed in the paper today are nothing new. Nothing wrong. The consultancy fee paid to Giles was above board, declared in the accounts and fully documented. It was a business arrangement. He brought in an agreement with the CRA which added significant value to Dedalus. The difference between the company being a mature publishing business and an exciting, fast growing, multimedia business. The value of the company increased from fifty million pounds to one hundred million pounds. Personally, I don't think paying four million for that increase is excessive. He did far more for me than you have done. I don't hear you saying that the Bank's fees are excessive. Do I?" He kept his voice steady, only a raised eyebrow betraying irritation.

"No, of course not. We believe we have a very equitable arrangement," said Gross.

"Good. Because if you do have a problem there are plenty of other banks out there who would love to get the fees that Icarus is going to generate."

Carter was not about to sack the Bank. Carpenter knew that. It would ruin any chance of launching the bid for CRA in the near future. However, the threat was worrying. Future fees could go elsewhere. The dismantling of the CRA could generate fees of at least £20 million.

"You can phone my auditor," continued Carter, "I think you'll find he's looked into matters thoroughly."

"Thank you, I will," said Carpenter.

"We need to do so for compliance reasons. Purely routine," Gross added.

"As you wish. My secretary can give you his number. It's Hogg Midgely. I'll let him know you will be calling. If that's all, I have a lot to do as, gentlemen and lady, I expect you have. We have a deal to do."

Carter and Bonnier stood as one.

"Oh yes," finished Carter, "if there are any more allegations regarding Giles or myself, I would be happier if they were referred to Byron Black. Understood."

They left.

"Happy?" remarked Gross.

"Yes," said Carpenter, though he was not convinced. The others stood to leave. "Claire, would you mind staying behind for a moment."

Claire sat down again as the door closed behind Gross and Forrest.

"I have been watching you now for sometime, Claire..."

Here it comes. Forrest has told him. I am fired.

"...I think you are doing very well. You have a bright future at the Bank. Promotion to Assistant Director next year I expect..."

Attention guaranteed.

"...tell me, what do you think of Carter and Bonnier?"

The Naked Bank

She ducked the issue. A policy which in hindsight she would regret. "I think they are valuable clients and will earn the Bank a lot of money."

"I agree with you there. The question is what do you think of them as people? Are they above board?"

Claire faced a dilemma. Her thoughts were full of half baked theories with only Josh's word to go on. And he was certainly persona non grata around here. Forrest had the chart. Carpenter was his boss. Was Carpenter in Forrest's confidence? He could be testing her. Play it safe. At least until Josh had a chance to examine the disk.

"I think so, Ian. There's nothing solid to indicate they're not."

"And something unsolid?"

"Not that I know of." The words slowly left her mouth.

Carpenter could tell she was not being open. "If there is anything, anything at all, let me know. Between you and me, I'm not sure if I trust Forrest."

Claire was shocked. Carpenter had recruited him. He was his right hand man. And yet behind his back he denigrates him? Something was wrong. She said nothing.

*****

Fergus tried to call Janet every place he could think. He tried home, he tried the theatre. He tried Jean who said she had not seen her. Fergus did not believe her. They were best friends. She was probably sitting with Jean by the phone, laughing. He only wanted to apologise.

Unsure whether he was miserable or ecstatic, Fergus resolved to forget both Janet and Christine, for today.

There was much work to do before a bid could be made. The Stock Exchange announcement was planned to hit the Reuters screens at about 2.30pm tomorrow. They would have preferred first thing, before the markets opened, but that was impractical. The press release would also go out then. The offer documents would be posted to the CRA members the moment the announcement hit the screens. That meant finalising and printing overnight. It would be tight but their printer, Jacobson & Co, had assured them it was possible as

143

long as they received the final changes to the draft by three in the morning. And so a process engineered by a team of ten people at the Bank, countless lawyers, accountants and brokers, would finally reach its climax. Tomorrow morning.

Contemplating the night ahead, Fergus almost immediately broke his pledge and called Christine. "Hello, its Fergus."

"Hello, Fergus. How are you today." She spoke as if concurrently reading 'The Radio Times', and finding it more interesting.

"Pretty good. How are you?" Enthusiastic.

"Snowed under. You'd better be quick."

"We'll have another draft of all the documents over to you shortly for vetting. With luck the client will agree it. Then we can get it out to the printers."

"You know as well as I do there'll be another three or four drafts before the deadline." Fergus had no idea. "That's what deadlines are for. Changing things until the last moment. Justifying existence." She sounded bitter.

"Is everything OK?" asked Fergus.

"Perfect. Get it over as soon as you can."

"Will you have time later for a quick coffee or something?"

"You've got to be kidding. I'm too busy. I'm surprised you're not. Last night was a one-off. You knew that. I don't want you getting sloppy on me. We have to work together."

"A one-off?"

"I don't need any shit right now.."

"My girlfriend left me last night because I was at your place."

"Fergus, I'm sorry, but I don't need this right now. Byron's coming. We'll talk. Got to go."

She went.

The afternoon passed with his head down. Claire returned from various meetings and checked through the draft, adding her own changes and incorporating the thoughts of Forrest, Carpenter and Gross, each amending the previous alteration, each conflicting with the others. Existence justification.

The Naked Bank

Late in the afternoon the phone rang. It was the messengers and there was a package outside for him. Assuming it was another marked up draft, probably from Giles, he passed through the security doors to collect it.

Dave the messenger had a huge grin on his face. He was holding a bunch of red roses.

"I didn't know you cared," joked Fergus.

"They're not from me my boy. From a lady, I expect."

"Seems it's my lucky day."

He took the flowers off Dave. Twelve red roses. There was a card. From Christine, apologising for earlier. He hoped. No. It was from Janet.

Dear Fergus, Something thorny for you to remember me by. I'll get the rest of my stuff on Saturday. I don't suppose you'll be there anyway.

"In luck then?" asked Dave.

Fergus's glum face betrayed him. "'fraid not." He made to toss the flowers in the bin.

"Don't do that," protested the messenger. "They're not cheap you know."

But I am. "I suppose you're right."

"Give them to someone else. Cheer someone up. Too many glum faces around here."

Idea. "You know, I think I will."

Re-entering the department, he strode straight up to Claire's desk.

"Present," he said with outstretched arm, "Courtesy of a secret admirer."

"Who?" she inquired, taking in their fragrance.

"I can't tell you. A delivery boy just dropped them by."

"I see," said an uplifted Claire, thinking they were from Josh. "You couldn't put them in water for me could you Fergus?"

"Sure," he said. Better than doing the photocopying.

Shortly after the roses, another thorny issue arrived at the Bank. Nicola Macintosh walked in. Having strode past the security on the ground floor without so much as a glance, she marched straight up to Dave the messenger.

David Murray

"I'm here to see Ian Carpenter. I have ten minutes and I suggest he sees me. Tell him its Mac the Knife."

"Can I help you," blurted Dave somewhere in the middle of her opening remarks. "Just a moment." Picking up the phone he dialled Carpenter's PA. "I've got an urgent visitor for Mr Carpenter....I know he's in a meeting...It's someone called Mac the Knife." He said this with a perfectly straight face. It was his job to stroke the ego of visitors, no matter how inflated or ridiculous. Mac was unexceptional. "He'll be right out. Would you care to wait in room 3?"

"Love to. Mine's a black coffee and a coke if you've got one. And none of that diet rubbish."

"I'll bring it in. Room 3's that one," he said firmly to Mac who had begun to leaf through the mail on the desk.

Mac entered the room and sat on a comfy leather swivel chair. 'I wish I had one of these' she thought. The view offered a beautiful sunset, the day's earlier storms having cleared. Mac admired the pink haze, only for a second or two, for her mind could not remain settled for longer. Nice view, she thought. Shame about the Bank. A once great institution flushed down the toilet. Bobs around like a rotten poo, but after three or four flushes it disappears forever. What is it that destroys so called pillars of the community? Answer - not moving with the times. Adapt or die. The world was littered with examples of companies, of countries, even Empires which fell foul of this rule. So simple, complacency chose to ignore it. The CRA and the Bank had much in common. She could just as easily be defending the Bank from a take-over by the CRA. The strategy would be the same. One as easily discredited as the other.

Opening her briefcase she took out a small button shaped device and stuck it under the table.

What she could not fathom was why she was having things her own way? She churned out adverse publicity against both the Bank and Icarus and neither responded. It was easier to demolish the CRA's record than say anything positive. Unless you were a Labour MP.

The Bank would be finished by the time this was over. A memory for the City history books. No love lost over its demise. Such sentiments do not generate a profit.

The Naked Bank

Carpenter entered the room with her coffee and coke. Big mistake number one. Being polite looked weak. "Hello, Mac. A bit of a dramatic entry eh. What can I do for you?"

"Milk, five sugars, for a start."

As Carpenter poured she reached across the table and grabbed the can of coke. Ignoring the glass, she pulled the ring and took a long, hard swig. Wiping her mouth on her sleeve, "That's better. Can't do anything without my coke. The real thing. Can't snort it though. Too many bubbles."

Carpenter had only briefly come across Mac a couple of times and had no idea how to manage her. Abandoned clients waited next door while this woman expected him to be grateful for the opportunity to alter his diary on a whim. His annoyance did not show as he handed her the coffee, which she left untouched. He waited in silence.

This was impressive restraint and was noted by Mac who, after finishing her coke, spoke first.

"I have it on good authority that your client is about to make a bid for CRA."

Carpenter said nothing. She did not expect him to confirm or deny her statement. He internally fumed at at the breach in confidentiality.

"I strongly advise you not to proceed with the bid," she continued. "Let's just say that we've gathered some incriminating evidence which we'll use if we have to. It will be very embarrassing to the Bank. Ian, may I call you Ian?..."

He nodded.

"Ian, if you proceed, I fear not just for your future, but for the Bank's."

"Would you care to expand?"

"We know about the documents. The stolen documents."

Carpenter's heart sank. How could she know? He gave nothing away. "I'm not sure what you're talking about."

"Yes, you are. I have warned you which is more than the rules require. Be very sure of your position before you move."

"Is there anything else. I've a meeting to return to."

"No," said Mac, "that's all. That's enough. You can't win. I'll see myself out."

And she did.

Carpenter sat for a moment on his own, deep in thought. He could not stop events on the whimsical testimony of the enemy. She had told him nothing of substance. So what about the documents, they had legal advice. All the same, he picked up the phone.

"Byron Black please. It's Ian Carpenter."

"Putting you through."

A few seconds of elevator music while on hold.

"Ian, how are you?"

"Well. We have a potential problem on Bluebird."

"Yes."

"I've just had a visit from Nicola Mac, of USB. She told me quite categorically not to go ahead with the bid."

"Well she would wouldn't she."

"Sure. But she knows about the documents." He paused to let the news sink in. "You are positive they are legal?"

"No doubt. Christine double checked it. You can't steal information, only the paper it is printed on."

"So there is nothing to worry about?"

"No..."

"You don't sound as positive as I would like, Byron."

Byron was not worried by his opinion. More what else Mac might know if she was aware of the stolen documents. He kept this thought to himself.

"No, I'm sure. I'm a lawyer, we don't give our opinions lightly."

"Good. How's the documentation going?"

"We're making progress. As long as you guys don't change anything drastic we can sign off before the deadline."

"Excellent. The champagne's on me."

Mac stood outside the Bank listening to the conversation through an ear piece. They were proceeding, confirming her guess. Fools. She would crucify them.

*****

2 o'clock in the morning.

The Naked Bank

There was no more coffee. How much longer could he stare at the same information without making the connection?

Josh stood to stretch his legs. He grabbed a packet of crisps and munched to both satisfy his hunger and rest his brain. The packet finished, he was by no means satisfied and quickly polished off another two bags.

He laid down on the couch staring at the ceiling. Anything for inspiration. He followed a crack from one wall to the other, caused by last year's party. A spider sat patiently in its web, waiting for a fly that would not come. Poor bastard, he thought, and then wondered why he cared. Why? And then he saw it, the answer to his riddle. So obvious why hadn't he thought of it earlier? What a story. Prizes. Promotion. Danger. He had to warn Claire.

Phone. Directory Enquires. Answer machine.

"Hello, this is Claire. I can't take your call at the moment. Leave a message and I'll get back to you as soon as I can."

"Hello, Claire. It's Josh. The disk is dynamite. Give me a ring as soon as you can. It's important. You may be in danger."

She could be at work. Possible at this hour. Take a chance despite recorded conversation. Too important not to.

Dial Enquires. Phone ringing.

"Hello, Corporate Finance. John Snead."

"Hi, is Claire Snow there?"

"No, she's not here at the moment. Can I take a message?" said Snead without pausing to consider the hour of the call.

"Do you know if she's gone home for the evening?"

"No, I think she'll be back later."

"Could you ask her to call Josh whatever the time. The number is 0171 423 6745."

"Will do."

"Thanks."

He put down the phone. So the bid was tomorrow. Why else would she be working all night. Someone needed to tell Mr Snead to be more guarded on the phone.

It was too late for the presses. The story would have to wait until tomorrow. Not much of a scoop if it was already announced. Josh was more concerned with the information which would not be announced to the Stock Exchange. What to do with it? It should be reported to an authority of some kind. But who? And when. He wanted to break the story before it reached the public domain. Think.

Returning to his PC, Josh opened up his e-mail. There were about five messages from his editor demanding his presence. Where was his overdue story? He'd better have a good excuse. The usual bullying of a maverick hack.

And then he remember the notice in today's FT. Josh routinely devoured the paper for story ideas. Grabbing the discarded pink paper, he yanked it open, folding and pressing the pages open at the relevant section.

Financial Times, January 14
On the Move

Lara Waters has moved to take up a post at the Bank of England. She is to be Deputy Head of the Bank investigation division, newly created in the wake of the government's drive for greater regulatory bite. This division is shortly expected to be subsumed within the Financial Services Authority (FSA), Gordon Brown's latest well meaning qango.

Miss Waters is on secondment from Goolie and Grimshaw, the Big Two Accounting Firm where she was a Director.

He had no idea if she was the right person, but hopefully she would be able to pass the information on to someone who was. She was the only name he had and at this time there was no hope of verifying his guess.

E-mail meant he could delay the message. Get the story out just as it was hitting Lara's desk. He could even speculate on the Bank of England getting involved. His editor might even become more sympathetic towards his unconventional methods.

Josh began to attach the files to his e-mail address in preparation for sending the message. No, he wanted it to be anonymous. He didn't want any link between story and information to be made. It could discredit one or the other. Like many people, Josh kept a second e-mail address. To be used when secrecy was essential. For a journalist it was often important to remain in the shadows. His alternative address was 'The Falcon'. He used the free

The Naked Bank

'fastmail' e-mail service. It was untraceable. No one knew The Falcon. He liked the name. It was his dark side, his alter ego. And while using it he was safe from discovery.

The Falcon would send Lara.Waters@BankofEngland.org a message. Again he guessed, logically, that this was her e-mail address. He placed a twenty four hour time delay on the message. Plenty of time. He sent only the information, not his analysis. That would follow to fill in her gaps. Let her use his upcoming article to piece the whole scenario together.

He signed off and fell asleep on the settee while reading the latest Darkman comic book adventure for all of thirty seconds.

*****

Two thirty in the morning. A scratching sound from outside the front door of Claire's apartment. The lock clicked, and after a second's delay, the door slowly opened inwards. A flash light shone into the dark interior, pausing briefly on anything of interest before resuming its flickering one hundred and eighty degree journey across the hall. A figure stepped inside and shut the door behind.

He walked quickly to the stairs and padded lightly to the landing at the top. The door to the main bedroom was open and he listened for any sound. Hearing none he went to the doorway and pointed his torch through. The room was empty.

Entering, he drew the curtains before turning on a bedside light. He would begin here before working the rest of the house. Byron had several hours before Claire would return from the printers. He had specifically asked her to oversee the printing of the document on behalf of the Bank. She was keen enough to have copied it by hand.

Dressed in dark trousers and a sweatshirt, he pulled his mobile phone from his pocket. Now certain of his solitude, he switched it on. His home phone was diverted allowing him to take any last minute panic calls from Christine. He was worried by her attention to detail, particularly her attention to him. Her call would provide an alibi, if needed.

"I didn't practice law to become a common burglar," he muttered to himself as he steadily worked his way through her cupboards and drawers, finding nothing. He was the unanimous choice to search Claire's apartment. Living next door allowed him to slip in unnoticed with the added familiarity of an identical layout.

He was looking for the disk. The disk that Bonnier had witnessed her steal from Forrest's PC. Or anything else that could be used against Claire. Blackmail material.

Working his way through the upstairs he found nothing. No pictures save the odd holiday snap, no dodgy videos. The woman did not even own any racy underwear. She was totally straight. Unlike Forrest. The man had become a liability. To have stored his files so carelessly on his portable was unfortunate. The circumstances of Claire's retrieval appalling. The man was a vital, but weak, cog, necessary for the completion of the deal. Then he was expendable.

He checked his watch. Fifteen minutes so far. He wanted to be out in another fifteen. Quickly, he worked the ground floor, the study his prime target. There were several computer disks in the desk. He placed them in a black bin bag he unstuffed from his back pocket. Again, nothing of interest. Same with the other rooms. He knew all the hiding places. In his house they were all used. Nothing. The woman did not even have a video recorder, never mind incriminating tapes. Very little of a personal nature. She was married to her job.

The phone rang. His phone.

"Hello," he answered totally aware of his voice in the empty house.

"Hi Byron, it's Christine. Where are you? I've been ringing the bell for ages."

What the hell.

"I'm round at the corner shop, picking up some supplies. I ran out of milk. What do you want?"

"I thought I'd bring round a copy of the final print mock up for you to look at."

There was no point arguing.

"I'll be back in five minutes."

He had to be quick. If he left by the front door she would see him. He locked it from the inside and proceeded to the kitchen. Checking the fridge he grabbed a full carton of milk. A Seven Eleven carrier bag sat on the side in which he placed his own black bag and the milk. He opened the back door and stopped. Check the answer phone. Retracing his steps to the study pressed 'play'.

"Hello Claire, it's Mum, give me a ring when you get the chance....Hi, Bridget here. Fancy going ridding this weekend...This is Doncaster Repairs. Your car is fixed and you can pick it up any time... Hello, Claire. This is Josh. The disk is dynamite. Give me a ring as soon as you can. It's important. You may be in danger"

He pocketed the tape. Closing the back door behind him, he looked down the row of houses. It would take too long to work his way around to the front. Instead, he hopped the fence, making a mockery of his passing years, and entered his own house from the back. He hid the binbag and placed the carrier bag on the kitchen table where it was obvious.

Memory flash. The study light was still on. Too late, he would return once Christine left.

He walked to the front door and opened it. Christine sat on the step and turned to look at him.

"I thought you were at the shop."

"I was, I came in the back way. It's quicker."

She bought the story. "Can I come in?" He did not want her here. More damage limitation was required. Someone had to get Josh.

"Sure, but only for a moment."

Christine looked crestfallen, and he did nothing to improve her mood. She went directly to the living room where the fire was almost dead. Odd for a man planning to stay up all night. Odd that he was wearing a sweat shirt. She had never seen him wear anything so casual.

"Are you all right?" she asked.

"Yes, fine."

"You seem a little flustered."

"Oh, one of my kids is unwell. My wife called to say she had to take him to the doctor. I'm worried. Would you mind while I make a call to check?" For a lawyer, Byron was an unconvincing liar.

"Of course not Byron. I hope it's not too serious?"

"I'll find out."

Byron walked out of the room and shut the door. Taking out

his mobile he dialled a friend on the Herald at home. The digital phone was secure and untraceable.

"William, it's Byron."

"Hell, Byron, what time is it?"

"Sorry to disturb you but it's important."

"It better be, it's three in the morning."

"Do you know if Josh Walker is running a story tomorrow?"

"What kind of half-arsed question is that?"

"It's important William."

"No he's not. He went AWOL and is going to get a severe bollocking when he gets back. He was supposed to post a story but we never got it."

"You're sure."

"Sure I'm sure. What's this all about Byron?"

"I'll tell you later. Oh, and you never got this call. Understand."

"If I can go back to sleep with luck I'll think it was a dream."

"Thanks William."

"Sure."

There was still time to stop the story.

Dialling again. "Giles, it's Byron. Our little problem has spread to Josh Walker of the Herald. He's AWOL from the paper and hasn't filed but is in contact with Claire. We have to assume he knows all."

"Thanks Byron, We'll deal with it. Any luck with the search?"

"No. I've got a few disks to check but I'm pretty sure I drew a blank."

"OK. Thanks."

Bonnier hung up.

"How about I make some coffee?" asked Christine standing in the doorway.

"How long have you been there?"

"Not long, " she said unconvincingly. "How's your kid?"

"He's going to be OK," he replied unconvinced.

The Naked Bank

Christine made the coffee while Byron stoked the fire and thought through the two conversations. He assumed she had heard everything. How explicit were his words? She would need a story.

The coffee brought Christine back.

Anyone can crack under pressure. Tonight Byron, the most delicate of lawyers lost his subtlety. Rather than relax, string Christine along, play it cool, he blurted straight into his explanation the instant she handed him the cup.

"That was Giles. I better tell you what is happening, seeing as you overheard. There is a leak and there may well be a story about Bluebird in the papers tomorrow." "And you think it's Claire?"

She had heard.

"We don't know. It's important you don't repeat this to anyone."

"I understand."

Christine's mind tried to piece all the evidence together. The back door. The sweatshirt. The calls. The milk from the shop which was past its sell by date. It didn't stack up.

Byron aware enough to recognise the need to muddy the water. On the spur of the moment one thought leapt immediately to the front of the queue. Whether rational or driven by his subconscious libido, who can say. On the surface he was in control of his animal passion. Beneath it bubbled.

"Christine, put the coffee down and come and sit next to me."

A puzzled Christine did what she was told.

"Why did you really come here tonight. You can tell me."

"I told you, the documents."

"Let me guess the reason. I think you're attracted to me. I hope you are. I think I've fallen in love with you. I want you."

She was confused. He was the one making advances.

"Byron, this is a surprise. You're married."

"Why do you think I sent the kids away?"

"Who cares," she said as she threw herself at him, her only thoughts of the sweatshirt now were how to remove it as quickly as possible.

The Naked Bank

January 15

Eleven o'clock in the morning.

Fergus and Claire entered the department together. The usual hive of activity was magnified five fold in anticipation of the announcement. They had been at the printers, checking changes, final proofs, the finished article, checking the mailing list and ensuring that the offer document was packed and ready to roll. Fergus was more impressed than ever by Claire's energy and commitment. He felt exhausted, and had done so for the past ten hours. Working in zombie mode he had simply done what she told him. The later the hour, the more she excelled.

Claire sat down and scanned the mess on her desk. There was a pile of messages which she was too tired to look through. And a photocopied article from the midday edition of the Evening Courier, which she read through glazed eyes.

Icarus Launches bid for CRA
by Denton Blackledge

It was announced this afternoon that Icarus plc had made a £1.5 billion bid for the troubled CRA mutual conglomerate. Members will receive the formal documentation in the post offering them around £2000 each. Membership of the CRA cost a mere £1 up until last week when membership lists were closed to deter so called carpetbaggers. The bid has been rumoured for some time now and some in the City were wondering whether it would ever happen.

The key to its success will be the response of the regional committees, whose votes represent 51% of the total. They have been offered shares in Icarus in return for their share of the whole company. Their stakes are valued in the millions. It is not yet known whether they will accept, but the size of the offer means they are certain to take it seriously.

Claire looked up at Snead. "How long's this been out?"

"Ten minutes. It seems our PR people fucked up and released the story early. The whole timetable's been shifted forward two hours."

"So we announce at twelve thirty?"

"That's the idea. There's a Bluebird huddle starting in two minutes. Room 1. Everyone's going to be there."

"OK, let's go. Fergus, you coming?"

"I wouldn't miss this for anything."

Snead, Claire and Fergus walked. Snead asked Claire,

"Did you get your message?"

She was so wrapped in her own thoughts she answered in the affirmative. She had seen the pile. "Yes."

"Was everything all right then?"

"What do you mean?"

"The guy sounded desperate to speak to you."

"Who?"

"I thought you said you got the message."

"Which guy?"

"Josh, I think."

Fuck. In the drama of the evening she had forgotten about Josh. Better call him after the meeting. Besides to call the press was impossible before the launch. Not that passing stolen information was particularly kosher either.

It was the big room. Gross, Carpenter and Forrest were there. Carter, Bonnier, Black and Edgerley sat on the other side of the table. Carpenter stood to speak.

"First of all, I'd like to thank you all for all your efforts. The work has been tremendous. No doubt you have all seen the article in this morning's Courier. Because of all the sterling work performed last night, we've been able to move the timetable forward. Its now eleven fifteen and we are going live in exactly one hour. The Stock Exchange announcement is being cleared by compliance as we speak. The Takeover Panel have seen it as have the Bank of England. We're almost there.

The Naked Bank

"I know how much you want to go out and tell your colleagues. Please refrain from doing so until we announce. There have been too many leaks. If anyone from the press calls, please do not comment and refer them to Wendy Perkins in PR. That's all. Go out and do your job. And be careful out there."

The room rapidly cleared. They all wanted to get back and study their Reuters screens. What was Icarus's share price doing? Shooting up, it had reached thirty pounds. There were no sellers. The market waited, a stalking tiger ready to pounce. Eyes trained on the Bank for the first time in many a year. This was their deal and it was going to be big.

Claire rummaged through her messages and found the one from Josh. She picked up the phone and then remembered Carpenter's words. It could wait an hour.

*****

A rap at the door awoke Josh from his slumber. He looked at his watch. It was almost eleven thirty. How the hell could he sleep for so long? Frank, his editor was probably here in person demanding his overdue copy.

Rubbing eyes, he remembered the other story. The story. Had Icarus launched their bid yet? He had to get to the paper and file his scoop. Frank would be impressed.

Another rap at the door.

"OK, I'm coming."

Still dazed from sleep, he opened the door. Not Frank.

"Hello," he said. They did not answer. "Wait a minute," he continued as two men barged into the room pushing him in front of them. One shut the door, the other kept pushing him until he fell backwards onto the settee.

"What's going on?"

"Shut up and you might make it through the day," said the shover. Josh guessed he was the boss. He was about five six, tanned, with a full mop of hair. His leather jacket creaked with his flexing authority. The muscle behind him was at least as wide as his boss

161

was tall. He almost stooped as he stood in the basement studio. He wore black leather gloves and looked like he enjoyed using them.

"Where's the disk?" asked the boss.

"What disk?"

"Tough guy." He motioned his number two over. "I hate to be a talking cliché kid, but sometimes the job requires it. Bert here, and remember that's not his real name, Bert here would like nothing better than to beat the shit out of you. If he doesn't beat you up he'll go home and beat the missus up. And I wouldn't want that to happen. Mrs Bert is a very lovely lady. So I'm not going to hold Bert back. And I'm not going to repeat myself more than once. Where's the disk?"

"Over there by the computer." Josh was no hero.

"Thank you, wasn't that easy. Now, who gave you the disk." The boss knew the answer. Josh did not know that he knew. So he kept stum. And Bert re-arranged his face. Not a lot but enough so that it hurt and ruined both their shirts.

And then he told them. Claire please forgive me.

"What other information have you got?"

"Nothing. Just the disk."

Thwack.

"Are you certain? No copies?"

"Positive."

"I'm glad to hear it, for if I find otherwise I won't be very happy."

Josh hurt. He would hurt until they finished him off. They could not risk freeing him. He was alone without help. Did Bert lock the door. He couldn't remember. He had to try to run.

The boss picked up the disk and placed it in his pocket. "Now, let's see whether you were telling the truth." The familiar whirring booting of the portable followed.

As the boss focused on the screen, Josh made his move. Bert reacted but not quickly enough and Josh was past. The door was indeed unlocked as a chair crashed just above his head. He legged it up the basement steps to the main road, Bert only steps behind. Josh looked one way and ran the other. Down the pavement past unfazed onlookers. Happens all the time in London. Best not get involved. Two rather large guys climbed out of a dark Mercedes parked twenty yards away. They could have been anyone. He could not risk it. He darted into the road. He darted in front of a bus.

"Christ," said the boss as he walked up to the squashed body. The bus driver jumped out to have a look.

"Its not my fault. He just jumped out at me. Its not my fault."

A crowd was gathering and the boss was uncomfortable. The situation needed resolving.

"Secret Service. This man is a wanted criminal," he said flashing a badge of some sort. "Back off." He knelt down to examine Josh.

The Mercedes pulled up by the bus.

"We'll take him to hospital. He's just unconscious."

The two goons placed him carefully in the back seat and jumped in. As did the boss. Lowering the electric window, he said to the bus driver,

"What's your name?"

"Arthur Perkins, sir."

"Well, Arthur. I have your bus number. I'll be in touch if you're needed. You've done your country proud. Carry on with your normal business."

"Yes sir."

"Oh, and Arthur, don't speak to anyone about this. It may affect your rights."

"Yes sir."

He raised the window, and the Mercedes pulled away. Punching his mobile, "Bert it's me. Set the answer phone. Grab the PC and search the flat. Then meet me back at base."

"And the mark?"

"He didn't make it."

*****

Robert Parsons entered his office and wondered where Susan his secretary was. He was late this morning, she was later. No matter, he walked through the outer office and placed his briefcase down on his side table. No Susan meant no coffee. Parsons enjoyed his coffee, it was one of the few delights of his working day. That and imagining who he would fire upon assuming control of the CRA. Carter had promised to stay out of his hair. Whittle would be the first to go, that no talented son of a concrete block. The man was driving the company into the ground. Annoyance. Parsons was cranky before his first cup of coffee.

Picking up the pot, he walked down the corridor to the kitchen. This path took him past the photocopier, where he seemed to spend most of his evenings these days. Still that was all over now. The bid was today. It was difficult to contain a whistle. The tap quickly filled his coffee pot and he returned, filled the machine and replaced the filter before switching and waiting.

Gordon from accounts walked past at one point, the first person he had seen in the office despite it being 11.30am.

"Morning, Gordon," he uttered but the man hastily walked past.

A few moments later he tried,

"Morning Jane," and she again paid no attention, almost positively avoiding him.

The puckering of the coffee machine soothed his paranoia.

Coffee in hand, he placed his feet on the desk and opened his copy of the Evening Courier whose headline leaped out at him. It had happened already. He picked up his phone and dialled Carter on his mobile.

"Carter."

"It's Robert here. Congratulations, I see it went through."

"Get off the phone you idiot. The story's a leak. A plant."

Parsons slammed down the receiver just as two men walked into his office. One was Christopher from Personnel. The other a security guard. Not the usual semi-retired variety but a big, mean, no nonsense type. He had the look of hired gun.

"Parsons, I'm afraid I'm going to have to search your briefcase," said Christopher.

"I beg your pardon."

"And then my friend here is going to escort you off the premises. Any personal effects will be gathered together for you to collect at a mutually convenient time."

Parsons was dumbstruck. He was caught. He had no defence and offered none.

The Naked Bank

Christopher enjoyed watching the suspect squirm. This was what being a personnel officer was about. Sod interviews and assessments. Canning a man was the pinnacle, only matched by mass redundancy. The latter's volume making up for any loss of intimacy.

A quick search of the briefcase revealed nothing but a clean pair of socks, woman's panties which Parsons had unfortunately kept as a souvenir, and a packet of condoms in case he struck lucky again in the photocopying room.

The guard with no name led Parsons out and towards the lift. Jean stood in the door to Whittle's office and watched. He raised his hand to wave. She ignored him, just stared.

He moved at the pace of an ant crossing the exit foyer. A crowd had gathered to bid him farewell. There were photographers and cameramen. Keen journalists, primed by those in the know, shouting, intruding on his nightmare.

"Mr Parsons. How could you steal from your employer?...Is it true you betrayed CRA?...Any comment?.....Will you give an interview...?"

These people refused to vanish as he shut his eyes to protect himself from the flash bulbs. The lot of the ant is a weary and dangerous one, hemmed in by predators it can only feel its way forward in search of sustenance. Eventually he reached the door and was thrust out into the street.

It was a bright day and the light shocked him. The pack followed and chased. He ran, hailed a cab, and fled for his sanity.

*****

Judges in England have a bad reputation. Doddery old men completely out of touch with contemporary society, making 'What is a television?' remarks very slowly. Mr Justice Barker was an exception.

He sat in his chambers, upright in his mottled leather chair, facing what amounted to legal overkill. With a barrister, three solicitors, two merchant bankers and a faded businessman all struggling to find space in his cramped quarters, he wondered what on earth could be so important. Looking forward to a comfortable

day of nothing, he had ambled into his office at 10.30am after a
rather rough night of claret and port. Stretching his abused mind
back to the night before also brought out memories of the odd gin
and tonic with the possibility of a beer thrown in. He had not seen
his old school chums, Piggy and Slapper for over a year, and they
had made the most of it, drinking well into the early hours. The last
thing he needed was some big wig barrister throwing his weight in
gold around. So he watched without comment as they all filed in.

"Good morning, your honour," opened Jenkins-Smythe, the
afore mentioned barrister and scourge of part time judges
everywhere.

"Get on with it," said the clearly out of sorts Barker, his ill
humour throwing Jenkins-Smythe's rhythmical patter for a moment.
But only for a moment.

"I'm sorry to disturb you at this early hour," continued the
brief, annoying the judge even more with his attempt at sarcasm,
"but something most serious has come up. Something which requires
immediate judicial action without which I fear for the reputation of
justice in this land."

Barker groaned. "Out with it then. What's going to end the
world this week then?"

"You may be aware of a company called the CRA?" Barker
nodded. "Well we have it on very good authority that documents
have been stolen from this company and are being used to launch a
take-over for this company in a few hours, at the most. These
documents are confidential and as well as having been stolen, have
been hawked around the City in return for a few pieces of silver."

"In English please Jenkins."

"Jenkins-Smythe. These documents are being used to raise
finance for this bid. Because of this immoral and illegal act, we seek
an injunction to prevent the bid proceeding while it relies on the use
of stolen goods."

"I see. And what evidence do you have to substantiate your
case?"

This was the cue for the three solicitors to step forward,
creating breathing room for Mac at the back while severely cramping
Jenkins-Smythe at the front.

The Naked Bank

"Do you have a video recorder?" asked the first solicitor, dreading the answer, 'A video recorder, pray tell what is a video recorder?'

"Over there at the back of the room."

Scramble as bodies press to open a route to this most holy of machines. Solicitor number two inserts a tape, while number three presses play. Nothing.

"Why don't you switch the TV on," said the technophile judge.

Number one, for it was his turn, pressed the knob and the picture sprang to life.

The video showed a grainy car park. The shot was trained on a green Jaguar. Nothing was happening.

"What is the significance of this please Jenkins?"

"Jenkins-Smythe. If your honour will bear with us for a few moments all will become apparent."

Barker accepted this and sank back into his chair. He was a tall man, prone to slouch. So much so that the natural height which had made him a prominent barrister in his own right, seemed to melt away. He was not inclined to be impressive today. He saved such demeanour for his days in court.

Fighting to prevent dozing off, he continued to watch this car. Finally, the door opened and out stepped a well dressed man.

"This is Mr Carter, your honour, the chief executive of Icarus plc, the company that is about to bid for CRA."

Carter carried a briefcase and shook the hand of another gentleman.

"This is Mr Robert Parsons, a senior employee of CRA."

The two talked for a few seconds before Parsons walked Carter to another car parked nearby. Opening the boot, he placed Carter's case inside and handed him a large cardboard box, clearly heavy. Parsons shut the boot of the second car and took the box off Carter before carrying it to the Jaguar and depositing it in the boot. They shook hands, Carter getting back into his car, Parsons walking off. The Jaguar drove off as the tape ended.

"I presume these are the documents you mentioned?" asked Barker.

167

David Murray

"Those we have on film. We suspect there are others."

"Tell me, who filmed this?"

"My client became suspicious of Parsons and hired a private detective to trail him. We have evidence that he called Carter on a regular basis and that he went so far as to sleep with Mr Whittle's," Perkins-Smythe gestured to Whittle wedged in the corner, "secretary. We believe this was to obtain information."

"I must say, this sounds more like James Bond than mergers and acquisitions. Is there any more evidence?"

"We suspect Parsons has been taking bribes. We believe the case passed to him was cash although we have no firm evidence. We have sworn affidavits from a number of City institutions stating that they were offered copies of the stolen documents by the Bank, Carter's advisor."

"No doubt only too keen to stick the knife into a competitor."

"That may be the case, but it does not invalidate their statements."

"No. I will have to think about this. Do you have a draft injunction?"

"Yes." Perkins-Smythe handed a three page document to the judge.

"Very well, get out and I'll look at it."

"You are aware of its pressing nature, your honour?"

"Yes, yes. Wait outside. Give me five minutes of peace for God's sake."

The posse trooped out leaving Barker with his thoughts and the stale whiff of body odour. The sweating of nervous solicitors.

The corridor outside was little more spacious than the judge's chamber. The solicitors stood together, whispering among themselves. The barrister kept his own company, while Mac's assistant was despatched to fetch coffees and cakes. Mac and Whittle stood by the door and waited together in silence. There was nothing to say. Both knew the bid was imminent and that their best chance of success lay in cutting it off at the pass.

Mac punched her phone.

The Naked Bank

"William, any news?"

"Nothing on the screen yet Mac. I'll call you if anything happens."

"What about Parsons?"

"Tossed out with the maximum of publicity. Its been playing on Sky and Reuters for the past half hour."

"Good - keep in touch."

She jabbed the off button and wondered where the cakes were.

Barker's door opened and he popped his head out. "Jenkins, please come inside. The rest of you stay out."

Jenkins-Smythe entered the room and the door closed behind him immediately. The waiting was unbearable. The judge just had to sign the paper. There was so little time. Mac's phone rang. The corridor looked up in disbelief. News of the deal? They were too late. Reluctantly she answered,

"Yes."

She listened as they stared.

"Make it a dozen eclairs and get back soon. I'm fucking hungry."

Relief. Relief, followed by the judge's door releasing Jenkins- Smythe.

"Got it," he said with a smile and a clutched piece of paper. "Boys, let's serve it."

As the three solicitors spend off to their pre-arranged destinations, it became obvious why they were there. Mac breathed a sigh of relief and dialled her contact at the Stock Exchange.

"Richard, its Mac. If you're about to release an announcement on behalf of Icarus, I suggest you stop it. We have an injunction and I'm sure you wouldn't want to break the law."

Hang up. Next call.

"Get me Ian Carpenter and I don't care if he's busy."

*****

John Snead was bobbing up and down in frustration. Ian Carpenter stood with a stunned look on his face. Claire could not believe it. Fergus looked at the three of them, accentuating the

169

disappointment of his first cratered deal. The rest of the department did its best to avoid them. The exception was Gross.

The smell of his cigar warned them of his approaching presence, its sweetness contrasting with their own bitterness.

"Cheer up troops," he said in familiar booming tones, "You've done a great job and you can be proud. Besides, it's not over yet. Not at all."

"What do you mean?" asked Carpenter.

"Well, there is a court hearing tomorrow when the judge will hear both sides of the story. There is nothing to stop us proceeding without using the documents in question."

"But how? All the names and addresses of the members came from Parsons. All the forecasts on which the finance is based."

"There is a way. If we can't put the offer to the CRA members, let's put it to the directors. It's so good that as directors it is their duty to pass it on to the members."

It was brilliant. Gross revealed in one instant why he was paid his enormous salary. Why his bonus was seven figures.

"John, Claire, Fergus," said Carpenter, "I think you've got some work to do."

They returned to their desk with a fresh sense of purpose.

Claire looked at the press releases sitting on her desk. A waste of paper and effort. She slung them in the bin and reached for her messages. Josh. She had forgotten to ring Josh. In the adrenaline charged atmosphere of the past few hours she had overlooked her suspicions. Now those concerns re-surfaced as she reached for the phone.

"You have reached the phone of Josh Walker. I'm afraid I am not able to take your call at the moment. Please leave a message after the beep."

"Josh, it's Claire. Give me a ring. I'll try you at work."

Claire thumbed her diary and found his card.

"Good morning, Herald," answered a woman.

"Hello, can I speak to Josh Walker please."

"Can I ask who's calling."

"Its Claire."

"Can I ask what it's concerning?"

"I'm his girlfriend," she lied to cut through the bullshit.

The Naked Bank

"I'm sorry Claire, Josh hasn't been into work for the past two days. We don't know where he is. You don't know do you?"

"No," said a worried Claire, "I just tried his home and got the machine. He called me last night and I haven't had a chance to get back to him."

"Well, leave your number and if I hear anything I'll let you know."

"Thank you. That's very kind." Claire sat perplexed at her desk. Where was he? What was so urgent that he called in the middle of the night?

It was now 2pm and she deserved a lunch break.

"Fergus, can you rework the offer document addressing it to the directors of the CRA? It shouldn't be too difficult. Run it past Byron and have a draft for me to look at in two hours. I've got to pop out for a sandwich. Can I get you anything?"

"I wouldn't mind a pastrami on rye." Fergus was tired. The thought of another two hours' work barely registered. Pastrami dominated his consciousness.

"OK, I won't be long."

Claire grabbed her coat and stepped out into the sunshine, her first fresh air for over twenty four hours. As she left towards the underground she did not notice a man, sitting on a bench across the road, stand and follow her. He wore a blue anorak, carried a small sports bag, and did not seem the secret admirer type.

The tube was uncrowded. There were few tourists at this time of year, the sales were over, and most people were at work. Claire had her pick of seats and took one without a chewing gum splodge. She opened the latest edition of today's Evening Courier and stared at the front page, greeted by a large photo of Robert Parsons running from the CRA building.

David Murray

Daily Herald, January 15
CRA ejects spy
by Peter Duncan

A little more light was shed on the shady world of corporate mergers and acquisitions today. Quite incredibly, invited journalists were treated to the most bizarre event this correspondent can recall. Robert Parsons, the operations manager at under threat CRA, was publicly ejected from the building with nothing but his overcoat to show for his twenty five years of service to the organisation.

CRA Chief Executive Frederick Whittle stated, "This marks a very sad day for the CRA. Robert was a trusted member of the senior management team. He betrayed that trust by passing numerous confidential documents onto Icarus plc and their advisors, the Bank. The exact extent of this espionage is unclear and we are taking the matter further through legal channels. There will be a further statement today."

Neither the Bank nor Icarus chose to comment on the event, a further twist in the increasingly addictive soap that is the CRA. Two days ago Mr Whittle wrote a public letter to Sir Wig Forthwright, the Chairman of the Bank, requesting him to withdraw his support for Icarus because of the dubious character of James Carter and his sidekick, Giles Bonnier. Rumours abound that a £4 million payment received by Bonnier was to bribe members of the CRA. It is unclear whether Parsons is party to these rumours. Sir Wig placed his full support behind Carter. That was, however, before this latest development.

Claire could not believe how badly the Bank was handling its public relations. The whole Parsons ejection was carefully manipulated for the maximum of publicity. The Bank chose to remain silent while the CRA, heavily guided by Mac the Knife, stole all the headlines. She turned to look at the crossword but was too tired to concentrate and instead drifted with the rocking of the carriage.

The anorak sat in the next section of the carriage reading a non-descript paperback. He showed no interest in Claire, not even a surreptitious glance. Not a glance at any of the other passengers. He was unmemorable.

The rickety Northern Line train trundled on, pulling into the dimly lit Clapham North station. Claire stood and alighted, her shadow doing so a few seconds later, as if an afterthought.

She walked through the grimy tunnels and stood still as the escalator struggled its way to the surface. The sunlight was still bright and it was with good cheer that she wandered across the Common towards Josh's flat. She had never been there but knew its location. A good friend of hers used to live in the same street and Claire herself had spent a couple of years in Clapham when her parents were using the Chelsea house.

The Common is never at its best in winter, the grass looks unwell and unrespected, chewed by impromptu games of football and rugby. Fouled by dogs on leashes whose owners would take great exception if one of the rugby players took a dump on the turf. The trees were stark, hiding from the cold. There were no birds save an occasional crow. The park lacked the vibrancy of summer frolics, sun worshippers and ice cream vendors.

On the other side of the common, she entered Josh's street, packed with cars, some double parked. The road was lined with empty wheely bins. A residue of trailing rubbish waited for the rain to wash it away. The trees lining the road were clipped and anaemic, waiting for the spring to repair the damage of an over-zealous council trimmer.

Stepping over a half chewed corn on the cob, Claire opened the gate, checked the address, and descended the ten or so steps to the basement door. She suddenly felt cold, having moved out of the sun, and vulnerable, as she waited in the damp semi-darkness. She rang the bell and there was no answer. The curtains were drawn and she was unsure whether the flat was occupied. She rang again and listened with her ear to the door. Still nothing. Where could he be?

'Go back and wait for his call,' she told herself. What else could she do? To wait around would be cold and unproductive. There was work needing to be done so she climbed the steps not noticing her follower twenty yards away across the street. Clutching her arms to her stomach to keep warm, she briskly began to retrace her steps to the underground. Her head was down as she walked, navigating the scraps of food which might ruin her new shoes. Her heels clicked out a rhythm as she went, unperceived by her, hummed by the anorak.

Someone else listened to those heel clicks. Two people to be exact, sitting in a Mercedes parked on the street. They had watched Claire walk past, ring the bell, and return back into the sunlight.

"We're outside the flat and a woman matching the description of Claire Snow has arrived," said Boss into his mobile.

"You're sure she's alone."

"Yes, guv."

"Pick her up and bring her back to base. Discreetly."

"Understood."

"And try not to kill her."

"No, guv."

So when the clicks reached the Merc, a door swung open. Bert jumped out from the front seat and the Boss from the back. Claire leaped back in surprise and struck her back against a railing. The two grabbed her arms as she dropped her handbag. Her legs flayed, catching Bert with a solid kick on the shin, causing him to exhale an expletive.

"Help," she shrieked before the Boss put his hand over her mouth. They bundled her with difficulty into the car, the Boss in the back struggling to hold her down. Bert jumped into the front and drove down the narrow street. He drove slowly so not to attract attention. The car windows were tinted, the interior sound proof. Claire could scream and struggle and no one would hear. Only Boss suffered as she scratched and hit him. He did not want to restrain her, loath to risk harming her. Instead he took her blows, doing his best to deflect them, before pushing her into the space behind the passenger seat, and sitting on her.

The anorak watched the car go, noting the number plate. He walked down the street and picked up Claire's bag, forgotten in the struggle. Placing his sports bag on the ground, he unzipped it and checked the camera was still running. Satisfied that he had captured the whole sequence on film, he turned it off, and placed Claire's bag on top. Re-zipping the bag he set off in the direction of the tube.

*****

The Naked Bank

Lara was used to the smell of emulsion. She was not used to sharing a desk with her secretary. Her office redecorating finally began today and was promised to be completed by the end of the week. Meanwhile she perched at one end of Sue's desk, a space large enough to fit a portable computer and a medium sized mug of herbal tea. Her own phone, fitted yesterday after much foot stamping, lay on the floor. She sat on a wooden upright chair, side on to the desk, her legs stretched to the side. Because of this acute angle she tried to restrict her time on the PC to minimise twisting her back. Fortunately there was little to do, John Greggor having barely spoken to her in three days, and certainty not having briefed her as to what the hell her job was.

Sue exuded energy and was constant motion. While Lara admired a go getting attitude, Sue's constant beavering became wearing, especially when in reflection. What her secretary typed all day was a mystery. No one else talked to her, or gave her any work. The phone never rang. Yet she kept typing, stopping only to make herbal tea, increasingly growing on Lara's taste buds, and disappearing down the corridor for her mid-morning and mid-afternoon bathroom breaks, as she liked to call them.

Now was no exception. Sue was bashing away on her wordprocessor. She resembled Jane Horrocks, on helium, over-dozed on Red Bull. Lara was amazed that anyone could wear leggings to work, particularly turquoise, with matching headband. Eyes popped behind bottletops.

"Tell me Sue," Lara said unable to resist for any longer, "What are you working on. I don't give you anything to do yet you display such diligence."

"Sorry?"

"What are you working on?"

"Oh, its a hobby of mine. I chat to people on the internet. Its amazing who you meet. One day I talked to Bill Gates."

"Of Microsoft?"

"I thought so for a long time until he said he had to go and deliver some pizzas. Must have been a different guy."

"And you do this all day?"

"Pretty much, except when there's work stuff to do."

David Murray

"When did you last do any work stuff?"

"Apart from setting up your office, seven months ago. I remember it well. Mr Greggor sent me out to get a sandwich. Cheese and pickle, with mayonnaise and no salad."

"Who are you talking to now?"

"Three people. You never just talk to one, it's too slow. So I talk to three and there's always a message coming in. Today there's Roger, who works in a dentist's reception, Marjorie, who is a librarian, and not a happy one I can tell you, and Dirk, who's a convicted mass murderer. If he doesn't win his appeal they're going to gas him tomorrow. Its quite sad."

"That's amazing - they let him talk from prison."

"Apparently it's his last request. He says he wants someone to remember him when he goes."

"How awful."

"Yes, he's a total psychotic. I'm pretending to like him which, I can tell you, is not easy. Still, at least he'll die happy."

For a moment Lara feared for the sanity of her secretary. No madder than most.

"Can I have a go?" she said to Sue.

"Sure. You need your own user id though. If you give me a minute I'll set you up?"

"How?"

"I'll e-mail IT department and they'll connect you up to the Bank of England server. It's quite simple really. In the meantime you can use my machine."

"But what about you?"

"I'll go and supervise the painting. I'm bored of Dirk. He's very morbid. And the guys next door are to die for. Give me fifteen minutes to set you up."

Sue returned to the computer and her typing, Lara to her dreaming.

True to her promise, Sue had Lara sitting in front of her PC a quarter of an hour later.

"Your log on name is Lara.Waters. If you type your password here, and verify it."

The Naked Bank

Lara did as she was told, noticing Sue looking straight at the keyboard as she typed the word 'rabbit' twice. Lara made a mental note to change it later.

"OK, you're into the system. You have no messages at the moment. If you want to go onto the internet you click on this button," which Sue did, "and then you can sign onto an on-line forum where people log on and chat. It's a good way to meet people for the first time. There are loads of different ones geared to different interests. Alternatively you can search the member database for keywords relating to interest, age, or sex and it will pull up a list of people you could mail."

"How did you meet the prisoner?" asked Lara.

"He met me. It seems we share a common interest in taxidermy. Mine was a joke, he apparently liked stuffing people."

"Really." It was more the need to say something than an interest in the man.

"Well, I'll leave you to it while I go and sort a few things out."

Sue left the room leaving Lara alone to sink into the comfortable chair and examine the bewildering number of options that faced her.

The phone rang. Lara had never answered the phone. No sign of Sue so she answered it.

"Hello, Lara Waters speaking."

"Hi, Lara, it's Sue. We've got a problem at reception. Have you got a moment?"

"Sure - what's the problem?"

"Mr Greggor's not here and there is someone demanding to see him. Says she won't be fobbed off. She refuses to come back later or even take a seat."

"I'll be right there."

Along the never-ending corridor and Lara was in reception, faced by the sight of the receptionist and Sue being berated by an enormous woman.

"Can I help you?" Lara said by way of introduction.

"And who might you be?" asked the woman.

"Lara Waters. I work with Mr Greggor who is unavailable at the moment."

David Murray

"I don't care if he's unavailable. I want to see him. If I don't there will be hell to pay. I've just briefed several journalists to rubbish one ancient institution. I have no qualms about rubbishing yours."

Lara felt like pointing out it was not hers, and she was only here by default. However, instead she resolved to solve this problem as easily as possible.

"Sue, do you know where Mr Greggor is?"

"As I've said to Ms Macintosh," she said overemphasising the Ms, "he's away all day and won't be back until tomorrow morning. I'm sure he'll be happy to see her then."

"Which is not good enough," butted in Mac. "Do you know who I am?"

"No," replied Lara which only further incensed Mac.

"I am Nicola Macintosh. You may have read about me?"

"Don't think so."

"I am defending the CRA against a hostile attack from Icarus. We have just obtained a court injunction against The Bank that proves grave wrong doing and misjudgement. As the regulator of banking, it is your duty to investigate."

Now this put Lara in a difficult position as she did not know what her job actually was. Moreover, this woman seemed unlikely to leave unless either Lara listened to her argument, and accepted it, or called the police and had her physically removed, not an easy task in itself. And if she was as important as she seemed to think...

"Very well, why don't you step into my office and we can talk about it."

"Glad to see you showing some common sense," patronised Mac. "Lead the way."

Lara took Mac down the corridor, past the workmen, and into Sue's office.

"Please take a seat," she offered, pointing at the old wooden chair. The chair looked nervous as Mac's considerable weight was applied. It creaked but held.

Mac was far from impressed with the surroundings. No surprise. "You have an unusual office," she said leaving her domination script for the first time in living corporate memory.

"Yes it is. What can I do for you?"

The Naked Bank

"You can get me a Coke for a start."

"I'm not sure we've got any of that. How about herbal tea?"

"I'll pass, thanks," said an unamused Mac beginning to despair at her situation. "I suppose doughnuts are out of the question?"

"Uh, huh."

"Never mind. As I said I am here to request you investigate the Bank for its role in the Icarus affair. It's very serious and will be hitting the press tomorrow. I have all the evidence you will need to get things rolling." Mac slapped a fat file down on Lara's laptop, which did crack under the weight, beeping frantically. "The court case is tomorrow so that will be a good day to begin."

Lara was dumbfounded at the woman's effrontery, and not sure of her ground. This could be completely the wrong department for such work. She assumed that, given Mac had asked for Greggor, this matter might relate to her new job. She therefore needed to stall.

"I appreciate you bringing this matter to our attention..."

"But?" interrupted Mac.

"If you would let me finish. I appreciate you bringing this matter to our attention. I cannot make any kind of decision until after discussing it with Mr Greggor. I'm sure you can appreciate that. If you leave your details we will get back to you with an answer. I'm afraid at this point I can offer no more."

"Fine," said Mac standing. The chair breathed out. "That's as much as I can ask for. I will call you tomorrow. It's easier than you getting hold of me."

"All the same..."

"My details are in the file. I must go. Other fish to fry. I'll see my way out. Thanks for your precious time. Oh, yes, one other thing. Read the papers before you make up your mind. We wouldn't want a constitutional crisis."

Lara had no idea what she was talking about and showed her to the door.

"Goodbye. I enjoyed meeting you," said Lara. They did not shake hands.

*****

David Murray

The room buzzed as the department gathered in meeting room 1. There were enough chairs around the table for about half the sixty or so people in attendance, the rest stood, leaning against the walls, or sitting on other pieces of furniture. The Commons on three whip night.

All looked forward to hearing Ian Carpenter describe the events of the past few days. Copies of the Courier had done the rounds and the television in the department was constantly replaying footage of Parson's eviction. Some had only seen the earlier edition of the Courier which described the successful launch of the bid. Others had heard of the injunction, which made the late edition. Those who could operate their Reuters screens had read of the day's events. Whatever each knew, there was plenty more for them to learn from Carpenter.

The stressed head of department entered the room and made his way to his customary place in the middle of the table, the only empty chair. He had better things to do than brief his men but felt it was important in case they were quizzed by the press.

"Good evening, everyone," he began. "Thank you for coming at such short notice. I know you're all busy so I'll keep this as short as possible. I really just wanted to give you the Bank's side of events on Project Bluebird before you read all about it in the press tomorrow.

"You may know we were launching the bid today and that it was reported in the Courier before we could. We are investigating how this happened. In any event, an injunction halted the bid on the grounds we relied on so called stolen documents to gain the debt financing. You will probably have guessed that Robert Parsons was the source of these documents.

"Now, I must say that we have taken legal advice which tells us that we have done nothing wrong. In fact, I am reliably informed that this sort of thing happens all the time in hostile take-over situations. The judge has ruled otherwise, even though we are not able to put our case until tomorrow. The injunction may therefore be lifted when we do.

"If it's not, we will go ahead anyway. We have a contingency plan which is being put into operation tonight. I am confident in the plan. As you know, half of our fee is contingent upon getting a bid on the table, regardless of its success. That remains our priority.

"The other matter that has received press coverage is the matter of a payment of £4 million to Giles Bonnier. We have investigated this matter fully and are happy with his explanation that it was a legitimate consultancy fee. He certainly generated far more than his fee in value for Dedalus. There is no evidence that this money was used to bribe Robert Parsons, or anyone else. As such, we stand fully behind our client. We are a relationship bank and will not drop a client once the going gets a little rough. For those of you who haven't been involved in hostile bids, this is par for the course.

"Any questions? Yes, Richard."

Richard Jackson was the Scandinavian sector director, also known as Wiggy on account of his outrageous hairpiece. "Tell me Ian, I think a lot of people are wondering why we are not making a better case for the deal in the press. Presumably we believe this company is ripe for break-up so why don't we highlight its inefficiencies and potential benefits to members?"

"Remember, we haven't made a bid yet. Nothing has been announced. It is therefore very difficult to make any comment. You'll be pleased to know, however, that Sir Wig himself will be taking charge of the PR effort going forward."

Silence.

"Good. Well if there are no more questions we all have work to do."

Fergus handed Ian the revised offer document for his final approval on his way out. It would be couriered to all the CRA directors that night.

*****

Fergus had not slept properly for three days when he finally left the Bank. The revised offer was completed and in the post. His draftings were easily agreed by all parties, in part due to the simplicity of the task, in part because of a reluctance to overcomplicate matters at this late stage. The injunction hearing was tomorrow and all longed for an early night.

David Murray

The cab waited outside the Bank. It was 8.30pm and as he climbed into the back and instructed the driver "Finchley, please," he realised he would be returning to an empty house for the first time in three years. He was tired, hungry and did not have the energy to fight despair. He knew it was his fault. He could have gone to the party. He could have done more to keep them together. For the first time since joining the Bank he questioned his career. Was it really all worth it?

This was far too philosophical for his current mental state and he settled back into the seat and watched suburban London race by. There was little traffic and they made good time. He looked at the couples walking hand in hand, at youth enjoying itself in pubs and restaurants. At smiles and laughs, the music of fun. He was the same age as them and felt washed up. He was sorry for himself.

"Where abouts, guv?" said the taxi driver.

On impulse he answered, "22 Palmer Street." Christine's address. After the past few days it was inconceivable she would not be home. Even a workaholic has to sleep.

The cab drew up to the now familiar house. A light was on, she was in.

"Thanks," said Fergus to the driver who chugged off with the distinctive diesel ticking unique to Hackney Carriages.

Fergus rang the bell. He was not really sure why he had come. He was drawn by the lack of alternative.

The door opened. It was Byron in his boxer shorts.

"Hello," he asked looking out on to the porch step, unlit since its light was smashed during the burglary.

"Byron!" said Fergus.

"Fergus? What are you doing here?"

"Err, I came to see if Christine was OK after the robbery," he lied. "Is she in?" he asked putting Black in a difficult position to refuse.

"Just a minute." Black returned inside shutting the door behind him.

After a wait, the door opened again. Christine stood with a robe on, and nothing else.

"Hi, Fergus. What can I do for you?" She played it perfectly straight.

The Naked Bank

"I thought I'd pop round on the way home." He was embarrassed by her lack of embarrassment.

"I'm sorry, but you've caught me at a rather difficult moment. Can I ring you tomorrow."

"Fine," he said as she closed the door without waiting for his response. He stood on the step and felt a chump.

Christine walked back into the living room where a half empty champagne bottle, a hardly touched tin of caviar (she hated the stuff) and a collection of exotic flowers once again greeted her. Byron lay stretched out in front of her on the couch, his wiry body surprisingly muscular for his age.

"Sorry about that darling," she said as she dropped her robe. "I'll make up for it."

"Don't let me stop you," said Byron in his deepest, sexiest voice, a voice to make Barry White seem choirboyish.

Christine knelt by his side and began to remove the boxer shorts with her teeth. Byron lay back and tried not to think of tomorrow's court case.

*****

Doug Youngblood leaned back and ordered a double scotch for himself and a double brandy for Geoff Thomas, MP for Sheffield South. They sat in the members' bar at the House of Commons, enjoying the subsidised booze and the warm ambience of power.

"This is what I like about the job, Geoff," Youngblood enthused. "Long hours in the bar with the occasional foray into the chamber. Very civilised."

"It was a lot better before that lot managed to stick their oar in," he said gesturing to a gaggle of women MPs, replete in designer shoulder pads and official party scripts. "They'll probably abolish Bitter from the bar next."

"Stop moaning Geoff. Move with the times. Change is an opportunity."

"For you maybe. I want to go back to the good old days."

"What, when we were a party of opposition," said Youngblood feigning astonishment.

"Sometimes I feel as if I'm in silent opposition now. That lot run things."

"I think you give them too much credit, Geoff. They may rule the roost in here, but we still hold sway where it matters. With the lobbyist. New Labour are so busy with their public relations they've forgotten how the game is played. Speaking of which, I've got something for you to sign."

"What is it?"

"Not like you to worry, Geoff. You have turned over a new leaf. It's a petition protesting against the bid by Icarus for CRA."

"I didn't know they were bidding."

"They were stopped by injunction today. This letter will help throw our weight behind the CRA."

"What's the inducement."

"The usual five hundred. Cash."

"Where do I sign?"

Youngblood placed a paper in front of his erstwhile colleague. "Below the last signature."

"You've done well with this lot," Thomas said as he scanned the names. "They must have a big budget."

"They do. It's a very important issue and they'll do whatever has to be done to win."

"A bit like that lot," said Thomas pointing at the Gin and Tonic crowd.

*****

In the street outside Christine's flat, an ordinary Ford transit van was parked. In the back a video recorder turned, slowly, quietly, efficiently, capturing everything for posterity. The level monitors flickered in time with the couple's passion. A television screen transmitted the action, offering the viewer a selection of camera angles. Bonnier leaned back in his seat and enjoyed, all the while puffing on one of Gross's cigars.

January 16

Daily Herald, January 16
CRA Saga takes further twist
by Jason Tweedy, staff writer

Yesterday was the most extraordinary day yet in the Icarus/CRA saga. While the Evening Courier was printing a story about a bid by Icarus for the CRA that never happened, lawyers obtained a high court injunction to prevent the bid being launched. The injunction was granted on evidence the bid was based on documents stolen from the CRA. It is alleged that Robert Parsons, the operations manager for CRA, passed key documents to James Carter of Icarus as well as staff of his advisors, The Bank. The judge ordered all stolen documents be returned.

Today there will be a court hearing giving Icarus and the Bank the opportunity to put their own side of the story. The judge's ruling is likely to play a decisive role in the success, or otherwise, of any attempted take-over.

As this was happening, Robert Parsons was publicly ejected from CRA House. He refused to answer any questions, and on a morning of light news, gave the networks a story they ran all day.

Sources close to the CRA also suggested that the Bank of England was considering investigating The Bank for its role in the matter. While no final decision had been taken, the regulator is understood to be closely examining all the facts.

The Stock Exchange suspended Icarus's shares at £35 pending the outcome of the injunction and any Bank of England enquiry.

Meanwhile the Evening Courier is forced to lick its wounds having jumped the gun on the bid story, no doubt prompted by an inaccurate press release from an overzealous Bank PR advisor. A number of reputations have been tarnished and the carnage may well get worse before it gets better.

The Times, January 16
Letter to the editor
from Doug Youngblood MP

Dear sir,

I write to express my outrage at the behaviour of James Carter and Icarus plc in its dealing with the CRA. As your readers are no doubt aware, the CRA was founded to help the poor and needy. In fact, for many years its stood beside the Labour movement in its fight against injustice in society. In this context, the high jinks of the past few days are thoroughly reprehensible.

A group of 50 Labour MPs, including myself, have written to Icarus demanding that they (sic) drop their (sic) bid. It is outrageous that such a fine and noble institution should be subject to a break up, launched solely as a smash and grab attempt, a bid to make money. What will be achieved in the long term by flogging off its assets except certain individuals increasing their already substantial wealth? The CRA belongs to the community. It is not a commodity to buy and sell. I find it most distasteful that the Bank, itself a respected and long standing institution, should align itself with these cut-throats and vagabonds. I hope your readers will inform themselves of the facts before lending any support to Icarus.

Yours Sincerely

Jack Youngblood MP
House of Commons

*****

Claire was disorientated. There was no natural light in the room to give any idea of time. She was groggy, waking from a deep

The Naked Bank

sleep. A sleep unconcerned by her circumstances, induced by the strain of days without proper rest. How can a kidnap victim sleep so soundly, you may ask? Simple. There is only so much adrenaline for any person to draw upon. When exhausted it is that adrenaline that keeps a banker going, striving to complete the deal before being overcome by the unhealthy lifestyle. When the supply is exhausted the person must sleep. At a certain point it makes little difference whether that sleep is in a bed, at one's desk or locked in an unfamiliar prison cell.

At first when bundled into the car she had struggled, fighting for her life. Kicking and screaming helped her come to terms with the situation but, she soon realised, achieved nothing in remedying it. And she was tired. After a few minutes of resistance she accepted her position. She was frightened, scared witless, terrified. But there was nothing she could do. So she accepted her fate, at least for that moment, and lay quietly on the spotless floor of the Mercedes, silently whimpering. A sight of the Boss's handgun was a contributory factor in her change of heart.

They blindfolded her and kept driving, the sound proof car leaving her guessing as to the route. There was no doubt, however, they were in the country, revealed by a familiar crunch of gravel when stepping out of the car. The air was still and fresh, bereft of the London cocktail of diesel and petrol fumes. Based on journey time, she was somewhere in the home counties.

They placed her in the room and returned her sight. Sleep soon overcome fear. How long did she sleep? Minutes, hours, a day? With no point of reference she imagined it was now tomorrow.

There were no windows and only one door, which was locked. She had a bed, en-suite toilet, and washbasin. Nothing else. She could walk around her bed without being cramped, and walk the four paces from the room's head to its door. An upmarket prison cell. The strip light was excessively bright and her head throbbed.

Standing, she walked to the washbasin and slapped her face with water. There was no mirror. She imagined her potential audience. Imagined how awful she must look. She stank, unable to properly clean herself after having wet herself when grabbed. It was hot in the room and she sweated. Ladies perspire, prisoners sweat. No air, just heat from a radiator she could not adjust.

David Murray

Sitting on the bed she felt sorry for her discomfort, watching a trickle of salted water run down her arm, feeling several more chasing it down her back. A small camera watched from one of the ceiling corners above the door. A red light torturing her, boring into her soul. Straightening her posture, she forced a smile and pathetically waved to her audience. No response. Perhaps no one watched.

She lay back on the bed and stared at the ceiling. A small spider's web occupied another corner of the room. There was no spider. She shut her eyes but this time sleep refused to rescue her. Her waking thoughts were filled with images of the car, her kidnappers and Forrest Hayden, tied to his bed. The prostitute laughed at her. The bell boy taunted her. Josh danced and Fergus comforted.

She thought of her family, unaware of her predicament, worried about her disappearance. She thought of her friends who she barely knew, so seldom did she see them. She thought of her ex-fiancé, the cad who traded her in for a younger model. She dwelt on how few people would miss her, she dwelt on her life and what a mess it had become. Everything flashed through her mind as she revisited her memories, the only company the prison cell allowed. So many memories, none vivid, none holding her attention for more than a few moments. And then her store was bankrupt, her mind empty, her life lacking. And in all that reflection she never once considered the Bank. Sure, she thought of Forrest, and Carpenter, and Gross. She thought of Giles and his cigarettes, of Carter and his mop. But never her work, her job, her career. In an inventory of her soul it failed to register.

There was no need for her to dwell on who was responsible for her predicament. She had guessed that the moment she was seized.

In another, more spacious, room of the house, the country location was apparent. Giles Bonnier looked out the French windows at a beautifully manicured lawn, and from the lawn out across the picturesque Weald of Kent, a huge valley taking in the heart of the Garden of England. He munched on his toast and slurped his coffee, washing the crumbs down his throat with a gulp. Then took a long,

The Naked Bank

hard drag on one of two lit cigarettes balanced on the side of his plate, the motivation for the second being absentmindedness.

The Boss walked through from the kitchen bearing a cooked breakfast and placed it on the table in front of Bonnier, who tucked in without a word. The Boss was not the type of man to take offence, not when paid this well. Bert sat in front of a screen, watching the prisoner.

"She's very pretty when's she's sleeping," he said.

Bonnier washed his latest mouthful down with more coffee tar. "Do you mean in a classical sort of way?"

"Huh?"

Bonnier delighted in proving his mental superiority of goons like Bert. The trick was to ensure they did not realise he was taking the piss. "Well, classical beauty as depicted in Renaissance art was always much more rotund than today's more waif like beauty. In fact, there is a bulk of evidence to suggest that the average ideal measurements of women are shrinking. But then are fashion models beautiful? Personally I do not find some anorexic sixteen year old attractive. If you take Claire, who has a fuller figure, you could say she has classical beauty. Would you agree?"

"I wouldn't mind shagging her, if that's what you mean," answered Bert.

"Not exactly. And I'd advise you keeping your hands off her. At least until I," he took a menacing puff as he pondered his words, "...say so."

"What's the plan then, boss," said the Boss, uninterested in this debate over the female form.

"We'll leave her to stew a bit longer. Can't afford to injure her, she's the only link with the disk. Besides, I like her. It would've been easier if you clowns hadn't killed the journo."

"Sorry boss."

"So keep watching and make sure she doesn't do herself any damage. Capice?"

"Sure boss."

Bonnier had never used the word 'capice' before in his life, but it felt right under the circumstances, and helped establish his authority with the hired help. "I'm going to check out Walker's computer."

191

David Murray

Computers were a hobby of Bonnier, and he liked to think he was pretty wired. The idea of calling in an expert had not yet crossed his mind. Josh's computer lay in front of his on the breakfast table. They had removed it from the apartment complete with disks and anything else resembling computer kit. Bert's definition of computer kit differed from the norm, so much so that Bonnier chuckled as he looked at the pile of junk littering the table. There was a calculator, clock radio and portable fan heater.

Switching the system on, he watched it slowly boot up with all the usual meaningless jargon of letters and numbers flashing across the screen. Once the thing settled down into Windows, he began to play, calling up all the Word and Freelance files on the hard drive, and reading each in turn. There was nothing relevant, although much of interest. Most of the files were newspaper articles. Josh's style was captivating and it took all Bonnier's discipline not to read a complete article before moving on to check the next. There was one file of great interest containing Josh's research on Icarus and Dedalus, none of which appeared to have found its way into an article. To Bonnier, he had all the information required to make the connection. Josh simply had not concentrated in the right area. It was fortunate he was stopped so promptly.

Doing the same, he worked his way through the computer disks, eventually coming across not one, but two, containing the stolen information. Must have made a back-up. But were there any more copies? He hoped Claire would be of assistance.

Plugging in the modem, he opened Josh's e-mail file. It took a moment to load before presenting him with a request for a password. Tricky. He typed in 'walker' expecting to be rejected. Incredibly he was in, looking at a record of all the e-mails sent by Josh over the past two weeks. Again he read quickly, this time dismayed by the boredom of the messages. All were routine and office related. Nothing remotely juicy.

This whole search had taken several hours and yielded two disks and some interesting research. No leads to other sources of information or people who might have received the incriminating data.

"How is she?" asked Bonnier.

The Naked Bank

"She's pretending to sleep, in a sort of classical manner," said Bert.

"What, you mean with her eyes shut," mocked Bonnier.

"Yeah," replied Bert wondering whether he should be offended.

"I think it's about time we asked her a few questions."

*****

The courtroom was small and undistinguished. Just like any of the courtrooms featured on soap operas or low budget dramas but without the baying gallery. Here there were only a few seats for journalists and well-wishers. There was no jury, the judge's word being final. A court recorder and a bailiff completed the home team line-up along with Mr Justice Barker, the overseer.

Representing the away team was Mr Jenkins-Smythe, scourge of Barker and all his contemporaries, once again equipped with rapier like points, honed and practised during the night in front of his over-sized mirror. Again a gaggle of solicitors sat beside him, marvelling at his every nuance, wishing they could be as expert and precise as he. But they could not, being mere solicitors, hope to match his exactness. It was not a feature of their jobs to be understood. Jenkins-Smythe was not only understood, but so admired that everything he said was instantly credible to the jury. In the presence of only the judge his task was more difficult. Barker expected reasoned argument.

Behind the solicitors sat the bankers, including Mac, and Mr CRA, Frederick Whittle. Mac itched to use her mobile to catch up with events while the court formalities were completed. Rightly, she assumed that mobile communication would not be tolerated by the master of the court. The tradition and pageantry of justice conflicted with the modern world of business and telecommunications. If the justice system was a private company it would have been broken up and sold years ago. Far too inefficient, from its ten to four working hours, to the number of hangers on attaching themselves to any particular case. Rather like the entourage of a prize fighter. No one knowing exactly why the others are there, only certain of the indispensability of their own role.

David Murray

The defence team, sat to the right of the judge. The lead striker was Byron Black, convinced by Carter of his ability to handle such a high profile position. Black's confidence was bolstered by the assistance of Christine, a woman of much beauty and sensuality, but whose expertise in court matters was unproven. Behind sat Carter, and the Bankers named in the injunction. Carpenter was serene. After facing hoards of blood thirsty Argie warriors during his time in the Falklands, the prospect of Justice Barker was undaunting. Forrest was nervous, both because of the potential verdict of the court and also because of the absence of Claire. His carelessness was responsible for her stealing the information and her subsequent disappearance. He was unsure of her fate. Bonnier was officially away on business and could not attend the proceedings, a situation which only reinforced Forrest's apprehension.

Fergus made up the contingent. He looked around worried - there was no sign of Claire. Never having returned with his sandwich, his stomach had cursed her for her cruelty. He had assumed she had gone home and fallen asleep. Besides, Christine had been on his mind that afternoon. Christine and the constant alterations to his document. It was only this morning, when the document was sent and Christine banished from his thoughts, that he began to worry. There was no answer from Claire's house. Not turning up to even a modest team breakfast meeting was out of character. Not attending a court session unthinkable.

The room rose as one to greet Mr Justice Barker, the man whose mood dictated their fortunes. Barker's early night put him in good spirits today, as had a quick scan of the morning's newspapers. He was a man in the limelight. While the session did not attract the kind of press rabble associated with murder or libel, there were enough respectable journalists present in court, and in the lobby outside, to gently stoke his great judgeship.

He looked around the room, making a mental note to put Jenkins-Smythe down at every possible opportunity. He did not recognise the defence team which was surprising, the stakes being too high to appoint rookie counsel.

"I've met Mr Jenkins-Smythe and cast, representing the prosecution. Many times. I would be grateful if the defence team would introduce themselves."

194

The Naked Bank

Byron nervously stood. "I am Byron Black, senior partner of Gilbert, Wilkins and Horsefly. My colleague is Christine Edgerley, an associate at the same firm."

"Would I be correct in assuming you are not a barrister?"

"You would, my lord."

"Your honour will do nicely, thank you. Very well," he said looking down at this impostor, "who am I to quibble?"

Carpenter and Hayden looked at each other wondering whether they should have taken independent counsel.

Barker continued, "I made my initial ruling yesterday without the opportunity for the defence to put its case. The reason for doing so was that I believed a bid for the CRA was imminent. If the evidence provided by the prosecution was in error, there is every opportunity today to challenge it. After all, what is a day in the life of a hostile take-over?" Barker and Jenkins-Smythe were the only two who found the joke amusing, the later guffawing loudly in an attempt to ingratiate himself. "Its not that funny, Jenkins."

"Jenkins-Smythe, your honour. My apologies, I found it very amusing."

"Quite...The defence team was presented with the evidence yesterday afternoon, is that so Mr Black?"

"Yes, your honour."

"And do you wish to challenge the authenticity of that evidence."

"No, your honour, but I must..."

"Thank you Mr Black. No buts in this court," said Barker. "Does the prosecution have any further evidence?"

"No, your honour."

"Very well. So we have established that the evidence is valid. Would the defence care to comment on the validity of the injunction given that it accepts the evidence...I assume that is why you are here...Mr Black, you may speak now."

"Thank you your honour." Black stood to make his pre-prepared address, practised while naked in front of, and on top of, Christine last night. "My clients have accepted the irrefutability of the evidence laid before the court. However they dispute its illegality." Black twitched. "If I may refer your honour to Dwain vs Goosebump, 1823, you will see that information cannot be stolen, only the paper on which it is written. As these documents were copied they are not stolen. But, given this is disputed there is still no reason for my client's bid not to go forward. The bid is based on the poor past performance of the CRA and the unsuitability of its management to effectively run the business. It has sat on its laurels for too long."

"Please spare me the speech, Mr Black. Stick to the relevant points."

"Thank you your honour. The bid is an attempt to unlock member value and to hand the CRA over to the appropriate management. The documents were used to confirm valuations of the companies rather than establish them and were used to verify that the value being offered to the members of the CRA was equitable. It is in the interests of these members that there is full and frank disclosure. As for obtaining a membership list, I think it is fair to say that the CRA management would not have given us this list and so would have denied their members any chance to examine the proposals.

"The Icarus team does not seek to impose any solution on the members of the CRA. It seeks to offer them the legitimate choice to which any shareholder of a public company would be entitled. The documents do not affect the making of this choice."

Black sat down pleased with himself. Christine offered a friendly stroke of his thigh in lieu of congratulations. The bulk of the speech was hers.

"Mr Jenkins-Smythe," droned the judge. "Would you care to counter this argument?"

"I would indeed, your honour." From Jenkins-Smythe this amounted to leaping in the air and screaming 'you bet' at the top of his lungs. Barker was taken aback by the man's vigour. "It seems pedantic for the defence to say that their bid did not rely on the stolen documents. If it did not, then it seems odd in the extremis that they rely on them, does it not?"

"Please do not direct rhetorical questions at me Mr Jenkins."

"No, your honour," and then as an after thought, "Jenkins-Smythe. It also seems strange to hide behind an obscure precedent when to the man on the Clapham Omnibus it is evidently wrong to have taken the documents. I am also reliably informed that the documents were photocopied at the offices of CRA, in which case unless Mr Parsons can demonstrate he brought his own photocopying paper into the office, it is clear he stole paper belonging to his employer.

"I think it mischievous for the defence to call upon the freedom to bribe the members of the CRA. The CRA is a long standing institution whose constitution was drawn up by its founding fathers. It is an institution more important than its current membership. It serves all future members. That is why decisions are taken by the executive committee rather than the membership. The executive committee has all members' interests at heart, both current and future. Current members may be tempted into taking a short term gain over the long term prosperity of the organisation. Icarus does not have the long term interest of the CRA at heart. It wishes to break it up by selling its parts to the highest bidder for a profit. Destroying a great British institution. Appealing to the members is their way of circumventing the internal rules of the organisation. Obtaining those names through theft would seem to greatly compound that backhandedness. Icarus is no more than a corporate carpetbagger."

"Thank you Mr Jenkins. Unless the defence has anything else it wishes to add I will adjourn to consider my verdict."

Black stood. "Only to say your honour that this is more than about technicalities. It is about the rights of CRA's members. It is about the right for organisations to be taken over. It is about the rights of the market."

"Thank you, Mr Black. You have more than made your point."

Barker stood, as did his audience, and then made his way backstage to his chambers where a pot of tea and a hot muffin awaited him. He always liked to ensure a recess in time for morning tea.

*****

Fear is relative. Fear should be confronted. Claire had no option but to face her fear as it opened the door and entered in the

197

guise of the Boss and Bert. No longer wearing the dark suits of the mob, they wore white tennis gear. Bert's was too tight, accentuating his muscular body, bulging in all the right places. Boss's was well cut to hide his less than athletic demeanour. Neither were welcome.

"Hello Miss Snow," said Boss, careful not given any indication of the time. All part of the routine.

"Hello," she said quietly. While she longed to rant at these thugs, it would achieve nothing and weaken her already non-existent hand.

"I'm glad to see you up and about. I hope you find our facilities to your liking."

Claire said nothing, studying the man and the fact that the door was ajar behind him.

"I wouldn't try and run, if I were you," said Boss reading her thoughts. "The last person who tried to run didn't make it very far. In fact he didn't live very long. I think you might know him."

Josh. "No!!" she cried.

"Yes! A bit of an accident. He ran straight into a bus. So if you're hoping for help I'd forget it."

"You bastards! Why have you brought me here?" she demanded.

"I would have thought that was obvious. Josh had some disks which you gave him. We want to know who else you gave them to and where you've hidden your copies?"

Claire paused to consider her position, in no doubt she would tell them everything they wanted. Already she was emotionally wrecked, overheated, and hungry. There was nothing to gain by stalling.

"I gave Josh the only copy. That was two days ago after I returned from Italy. I haven't spoken to him since. I was working. He called me but I never got back to him." The last words were accompanied by a tear of regret.

"That's it?" said the Boss with no remorse.

"That's the truth. I can't say any more than that. Who are you and when are you going to let me go?"

The Boss kneaded his plump chin, encouraging the poor growth on his face which he liked to call a beard. "Who we are is unimportant. You have upset some very powerful people. People who do not like being upset. Bert here thinks that you are a very attractive young lady. I am not convinced, but then I'm not that way inclined. An advantage in this business. I've no qualms about beating up women. I guarantee by the end of this not even Bert, not known for his selectiveness, will want to even buy you a packet of crisps. So I suggest very strongly that you talk."

"But I've told you everything." Claire was desperately scared. "Can I have some food?"

"Did you hear that, Bert, the little lady is hungry. Well perhaps you should have thought of the consequences of your actions. There will be no food, no champagne, no change of clothes, and I must say you reek, no nothing until you tell me where the disk is. If you don't I may have to leave you here with Bert, alone."

Bert slobbered a grin.

"Please don't talk," he said.

"I don't know," she said in tears, "I gave the only copy to Josh. Search my flat if you don't believe me."

"We have," replied the Boss. "I'm afraid we had to mess it up a little," he lied. "Seems the door won't shut any more."

Claire did not care. She would have told them anything. She had nothing to tell.

The Boss realised this, but was professional enough not to reveal his instinct. "Why don't you think about it a bit longer. Next time I come back I may not be so tolerant."

The thugs left the room with the Boss saying to Bert, "Do we still have the pliers lying around?"

And Bert replying, "Why did you have to say I fancied her?"

The door closed and she heard the key turn. She was alone again.

Bonnier watched all this on the monitor. He suspected she was telling the truth. She was not a liar. She was a merchant banking automaton, programmed to carry out orders. Why would she lie? There was no one to protect except herself. She would co-operate. It would be grim to dispose of her. Unlike the Boss, he did have a conscience, of sorts.

David Murray

If Bonnier had been working at the computer he might have noticed the modem register activity. On a free-standing modem there are a number of lights. When communicating most of them flash. In this way the user can tell whether he has a connection. This is the main advantage over one contained within the machine. The flashing of the lights for a few seconds indicated the time release of an e-mail. Not from Josh's normal e-mail account. This one was from The Falcon and by the time Bonnier resumed hacking at the PC it was long gone. The Falcon was anonymous and Bonnier unaware of its secrets sent.

*****

Lara's first proper meeting with John Greggor was a bollocking. She stood in front of his desk, in his plush office, and listened to him rant. No invitation to sit down. No how's it going so far? Just grief.

"How the hell did you get into this mess? I'm only gone a few hours and you've committed us to an investigation I know nothing about and, is probably completely bogus. I've got the press calling me every five minutes wanting to know the details of something I've never heard of. What the hell am I supposed to do? How could this happen? I took you on as a favour to Hogg and look what's happened. How long have you been here, a week at best. This is amazing. I'd be better off without you. Why should you stay? Give me one good reason?"

Lara fumed inside. This guy was an asshole. Not in the Hogg Midgely class, but an asshole nonetheless. His offer was tempting. Walk out and never come back. But to do so would end her career just as effectively as decking Greggor right now. Out on the carpet. Blood on the floor. Tempting for a second, but by quitting Hogg's opinion would be confirmed. She would end up stuck in the backwoods, no hope, yokel office trying to make partner while less able people were promoted in preference. With nothing to lose by staying she stuck her heels in. After all, this guy was an asshole. And five assholes in one paragraph is a lot of assholes.

"I don't think that's fair John. You are right, I've been here a week. Doing what? You give me a run down office and I'm expected to get it decorated. That takes time. You have yet to tell me what this job's all about. Yet to give me any assignments. I don't know what you do, how we fit into the Bank of England in general. I don't even know what my hours are supposed to be. So don't give me this shit. A woman who I've never met walks in off the street and demands to see you. Won't go until she does. No one has a clue where you are. What else can I do but agree to see her?

"She asks me to investigate this CRA affair. I've never heard of it. I don't know whether that's because it's something new or because you haven't told me about it. What can I do? I say I will ask you, that we can't make a decision at the moment. Is it my fault that the papers then report that we are considering an investigation? We are, I just don't know how strongly we are considering it. Perhaps if you had been around a bit more, or rather at all, I would have had a better idea of how things work. I didn't even know if she came to the right department. Did she?"

Greggor was transfixed. "I guess we've got off on the wrong foot."

"You could say that." Lara was in no mood for surrender. He should not have had a go at her without hearing the facts.

"I'm sorry if I over-reacted but we're in a difficult position." Greggor's tone was conciliatory. "The matter is currently being considered in court and whatever we decide the press are going to jump all over us. I guess you weren't to know how manipulative this woman was or that you should have let her stew until I got back. Basically, don't say you will even think about something. That's all these sharks want. Great publicity for their cause is gained by us thinking about things. You'll learn. And I'm sorry I haven't briefed you, you would not believe how busy I've been. That's why I took you on I the first place."

"Then let me help. That's what I'm here for."

"You're right. For the record, we do investigations here, fraud and anything else that falls under the Bank of England's remit. We second auditors with your investigative skills, although as you've already discovered, the job is far higher profile than your average company accounts."

"I'll do it," said Lara jumping the gun..

"What's that?"

"The CRA investigation."

"Hold on now. First of all, we haven't decided to investigate. Second, you don't know the first thing about it."

"I can learn."

"Sure." The woman had enthusiasm. "Why don't you bring Macintosh's material in and we can look it over. If I think there's a case, you can have it."

"Fantastic."

"But only because I have no time. It'll be tough."

"I'll do you proud."

"Well, until I look at the file there isn't a case," said Greggor.

"Just a mo," said Lara. She disappeared down the corridor to her makeshift office.

"Do you have the CRA file, Sue?" she asked.

Sue looked up. "You only have one file."

"I know. Can I have it please."

Sue handed it across the desk. "You've got your first e-mail," she said.

"I'll read it later. I'm sure it's not important."

*****

Barker took his accustomed place in front of an expectant audience.

"I have reviewed all the evidence and submissions placed before me with great care. I must say that rarely have I seen such dishonest behaviour shown by such respected folk. This entire bid seems in have been based on iniquitous conduct. Mr Parson's behaviour in all of this appears to be a serious, gross and wilful breach of conduct. The advisors to Icarus have behaved appallingly. To pass stolen documents around the City like pieces of candy was inexcusable. While technically such an act might be deemed legal, it was obviously wrong and immoral. To hide behind legal precedent is no excuse. The whole affair was clearly dishonest.

"As such I have no hesitation in extending this injunction indefinitely, banning the named parties from using any of the confidential information clearly stolen from the CRA for any purpose including using it to launch a bid for the CRA.

"This court is adjourned."

Mac punched the air in jubilation, turning to Whittle and bear-hugging the man, lifting him off his feet with her enthusiasm. Dropping him to the ground she uttered the now predictable line, "How about lunch?"

"I'd be delighted," coughed Whittle, even more crumpled than usual, or indeed a few moments ago.

"Great. I'll meet you outside. I think a quick word with the opposition wouldn't go amiss while you chat to our friends in the press." Turning to her assistant she said, "Come with me son, and bring the box."

Her assistant was wide and starry eyed, and relieved at not being despatched on another bun-run in the midst of all the action.

Across the gangway there was only disbelief and recrimination. Carter had already slunk out a back entrance, intent on avoiding the media. Black stood stunned by his defeat, wondering whether shagging Christine last night represented the ideal preparation for his court debut. Christine smiled meekly, with a shrug, as if to say things could be worse. Which they soon would be.

Carpenter and Forrest chatted quietly, mulling over their next step. Fergus sat on the bench ignored, staring at Christine and wondering how long she had been seeing Black. Was she sleeping with him before the burglary?

The crowds bayed around the triumphant Whittle, who spoke freely, enjoying his moment of glory. The defence team were ignored with the exception of Mac, who strode up to Carpenter with her customary directness.

"Commiserations, Ian. You put up a good fight." Hers was the generosity of the victor.

"It's not over yet," responded Carpenter. "We have a few aces up our sleeve," he said defiantly. Forrest looked a little more sheepish.

"Sporting words, that's what I like to hear," said Mac. "Son, would you pass the box over please."

Her personal hunk handed across a large cardboard box, the weight of which was only apparent when Fergus received it from the six foot five banking Adonis, and dropped it, the contents spilling across the floor. A number of bulky brown foolscap envelopes, each addressed to a director of the CRA.

"I'm afraid we cottoned onto your little ruse, Ian. None of the directors have opened your correspondence so I'm afraid none of them have any idea what was inside. They are under no obligation to pass on something about which they have no knowledge."

Carpenter was silent, and knew he was beaten. With a bow, he walked out through the front of the court room, passing journalists all too interested in Whittle to pay any attention to an anonymous suit. Forrest, however, snapped.

"Why don't you just fuck off, you ungracious cow."

"Sorry if I upset you Hayden, you always were too stressed to concentrate properly on your job. You should have learnt from me when you had your chance."

"Oh, just fuck off."

"And so eloquent."

Hayden aggressively moved towards Mac, forgetting there was a bench in the way. He tripped, finding himself among the documents on the floor. He stood, brushed himself down, to an audience of the now attracted press, and stormed out, the veins in his forehead full to bursting.

Fergus was left to gather the documents and listen to Mac making her lunch reservation on the mobile.

*****

The Naked Bank

London Courier, January 16
Finance backs out of Icarus Consortium
by Wilhard Attwater

Republica Bank of Italy today announced that it has withdrawn its debt facility from Icarus for this bid for CRA. This follows the upholding of the injunction by Mr Justice Barker prohibiting the use of allegedly stolen documents in any bid. In a statement, Republica said it had sought assurances from the Bank, advisors to Icarus, that the documents were legitimate. It also sought clarification that an earlier payment made by Dedalus to Giles Bonnier, James Carter's right hand man, was above board. Press rumours suggested that the money had been used as a bribe to staff at the CRA to conclude a favourable deal. Robert Parsons was expelled yesterday from CRA House alleged to have passed stolen documents to Carter. He was central to the Dedalus/CRA negotiations in question.

Receiving no satisfactory clarification from the Bank, Republica says it was forced to withdraw from the bid, effectively killing it off.

*****

Sir Wig was nervous of events. As a traditional banker, he enjoyed nothing more exciting than choosing the vintage of his claret over lunch. The mess the Bank now found itself in was abhorrent. He had known, of course, what was happening, having been thoroughly briefed. It was his appreciation of the seriousness of the situation which was lacking. He had understood the documents were legal, that the client was reputable. His image was now tarnished by his letter to Fred Whittle defending the Bank's position. Now he prepared to meet the vile Macintosh woman. Someone who stood against everything in which he believed. The sanctity of banking.

His phone rang. "*Mrs* Macintosh is here to see you." In his office woman of a certain age were assumed to be married.

"You'd better show her in."

Sir Wig stood as she entered his office, not having time to cover the vast stretch from his desk to the door.

205

David Murray

"It's a pleasure to meet you, Mrs Macintosh," he said extending a hand as she moved quickly across the plush blue carpet to seize it. Sir Wig offered his handshake for women, a weak, polite grip designed to comply with formalities but not offend ladylike fingers. Mac grasped his hand with force, squeezing his arthritic hands tight, forcing him to fight back a squeal.

She released and sat without bidding. "I'm surprised we haven't met before, Sir Wig. I guess you don't get out and about as much as you did in your heyday."

This was Mac's attempt at small talk, but as Sir Wig cradled his crushed hand behind the screen of his enormous desk, he only felt more aggrieved at the aggressive nature of this *woman*. For indeed this was no lady. Mac would have regarded that as a compliment rather than insult. They were generations apart.

"I guess we don't move much in the same circles," said Sir Wig.

"I guess not. I'm not into shooting and fishing, I'm afraid. I enjoy hunting mind you. Hunting business opportunities, shall we say." Mac smiled for she was in charge.

Sir Wig was tired with the preliminaries. "What can I do for you, Mrs Macintosh?"

"Please, call me Mac. Well, Wig, if I can cut through the formalities, I wouldn't mind a coke and a cup of coffee. A few cakes would not go amiss either."

Sir Wig was appalled. Where were this woman's manners? Being a true gent he obliged, picking up the phone,

"Mary. Could we have some coffee please? Cakes or biscuits and a....can?...of coke. Thank you." He replaced the receiver. "It will be right in."

"Thanks Wig. I can call you Wig can't I?" she continued without offering him the chance to respond. "I can't do anything without my coke. This is a wonderful office. I'd hate to think what the overheads are like on a place like this."

"I'm sure you could take a stab."

"I could indeed. Couple of million a year, I'd say. Not to mention furniture maintenance."

"Now would you expect me to comment on that?"

"Not really, but I wouldn't have been surprised if you had."

The Naked Bank

Sir Wig fumed. Mac let her gaze wander across the ornate ceiling, transferred intact from the Bank's previous headquarters in the heart of the City. It had previously been in the board room. On moving, Sir Wig thought it more appropriate to be in his office. After all, he was Chairman, Chief Executive and General Big Cheese of the institution. What he said, went.

The coffee arrived carried by a woman more resembling a cat walk kitten than a secretary. She placed the tray on Sir Wig's desk and left, after receiving his gracious nod.

"She's a bit of all right, eh Wig. Hand-picked perk of the job I suppose. I bet you and her have shared a few good times on top of your antique mahogany desk. King sized by the look of it."

Sir Wig exploded. "Who the hell do you think you are to come in here and insult both me and Mary like that? You are out of order Mrs Macintosh and I suggest you come straight to the point before I ask you to leave."

"Apologies. Touchy subject." Mac slurped her coke, half deliberately playing the role of slob for her audience. "OK, Wig here are the facts. You've been caught with your trousers down behind the bike shed. My clients are none too impressed by your behaviour and are going to take civil proceedings against you, and the Bank. That will mean dragging the whole affair through the press for months and will mean you personally taking the witness stand."

"Me?" said Sir Wig spilling his coffee.

"You are in control of this place. Aren't you?"

"Well..yes, but I had nothing to do with stealing documents?"

"You did write that letter didn't you? Well, I assume you at least read it before you signed it."

"Yes, but that doesn't make me a crook."

"I'm not sure others will see it that way."

Sir Wig was being taunted, and despite generations of in-breeding, recognised it. Regaining his composure he asked, "So you have a proposition?" He began to light one of his customary fat cigars.

If there is one thing a career in the City teaches, it is that no matter how dire a position is, there is always a deal to be done, a favour to be granted. Nothing is irredeemable.

207

David Murray

"Having talked the situation through with Fred, he agrees that it would be best for both parties to draw a line under events," said Mac.

"Agreed." Three rapid puffs and he sucked air through the hand rolled tobacco, now once more in his element.

"I would appreciate it if you didn't smoke those things," said Mac as a sweet smelling haze began to descend. "I do have my health to consider."

"Sorry, I should have realised you're pregnant," shot back Sir Wig in a cheap jibe about Mac's size. Larger than the average bimbette.

She was unfazed. That was the name of the game. Put your opponent off balance. Those who remained calm won.

"No, I'm just fat. However my only vice is not to smoke so it would be somewhat tragic, not to say ironic, if I died from passive smoking."

Sir Wig stubbed out his cigar. It would keep until the banshee left.

"Thank you," said Mac in a moment of grace. "The deal on the table is this. You write a letter apologising for the Bank's mistakes in this affair and stating they will never happen again. You will pay the CRA the sum of five million pounds in full and final settlement. Your letter will be published in the FT, and we will graciously accept it. And of course you will disavow Icarus and Carter as clients. There will be an internal investigation to find a few scapegoats but we are quite happy for you to remain untouched. Likewise, we will ensure that you are not blamed in the Bank of England investigation."

"What investigation?" asked the punchy Wig.

"Oh didn't you know? They are to investigate matters for themselves. I'm sure their activities can be co-ordinated with your investigation. I understand a rookie on secondment is leading the enquires. I'm sure there is nothing to worry about. They prefer to avoid embarrassment."

"For them or for us?"

"Both. They regulate you...Just as you are responsible for your staff. You are both equally to blame so you can see the incentive for them to find no blame."

The Naked Bank

Sir Wig leaned forward and stared at Mac. She was tough. He had no choice but to accept her terms. The Bank could not be dragged through the courts. He could not be disgraced. They would hide the payout in the accounts and no one would know. Unless it was leaked.

"Agreed on condition we have a binding agreement maintaining full confidentiality."

"Not an issue. Very few people will know of the size of settlement."

"Where would you like it paid?" asked Sir Wig.

Was this an attempt at bribery? "The CRA will give you its banking details when appropriate. Right now you need to sign this letter." Mac pulled out something she had prepared earlier.

"What is it?"

"Your apology. I thought I'd save some time and energy by drawing it up for you. It's not negotiable."

Sir Wig slipped on a pair of half-moon reading glasses and quickly skimmed the letter's contents. His face noticeably brightened though his subsequent tone of voice maintained its stability.

"Hobson's Choice. I suppose you have a legal agreement as well?" It found its way onto the table. "I'll need to run this by our internal lawyers and will get back to you in the next couple of hours."

"Good, my number's on the front...A word of advice if I may. Don't run the agreement past Byron Black. He has yet to settle with us although I'm sure it's only a matter of time."

"You're going for Gilbert, Wilkins and Horsefly as well?"
"Why not?"

"Why not indeed. And what about Carter and Icarus?"

"Not your concern. As of today they're no longer your clients."

*****

Rounding the corridor, Bonnier was faced with another five monsters, each heavily armed. He was low on ammo and his body couldn't take much more. In the last room he had received several glancing hits and unless he received medical aid shortly, was doomed. The monsters spotted him and rushed in for the kill. Bonnier's shot gun blasted the first, continuing to shoot when the creature fell. He needed to ensure the thing was dead. Turning ninety degrees he fired at two more. Bang. Bang. With satisfaction he noted the blood burst from their bodies. Full hundred and eighty degree turn and more rapid firing. Two more monsters down. Somehow he had survived.

Stumbling on he saw the lift, and a route out of this hell hole. There could be medicine further down. He opened the lift door and walked in. Bam. He felt the full force of the machine gun from behind. His life-force oozed away in front of his very eyes. He had not even seen the thing coming. Bonnier was dead. He'd remember to look for the beast next time.

He closed the computer game, his adrenaline pumped. It was amazing how realistic the graphics were these days. Time to continue with his search through Walker's computer records. He had gone through all the obvious ones, but was in no mood to take a chance. Entering file manager he started to methodically read every file on the hard disk. He felt sure he had overlooked something and this was the only way, very slow way, of finding out.

A quick glance at the monitor as he worked showed Claire pacing her cell. Good. She was beginning to crack. While he doubted she had anything to tell, one never knew. In this game he was often surprised, no more so than when the woman stole the information in the first place. He enjoyed breaking people. She would be his. He would own her, which was all a power hungry, racketeering bully boy like Giles Bonnier sought in life. He owned Byron Black. He owned Forrest Hayden. Soon he would own Claire Snow.

The routine of the computer was dull. Mind numbing. Slowly he worked his way through the hundreds of files saved on Walker's PC. After an hour he was about to return for a re-run of Quake, when he found something unusual. He assumed it was software for another Internet Service Provider. Probably an old subscription which Josh had cancelled but not deleted. A common enough occurrence.

He found the execution file which started the 'fastmail' program. Similar to other Internet Service Provider front pages, it presented him with a space to type his password. He typed in

'Walker' again and waited. The modem made its customary imitation of a strangled cat and he was in. Then he was out. The system rejected him. Incorrect password. Interesting. It had accepted the automatically posted user name but not the password. It was only then that he noticed the user name. Simon Worthy. Who the hell was Simon Worthy? Bonnier changed the user name to Josh Walker and tried again. Rejected. Unknown user name. He was right. This was an active account for which he did not have the password. An active account which may hold some of the secrets for which he was looking.

Bonnier began to try different passwords to no effect. He banged his fist on the table in frustration.

"Shit."

"How can things be worse for you than me?" asked the familiar voice of James Carter from behind him.

"James," he said with a warmth that was genuine. "How did the court case go?"

"Your own words would sum it up well. We got the shit kicked out of us. It's hard to see how the bid can go ahead."

"Shit," said Bonnier.

"Shit."

"That's a lot of shit."

"No shit," said Carter. "What's been happening here?"

"The girl hasn't told us anything. Frankly I don't think she knows anything. She's so green around the ears it's frightening. I'm letting her stew a bit to see what comes out."

"Shit, I expect," laughed Carter.

Bonnier almost found that funny. "I suspect the journalist had another e-mail account. He may have sent some stuff we don't know about."

"Jesus."

"Yep. I'm trying to crack the password but we've had no luck so far. We may need to get a professional in."

"Leave it for the moment. Keep trying yourself but things are a bit dodgy to bring someone else in. We've still got to decide what to do with the girl."

"You're not thinking of losing her are you?" asked Bonnier. She could not be his if she were dead.

"It crossed my mind.."

"She doesn't know that we're involved. She's only seen the goons to date." *Although it would not take much to put two and two together, she could prove nothing.*

"Good," said Carter hearing the first decent news of the day. "Keep it that way."

Carter's phone went. "Hello....yes. Hold on a moment. I've Giles here. I'll put you on speaker."

A moment later they were ready.

"Hello, can you hear me?" said Carter.

"Loud and clear," replied the distinctive voice of Ian Carpenter. "I've got Hayden here with me."

"Hi James, Giles" said Forrest.

"Hi Forrest," said Giles.

"So what's the game plan after today? I can't see where we go," asked Carter.

"No," said a subdued Carpenter. "I've got more bad news. Republica Bank pulled out this afternoon. The deal looks pretty dead."

"They what!" exclaimed Bonnier. These were his contacts. These were the people behind the deal. The people he had made a fortune for on the Dedalus deal. Carpenter was unaware of the full connection.

Carter was more resigned. "I see," he said. "So we're alone to face the heat. I'm sure it'll blow over. The City has a short memory. We can re-launch in a few weeks without using any of the documents."

There was silence at the other end of the phone.

"Hello," said Carter, "Are you still there guys?"

"Yes," said Carpenter, hesitantly. "I'm afraid there is more bad news."

"I didn't think it could get any worse."

"I'm afraid so. I just want you to know that Forrest and I had nothing to do with this."

"With what, Ian? I don't think I like the sound of this," said Carter.

"Sir Wig has reached a settlement with the CRA."

"What!!"

The Naked Bank

Carpenter was glad he was on the other end of the phone. This was difficult. More difficult than when he asked his first wife to marry him. Or his second wife to divorce him.

"He didn't consult us. He's agreed to print a full apology in tomorrow's FT. He's paying them off."

"The bastard."

"Your words, not mine. I must say they reflect my own sentiments at the moment. But there's worse."

"How the hell can there be worse?"

"As part of the settlement we resign as your advisors."

Carter stared at the speaker phone in disbelief. After everything they had been through, the Bank was just going to walk away.

"I think you are making a huge mistake guys."

"It's not us," Forrest. "I'd back you all the way, you know that."

"Well fuck you," exploded Carter as he punched the phone cutting off the Bank men. "Fuck em," he shouted at Bonnier who knew when to keep quiet. "I need a drink."

Three tumblers into a bottle of eighteen year old single malt The Maccallen, the phone rang again.

"Hello," punched Carter.

"Hello, Mr Carter. This is Nicola Macintosh. You might have heard of me?"

"Sounds like a whisky to me. Lowlands or Highlands, I can't tell from the sweetness, or lack of it, in your voice."

Mac ignored his ramblings. "I am the advisor to the CRA."

"What the hell do you want? Phoning to gloat?"

"Not exactly. I'm phoning to make your acquaintance. I always believe it's much better to make friends than enemies."

"What are you talking about, woman? You've just shafted us so get to the point or get out of my face."

Mac was not used to someone more abusive than her. "Fine. I know you have Claire Snow."

Carter did not flinch. "Who's she?" Wrong answer for someone who worked with her.

213

David Murray

"You may recall the video evidence of you and Parsons in the car park. As routine, we had PIs follow Bank staff just in case it led anywhere. Well, I have a video of two of your goons bundling Miss Snow into the back of a dark Mercedes sedan. I hope its not traceable to you."

It was not.

"I repeat, I don't know what you're talking about." Carter was aware this woman might be taping the conversation. First rule - admit nothing.

"I'm not surprised. Hypothetically, if Claire Snow was to re-appear at her flat I'm sure the tape would be destroyed."

"Why do you care?" asked Carter.

"Let's just say I have a cunning plan. A plan so cunning you would not believe it. If you do what I say, I guarantee you will get your own back on Sir Wig and his cronies."

"I'm listening," said Carter using a second sitcom catchphrase in the space of two paragraphs.

"I'll meet you in half an hour and I'll explain. This line may not be secure."

"Make it an hour. I'm enjoying the country air."

Claire sat in the back seat of the Mercedes, blindfolded. They had been driving for some time. The gentle motion of its smooth suspension then stopped. She heard nothing but the breathing of the driver and his partner.

"Where are we?" she asked nervously. Visions of being dumped in a forest, never to be found. Of stabilising a motorway concrete pylon. Of fuelling an out of the way furnace. She hoped it would be quick.

"Listen," said the Boss. "Now I don't want you to think we're soft. This is not my idea. I wanted to bump you off, like in the good old days. But no, we're living in the twenty first century now. If you laugh at me I will not be happy." There was no chance of Claire so much as smirking. "We've brought you home."

Claire did not believe it. A ruse to relax her before a bullet in the back of her head. She'd seen the movies. A penny for every time that stunt was pulled. Her head dropped at the finality of it all. It was over.

214

The Naked Bank

"She doesn't look very happy," said Bert. "Tell her about the money."

"Oh yes. My employers, being even more wet than I dreamed possible have decided to compensate you for any inconvenience. You will find in your pocket a scrap of paper with the name of a Swiss bank and an account number. In that account is two hundred thousand pounds. More than my fee I might add. This is supposed to cover loss of earnings, mental torture, all that kind of thing. You could do with a new suit for a start. And some deodorant. The money's being paid, how did he say it, in full and final settlement. That means you tell no one, including, no, especially the police. If you do, I think you'll find it difficult to explain the account which includes deposits over the past six months. Oh yeah, and I'll kill you. So I strongly recommend you forget all about this little adventure. Relax. Take a nice long holiday. Somewhere hot. You look like you don't catch the sun enough. Do I make myself clear?"

Claire nodded her head.

"Bert, be a gentleman and get the door."

Bert opened the door and pulled Claire onto the pavement.

"The paper Bert."

He then dropped the Bank details into her pocket. Spun her around three times as if this were a party game, returned to the car and drove off.

Claire stood still listening. Her hands were free but it was sometime before she moved them. She took in the sounds of the traffic around her. Although it had been raining since she exited the car, it was a moment before she recognised the wet splashes on her face. There was no shot. No bump on the head. She reached for the blindfold which was a simple mask, and removed it, lifting it above her head. Her blurred vision gradually focused onto the street, at night, half lit by lamps. The moon was full and she was again alone. As her senses returned she recognised the street. Not her own but very close by. Around the corner. 'Didn't want to get caught in the one way system,' she mused thinking clearly.

The rain was heavy and prompted her to action. She wandered slowly to Palmerston Street. Her legs were quite numb having lacked any proper exercise for the last two days. And no food either. She felt faint as she climbed the steps towards her front door.

215

David Murray

Hearing a noise she turned to its source and recognised Byron Black opening the front door to the house opposite. 'I didn't know he lived there,' she thought. Byron looked at her as she stumbled against the door. He knew her, smiled, and entered his house. The door shut behind him.

Claire looked at her own door. She had lost her handbag. Her key was gone. She sat on the uncovered step and watched the rain fall. Only then did she realise it was winter and she had no coat. She pulled her jacket about her body and felt ill. She felt lost sitting on the step of her own house. Her feet were sore from the cold. Her legs tingled as she pushed them tightly together, her designer suit not practical for outdoor survival. She cried.

Another sound from next door. It was Christine.

"Claire," she exclaimed. "What are you doing out here? You'll do yourself some harm."

Christine trotted up the stairs to help.

"What's the matter?" she asked. "You're in a right state." Christine pretended not to notice the smell. "Let's get you inside. Where's your key?"

"I lost it," sobbed Claire.

"Don't worry. It's not the end of the world. Do you have a spare?"

Claire could not think.

"Wait a minute," continued Christine, "What's this?"

Stuck in the door lock was her front door key.

"You must have left it in the door." Turning the key the door opened and she took Claire in. The heating was on, but Christine still wrapped her own coat around Claire. It could be cleaned.

"I'll run a bath for you and get you to bed. Don't worry. Don't explain. Everything can wait until tomorrow."

Claire hoped her ordeal was over.

*****

The Naked Bank

The Naked Bank

Daily Times, January 17
Bank meekly surrenders
by Gibbony Lee

The City today was rocked by the apology of Sir Wig Forthright, Chairman, Chief Executive and General Big Cheese of the Bank, to CRA published on the front page of the Financial Times. The Bank was the advisor to Icarus plc in its ill-fated bid for the CRA. The golden rule of financial advice is admit nothing. By taking responsibility the Bank may well be laying itself open to legal claims from suffered parties. Although it seems sure that the Bank settled out of court with CRA, there is the possibility that Icarus will sue claiming poor advice. Sir Wig announced there will be a full internal inquiry into the affair, a move which has all ready sparked cries of 'cover up' from several city sources.

It is also rumoured that the Bank of England is looking into the matter. If this is the case, a further question mark hangs over the Bank's tattered reputation. The Bank's Corporate Finance department was quiet yesterday evening and made no comment. James Carter issued a statement to say that "the Bank had dumped him as soon as the going got tough." He was reputed to be seeking legal advice.

In a related development, Gilbert, Wilkins and Horsefly also issued an apology to CRA. The city law firm were legal advisors to Icarus and to date have stayed clear of criticism. It is believed that it was on their legal advice the Bank passed documents stolen from CRA around financial institutions when seeking to raise funds for the bid. It was these documents that were the basis of an injunction granted against Icarus and the Bank, effectively stopping the bid cold in its tracks.

David Murray

Lara Waters finally moved into her new office. Not much, but at least she had her own desk. The walls were white, the floor carpeted. A damp patch in the ceiling was the last remnant of the leak. There were no windows to allow her to watch the world pass by, but at least she had her computer to gaze into, an interactive Brad Pitt screen saver providing some entertainment. And apart from the Sue's hourly herbal tea deliveries, so punctual Lara had no need for a wall clock, there was silence. This allowed her to think without interruption, now that she had something to think about.

Her instructions were to adopt a softly, softly approach. Sir Wig had appointed the lawyers Fitchkins & Snot to conduct an independent internal inquiry into the CRA affair, as it was now known. There was no need for Lara to duplicate that process. Besides, she was far more interested in the substance of the transaction rather than any individual acts of the Bank's staff. It was the guiding hand behind events that attracted her interest.

Greggor did not think there was a case at all and it took all her nagging enthusiasm to convince him otherwise. For Lara it was better than doing nothing and would prevent certain press allegations of the Bank of England sweeping the whole mess under the carpet.

The investigation was hers and hers alone. Her mandate was free, Greggor having no confidence in defining it. The only condition was that it was an off the record inquiry. The public would not be told. If she screwed up, to use Greggor's own words, no one would know. How reassuring.

Lara said goodbye, for a moment, to her montage of Brad Pitt action scenes as she touched her mouse, dissolving his images into nothing. She had been so enthusiastic about winning Greggor over last night, she clean forgot her e-mail. Probably from the system administrator anyway, welcoming her to the service. Or her first junk e-mail.

No matter, she clicked into her mail box. Still just the one message, from someone called The Falcon. With curiosity, she read.

The Naked Bank

To: lara.waters@bankofengland.org
From: the falcon@fastmail.com

I am not sure whether you are the right person to send this information
to. Please forward it to the appropriate authority as it is very important
that the truth is told. I have attached a file that came into my
possession today which you should study closely. It has come from a
source close to the Bank and Icarus, the former who are advising the
latter on their bid for CRA. It is information not in the public domain. I
will send you another e-mail shortly once I have set out my thoughts in
some kind of logical order.

Love and kisses

The Falcon

Attachment

Icarus plc is a publicly quoted company on the Alternative Investment
Market (AIM)

Shareholdings:

James Carter		20%
Barracuda Trust	20%	
Cluny Trust		25%
Dashiell Trust		10%
General Public		35%

These trusts are controlled by Carter, Bonnier and Black respectively,
although in the accounts Black's name is not mentioned, rather Carter's
wife.

The ultimate control of these Trusts rests with the Bermudan Eduardo
Trust, itself controlled by Foxtrot Trust.

Foxtrot Trust is controlled by Moscow Chetnik Bank, 50% owned by
Republica Bank, Milan (undeclared).

Republica Bank is a 20% shareholder in the Bank (declared). It also
owns a 20% stake (declared) stake in Banco de Bogota of Columbia.

Attachment ends

David Murray

For someone who had just had information relating to her only case literally drop out of the sky, Lara was very matter of fact. Her first thoughts were how this information fitted into the jigsaw which Mac had already assembled. The information on Eduardo and Foxtrot trusts was new, as was the involvement of the Russian Bank. And why did Banco Republica have an indirect role in both Icarus, and its advisor, the Bank?

It was also apparent there was an another e-mail to follow. Perhaps it would enlighten her more. But who was The Falcon and when would it arrive?

Then she had an idea. Simple ideas are generally the best. Why not send a return message? She pressed the respond key.

To: the falcon@fastmail.com
From: lara.waters@bankofengland.org

Dear falcon,

I found your last message most useful. I am investigating the Bank in relation to the CRA affair. I would be grateful if we can meet, or If this is not possible, then please send me any other information you might have.

Love and kisses

Lara

She was uncomfortable with 'love and kisses' but somehow the internet lowers inhibitions. She wanted to encourage The Falcon. Should she address him as 'The Falcon', or Mr Falcon or just plain 'Falcon'? Her understanding of protocol in these situations was limited.

Mac's papers filled a standard box file. Lara opened the lid and pulled the relevant evidence out piece by piece. She had spent all evening sorting through it but in the light of the e-mail decided to refresh her memory of its contents.

There was a video showing Parsons passing the stolen documents to Carter. There were phone company records of conversations between Parsons from his office and Carter's mobile phone, though unfortunately no transcripts. There were photos of

The Naked Bank

Claire Snow and Fergus McKay delivering documents to other banks.

She recognised Fergus as the man she had left in his bathtub a few months ago. In the photos he looked more haggard than she remembered and he had been pretty wiped out that evening. Then there was the row in the restaurant. Were their lives destined to entwine? A fanciful notion of romantic fiction. Claire looked vaguely familiar but she could not place her.

Next out of the hat were the minutes of negotiations between the CRA and Dedalus to secure ownership of the former company's map rights. Hayden Forrest, James Carter and Byron Black were all involved. Giles Bonnier made his appearance right at the end. There was no mention of the Seychelles Company, Dynasty Inc, which received the four million pound payment from Dedalus.

A couple of typed pages detailed the movements of the principal players in the Icarus camp. The movements of Bonnier were highlighted, having travelled to Milan five times in the space of a month. Presumably because Republica Bank was providing the funds for the bid. Interesting. Republica Bank at the centre of the web. A spider whose reach she did not fully understand.

Finally there were details of trading in Icarus's shares. Mac's notes seemed to indicate an unusually high turnover for a company of its size. In fact more than fifty times normal. Presumably why the shares rose so much before eventually being suspended. Enclosed were the complete share trading records. A number of transactions were highlighted, all by off-shore trusts. Lara checked them against those named in the e-mail, though none matched.

Placing this all back in the box, she again read through the press search on Icarus and the Bank run by Sue. Nothing new but it helped to put everything she had just read in context. There was a lot to learn and she was feeling her way forward, unsure of her ultimate, or even immediate destination. Sitting at her desk would achieve nowt, even if the freshly painted smell was lulling. She picked up the phone,

"Sue, get me Roger Warton from Fitchkins & Snot on the phone. And then can you try and track down Fergus McKay at the Bank. I think it's time he and I had a little chat."

225

Another day, another departmental meeting. The deeper the trouble the more often the troops were gathered together to be informed about nothing. Fergus felt just as in the dark as the others, and he was regarded as an insider. Secrecy prevented anyone from feeling comfortable with their own position, and in a crisis that allowed the department to controlled.

As the bankers filed once more into the meeting room, a sense of lethargy prevailed. Already two clients had dropped the Bank as a result of the CRA troubles. Clients who could not afford to become embroiled in any controversy. Still fully supported the Bank, of course. *'You must come for lunch sometime. Play some golf. We'll ring you. A little busy at the moment.'*

Fergus was worried about Claire. She had not rung and no one knew her whereabouts. He looked around the room and noticed Forrest Hayden also missing from the massed ranks of the great and the good. There was no space saved for the director, an ominous sign. It was as if the wolves had consumed his memory. Their teeth now bared with a snarl for Ian Carpenter whose manner was strained, perhaps aware of his fate, perhaps aware of the power struggle freshly begun behind his back.

Carpenter hushed the room with a gesture. He was in charge until replaced.

"Thank you all for coming. No doubt you have seen the papers today and are wondering what is happening. No doubt you all have questions. First can I say that the Bank have launched an internal investigation which will be conducted by Fitchkins & Snot. Until the results of that emerge there is very little I can say that you haven't already read about. I ask for patience. Of wider concern at the moment is the reaction of our clients. It's important we present a unified front, an optimistic front. I have received a number of letters and phone calls today from clients expressing their support. I know Jonathan and Sir Wig have also. Jonathan will be coming down to address us in a few minutes.

"Some of the directors have asked if they can address the meeting and I thought it would be a good idea for them to express the positive steps they are taking. We must keep up the momentum we have developed over the past two years and not let this thing get us down."

No one believed him.

"Its time for the leadership beauty parade." muttered an unknown source close to Fergus at the back of the room.

It was loud enough that a few of the executives and managers stifled a laugh.

"Roderick, would you care to say a few words?" asked Ian.

"Yes, thank you Ian." Roderick Winston, alias young Mr Winston, had been with the Bank for thirty years and was the former head of the department. No one suspected him of being involved with the CRA affair. No one suspected him of being involved in anything. He was dull, conservative, crusty and moved with the speed of a geriatric tortoise. So in the department's hour of need, it was to he they turned. He was Young Mr Winston, the voice of reason.

The voice rose from a forgotten era. His was a speech of Empire, of the Raj, of Neville Chamberlain and peace in our time. Antony Eden, Harold Macmillan, a long forgotten Tory grandee. The words of wisdom, belonging to the past, but sometimes relevant to the future. Great sadness, for the voice had seen much in its life, inherited much from its upbringing, and did not expect to see much more.

"I think Ian is right," hesitated Young Mr Winston, "many of the clients I have spoken to have offered their full backing. They understand these things happen, these things pass." Perhaps he remembered the last crisis, the last tragedy. This a mere blip in the prospect of life. Perhaps he remembered no such crisis, his memory lacking the clarity of earlier years. Instead he might have felt disappointment in the betrayal of his legacy. Why hadn't they consulted me? Is their disrespect for age so great not to call upon my experience? It was impossible for the audience to tell, sniggering at his sonorous delivery, as he stumbled from one phrase to the next. Winston shaped to say more and then seemed to lose his way. He groped for the thought that only a moment ago appeared crucial. He exasperated at his own frailty. A prompt from Ian gently moved him along.

David Murray

"Ian is going to be busy for a little while helping the inquiry. He has asked if I will take on the day to day running of the department in the interim. I am delighted help in any way." Delighted to be offered purpose though sorry the offer was not sooner.

"Thank you, Roderick. We all appreciate your help," said Carpenter. Not. Carpenter regretted relinquishing his duty, his baby slipping from his grasp. The first step on an elevator out of there, needing to run upwards to stand still.

Douglas Montgomery, a man with both eyes on Carpenter's job, was flabbergasted the caretaker role was not his. Roderick preferred to him? Roger Thomas was sadly deluded, upset he was not party to the decision. Only Bruce Andrex fully understood Winston's temporary nature, his underswell of leadership pretensions remaining unfazed.

"May I say something, Ian?" said Andrex.

"The floor is yours." Ian recognised a rival. To prevent would seem churlish.

"Thank you. For those with less experience than me," he began patronisingly, "this will seem like a great disaster. I have lived through several such disasters, the key word being lived. They come and they go. Life goes on. We must forget about it and get on with our work. The real disaster will be if we allow it to affect all our other endeavours. If you look at my team, they are all working flat out to win more mandates. No time for sulking, it's a time for action. Follow this lead and we will flourish." Andrex stopped, realising his speech was in danger of prematurely launching his campaign.

"Thank you Bruce, I'm sure we all share your chivalrous sentiments." A put down although Carpenter was unsure of its meaning. Looking to the back of the room, the reassuring presence of Jonathan Gross entered. Time to shift the spotlight. "Jonathan, would you care to say a few words?"

Eyes shifted backwards as Gross's hugeness worked its way through the parting crowd, brushing them back with a flick of his regal cigar hand. Standing at the front of the room he gazed out on his army, most of whom he did not recognise. No matter, most were expendable, intent on seeking higher salaries and would jump ship when the time was right. Mercenaries lacking loyalty to the Bank, to him. Not that he took it personally. He merely ignored them.

"I just thought I'd take a moment" (of my extremely precious time) "to explain the CRA situation. It's a set back, there are no two ways about it, and there will be a lot of publicity in the press over the next days and weeks. Don't worry about it. That's why we are here. Ian, Roderick and myself can handle it. You should get on with your jobs and keep bringing in the fees. That is after all what we are paid for" (well not me).

Gross puffed his cigar and let his belly hang loose. After allowing the department a few seconds to absorb his greatness, he left as impressively as he arrived. Mission accomplished, now they all aspired to be like him. Why ever would they want anything else?

Carpenter wrapped the meeting. "The internal investigators will be questioning some of you over the next few weeks. I expect you know who you are. Please give them every co-operation. Those who are working with those involved with CRA, please bear with them as I'm sure they have plenty on their minds. They are likely to feel some pressure. I know I do. Be careful out there."

The meeting adjourned in silence, re-convening in small groups around the coffee and photocopying machines, in the staff canteen, the pubs and bars around the Bank. Recruitment agency phone numbers were much in demand.

*****

Fergus looked at the door and wondered if he had the correct address. After the department meeting a Lara Waters had called from the Bank of England. She had asked him to meet her here, and not to tell anyone. Strange, but who was he to question the bizarre practices of the City. With plenty of free time, his services at the Bank about as welcome as a leper with diarrhoea, he popped along. She might buy lunch, the junior executive's Holy Grail, or even offer him a job.

He was in a side street behind Victoria Station. While one of the more salubrious stations in London, it was still seedy, as was the surrounding area. Many shop fronts housed bucket travel shops, burger joints, both the large chains and the mad-cow establishments aimed at the never to return tourist, shoe repair shops selling everything from laces to maces, both the spray and the medieval weapon, pizza parlours, havens for laundered drug money and overweight venture capital buyouts, lingerie shops with dirty windows, sock shops with no customers, pawn shops, porn shops, second hand book shops more adult than literary, up-market greasy spoon caffs and condemned office blocks, the staff inside unaware of their pending move to the spanking clean, totally inaccessible, Docklands. And then there was Fergus's building.

The ground floor housed Joe's American Pool Hall, a spangley place lacking in pool tables. Through a large plate glass window he saw a bar, a few tables and chairs, and a bored waitress picking something out of her hair while consuming an over-stuffed bagel. One pristine pool table awaited its first punter of the day, or the month.

There was a bell next to the door which descended to the basement. This was the given address though there was nothing to indicate it was the property of the Bank of England. What chance of the most venerable financial institution in this, or any other country, being here? He rang the bell.

"Hello," it replied after a wait.

"I've come to see Lara Waters," he said adding, "of the Bank of England."

"This no bank honey."

"I'm supposed to meet Lara here."

"Just sec."

The door buzzed and he pushed. Stairs led down into darkness. Stale, bald carpet, his eyes adjusting to find himself in the alter-ego of Joe's American Pool Hall. This was more Ma Parker's seedy clip joint. There were pool tables neatly lined up with little space for anything but a drink at the bar or a conversation with one of the friendly looking hostesses. It was far too early in the morning for them to bother with Fergus, preferring to nurse hangovers and exchange stories from the night before. His clean cut suit was enough to raise a false eyelash or two.

"Fergus," said a voice while the eyelash's lips did not move. "Over here." At the corner table stood a woman, pool cue in hand, balls already racked. "Grab a cue, they're on the wall over there."

The Naked Bank

Doing as he was told, he weighed several cues in his hand, sighted the best for straightness, and walking towards the table, the walk of a gunfighter returning to Dodge City after a long period of absence. Contemplating the mustiness of his trigger finger.

"Why are we meeting here?" he said not at all disappointed, removing his jacket to demonstrate.

"I often come her to relax. Surprised? My father was a pool hustler. Taught me everything I know."

"Was?"

"Yes, he died. I thought we should meet here. No chance of anyone in our circle stumbling across us now, is there?"

"No. Sorry about your dad."

"Don't be. He beat my mother."

Fergus rapidly changed the subject. "So why are we talking?"

Lara stepped into the light. "You don't recognise me do you?"

"Should I?"

"You fell asleep on me in your bathtub. Given your state, I can believe it if you don't remember."

"Uh, yes. It's a bit of a blur but do you look familiar. God. That was my first day at the Bank and I've never drunk so much champagne in my life. Not before. Certainly never since. Had a hangover for two days. Sorry, at first I didn't recognise you. No offence."

"None taken. Heads or tails." Lara brandished a shiny fifty pence coin. "Call it in the air." She tossed it.

Fergus called "Heads" as it vanished into the darkness created by the brightness of the table lights.

Tails.

"My break," said Lara bending to play the shot. She wore a long sleeved blouse, her skirt was long and did not reveal much, itself a novelty in the City. But then they were not in the City, rather a seedy pool hall where women's legs had been known to start gang wars. Lara pulled back the cue and crack, the white ball sent the others crashing into the cushion, each other, and two fell into the right bottom pocket.

David Murray

Lara did not speak as she played. Taking each ball in turn she quickly cleared the table, potting the nine ball last.

"I've never played Nine Ball," remarked Fergus as it fell with a clunk into the deep, wide pocket. "I used to play at university but that was spots and stripes."

"This is real pool. My father won several tournaments in the States. He won a bit of money. The real cash was made in the halls around the tournaments, or in halls as far away from the action as possible, where the people had cash and little imagination."

"Normally the winner breaks again. But we can play rotating breaks. Otherwise you won't get much of a game." She was confident. A pint sized, mousy haired pool demon.

Lara racked while Fergus prepared to play his first shot. "Do you mind telling me why I'm here?"

She removed the triangle. "I'm investigating the relations between the various parties in the CRA affair. The payment from Dedalus to Bonnier, the role of Republica Bank and the use of off shore trusts. Know anything?"

"Not really. Just what I've read in the press. The big-wigs keep things to themselves."

Fergus broke. Nothing went down.

"You were involved in the CRA bid, right?"

"Yes - but that doesn't mean I know anything."

"I'm not surprised." One onto nine ball combination. End of rack. " It's unlikely you can tell me anything I don't already know. I thought it would be interesting to meet again. Quite frankly I've been in my job for a week, am not totally sure what I'm investigating, and have no one to help. I was hoping that you could help. Off the record of course. Rack 'em up."

He pulled the two balls out and re-set the balls. "I'm not sure what you expect from me. Like I said, I know nothing."

The white ball crashed into the pack, sending them spinning. Three balls down.

"It will be useful for me to bounce ideas off you. You must realise your career is severely limited now. Any help offered can only help you."

Fergus's naiveté protected him from such thinking. He now watched his future disappear into the pockets with potted precision.

The Naked Bank

Another rack over. "Why don't we have a drink?" he suggested, "I think you've probably bashed me up enough."

"Sure. What will you have? On me."

"Diet coke thanks."

"I don't think they'll serve that here. Girly drink. How about a beer?"

"Half pint then."

"It comes in bottles."

"Why don't you get me whatever you're having." Fergus was out of his depth and had the sneaking suspicion she was taking the piss. He felt annoyed at losing three frames of pool to a woman having only played one shot. His ego needed stroking.

Lara fetched the drinks and brought them to the dirty table at which Fergus sat. "I got you a beer. I didn't think you'd want a barcardi and coke."

"I thought you..."

"I said no diet coke."

"Oh." There was an awkward silence.

Lara spoke first. "Have you ever heard of someone called The Falcon?"

"He's a comic book character, isn't he?"

"I've no idea. I received an e-mail from him yesterday."

"You're kidding."

"Yes, he, or she, sent me some very interesting background on Icarus plc and its structure. Did you know a large chunk is owned by off shore trusts?"

"Yes. Don't they represent major shareholders like Carter."

"Apparently, although the info I got yesterday seems to suggest otherwise. These trusts seem to be controlled by others, indirectly linked to Republica Bank."

"That makes no sense. They own 20% of the Bank."

"That's right. And were to finance the bid. Seems they had all the bases covered."

Fergus hated the use of baseball analogies. Most British assumed they were part of a legitimate business language. They didn't understand the real meaning. Given her pool play, he suspected Lara was different.

"And that's a crime?"

David Murray

"It's a start. Well it breaks stock exchange rules as far as conflict of interest is concerned. There must be more to it than that. I'm sure the payment to Bonnier is tied in as well. Off shore trusts are the key."

"That would seem logical," (Captain) said Fergus as an image of Mr Spock leaping into his head. "But why are you telling me?"

"I'm hoping the facts may trigger some memory, some recollection of events. Something that may not have made sense then, may have been inconsequential, but when pieced with my info might click. Might give us a clue."

Lara was fishing. Fergus knew it. She knew it. Unfortunately neither knew what she was hoping to catch.

Two beers and a dodgy roast beef and pickle sandwich later, Fergus left the pool palace. Lara remained behind. A good place to think, she insisted.

Upon reaching the street, he called the office on his mobile. He used it as inconspicuously as possible, not so much worried about the social ridicule he might receive for openly flaunting it on a pavement, more concerned about its swift removal by a passing aficionado.

Claire was still not at work. Someone had phoned in sick on her behalf. He tried her home and spoke to the machine. Hailing a cab, he asked for Chelsea, her address written on a card in his wallet. For office emergencies. The cab driver immediately recognised the street name and after taking a detour on account of the one way system, dropped Fergus at the door.

The size of the house was even more impressive by daylight. Claire once told him about her parents. Her father was a senior partner in an accountancy firm. As had her mother been before retiring to raise three children. Now in their sixties, the couple spent most of their time travelling. When in England, they stayed in the shires. Shooting birds, that kind of thing.

He rang the bell with less apprehension than at the pool hall. No answer so he rang again. Nothing. If there was movement in the house, the solid door and double glazed windows masked any

234

sound. The windows were too high for him to get a decent look into the house. There must be a back entrance. The trick was to find it.

The street was terraced. He walked to the end of the row, rounding the last house. There was a path splitting the houses in Palmerston Street from those in the next road, gardens facing each other. An end wall prevented access, keeping out riff-raff, tramps, burglars and life insurance salesmen.

Unable to categorise himself as one of these undesirables, Fergus determined to climb the wall. With a struggle he reached the top before dropping over onto a hedge. Extricating himself, he uncovered the path and walked towards Claire's house. Counting back carefully he found what he assumed was her door. He banged on it. A light was on.

Auto re-dial on the phone. Machine. Try again. He repeated this several times before a voice answered. "Hello."

"Claire, its Fergus. I'm at your backdoor, can you let me in."

"Its Christine."

"Well can you let me in then. What are you doing here?"

"I could ask the same question. Just a moment."

Fergus waited and noticed a mark on the paint by the door, which soon opened. Christine stood in the doorway. Fergus spoke. "Someone's tried to jimmy this door. Judging by the flecks of paint I'd say it was fairly recently."

"What do you want?"

"I came to see Claire. We're worried about her." He was. The other Bank staff showed no concern. Too busy.

"She's not well. Can you come back tomorrow?"

"Not easily. You should see the size of the wall I had to climb to get in."

"Wall?" For a moment Christine replayed the events of the night Byron went shopping to 7-11. Why would he climb a wall? Her thoughts were broken by a voice behind.

"Its OK Christine, let him in." Looking through Christine, Fergus saw Claire enter the kitchen. She wore a grey track suit with bare feet. Stack contrast to Christine's pristine business suit. Christine stood aside with a swish. "You'd better remove those shoes and don't sit on anything." Looking down he saw his shoes were muddy, his trousers grimy from vaulting the wet bricks. He had a habit of destroying his new suits.

Claire looked different. He had never seen her so casually dressed but that was not it. Her face was tired. The lack of any make-up revealed the shadows under her puffy eyes. Her skin was white. Unhealthy. She looked ill, tired, stressed. Stripped of her corporate image, the truth lay bared. She worked too hard. He wondered whether Christine was similar. Trying not to think of stripping off her corporate image, he was convinced she was placed on this earth as a legal workaholic, temptress and man-hater. This was etched on her soul. Even if stripped to her heart, its last dying beat would spit at him in contempt.

Christine recognised his daggers and made her excuses. "I'd better get to work. There's a lot to do." She was not under investigation. Black had taken full responsibility, only enhancing her admiration for him. She must work to repay that faith.

"Thanks for everything," said Claire reaching out for her new friend. "I'd have been in trouble without you."

Christine reluctantly bore the embrace.

"It was a pleasure. Maybe you will return the favour one day." In Christine's world, life was a collection of favours, to be played at the opportune moment. She was at a position in her career where she did not need favours, so she saved them. "I'll let myself out."

"Goodbye," said a weary Claire. Weary through lack of sun, sleep, diet. Weary of corporate games. Weary over the loss of Josh.

They sat in the living room, shaped the same as Black's. Decorated the same. De ja vu if either had set foot in the house next door. The fire was not lit, the rattling central heating system struggling to heat the old house. Claire sat with her feet under her, leaning against the back of a cloth covered sofa. Fergus perched anxiously on an armchair opposite.

"Where have you been?" he asked quietly.

"It's hard for me to say. I don't know what to say. Or do."

"What do you mean?"

"I'm in a difficult position. I don't know if there is anyone I can turn to," said Claire with welling eyes.

The Naked Bank

Fergus reached deep into his bedside manner. "Let me help. I can't help if you don't tell me what's going on."

"It's not that easy."

"You seem to have trusted Christine. Why did you let her in here?"

"Christine saved me. She found me and helped me into the house. She looked after me. I owe her a lot and you must understand that, whatever your grudge is against her. She's has a kind soul..."

Fergus silently tutted.

"...She didn't ask what happened. I didn't tell her. It's not a question of who I trust more. It's whether I tell anyone. OK?"

"OK." Fergus moved on. "I waited a long time for my sandwich the other day. It's so hard to get decent help these days." .

Claire put her hand to her mouth. "Sorry, I forgot all about it." She visibly relaxed, the innocence of a forgotten sandwich therapeutic. And she did need a confidant. "If I tell you, you must promise not to tell anyone. Ever."

"I guess."

"I mean it. It's very important that you swear."

"You have my word."

"Do you remember the man I met at the Christmas ball, the one who walked out on me?" Fergus nodded and listened as Claire recited the whole adventure.

Claire finished her story for the second time. It flowed better than the first telling. Much less patchy. Plenty of opportunity to embellish for dramatic effect. It included Forrest and his amazing contortion act in Italy. The disk. Josh. His disappearance followed by her own. Her miraculous release and how Byron Black had ignored her. Essentially the facts were the same but this time the audience included Lara. Shortly after Fergus heard her story he insisted on inviting Lara around. At first Claire protested but lacked the willpower to hold out for long. She was exhausted and desperately wished to relieve her burden. Now that she had told someone in a position to help, she felt better. She wanted to sleep, and then to wake with her troubles gone.

Lara was amazed. Kidnapping belonged in the movies, not cosmopolitan Chelsea. It was for mobsters and hoodlums, not pin

stripes and pearls. While there was nothing to link Forrest, or
Bonnier, or Carter to Claire's ordeal, Lara was in no doubt of their
role behind the scenes. The jigsaw edges fitted.

Lara sipped her cold coffee, ignored until now. "Thanks for
placing your trust in me. I won't let you down."

"Should I go to the police?" asked an anxious Claire.

"For the moment, no. Let's keep this our secret. Do you
have the bank account details they gave you?"

"Yes, somewhere. In my suit pocket."

"Would you mind getting them for me?"

"Of course." Claire stood, still a little unsteadily, and
walked up the stairs under her own power.

"Was that necessary?" asked Fergus.

"I think the bank accounts details could be crucial. I also
wanted to ask you your impressions of the story. Can you corroborate
any of it?"

"I believe her although I can't confirm any of it, except she
was missing for two days. And why would she come up with
something so absurd as an excuse for missing work?"

"Presumably Christine can vouch for her."

"How reliable is that?" asked Fergus.

"I don't know. We need to track Josh down."

"We?"

"Yes, we. I need your help on this. Keep you out of
trouble."

"What's that supposed to mean?"

"If you co-operate the report can exonerate you."

"But I haven't done anything."

"In these situations it's the innocent who are most at risk.
It's much harder to punish the guilty."

"I don't follow."

"You will. In the meantime, I need some help. I'm working
on my own and my boss isn't interested." This was her chance to
prove him wrong.

Claire returned with the scrap of paper. "This is all I have."

Lara examined it and noted the bank account number and
bank name in her pocket diary. "This may prove very useful. I have a
hunch." Claire and Fergus looked at her for more. Instead she

changed the subject. "I don't suppose you've heard Josh referring to himself as The Falcon?" *It must be him.*

"No," replied Claire. "Why?"

"Another hunch. Given everything you have told me, either he, or someone close to him sent me an e-mail using the name Falcon. He was due to send me another message but it never came."

"Well Josh is dead. That would explain it."

"Yes. If I could get his user name we could access his account. You don't know any alias he might go under?"

"Sorry. I barely knew him. Do you think he really is dead?"

"I don't know," said Lara. "Fergus, can you get onto a company called Fastmail and explain who I am and that I need to get access to The Falcons's e-mail account." Fergus nodded unsure where to begin. Lara continued, "I think it's about time I asked the police to help track him down. Don't worry, Claire, I won't mention you."

Claire leaned back into the comfort of the settee. She was not sure about this woman. How could she possibly help? Did Claire want any help? She remembered the Boss's chilling threats. At the moment, however, there was no one else to trust.

*****

Dick Johnson was an ex-copper, ex-hard man. His name was Dick. Not short for Richard, just Dick, named in an era without today's connotations. No one sniggered to his face. No one laughed behind his back. Dick Johnson commanded respect, especially within the professional circles in which he now moved. Because he was hard.

Johnson worked for Fitchkins & Snot, the law firm. Having retired from the force due to ill health at the age of fifty, quite by accident he stumbled across his new job. It was at a party his wife dragged him to. Full of her high flying friends. She was a legal secretary who liked to mix with her superiors. He hated these dos and would have preferred a night in front of the telly. Mr Wenton had been politely interested in his background. Then, quite out of the blue, he was offered a job. More money than he ever earned in the force. That was two years ago and he'd had three pay rises since.

David Murray

Forensic investigation was a cinch. Johnson knew little about the subtleties of high finance. He did not need to. His strength was in interviewing. Used to dealing with pimps, drug dealers and general riff-raff, interrogating an uptight professional was a joy. They were so easy to intimidate. Most confessed without prompting. And if there was the need for a detailed question, his partner, Mr Wenton, would be on hand. Johnson was the psychological muscle. He could scare the willies out of suspects without even trying.

Today he began the Bank investigation. Seated to his left, as usual, was Mr Wenton. On the other side of a small table sat Hayden Forrest. Two tape recorders were rolling. One tape for the interviewee, one for them. No different from today's police procedure. He preferred the old ways, schooled in closing the door and not opening it until the conviction was secured. Times change.

Forrest was rambling.   "...from James Carter. We had no contact with Parsons at all."

"You knew the documents were stolen?" asked Wenton.

"We knew their source. As I've said, we took legal advice."

"Don't you think there was a conflict of interest taking advice from Carter's own lawyers?"

"Banking is full of conflicts. Our job is to manage them." said Forrest coolly.

"Don't be so cocky. You're in the shit up to your neck. You're the man who's going to take the fall unless you dish the dirt."

Wenton was always amused by Johnson's approach. He hired him to play the bad cop role in their interviews. He was more successful than anyone Wenton had ever worked with.

Forrest was confused. "I didn't realise I was accused of anything." His tone was smooth.

Johnson continued. "Let me get this straight. You accept stolen documents. You take legal advice from the brief of the guy who's stolen them and who has most to gain from stealing them. And you don't question this?"

"No, we were all happy."

"Who's we?" Johnson looked straight at Forrest, a vein in his forehead throbbing with anticipation.

The Naked Bank

"Carpenter."

"And?"

"Gross."

"And?"

"That's all apart from Snow and McKay. They were junior and there's no need to bring them into this."

"Your loyalty's touching. What about Sir Wig? What did he know?"

Wenton shifted uncomfortably in his chair. Johnson had left the script. Sir Wig, after all, paid the bill.

"I expect so. Gross told him everything."

Wenton jumped in. "But you never told Sir Wig yourself?"

"No, we never talked about anything. He was too important to be concerned with me." There was a hint of bitterness in Forrest's voice. He felt just as betrayed as Carter by Sir Wig's letter. He also knew he had no chance of survival. Forrest poached the client. Forrest was the main point of contact. Forrest would soon not even be history, his name removed from all Bank records with a thoroughness of Orwellian double think. At least his secret retirement fund was intact.

"How much did Carter pay you?" Johnson asked as if rummaging through Forrest's mind.

He turned pale. "Sorry?"

"What was your fee?"

"The Bank's?"

"Yes, who else's would it be?" Johnson sensed discomfort. Forrest clutched his hands, their knuckles gripped white.

"Uh, a few million. I forget the exact details."

"That's quite a fee. How could you justify that?"

"We can justify any fee," be began flippantly. Johnson leaned forward prompting less flannel. "It's normal in the City. We worked hard for it."

"I see. And were there any other fees?"

The moment passed and Hayden's poise returned. The man was fishing. The retirement fund was safe.

"Yes, we received a million for the Dedalus deal."

It was Wenton's turn. "Wasn't that a lot for the size of deal?"

"I suppose it was. Carter was pleased with our work."

"He wasn't bribing you?"

Hayden retaliated. "How dare you suggest such a thing." It was paper anger.

"I'm sorry," said Wenton. "Let me re-phrase that. He secured your loyalty for the difficult days ahead. When it got tough, you backed him."

"We back all our clients."

Johnson again. "And when did you learn of the payment to Bonnier?"

"It was in the Dedalus prospectus, I think. I knew about it from the beginning."

Wenton. "And you didn't feel it was worth looking into. As part of your client due diligence."

"No," said Hayden. "We relied on the work done by USB when they floated the company. It's normal procedure."

"USB floated the company when you worked there. Correct."

"Yes."

"And then you brought Carter with you when you moved to the Bank?"

"Yes."

"So what due diligence did USB do?"

"You'll have to ask them?"

"You looked after him. Can't you remember. Didn't you refresh your memory?"

"It was in the past. There was no point going over old ground. If it was good enough for USB, it was good enough for us."

"And did you mention your past due diligence to any of your colleagues. Did you tell them about the payment?"

"No."

"Why not?" Johnson smelt a rat.

"It didn't seem relevant."

*****

Jaffe was an inspector in the great tradition of Sherlock Holmes. Bumblingly effective when pointed in the right direction.

The Naked Bank

He listened patiently while Lara told her story, leaving out any mention of Claire or Fergus for the time being, and stressing the difficulty of linking any crime to Carter or Bonnier, even though she had her suspicions. Jaffe listened quietly, taking the occasional puff on his trade mark pipe. It helped him concentrate and perpetuated his myth, which few others bought into, of being clever. In fact he had only reached his current semi-lofty position in the force by way of his immediate superior being suspended for 'bank account irregularities' and his nearest rival leaving the force to spend more time with his family. Jones was suspended for his propensity to slap unsuspecting WPCs on the bottom and his only woman rival was relieved of duty for punching Jones' lights out. When the vacancy arose, of five candidates there was only Jaffe left, a fact that gave him no end of pride in his own political prowess.

"I see," he stressed, pulling on an imaginary goatee beard. "Well we in the force naturally wish to co-operate with such a hallowed institution as the Bank of England." He said this in all sincerity without fully understanding the function of the Old Lady of Fleet Street, or was it Threadneedle Street? Something like that. He had once driven past the place on an open topped tourist bus while showing his Aunt Gladys from Canada the sights of London. Who would have guessed that her highly inconvenient visit would later bear such dividends? "I'd better get over to Mr Walker's residence straight away. We'll contact you as soon as we learn anything."

It was not far from Scotland Yard to Lara's office according to the map. On the ground, it was half an hour's drive for those reliant on London traffic. Jumping in a cab she thought for a minute, before re-introducing herself to her mobile phone. She shut the glass, to separate the driver, as the number rang.

"Yes."

Why is it that when answering the phone in the office people politely introduce themselves, while on a mobile they dispense with years of phone protocol? It's as if phoning a mobile is an invasion of a holy place, an inner sanctum where people disappear to hide, neglecting the fact they have given their number to all and sundry. All serious business people make themselves available twenty four hours a day through mobile phone, car phone, three fax machines, e-mail and pagers. Yet mentality has yet to catch up with practice, for why else do people sound so churlish when rung out of the office? If inconvenient, turn the damn thing off.

"Is that Mac?"

"Speaking."

"Lara Waters here. Can you speak?"

Another thing about these phones. Why the need to ask if they can speak? If they are in the middle of a meeting, switch on the answer phone. If not, it tells your host that you are expecting far more important people than him to call you. Maybe that was the point.

"I've got a couple of minutes. How can I help?"

For Mac a call from Lara was the highest priority. She sat with her feet on the Board table of another faded institution, its Chairman tolerating her sweaty feet in exchange for her sound advice. In fact he quite enjoyed Mac's forthright nature, a welcome change from the usual toadying of bankers, not to mention his own minions. He left the room to allow her privacy, and his nose a chance to recover.

Lara, unaware of Mac's setting, proceeded.

"I have a favour I'd like from you."

Mac smiled to herself. A favour meant power. "Fire away, it's always a pleasure."

Never having asked Mac for anything before, Lara was slightly confused by the woman's familiarity. Nevertheless, she continued.

"I have the details of a Swiss bank account. One held by your bank. I have the account number and need to know details of who deposited money into it."

"You know that's highly irregular?"

"I realise that. As is my next request. I have the names of a number of off-shore trust companies. I am interested in knowing if they have any links to your private Swiss bank as well. In fact, whether there is any link to Icarus, Carter, etc."

"You're asking a lot of me," said Mac, already calculating the permutations of her actions and how they would affect the overall plan.

The Naked Bank

"I know, but I'm sure you realise what a bind you placed me in when I took your Icarus file. I almost lost my job within a week of starting."

Mac said nothing.

"This seems an adequate recompense for my inconvenience. Plus it helps the inquiry you're so keen to see go smoothly."

The girl was learning. One favour deserves another. "I'll see what I can do, though I can make no promises."

"I understand."

"Give me a day or two. I'll get back to you. Fax the details to my office."

Mac hung up and made another call. "Sandy, get me the number of the President of Private Banking in Switzerland and see whether we've any dirt on him in the files. I'll call back in any hour."

Mac clicked her phone shut and wondered whether Lara might be a bit too competent.

Lara made another call, this time to Fergus. She leant back in the taxi enjoying the sense of efficiency reeling off numerous mobile calls gave her. She played with the big boys. Played with the piranhas.

"Fergus, its Lara. Any luck with Fastmail?"

It had taken Fergus several hours to track down the company, using the Bank's facilities for his research. Eventually he had found it, and a called Monaco number.

"Some, in that I tracked them down."

"But?"

"There's no dice. They won't deal. Unless we can prove the falcon's identity they will not release any details of his account. I tried hard, but they were determined to ensure client confidentiality."

"What if we serve a warrant?"

"I asked that and the bloke questioned any jurisdiction we might have. It sounds like it would take us months to get anywhere."

"I feared that might be the case. Thanks for trying, Fergus. I appreciate it."

Receiving an act of thanks was a novel concept to Fergus.

"You are very welcome. Can I do anything else?"

"For the moment, no. Why don't you keep an eye on Claire?"

"Sure," he said unsure whether that would involve another encounter with the she-devil Christine.

"Thanks," said Lara, "Got to go."

The taxi pulled up outside the grim concrete office that Lara now called home. She stepped out and paid the cabby, tipping generously. It was on expenses, allowing the taxpayer to cover the bill. As she prepared to enter the large glass fronted reception area, her phone rang. She answered, standing in the street with a finger in her ear as she battled to hear the caller above the traffic.

"Hello, Lara Waters speaking."

"Miss Waters, its Jaffe here. Jaffe of the Yard."

For a split second the name meant nothing before she recalled the pipe-smoking features of the policeman.

"Hello, Inspector. I didn't expect you to get back so quickly."

"All in a day's work," he replied extracting full value from his first edition of The Bumper Book of Old Bill Banter. "I thought you might like to know that we've entered Mr Walker's flat and can find no evidence he's been here for the past few days. In fact, quite the contrary. The place would appear to have been burgled. The crime lab boys are giving it the once over but I would be surprised if they find anything. It looks like a professional job."

"May I come and have a look?" asked Lara. She hoped for a lead on the e-mail.

"Just a moment." She was put on hold to the strains of the Z-Cars Theme song. Nice touch. More original than Vivaldi's Four Seasons. Then he was back. "Give us half an hour and then you will be most welcome."

"Thanks, it'll take me that long to get there."

She hung up and whistled at her departing taxi, only now turning in the road to return to the West End.

The scene of Josh's flat resembled Inspector Morse after a particularly grizzly murder. Police officers loitered everywhere outside the building performing no perceptible task, their presence giving the whole proceeding an air of gravity. Four panda cars and a van obstructed the road causing a minor tail back as traffic attempted to squeeze through the already crowded road. An earnest police woman in a non speaking role intercepted Lara as she arrived at the basement stairs, only to allow her to proceed on the beckoning of Jaffe inside.

Inside the flat was a mess with furniture, paper and books strewn across the floor. There was no sign of the forensic boys with the exception of numerous dustings of finger print powder.

"Hello Miss Waters." The voice was Jaffe's. "I'm afraid we have no real leads. The only fingerprints are Walkers. No others which is surprising in itself. The burglars wore gloves."

"Is his computer here?"

"No sign of it. You can see from the house dust that it was placed at the desk over there. The intruders must have taken it."

Lara was disappointed, her main lead disappearing. "Anything else?"

"Well, the place has been pretty thoroughly turned over. But there's no sign of blood, and no body. The answer phone is blank."

"Any notes or papers."

"No. Nothing that would seem relevant to your investigation."

Lara sat without speaking. The sofa was surprisingly comfortable given the hunks of leather that had been ripped out, no doubt part of the search, the success of which was unclear.

"We're finished here, but if you would like to look around that can be arranged."

"That's very helpful. I'll stay a while if I may."

"Certainly. The WPC outside will lock up when you finish. We have to get back to the station but you can rest assured that we are treating this very seriously and will immediately start a full search for the man, or the body."

Lara found the cold manner of Jaffe's tone rather chilling. "Let me know if you find anything. Please."

"We have your number."

Sheriff Jaffe and his deputies left Lara to her thoughts and the new found redundancy of Josh's self assembled furniture.

Somewhere in this flat she knew there was a clue to Josh's password. She had his user id. It was a Fastmail address which, Sue had reliably informed her, meant it could be accessed from anywhere in the world. She had to find his password and access his files before the burglars did. Before Carter and Bonnier. But first she needed a computer.

Another phone call. "Sue - I'm going to need your help. Can you get yourself and an e-mail friendly PC over here as soon as possible."

"Where are you?"

"A little lost."

The Naked Bank

South Downs Express, January 18
Body found in Shallow Grave

In a scene reminiscent of the film Shallow Grave, a man's body was discovered buried in woods outside Guildford yesterday. The hands, feet and head of the body had been removed giving the police no identifying features. Police are looking for leads from their missing person file but admit there is little chance of learning the victim's identity. This is the second body in sixth months to be discovered in these woods. A police spokesman said that the mutilation resembles a gangland killing rather than the actions of a serial killer. He said that local residents need not worry and that the man was probably killed outside the area before being disposed of in the woods.

*****

Sue went home leaving Lara seeking inspiration. For the past five hours she had tried, and failed to enter the correct password. Sue had set up the laptop enabling Lara to enter guesses at Josh's e-mail file. Each attempt took thirty seconds as the modem whirled and chugged its way into the fastmail centre. Initially it was slow going as Lara bombarded the system with woman's intuition. All the obvious passwords. All the off the wall ideas. Now she was so short of ideas the delay was no longer enough time for her to think of another guess. Minutes were spent gazing around the room seeking inspiration before the next failed input.

It was now twelve thirty in the morning and she was tired. The WPC had left, giving the keys to Lara. Her eyelids felt heavy

251

and the lack of success was depressing. Without Josh's clues her investigation would flounder. She resolved to stay until it was cracked. She was sure there was more to learn. There had to be. Otherwise nothing made sense. Why had Josh been killed? Why had Claire been kidnapped?

She drifted towards sleep, nodding in deference to the computer. Suddenly she was brought fully back to alertness by a scratching at the door. They had returned. Who had returned? She froze, her senses heightened by rushing adrenaline, each second stretching out into minutes. Scratch, yet the door did not open. Carefully she stood and walked towards it. The curtains were closed. Anyone outside could not see in. The light, however, betrayed her presence.

Peering through a spy hole in the door she saw nothing. Nothing. Yet the scratching continued. She turned off the main light and peered out through the edge of the curtain. There must be something out there. Still nothing.

What else could she do but open the door? Don't be silly cried her sub-conscious, the same jaded sub-conscious that has witnessed too many horror movies, seen too many Scooby Doo cartoons. First rule of safety is don't split up. The second is not to open the door when there are scary scratching noises outside. Perhaps it is a ghost, an alien, a huge invisible field of energy reminiscent of the creature from the Forbidden Planet. Who knows, but in a moment of tension such foolhardiness has been the downfall of many an American teenager.

All the same, she turned the handle of the unlocked door and pulled it slowly towards her. Quiet. Once open she stood in the doorway, fully exposed to the forces of evil, and looked out into the night, at least that portion of the darkness that represented the bottom of the basement stairwell.

"Shriek," was the wail of a ferocious banshee as some hideous creature leap at Lara, knocking her back with a force that was less than anticipated. Lying on the floor stunned, she waited for the tell-tale blow that never came. Instead a gentle purring was followed by a fuzzy, weather-beaten cat rubbing itself along her leg, enjoying the static of her intensely shocked body and the friction generated by her nylons rubbing along the carpet as she had slid

The Naked Bank

backwards. A human Van der Graaf generator. She jumped as the sparks flew from feline contact. And then stroked the cat that looked sorely in need of a good feed and slightly suspicious of this electric woman.

It was drafty and Lara closed the door, ignoring her pounding heart, and entered the kitchen. The cat followed continuing to rub against her legs, purring with anticipation. Opening the cupboards in a random order she quickly located a supply of tuna. Josh was an animal lover? The search for a can opener took longer. Eventually the mangy mog was gobbling down its second can of premium dolphin friendly fish, no longer interested in her feeder.

Then Lara had a brainwave. Waiting for the beast to finish its meal, for even she knew that to deprive an animal of its kill was asking for trouble, she examined the satisfied cat's neck. Among its frayed hairs, as she expected, or had hoped, there was an identification tag. Molly. The cat's name was Molly. That was it, the password, it had to be. Taking off, she ran to the computer with a speed that surprised even her own exercise resistant body. Typing 'Molly' she waited. The modem cracked. The system read the password. She waited.

"Incorrect password."

"Bugger," she exclaimed and sent the cat, which had sneaked up behind her, running for cover behind the sofa. "I bet you're not even his bloody cat."

The cat sulked, unaware of precisely how its crime had been revealed.

"I'm going to bed, Molly. You'll just have to fend for yourself."

The sofa did not look too inviting. The bedroom was a mess but Lara only needed a pillow and a blanket. After settling once, then removing the cat and shutting the door, she settled again, then remembered the front door. She rose and locked it, removing the cat again as she finally settled and lay back . By the bed was some reading material. She always liked to read before falling asleep and so picked up the magazine. Only it wasn't a magazine, more a comic.

David Murray

An adult comic, for this was no superhero in tights adventure where good triumphs over evil by wearing their pants in unorthodox fashion. It was the story of The Falcon, one of the most mixed up characters she had ever come across. OK, he was fictional, but after his entire family were wiped out by a chemical factory explosion, he developed super powers from the radiation of the blast. He was miraculously thrown clear, blaming himself for the death of his parents and siblings. Maniacally dark, he was a loner, sworn to avenge corporate greed and exploitation. He named himself The Falcon after the way he flew clear from the explosion. As Lara read on she was strangely fixated by this tale of battling against corruption and fraud. Somehow she identified with this man and quickly realised that Josh did so as well. A zealous reporter of corporate wrong doing, he was The Falcon. He was Simon Worthy, the real name of the comic book hero. He was Simon Worthy she thought as she drifted off to sleep to dreams of falcons and moustachioed villains, interspersed with Indian song and dance routines and plenty of curry sauce. It was after all a dream so why should it make sense?

Morning was greeted by a wet lick of Molly's tongue. The door was wide open. How had that cat got in? She sat bolt upright before remembering that the door did not shut properly and the cat must have pushed it open. She hoped.

Simon Worthy brought her out of bed and back to the still humming computer. This time she was sure. It had to be. After the prerequisite wait she was proved correct.

"Bingo," she cried as she was in.

"One new message," she was informed by the system.

"Read new mail," she clicked to uncover her own response to the dead man. She cringed at her message of love and kisses.

Returning to the menu she clicked on "Mail saved."

A long list of messages scrolled in front of her, and much as she suspected there were two addressed to her. She knew the contents of the first, and after batting away the attentions of a curious cat, opened the second.

A quick read and she whistled. If what he said was true, she certainly had plenty to go on.

The Naked Bank

Phone. "Fergus, its Lara. I'm at Josh Walker's flat. I have something. I'll meet you for breakfast.... At Luigi's....Where you had that row with your girlfriend....I just know...I was at the next table all right. I'll see you there in an hour."

*****

Interview of Jonathan Gross (JG), 10am January 18
Interviewed by Dick Johnson (DJ), Roger Wenton (RW)

DJ: Thank you for coming today Mr Gross. We appreciate your co-operation in our enquiry.

JG: You are most welcome, though I'm not really sure what help I can be.

DJ: You'd be surprised.

RW: If we begin, I understand you hope to attend a meeting in an hour, although if we run over you may have to cancel it.

DJ: I think there is a good chance you will have to cancel it.

JG: Well, let's see how things go.

DJ: Perhaps you would like to tell us about your role in the CRA affair.

JG: As you probably know, I am Deputy Chairman for the Bank which involves overseeing all the Divisions. I sit on the Heads of Division Committee which meets once a week and am always available for consultation by not only heads of department but any other director, or come to mention it, any other staff member.

DJ: How often do non-heads of departments consult you?

JG: Pretty infrequently, although my door is always open.

DJ: Please continue. Apologies for interrupting.

JG: Ian Carpenter has full responsibility for the running of the Corporate Finance Division. He only consults me when he needs advice. You will understand that there are Chinese Walls within the bank.

DJ: Chinese Walls?

JG: Because of the price sensitive nature of the work conducted by corporate finance, no one from other areas of the Bank is told what they are working on.

DJ: Was this the case with the CRA?

JG: I assume so.

DJ: Were you told?

JG: In my overseeing role, I was informed of the deal.

DJ: And you gave it your blessing?

JG: It was not mine to bless, or otherwise.

DJ: Or otherwise. Presumably if you did not like a particular deal you could disapprove.

JG: Technically, yes. Though as I've said responsibility rested with Ian.

DJ: But your view carried considerable weight?

JG: I used to be head of the department so I think it is fair to say my view was valued.

DJ: And did you express a view on CRA?

JG: It seemed like an exciting opportunity.

DJ: But did you support it?

JG: I did nothing to dissuade Carpenter from pursuing it.

DJ: And when did you hear about the stolen documents?

JG: When I read about them in the press.

DJ: No one told you about them before that?

JG: Not stolen documents. I was aware that we had obtained some documents and that the lawyers had said they were legally valid...I did not specifically enquire about their source. That was a judgement call for Carpenter. I cannot spend all my time second guessing Divisional Heads.

DJ: But surely you are responsible for his decisions?

JG: Not at all. The Bank operates as a series of independent units. Responsibility is Carpenters'.

DJ: Who else was involved?

JG: Err, Hayden Forrest was the director. There was Claire Snow. I don't know the others. I only had limited contact so I'm not sure of the more junior staff.

DJ: When did you look into the issue of the stolen documents for the first time.

JG: I can't say I have. When the issue was raised in the press and the CRA wrote to Sir Wig he took matters into his own hands. As you know he apologised for the actions of the Bank.

DJ: And he didn't consult you, his number two, and theoretically the man responsible for the Division concerned.

JG: No, he went straight to Carpenter, who knew all the details. He's my boss, he can do that.

DJ: And when did Sir Wig first know about the documents?

JG: You had better ask him about this. I haven't discussed this with him.

DJ: I find that hard to believe.

JG: You can believe what you want.

Interview suspended for coffee break.

*****

Giles Bonnier rapped at the unfamiliar door. He found himself in that part of Chelsea where connections matter more than money when buying such an exclusive town house. Byron Black had both. When a man has a reputation to lose he is dangerous. In certain circles, Black's reputation was immense. With his good name now at risk, Bonnier believed a little chat was in order. Just to convince the lawyer where his priorities lay.

He stood anxiously at the front door. Giles knew very well that Claire Snow lived next door and felt exposed should she happened to look out of her window, or leave to go to work. He did not want any questions raised over his presence, questions that would be difficult to answer now that Gilbert, Wilkins & Horsefly had resigned from the service of Icarus. Another matter he intended to raise.

He listened for a response knowing he would hear nothing, the black door too sturdy to emit any sound of habitation. A click and in front of him stood Christine, to all intents and purposes the butler. Dressed and ready for work she looked somewhat bemused at

The Naked Bank

the sight of Bonnier, who although taken aback at her presence, maintained a suitable composure. A trick he'd learnt from Black.

"Good morning Christine. It seems early breakfast meetings are the vogue these days."

Christine's neck blushed behind a white frilled collar. "We often have breakfast meetings. Byron's diary is always free early on." She saw no need to expand further.

Bonnier saw no need to press. She had explained enough. "Is Byron free then?"

"Yes, why don't you come in. I'll see if I can rustle up some more coffee."

Bonnier stepped into the hall. The lounge was the next port of call and he was soon enjoying his first drink of the day, having left his hotel that morning without breakfast. Normal for Bonnier who only saw sustenance as an opportunity for a business meeting. Otherwise it merely obstructed his day.

Christine reappeared at the door. "He'll be hear in a couple of minutes. I have to go back to the office." Her manner was frosty, recalling Bonnier's past abuse.

"Wait." said Bonnier, "Why don't you join me for a moment. I've never taken the time to thank you for all your hard work on the deal." He smiled an attempt at reasonableness, and almost succeeded.

Christine was now confused, her sharp legal mind unable to neatly sort all the facts. Why was this man here to talk to Byron when he was no longer a client? Why was the smarmy git suddenly trying to be friendly. Wearing her firm hat she had little choice but to humour him, at least until his motives became clearer. Wearing her own hat, she restrained herself from gouging his eyes.

She sat opposite Bonnier who struggled to look her in the eye, an inner sense forcing his wandering gaze towards her legs. He refrained, satisfying himself with the memory of the video he watched last night. And the night before that. All night. Christine and Byron's extra-curricular activities had providing Bonnier with several nights of satisfying voyeuristic pleasure. Lately she spent little time in her flat, presumably staying in this house.

"You're a very talented lady," he began. "Very talented."

Unaware of the context of Bonnier's comments, Christine took the statement as a compliment. "Thank you."

"Do you enjoy your work with Gilbert, Wilkins & Horsefly?"

"I find it very satisfying."

"I'm sure you do. Have you ever thought of leaving?"

"Leaving, why?"

"Well as far as I understand law firms, you either make partner or you leave."

Christine was not sure what he was getting at. "I will make partner. I'm the highest billing associate in the firm."

"That doesn't surprise me. You strike me as highly ambitious. But have you ever thought about going into commerce - fewer glass ceilings." *More mirrored.*

"Not at the moment, although I'm keeping my options open." In typical lawyer fashion Christine did not wish to close any avenues.

"Did you know that we are looking for an in-house lawyer at Icarus?" She did not. Bonnier had just created the vacancy. "We could use someone with your dedication and loyalty." *Someone with your propensity to sleep around.*

"Are you offering me a job, Mr Bonnier?" A little blunt for an accomplished solicitor.

Even Bonnier was taken aback by the directness of her question. The girl had some spunk. That was why he wanted her.

"You must know that I would never seek to poach a friend's best employee. Byron has spoken very highly of you," he lied. "But if you know anyone who might like this job, we would of course look very favourably upon someone recommended by as highly regarded a person as yourself."

He was offering her the job. "That's very kind." Christine had no intention of leaving Byron but still was curious. "And if I did know someone, what sort of remuneration are we talking about?"

Greedy as well. Even better. "I don't like to discuss remuneration. Let's say our basic package would be a fifty per cent. raise on your, sorry, the candidate's existing salary, with a performance related bonus potentially reaching seven figures."

"Seven?"

The Naked Bank

"Seven." Bonnier replied with the reassuring smirk only such a sum can produce.

Staggering. Christine allowed her guard of indifference to slip for a moment as she absorbed the magnitude of the offer. She might even have accepted if Black had not entered the room.

"Good morning Giles. To what do we owe the pleasure?"

Christine quickly re-entered earth's orbit, wondering whether Byron was using the royal 'we', or now referred to he and her as a collective team.

"Good morning Byron. I'm sorry to bother you at home but I have an urgent matter to discuss with you...in confidence." He looked at Christine who knew she should leave.

Black's glance reinforced her impression he used the royal "we."

"I was just going back to the office. I'll see you later Byron. Don't forget your nine thirty meeting."

"No of course not." There was no meeting but it was standard procedure in case Byron needed an excuse to leave. If he wished to prolong the conversation, cancelling his 'meeting' helped create an impression of commitment.

Christine left the room resisting the temptation to kiss Byron. Or 'seven figure' Giles, his offer placing him on first name intimacy. As she retreated, her latest fan could not resist the temptation to drink in her rear profile. Black was not so unobservant as to miss the blatant ogle.

When the door closed leaving them alone, he asked with a touch of exasperation, "How can you so crudely stare at women like that?"

Bonnier looked at Byron like at a man from another era. An era of manners and breeding, so out of date in today's winner takes all world.

"What's the downside?" he casually responded.

Black was unable to counter this riposte and so returned to the plot. "How can I be of service, Giles, at this time in the morning?" He expected a row over the firm's resignation.

Black's expectations were the undercard, a prelude to the main event.

David Murray

"It was with great distress that James yesterday learnt of Gilbert's resignation after many years of fine service. I must say I expected greater loyalty from you, of all people. That is after all why we pay you. Not Gilbert...you."

"I'm sorry. What can I say. The other partners voted to dump you. It was that or face an expensive and potentially crippling law suit against the CRA. That woman Macintosh forced our hand. I defended you, I did," Black's speech hinted of desperation, "but my own reputation has been severely tarnished by this whole affair. I am being investigated by the Law Society. I might be disbarred. The Bank's investigation wants to question me and it can only be a matter of time before that woman from the Bank of England tries to sink her teeth in. You see, I have no influence. I may have to resign."

"My heart bleeds. So where are you planning to retire to on Mr Carter's money?"

"That's an unfair question. You know I will help you if I can."

"Will you?" asked Bonnier even more sceptically than usual.

"What's that supposed to mean?"

"Well, I've been in this business for many a year now and understand the facts of life. One is that ambitious women are a good shag. But then you know that one." He paused for effect. No effect on Black, just his veneer of passivity. "The second is that toffs like you do anything to wriggle off the hook. The only loyalty you show is to your own good standing. Not to lowlifes like me."

"That's not true," said Black protesting a little too much.

"I'm glad to hear it. However, Mr Carter does not feel one hundred per cent confident in your loyalty right now. We've done many things together over the years and if word got out about them, say in return for a deal to save your skin, it could be somewhat embarrassing to him, and I might add, to me. That's why I thought I'd leave you with a copy of our insurance policy."

Bonnier opened his briefcase and tossed a video cassette on the coffee table.

"What is it?" Black was anxious.

"I am leaving this for your viewing pleasure. Needless to

The Naked Bank

say it is not the only copy. I'm sure your wife and children will be most interested. Your wife who owns most of the family money as well as the family seat in Surrey. Convenient that she spends so much time down there isn't it. I wonder what she would say if she knew about Christine."

"Oh God."

"Yes, but I'm afraid he won't be much help. I've made a few discreet inquiries. You get nothing in the event of a divorce. Very sloppy for such an accomplished lawyer to allow the family fortune to be held in trust for your children. Of course if we go down, you can kiss goodbye to your retirement fund as well. So unless you remain true to the cause, I'd start finding a nice spot under Waterloo Bridge. I hope you enjoy the tape, I certainly did. She has a lovely ass, and I must say, so do you for a man of your age."

Black was devastated. "I think you'd better leave now."

"With pleasure. Thanks for the coffee."

*****

To: Lara.Waters@BankofEngland.org
From: the falcon@fastmail.com

Sorry for the delay in sending this second message. Its late and I must have drifted off to sleep for several hours.

I have been thinking about the structure details I sent you. These have been taken from a reliable source close to Icarus. On the surface there is nothing new about Trusts owning Icarus. It is the ownership of the Icarus Trusts that is interesting. They are controlled by Moscow Chetnik Bank, which itself has links with Republica Bank, both a major shareholder in the Bank as well as the lead financier for the CRA deal. There is clearly some kind of conspiracy going on here deeper than would first appear. It took some thinking to get to the bottom of it all but I think finally it has clicked.

I won't bore you with attaching share trading volume in Icarus · I'm sure you can dig that out for yourself. What is interesting are the very high volumes. Ridiculously high. Of course that is one of the reasons the shares have risen so high · far higher than any rational asset or profit valuation. The company would have to make several enormously value adding acquisitions to justify its price. So if the price is so out of line with fundamentals, why does it continue to go up?

David Murray

You will notice from the shares traded in Icarus over the past six months that the bulk of trades have been conducted by a series of off shore companies, none of which ever hold over the 3% limit, where they have to disclose their stake to the stock exchange. Each company is selling as many shares as it is buying. Why?

It is my guess, and you will need to do some digging to validate this theory - as a journalist I do not have access to this kind of information - that these companies are somehow related to the Icarus Trusts - maybe not directly, but possibly through the Moscow Bank, making proving any link very difficult. These guys are smart. By pushing the price higher they realise profits by buying and selling amongst themselves. In the short run it would appear to be a classic money laundering scheme. Drugs money, say, is washed through the system. First company A buys shares in Icarus. The shares go up. It sells to company B. The money from the sale is clean. Company B sells to company C at a higher price. It now has clean money. And so on. As long as the price keeps going up they make money, and swap bad money for good.

But how do you end the cycle - at some point the shares will surely collapse. How about this though. Icarus is used as a vehicle to buy other, undervalued companies such as CRA. CRA, say, is bought for high value Icarus paper. In return for valueless paper, the shareholders gain a company. The company is de-merged on the stock exchange and then the shareholders gain shares in a real company, which again they can sell, thus breaking the loop. Or sold, with sale proceeds returned to the shareholders. What they did with Dedalus.

In effect they gain in three ways:

1. Make money from selling Icarus shares in a rising market
2. By selling they are laundering dirty money
3. Buying undervalued companies and then spinning them off allows valueless paper to be swapped into proper assets.

Seems quite simple and very difficult to identify. Goodluck.

Love and kisses

the falcon

PS I will check in when I get any further leads. I plan to publish my findings in the Herald tomorrow. Should give you enough time to find a few leads.

The Naked Bank

Fergus placed the printed e-mail on the table and took a sip of his high powered orange juice.

"It sounds like an interesting theory - but is there any proof?"

Lara leaned across the red and white table cloth.

"I have trading volume data which agrees. What he says about the offshore companies is true. At the moment there's nothing to link these companies with the Moscow Bank, Icarus or anyone else. They are all Liberian registered which means it is impossible to do any detailed digging on them."

"So where do we stand?" asked Fergus.

"We know that Claire acquired some information from Forrest, who to have such sensitive information must be working very close to Carter. We know that Josh received this information from Claire which forms the basis of his theory. We know he has since disappeared which helps corroborate his theories to a certain extent. We have no proof as to who kidnapped Claire although the chances are pretty good it was Carter. Which means he was up to no good but we can't link him with the money laundering, if that was what it was."

"So what you are saying is that we have no proof to link Carter to any crime."

"Nothing except the stolen documents, but then the Bank and his lawyers advised him that they were legal. At the moment we can't get him for anything."

"And if we can they will hurt Claire."

"That would seem likely."

"I think we should bring in the police."

"They're already involved."

"What! I thought you promised Claire not to involve them."

"I didn't tell them about her. They're investigating Josh's disappearance. I told you about it, didn't I?"

"Now that you mention it..."

"Wake up Fergus, keep up."

"Sorry, its too early."

David Murray

"There's one more lead," said a slightly exasperated Lara as Fergus looked up from his breakfast nodding. "And if I'm right, Carter has just made his first mistake."

*****

The door plaque was discreet and read "Greenhalgh Limited". The building was not a three a penny concrete monstrosity, rather a Tudor Cottage of some few hundred years age. It sat perched by the river Thames in Henley, a town near London, more famous for its rowing regatta than its financial prowess. A sleepy town for fifty one weeks of the year, the exception being seven days of drunken revelry that constitutes a City exodus of sorts, the worst excesses of champagne bars transposed on semi-rural beauty. That was the week that Walter Greenhalgh took his annual holiday. Back to the Minnesota suburb where he was born and raised. For the rest of the year he preferred his simple life as an English gent.

Given his reputation for corporate raiding, Greenhalgh was not an extravagant man. His Spartan office demonstrated the moral that companies are run for their investors rather than their managers. His own investors backed these values with billions of pounds. Managers of firms who ignored these values found themselves bought out. The company benefited as Greenhalgh slashed the corporate jet, expense accounts, taxis and travel budgets. Non-core executive toy businesses were sold off and the company's shareholders did rather well. Life became a good deal tougher for those managers fortunate enough to stay.

Today was a non-eventful day for Greenhalgh, as were most days. He had bought an option to sell shares in a medium sized retail outfit, Boxco, that had just launched an expensive bid for a rival. Shares he did not own. He would buy the shares he needed to sell once the price fell. If indeed it did fall. That was a risk he could live with.

The Boxco take-over deal was not earnings enhancing, merely power enhancing, as he liked to call it. He bet the deal would fail and the shares would become good value. He would make a lot of money, maybe even break-up the company. If there wasn't a Test Match on.

266

The Naked Bank

For the rest of the day he had read the newspapers and then watched recorded highlights of the cricket in Australia. He loved cricket and what it represented. When a game lasted five days a long term strategy was required. Sometimes it worked, sometimes it did not, and sometimes one could not tell. Any game lasting five days without a result grabbed his attention.

Today the Henley calm was shattered. It took approximately thirty seconds for the storm to hit, approximately the time Mac took to walk from her taxi to reception.

"Hello," she shouted into the air. Used to a bevy of attendants meeting her every need, Greenhalgh Limited was unique. There was no one. No doorman, no secretary, no receptionist, no messenger. Not even a friendly dog looking for a pat. "Hello, can I have some attention," she called. Silence. "I wouldn't mind a diet Coke, and a cake would be nice." Nothing. There was only one door and Mac was never shy of putting her best foot forward. Straight into Greenhalgh's office.

"Hello," she called as he turned towards her from his television.

"Can I help you?" he asked.

Now Walter Greenhalgh was a publicity shy individual, rarely interviewed and never photographed. He valued his privacy. He did not want some disgruntled middle manager assaulting him at the local Waitrose. The only people who he met were a few carefully screened investors, usually American, and always very rich. Because of this policy Mac had no idea of Greenhalgh's appearance. She had no appointment and was not expected. Indeed it was only through her extensive network of spies and informants she had even discovered his office location. Standing in front of this unassuming man, dressed in a checked sports jacket and brown trousers, brown trousers for Gods sake - City fashion death - she thought he was the janitor.

"Hello - there's no one on the desk outside you know."

"Yes, I'm aware of that. Janice is at lunch," said Greenhalgh good naturedly, longing to watch the cricket.

"Oh, well. Maybe you can help me."

"Perhaps. Who are you?" He was not rude, merely direct.

David Murray

"I'm Nicola Macintosh. Here for a meeting with Walter Greenhalgh."

"Do you have an appointment?" he asked aware she did not.

"He's expecting me," said Mac wishing to get past this antiquated sentry and meet Greenhalgh. "Have I come to the right place?" There were no other doors and the office was not that of a billionaire.

"Oh yes, you have, you have. May I ask what your business is with Mr Greenhalgh?" The speaker was beginning to enjoy his home field advantage. He always played at home.

"Its confidential. For his ears only. Is there any chance of a Diet Coke and something to eat?"

"Well, Mac, if I may call you that. That is what you're known as, at least in the papers?" She nodded. "Please have a seat and I'll see what I can rustle up." He spoke with a craggy wisdom, a guardian of take-over truth. Mac's stomach was too preoccupied to recognise this.

She sat herself in the faded armchair, across from the television, as the man stepped outside. She looked at the cricket for a moment and wondered why they were playing in the winter. She did not understand, or have time, for such trivialities. With nothing else in the room, her eye constantly wandered back to the television, drawn, if nothing else, by the tall bronzed cricketers whom she quickly decided could not be English.

The door opened and a head popped round the door. Janice. "Have you seen Walter?" she asked.

"No, I'm waiting for him to arrive."

"Oh, if I see him, I'll let him know you're here. He should be about somewhere." The door closed.

Mac thought for a moment. Her gigantic brain placed nourishment to one side and began to tick...If there were only two rooms....She stood and looked across at a table placed by the window, barely noticing the magnificent view across the Thames. A photo on the desk showed the old man and Margaret Thatcher. Another with George Bush. A well connected janitor.

Mac rushed to the door to halt her order. As she opened it, Greenhalgh entered with a tray, accepting her unintentionally polite gesture.

The Naked Bank

"Thank you. I could only find some doughnuts. I hope that's OK?"

"Yes, thank you, Mr Greenhalgh."

He smiled. "So I see you've discovered my little secret." Sensing discomfort, he sought to reassure. "Don't worry, I haven't had any lunch yet. You reminded me I was hungry."

"I'm sorry, I had no idea."

"You're not the first to mistake plainness for lack of authority. I hope you've learnt your lesson."

"I have," said a contrite Mac who recognised the man's skill in gaining the upper hand. It was a rare treat to be bettered. "and would be grateful for some of your valuable time."

"Oh, it's not really that valuable. What brings you all the way out to the home counties then? It wouldn't be something to do with the CRA, or the Bank by any chance."

"It is." Picking up a doughnut, Mac relaxed a little with the comforting feel of sugared food in her hand. "It's about the Bank. The Bank is in play, and as a player I thought there were a few areas of mutual interest."

"Have another doughnut," said Greenhalgh as he switched off the television.

The Naked Bank

January 20

Two days later

Claire was first up at the plate this morning, her first day back at work. Unsure of her position with Forrest Hayden, and indeed unsure of his position within the Bank, she decided to play a straight bat, this mixture of cricket and baseball metaphors reflecting her confused state of mind.

The room was the same. The interrogators, if that was the correct term, were the same. Wenton preferred the word investigator to describe his job. Johnson would have enjoyed 'torturer', but then that was illegal now he was no longer on the force. The stairs were too far from the interview room to use as a convincing excuse for any facial damage.

Claire was not nervous having already faced far worse over the past few days. They even brought her a cup of herbal tea. How could a Bank internal investigation team hope to match a gang of international criminals?

Sitting calmly, her hands on her lap exhibiting no signs of tension, Claire answered the questions directly and truthfully. Yes, she had known the source of the letters and had been involved in seeking out the legal opinion from Black. Yes, she had been responsible for sending copies of these documents out to financial institutions interested in funding the deal. No, she did not see anything wrong with this given the legal opinion. No, she had not operated independently. Both Forrest and Carpenter were fully aware of her activities. Yes, Gross had been involved and was kept informed of all major issues. She did not know Sir Wig's involvement, but was unsure of his role under more normal circumstances. Head of cigar procurement perhaps, she ventured, half tongue in cheek. Department fumigation?

The questioning did not cover Milan, Josh Walker or her kidnapping. They did not learn of Josh's conspiracy theory. There was no reason to, and if they had, she would have been unable to detail any facts, only once having glanced at the document which killed Josh.

When she left, Claire was relieved, her shadowy truth intact. So determined was she to hide the truly embarrassing and painful, she gushed to Johnson her full involvement in the Bank activities. While others were cagey and admitted nothing, she walked straight in off the street and gave Johnson, and particularly Wenton, something they desperately wanted. Someone who freely admitted culpability. Claire was unaware at the time, but she had inadvertently lined herself up for the fall.

*****

Lara was in the mood to stare out the window. Sadly her office was unaccomodating. She made do with a poster of the 'Usual Suspects.' In front of her lay the transcripts of Johnson and Wenton's first two days' interviewing. At this time of the morning they made hazy reading, only invigorated by the effort required to skate around coffee blotches, the result of a half awake arm releasing a tide of caffeine across the dusty desk. Even now the remnants of the dust sludge made working sticky. The cleaner came only twice a week. The dust from the building site down the corridor would pile higher before being relieved.

Checking her coffee for foreign particles, Lara took a swig before gazing again at her imaginary window. She knew she could not win. Either she found nothing, in which case she would be castigated for her naiveté in allowing herself to be manipulated by Mac in the first place, or, as now seemed likely, she would find circumstantial evidence for an improbable international conspiracy.

She placed her feet on the desk and allowed the cheap strip light to permeate her being. Her vision grew fuzzy as she pondered her predicament and the responsibility she owed to Josh Walker and Claire Snow, both of whom had placed their trust in a woman they

The Naked Bank

didn't know. In a woman who had been banished from her accountancy firm for lack of ethical depravity, who had been imposed on a reluctant boss at the Bank of England. A woman who knew one slip up represented career hari-kari. And for some indeterminable reason, she did not seem to mind. A calmness spread from her toes to the tips of her hair, as if the blood from her raised feet was spreading an enlightenment of sorts. She could not explain it. It was as if some greater being had whispered in her ear and told her it really does not matter.

Placing her feet firmly back on the floor, she abandoned such thoughts, taking her eyes from the artificial light, remembering this room possessed no window to the world, and that other people's reputations were dependent upon her efforts. The momentary lack of ambition was disturbing.

There was no time to dwell as an unexpected guest swept into her re-defined consciousness. Always the showman, Mac believed the best entrance was the surprise one. After her encounter with Greenhalgh, she was back to her best. Walking into Lara's office, the door was after all open, she placed herself on a dusty chair unconcerned for her Armarni creation already sporting the stains of egg yolk and donut jam. It was destined for the cleaners and any further dirt accumulation would only grant her better value for money from the overpriced con artist who picked up and delivered her clothes on a very regular basis. The can of Diet Coke in her hand was half empty, or half full in Mac's syntax, as her bottom hit its target.

"Good morning," said Lara to her unusually quiet guest. She welcomed the company but took several seconds to realise the origin of Mac's silence was the remains of two, maybe three, jam donuts simultaneously working their way down her gullet.

"Good morning to you," Mac finally managed. "You must forgive me for my dramatic entrance. It seems your security recognised me from last time and let me in, but if I were you I'd have a word with them. I could have been a terrorist or something." Lara found the image amusing. *'Hang on a second, I'll detonate the bomb once I wipe the jam off my fingers.'* Mac continued, "I have found something out which will interest you. I thought it would be better to discuss it face to face."

275

"About the bank accounts?" asked a hopeful Lara.

"Yep." Mac revelled in her information.

"Well." She was expectant.

"I managed to speak to a well placed source within our Swiss private bank. Would you care to tell me whom this account belongs to?" asked Mac.

"Not just yet - its confidential."

"I see. Well here's something that's very confidential, but of course if it were to aid your investigation it could be validated, eventually, through the international courts."

"Get on with it." said Lara in her most irate Margaret Thatcher voice, before placing her hand over her mouth. "Excuse me, but my fuse it rather short this morning."

"So I see. Funds were deposited in the account in question, considerable funds, four days ago. They were transferred by a Seychelles Trust Company, Foxtrot Trust."

"That's very interesting. Not from the Moscow Chetnik Bank?"

Mac made a mental note of that name. "No. But you may be interested to know that there are four other numbered accounts that Foxtrot has transferred funds into over the past two years."

"Really. Who?"

"As you will know, numbered accounts do not have names associated with them. There is no way of knowing who they belong to. However, two of them have transferred funds to Barracuda and Cluny Trusts respectively, which as you know are the holding companies for Carter's and Bonnier's interests in Icarus."

"So, Foxtrot has allowed them to fund their apparent holding in Icarus. That could mean they are only a front for someone else, someone who really owns Icarus. Moscow Bank perhaps."

"Sorry, I'm a little dense. What's the significance of Moscow Bank?"

It was only fair to share her hunch with Mac. "I have no direct proof, but I believe that Moscow Chetnik Bank is the sole shareholder in Foxtrot Trust, which in turn is funding the shareholdings in Icarus."

"You realise that Moscow Chetnik Bank had its UK banking licence withdrawn under suspicion of money laundering?

The Naked Bank

The Bank of England, you guys, thought it was a front for Russian Mafia money."

"I didn't. They don't tell me anything. Although I didn't ask. So why would Bank Republica own a 20% stake in Moscow Bank?"

"I had no idea they did. It's not disclosed in their accounts."

"How do you know that?"

"I've been looking for ways to attack the Bank to defend CRA, remember."

"And Republica owns a 20% stake in the Bank."

"Exactly. It seems we have a real web of intrigue. One final thing." Mac always enjoyed leaving a tasty tid bit until last. "One of the four accounts was emptied two days ago. Five million Swiss Francs withdrawn in cash."

"Cash - why?"

"Don't ask me - it seems a foolish thing to do, especially as he was caught on the security cameras. And I have the tape." Mac beamed, exhibit A thrust skyward.

Somehow Lara was not surprised. Her VCR was ten years old and untried.

"You do have a copy of this?" she asked fearful of the machine eating the evidence.

"Naturally," said Mac whose secretary was in the process of running off ten.

Lara placed the tape into the video recorder and pressed play. After extensive fiddling she sat back and enjoyed the rather stern face of a man emptying his account into an unremarkable sports bag. The picture could be clearer, the quality was grainy. She strained to recognise the face and then she had it. As he turned to leave he looked at the camera. Mac hit the pause button on the VCR, anticipating the climatic moment. There was no doubt. Lara was looking directly into the slightly distorted eyes of Byron Black.

*****

Help was now needed. Lara felt out of her depth. Confronting Black and hoping he would talk was one thing. Confronting him on her own quite another. To trust someone else meant breaking Claire's trust. There was no other option. The police was out of the question, the last thing her delicate investigation needed was Inspector Jaffe leading the charge. Fergus was compromised. Black knew him and there was no guarantee he would not be dragged into the investigation. Dick Johnson was the answer. An ex-copper, he knew the ropes and would offer her the muscle her own slender frame lacked. A spirit of co-operation between the two investigations. Pool information. Given the circumstances, Lara felt she now had no alternative.

Johnson was due to see Black at Gilbert, Wilkins and Horsefly that afternoon. Wenton's child had the measles and he had eagerly volunteered to stand aside. Lara was on the team, finding herself in the lift next to the fifty-five year old former policeman. He was broad, and looked younger than his years.

"You've got the tape?" he asked for the third time, showing uncharacteristic pre-performance nerves. This was the opening he sought. A small gap, but one he planned to force. There was no Wenton to deflect his best questions, no diplomat whose interests were as much with his paymasters, the Bank, as they were in determining the truth. Johnson felt Gross was hiding behind procedure. If Black would implicate him, then maybe, just maybe, he could nail the big man.

Lara had briefed Johnson and Wenton over the speaker phone. She could hear the smile cracking across Wenton's face when she revealed details of the bank accounts.

"Five Swiss accounts," he mulled. "One belongs to Snow, one to Black. There seems little doubt that two belong to Carter and Bonnier. So who does the fifth belong to?"

"Gross?" suggested Johnson.

"Don't be absurd," retorted his superior. "It could be another Carter employee, another Bank employee, Christine Edgerley or someone else."

"It could be anyone," was Lara's input. "And I think its unfair to lump Claire in with these crooks."

Wenton was firm. "For one thing, we have no evidence that Carter and Bonnier are crooks. For another, all we have is Claire's word that she was kidnapped and the money planted in an account. She could be an accomplice to your theoretical money laundering operation, or maybe she was paid to keep the deal going. Who can say?"

"Look," said an unhappy Lara, "If Claire was involved, why would she pass us the bank account details?"

"Good question. Let's see what Black has to say for himself."

Black was thin, thinner than even his normal. His face was drawn and grey. His hair unkempt, that which had survived being uprooted by nervous and frantic hands.

"Please come in," he said without standing. "I'm afraid I can only offer you instant coffee, our machine exploded at lunchtime." It was not a joke.

"I'm sorry to hear that," said Johnson and he sat without invitation. "I'm Dick Johnson, a member of the internal Bank investigation into the CRA Affair. This is Lara Waters, who heads up the Bank of England investigation. I thought it would be better if you saw us simultaneously as I'm sure you are a busy man. If you have any problem with such an arrangement, we would, of course, be happy to see you in turn."

"No, I have no problem," responded a clearly dispirited Black. "I must add I am perplexed as to what I can offer you."

"Mr Black," said Lara, "it is important for us to speak to all the key players. You are at liberty to refuse but your co-operation is greatly appreciated. You are also entitled to the presence of a solicitor."

"Rest assured, Ms Waters, I'm quite capable of conducting my own defence." He quickly added, "If one is required."

Johnson produced the tape recorders from his briefcase. "It is customary for us to record all our interviews. It creates a formal record. We will send you a copy of the transcript to ensure you are happy with it in due course."

Black grunted his acceptance, familiar with the procedure, having on many occasions sat on the other side of the recorder. He twitched as he lamented former glories, his neck spasms attracting great interest from the former policeman. Body language is a key betrayer of guilt and Black placed a neon sign above his head flashing "Guilty, Guilty." But then Black always twitched so it was fortunate he was not innocent.

Johnson began, keen not to waste time. His opening gambit lacked aggression. "I would be grateful if you could confirm that the legal opinion regarding the documents received from the CRA was your own."

"It was this firm's."

"But you wrote it."

"I signed it although if you ask Miss Edgerley she will confirm its validity. She did most of the background research."

"You are not blaming her, are you?" asked Johnson, unsure from where the man was coming.

"Not at all. I signed the letter. Nothing has convinced me it was the wrong opinion. Have you taken another legal opinion?"

He had not. "I'm afraid I can't comment on that at the moment. I'm sure you understand."

Black nodded.

It was Lara's turn. "Mr Black, how long have you worked for Mr Carter?"

"I do not work for him."

"Try not to be pedantic. We know your firm resigned as legal advisor to Icarus. Personally, in a professional capacity, how long have you known and worked with Mr Carter?"

"Several years. It's impossible to remember exactly. Say, three years."

"And how many deals have you worked on together?"

"Three."

"Including CRA?"

"Yes."

"And what sort of fees, roughly, has your firm received from Carter and his companies."

"If I had to guess, maybe three million pounds."

"That's a lot of money," said Lara, beginning to grow into her new role. "And how much have you received personally?"

Impassivity. "My share of the partnership profits naturally, and a 10% bonus of all fees earned. There are fifty partners, so what does that make it - three hundred and fifty thousand, something like that."

The Naked Bank

Now for the kill. "Sorry, I did not make myself completely clear. How much have you personally received from Mr Carter and his companies. That is not in fees to your firm, but personally into your own bank account?"

"I'm not sure what you're getting at."

"Look Black," said Johnson, "the question is perfectly simple. How much money has Carter given you? How much has he paid into your Swiss Bank account?"

The sledge hammer approach. Black did not crack, though the volume of his voice declined.

"Nothing."

"Could you repeat that louder for the tape?" said Johnson.

"Nothing."

"OK, Black. Let me ask you again whether you would like legal representation. These tapes are admissible in a court of law."

"No." The no was barely a whisper. This time Johnson did not press Black to repeat it.

"I take it you have a VCR, Mr Black." It was Lara's turn. Enough circling.

"Yes." He knew all about video cassettes.

"Perhaps you would like to play this one."

Black looked surprised. "What is it?"

"This is a tape from the security camera at the USB Private Bank in Geneva. You appear making a withdrawal of five million Swiss Francs. Would you care to comment on how such a sum happened to be in your account?"

Deny. Deny. "You must have be mixed up with someone else." The man was cool, although the beads of sweat were beginning to drip.

"Is it hot in here," asked Johnson, "only you seem to be sweating."

"I have 'flu'."

Lara again. "Look, Mr Black. We have video evidence of you making the withdrawal. We know your funds were transferred from an off shore company that also paid money to Carter and Bonnier. We know that money was paid into an account to keep Claire Snow quiet, who was incidentally kidnapped. Know anything about that?"

"No."

"Heard of Josh Walker?" she asked.

"No."

Johnson looked at Lara. Who was Josh Walker? He stored the reference for later.

Lara stood for effect and paced the room. It worked for Perry Mason.

Black remained composed despite the occasional drip from his glazed forehead. "Look unless you can prove anything I think you're just trying to wind me up here. If a security video is all you have, then you have nothing. You can check my passport, there are no stamps."

"Switzerland does not stamp UK passports, Black," said Johnson. We can easily find out if you visited through airline records. It might take some time, and a warrant, but we'll get there. Alternatively we can ask your secretary if she booked you a flight to Geneva."

Black was on weak ground.

"OK, so I was in Geneva. That doesn't mean I went to this bank."

"No it doesn't, but the evidence seems pretty conclusive to me." Johnson was winning.

It was only then Lara noticed the photos on the office walls. There was a familiarity about the diverse group of boats that patterned his working environment. While her brain screamed connection, her eye wandered across their architectural design, wondering what all the fuss was about. Call it intuition, call it intervention of the Gods. Lara felt there was something here. Something significant. It was in defeat she gained victory. Despairing of a subconscious intent on leading her astray, she glanced back towards her prey. As she did, her gaze flicked across a name. The name. The names were all around her, underneath each picture, proudly boasting their heritage, their passion betraying their master.

Both Black and Johnson stopped talking as her interest grew. Waiting for the judgement of Solomon.

"Are these your yachts, Mr Black?" were the words she launched across his bow, breaking the drifting calm.

The Naked Bank

"Yes, I've owned them all at one time or another."

"Really. The names are very interesting." Lara started walking around the outside of the room, as if in an art gallery. "Abagail, Barracuda, Cluny, Dashiell, Eduardo, Foxtrot. All names of off-shore companies we believe have been laundering money. Now you wouldn't know anything about that would you?"

Black was holed beneath the water line. "What do you want from me? A deal?" He had not admitted his role. He was too canny for that. Not while the tape recorder was on.

"Interview terminated for a coffee break." Johnson switched the machine off. "Mr Black. The evidence is steadily mounting up against you. However you are not the main object of our investigation. We need you to testify about who you were working with. In return we can cut you some slack. Can't promise immunity, but you know how the system works."

"Yes...yes, I knew, I knew this day would come. Why? Why did I do it?" He buried his head.

Lara and Johnson looked at each other. Was it an act?

Black raised his head, again in control. "I'll give you a full statement once I've taken some legal advice."

"That's reasonable," said Johnson.

"Tomorrow morning at nine."

"Why not tonight?"

"I'd like to talk to my wife and warn her of what is to come. The scandal won't be easy for her."

"Oh, I don't know," said a relieved and victorious Johnson. "If you co-operate, it may not even make the press."

"You're assuming there is nothing more to tell."

Once again Lara and Johnson looked at each other.

A street is an unwelcoming place to have an argument. As Lara hailed a cab to return her to the Bank of England, Johnson prevented her from opening the door.

"Before you go, perhaps you would tell me who Josh Walker is?"

She had hoped to leave before the subject was raised, trusting to the excitement to bury the passing mention of a name which until now she had neglected to reveal. Her tale of Claire Snow was incomplete, leaving out the missing journalist to simplify events. There was no need to mention Josh.

"Uh, did I not mention him this morning?" she stalled, "I'll tell you later."

Johnson firmly, but politely, held the door for Lara in the closed position. "One moment, mate," he confided to the cabby, putting the Eastender at ease.

"Perhaps you could find a couple of minutes to explain while I'm here."

There was no escape and Lara relented. "Josh is a journalist. Was a journalist. I don't know. He's disappeared. Claire Snow passed him information on the structure of Icarus which he passed onto me using an alias. The falcon. He has not been seen for days and I fear for his safety. I suspect the same people were responsible for his death as for Claire's kidnapping. That's all I know."

"And when were you going to share these messages with me? Anything to do with the names of the boats."

He was sharp. He guessed the imponderables led back to Josh.

"Yes. Come and see me tomorrow morning and I'll explain things fully. There's something I must do first. Before Switzerland closes. You'll have to trust me."

"I hate that word," said Johnson as he opened the taxi door.

*****

Carter did not often enjoy the company of thugs. That is, he did not relish the time in spent in their company, which was unfortunate, for lately he was enjoying their presence on a daily basis. He sat in his Mayfair flat all too aware of Bert, the heavy, placed in the corner of the room, headphones on, listening to the bug placed in Lara Waters' briefcase. A precaution in case damage limitation was deemed necessary.

The flat was typically plush, decked in wallpaper, the cost of which would make even Lord Irvine blush. The carpets were too expensive to walk on. Well, Carter was allowed to, but then his footwear was too expensive to be dirty. The heavies, even Bonnier,

The Naked Bank

were required to leave their shoes at the door. Healthy doses of air freshener kept Bert's foot odour within manageable proportions. He tended to waft his feet around the room when listening to the boredom inducing conversations between Lara and her secretary concerning computers, videos and the winter sales. Now Bert was hardly an intellectual giant, but he could listen to most conversations without stifling a yawn. That was why he was so good. However, he had now been listening to Lara for a day and a half, sleeping when she slept, alerted to any noise by the sound sensitive microphone. That meant any snore, any cough, set his alarm bells ringing. He felt justified in wafting his feet.

"Boss, I think you should hear this," he suddenly said, the first words he had uttered for several hours. Experience taught not to interrupt Mr Carter when listening to Wagner unless absolutely necessary. If Carter judged the intervention unwarranted, a kick up the backside with the boss's patent leather cowboy boots was the minimum reward. Tea cups, plates and once a plastic baseball bat were all past examples of flying objects. Today Bert was relaxed with his judgement.

Carter paused Tannenhausen as the chorus neared its crescendo. He felt confident in Bert given both parties' awareness of his nutcrackers. Bert winced as Carter reached for a walnut, cracking it with the masterful art of a pro.

"This is good, boss," reinforced the much put upon, extremely well paid, and slightly nervous, muscle.

Bert tossed one of the tapes from the double cassette machine which recorded every sound emitted from the lips of Lara Waters. Carter placed it in his ludicrously expensive hi-fi, neglecting to initiate any one of the five alternative sound systems currently at his disposal. He could dampen or amplify, tweak or twist. Or something like that. He settled for 'play'.

It was the pavement conversation. And it revealed Josh Walker's user name, The Falcon. Carter was pleased and replaced the nutcracker on the sidetable.

A much relieved Bert grew more adventurous. "If you re-wind five minutes, boss, you can catch the end of Black's interview. It sounds like he's going to cut a deal."

It was fortunate Carter no longer fingered the nutcracker for at that moment he may have inadvertently hurt himself, such was the intense feeling of rage that surged through his body at the mention of 'Black' and 'deal'. He found the passage and listened, his hands gripping the expensive upholstery of his armchair, fabric which would never quite recover from the shock of Carter's sweaty palms scrunching it like a piece of waste paper, popping the stitches.

"The bastard," screamed Carter. "He's dead."

An inopportune moment for Bonnier to enter the room, forgetting to remove his shoes.

Carter ignored the indiscretion. "Black's going to sell us out."

Bonnier was not surprised. "I guess he values his freedom more than his wife. Shame. Perhaps we should threaten his kids. That would shut him up."

"No. The time is passed for niceties. I've got the journalist's user name. See what information he sent that bitch. We need to clean up. Make sure there are no loose ends."

"Sure," said Bonnier.

"Remove the evidence," thought Bert.

Bonnier logged onto The Falcon's e-mail address and downloaded the files sent to Lara Waters. Printing them, he handed the copy to Carter while reading them himself on the computer screen.

Carter snorted. "If this is all they've got they can't prove a thing."

"Unless Black talks. Or Forrest."

"Black's not going to talk." He looked at Bert. "Make it look like suicide. And Giles, I think you'd better arrange to visit Hayden. Convince him to take a long vacation. He can afford it."

"And if he's unwilling...? He may want to clear his name."

"How can he clear his name? He's fucking guilty. Remind him of his vulnerability."

"With pleasure. And the woman?"

"Leave her. Without Black she has nothing. They can't touch us. Then its time for Plan B."

Bert wondered what plan B was. But then he did not understand plan A.

*****

The Naked Bank

"Mac, its Lara."

"Hi. What's up."

"I've got a lead on the off-shore companies. They were set up by Byron Black for Carter."

"He told you that?"

"No, not exactly. He will tomorrow though."

"I seems I underestimated you. How can I help?"

"Can you go back to your source and see whether USB transferred any funds to any of the off-shore trusts. The money launderers. It might link them back to Carter."

"I've already asked. Anticipation. They'll get back by tomorrow lunch."

"You're good, Mac."

"No kidding. But don't hold your breath. They'd have to be very sloppy to use the same bank. If you can get Black to reveal the other banks they used we might trace the funds, though it will take time."

"What about the money for buying the shares? We must know where that came from"

"I'm ahead of you there. Liberian banks. It's untraceable. We need to work further up the line. Find out who transferred the money to the Liberian banks in the first place. That means names from Black. Or a mistake."

"They've made one already. With Claire."

"Are you sure about that?"

"What do you mean?"

"The money in her account doesn't look good unless you can prove the kidnapping." Mac could. She had the video. That was beside the point.

"You don't think she's going to carry the can do you?"

"This is the City. You don't think Gross or Forthwright are going to take the blame do you? They need a chump. She looks good. If they're really pressed, Hayden and Carpenter will go as well. You're naive if you think otherwise."

"Well I for one will do everything I can to protect her."

"Good luck," said Mac. "I'll get back to you tomorrow."

"Thanks."

David Murray

Lara hung up, fuming as the taxi returned to her house. Then she realised she had left her briefcase in the office. As annoying. It contained all her papers. While she cursed, Bert listened to the office cleaner vacuuming her dusty building with a vigour that both strained both the Hoover and his ears.

*****

Hayden Forrest was technically on gardening leave. After his interview with Johnson and Wenton, he had asked to be relieved of his duties, a request the Bank gladly agreed. He was an embarrassment, his name splashed all over the newspapers as the vanquished foe of Nicola Macintosh . The press blamed him for the whole fiasco. The office knives were out, blaming him for the demise of the department. Business completely dried up, several deals being put on ice by clients nervous of the Bank's reputation. His angry colleagues saw their bonuses withering away. Angry at the Bank for managing things so badly, angry at the Directors who ran for cover the instant the 'shit hit the fan', and angry at Forrest for creating the problem in the first place. An overnight transformation from Big Swinging Dick to major league overhead.

Preferring to avoid the vultures, he retreated to his country cottage, away from the big city. Away from a wife who married him for his money. From his kids who were mocked at school. Away from a press that soon forgot him and pursued the latest Royal Family scandal as if a mere continuation of the inevitable downfall of society. Corporate greed, marriage infidelity. No difference, both sold newspapers.

Now he relaxed, putting this unfortunate event behind him. He would lose his job, probably be suspended by the Securities and Futures Authority. Never working in the city again was an unforeseen mercy. He was alone, friends preferring to be colleagues. Goodbye with a never to be seen again slap on the back. Too busy to be associated with a loser, afraid of looking into their own crystal ball. Alone. Alone with the exception of the local escort agency, whose services were refreshingly honest in comparison with his bygone golden days.

The Naked Bank

The television played a satellite re-run of The Generation Game. He watched as Bruce led the contestants through inane, yet strangely compelling games with a style that justified his title Britain's Mr Entertainment. Hayden sipped his whisky, the third of the young evening, watching the nubile form of Bruce's latest assistant, hoping tonight's company would be as pretty. He knew she would not, not that it mattered. He paid, she stroked his bruised and battered personality.

"...and Carol, who are the next contestants."

Carol was new, or had been when the programme was first recorded, ten years ago. She painstakingly ensured she stood in the correct spot before robotically reciting her cue. *"From Maidstone we have Sheila and Bryan. Sheila is a postmistress and Bryan, her son, is currently out of work."*

Carol retreated allowing Bruce the limelight. If she was the tinsel, he was the fairy on top of the tree. It was evident her auditioning skills lay in areas other than showmanship. Hayden wondered what a faded Carol was doing now. No longer treasured for her looks, perhaps she drew upon a previously untapped reservoir of talent. Perhaps she was washed up, her faded beauty repelling the nouveaux riche she once courted. Perhaps she was happy.

As Bruce began his pre-prepared jokes, only he able to display the kind of spontaneity necessary to fool most of the people, most of the time, the door bell rang.

She was here. Early but no matter. He went to the door.

".....so I understand you once had an embarrassing accident," said Bruce.

He opened the door. "You're early my dear." Only it was not his dear. Nor Carol.

"Yes, Bruce. I was serving in the post office one day..."

It was a tall man, protected from the elements by a black raincoat, wearing a black baseball cap to protect his sunglasses from the rain. It was unusual to wear sunglasses in the dark. Hayden did not dwell upon this thought as the man shot him through the head at close range.

"...when this strange man came in and asked if he could give me his package..." Stunted studio laughter.

"He wanted to give you his package," repeated Bruce so

that slower viewers could appreciate the double entendre.

The cottage was isolated. There was no one to see the stranger drag Forrest from his flat and place him in the boot of a car, stolen half an hour ago from the station car park. The man returned, went inside to check the house, re-emerged and closed the front door behind him. Then drove off.

A matter of minutes later a taxi pulled up, bearing Forrest's companion for the evening. Dolled to the eyeballs, she tottered on her heels to the door, feeling the draft beneath the thin raincoat. Black, which was in fashion. She rang the doorbell. This time only Bruce heard it. She pushed open the door. No one locked their door in this area. A quaint old custom of rural England. As the door swung, there was a click and the cottage was engulfed in exploding flames. Both she and the taxi driver were killed instantly as an intense fireball illuminated the night sky. Bruce lived to fight another day. Carol left at the end of the series to become a presenter on cable television in Arkansas.

*****

What drives a man to despair? A man so driven his entire life is based upon shaky foundations. A life solely dependent upon a career is a life in danger with every turn of the screw. Every turn of the wheel. If that career disappears, there is nothing. Many have family to fall back on, though if that family is part of their career aspirations, built on ambition rather than love, it will also fail. If marriage is for money, or for status, or to fit the mould, it depends upon the success of the overall strategy to survive. When simultaneously attacked by adultery and loss of career there is no chance.

Black sat in his lounge. He slugged the same brand of whisky which moments earlier Forrest had sipped. The room was quiet, the television unplugged. The second video of the day turning Black from the moving image forever. You might surmise forever is a long time for a middle aged man. In this case it was half an hour, an hour, the exact duration irrelevant. Enough to compose himself before the inevitable house call by the Angel of Death.

The Naked Bank

Our disgraced adulterer chose this time to pen his memoirs. They would never be published, though if a publisher learnt the full story behind them, a moderate bidding war for their rights might ensue. Perhaps Kevin Spacey could play his role in the film. Candice Bergen would be his wife, her influence little seen, but felt through the force of his actions. Actions yet to come. Robert De Niro would play Carter, his portrayal in the Godfather an adequate preparation. And Christine, the temptress. Sandra Bullock? Sharon Stone? Kim Bassinger? Helena Bonham Carter? She would do. If, as a reader you are wondering where the image of Ms Bonham Carter came from, rest assured, you have not misunderstood the character of Christine. She is nothing like Ms Carter with the exception of both occasionally wearing a corset. Ms Carter in every film she has ever made, Christine, tonight, in a desire to please her lover. That grand entrance only moments away.

Returning to the memoirs, they were short, and to the point. A suicide note of sorts. No, definitely a suicide note, outlining his infidelity, his legal indiscretion and how he would rather die than bring further dishonour to the family name by dragging it through the courts in return for a sleazy deal to keep him out of prison. He was bitter. Bitter of his wife's requirement for a pre-nuptial agreement, his lack of financial independence forcing him into the clutches of Carter. Bitter of Carter for placing him in this fatal position. And bitter of his temptress, Christine, the marriage wrecker. They would all suffer. His letter told all. Enough to send Carter and Bonnier down for good. Enough to shame Christine into leaving the firm, unemployable. Enough to form guilt in the mind of his wife who was too interested in playing with her horses to spend any time in London. To be around would have removed temptation.

He signed the page with his customary flourish, perhaps even with more of a loop in the 'l' of 'Black' than usual. Placing the letter on his desk he saw no need to re-read it.

Finishing his drink with a double gulp, he glanced at his watch. Seven thirty precisely. He walked to the door and prepared to open it. On cue the knocker rapped. Christine, as punctual as a Swiss clock. As reliable as a Swiss security camera. How could she allow Carter to place a video camera in her flat? Not just one either, judging by the numerous angles on the film he had recently finished watching for a second time. He could have mistaken it for a porno film. If he had not been the male lead. But then there was dialogue, albeit the bland and sickly sweet whispers of new lovers, an annoying distraction for any true flesh-flick aficionado.

As these images swirled, Christine was in the hall, leading him upstairs towards the bedroom. It was a blur and he followed, no longer feeling anger, only the vague inevitability of it all.

The bedroom was large, fluffy and adorned with the type of family photos which would in normal circumstances make indiscretion impossible. In this case, the sight of his framed wife looking on only further helped distort Black's thoughts and feelings, driving him to the act of selfish depravity that was to come. What drives a man to damage another human being for life, to scar them permanently with a sense of guilt and despair? To plant seeds of doubt in their own right to exist? Who can say.

Christine led Black into the bedroom and placed him on the bed, correctly recognising his passivity as depression. Incorrectly diagnosing the cause.

"You've been under pressure too much lately, Byron," she said, "You need cheering up."

Christine removed her raincoat and flung it across the room, upsetting a table lamp in the process.

"Oh, I'm sorry," she offered.

Black said nothing and she took it for forgiveness.

"Are you going to help me with my clothes?" she coyly asked, perceiving it as rhetorical.

"No, my dear," said Black. "I am going to pay you to strip. Does that turn you on?"

Christine could not say that it did. Despite her image, she was sensitive to his feelings. She was not a performer, a plaything. But she loved him so she humoured her lover, "Yes."

If one word was worth an academy award it was that one. This time there was no film to record her performance.

Black reached under the bed and pulled out a black sports bag. Placing it on his knee, he unzipped it and pulled out a wodge of bank notes.

The Naked Bank

"These are Swiss Francs, Christine. They were given to me for services rendered. I think its only fitting that I share them with you. For services rendered."

Christine was impressed by the cash. She ignored the words. He was upset. "What do you want me to do?" she whispered.

"Remove your jacket."

Which she did with less than total reluctance. He tossed the notes at her feet. "That's worth twenty thousand francs. Now your skirt."

Another pile of cash found its way to her shoes.

The process continued. One item of clothing. One pile of cash. For her underwear, which included the aforementioned corset, the stakes were raised. Stockings received two bundles. The corset four, plus another couple due to the length of time it took to remove it. Five for her panties. Christine stood naked, in a pile of money. Black threw the rest at her.

"What do you think of that then?" He was aggressive, drunk, not himself.

Christine was perplexed. "Where did you get this money from? Are you all right?" Perplexed and concerned.

"Never better. Have you ever fancied sex on a bed of cash? It's a fantasy of mine. An ambition before I die."

Now he was talking.

Black tossed the bag on the floor and began to strip off. Christine knelt in the cash and watched. It did not feel right. Nothing felt right.

Then he was on top of her, his wiry frame always surprising her with its agility. He kissed her and she let him, any notion of passion strangely gone. She just wanted to finish and leave. The romance of the affair disappeared with her striptease, the vulgarity of payment helped her understand what she meant to Black. No more than a thing to be bought. No different to one of his companies, she was a commodity, her reward for gratifying him a pile of cash, and a promotion to partner. It stank. He kissed her and tasted foul. An altered taste, which she could not place. With hindsight, the taste of death.

His penis failed and she felt relief. He began to cry. "Goodbye Julia," he sobbed, and Christine's intuition told her to get out. He was sobbing the name of his wife and she was underneath, pinned, on top of a pile of cash. What is wrong with this image? She did not notice him reaching for the bag, nor reach for her revolver. He kissed her again and she shut her eyes, inhaling his last breath.

Bang. A tremendous noise. For a moment she thought she was dead. Her heart stopped for two beats. There was blood in her mouth. There were brains over her face. He was heavy, heavier than normal, and after several seconds she realised he was dead. A smoking gun thumped to the ground. He was heavy. She pushed him off with effort, the money providing no purchase, rolling him onto his back. His eyes stared at her. Blood streamed from his mouth and the back of his head was on the wall. There was blood all over her, all over the money all over the carpet. All over her clothes. She knelt in the money and looked at him, in horror. He could have shot her. Why? Why did he kill himself? And then suddenly, without warning, she burst into uncontrollable sobs.

Bert entered the property, quietly picking the lock. He wore latex gloves and carried a small silenced revolver in his hand. He looked into the lounge and noticed the note. A quick scan told him it could never be published. He placed it in his inside pocket, along with the pad on which it was written, taking no chances with impressions. He moved to the stairs and heard talking.

For a big man, he moved silently up, gun poised. Reaching the bedroom door he was faced with the decadent scene. Black was on top of a naked woman, rolling in a pile of money. A gun in Black's hand. Bert raised his own weapon, something Black was clearly struggling to do, and prepared to fire. Black looked up and saw him and smiled. He then kissed the woman, raised his gun and shot himself in the head. The action took Bert as much by surprise as Christine. He stood in the doorway and watched as Christine rolled the body over and stared in disbelief. And then she began to cry, all the time facing away from the door. If she had turned, she would have seen him, and he would have killed her. She did not and he retreated, aware that the sound of the gun would soon attract company. He returned to the ground floor, and hearing footsteps, left through the back door. His job done, his conscience clear. He smiled.

The Naked Bank

The door was unlocked. Claire was worried, having heard the bang. Growing up in the country she recognised the sound of a gun. And now the door was open. Fearing the worst she did not announce her presence as she entered. Her previous experience made her rightly paranoid. She crouched catlike by the door in the semi darkness listening for anything. There was only sobbing from upstairs. It was not Black so she assumed it was Christine. Running up the stairs she stumbled across the scene. A dead, naked man, with half his head missing. Blood everywhere and Christine, also naked, sobbing in the middle of a pile of pink money.

Claire felt remarkably level headed. "Christine?" she ventured.

The woman raised her head and turned to see Claire.

"He shot himself. We were making love and he shot himself."

Unsure what to do she went over to her friend and hugged her, trying to offer her strength.

"Why? Why?" Christine kept repeating.

After several minutes of sobs, Claire gently pulled back. Totally calm. Almost out of body.

"I'm going to call the police now. You'd better get dressed."

"Yes," said Christine, "you're right."

As Claire stood and dialled '999', Christine returned to her sobs, using the notes as a handkerchief. Claire looked at her distraught friend and mourned for her in much the same way as she mourned for herself.

The Naked Bank

February

The worst snow storms for several years would normally have postponed the divisional meeting for a least a day. The roads were impassable, with the exception of those directors able to blood their urban Land Rover Discoveries in conditions other than on tarmac. Public transport was infrequent. Taxis in hiding.

Wilfred Kite, Assistant Director in charge of Administration, or ADA, was in his element. His title was permanently attached to his name, so much so that his official Bank initials were WAKADA. Rumour had it that the 'A' which was his middle Christening initial, stood for asshole, and this had never been denied. Those who did not refer to him as Captain Peacock, pea brain, fuckwit, dildo breath, dickhead, or the jerk that lived in the corner, their numbers in the low single figures, called him Wakada, after a long forgotten Jedi knight. With no part to play in the new Star Wars movie, Wakada resolved to use his powers in the pursuit of a smooth and efficient administrative system for the department. The Force truly does move in mysterious ways.

Wakada Kite had spent the entire morning cajoling, barracking, intimidating and sweet talking the Department's staff out of their cosy flats, houses and love nests and into the office. His methodology varied with both the grade of the recipient and his perceived status within the new regime. Kite was advantaged for he was held in Carpenter's confidence. Others suspected resignations upon completion of the internal review. Kite held firm intelligence, having arranged accommodation for Carpenter's successor. Kite and Carpenter had never particularly liked each other, yet it was with a tinge of sadness that Kite dwelt on his boss's probable passing. Only a tinge, for the sweep of the Bank's broom would surely return the department to the old guard, the old methods of who you know, rather than how hard you work. It was these attributes that secured Kite his job in the first place. His Jedi powers on the wain, he craved for the freedom to see out his remaining working days the old fashioned way. Expense lunches, fine wines and a desk to snooze at.

But then Wakada was to be made redundant three months later, and it was ironic that his last meaningful act, some would say his only meaningful act, was in gathering the troops to the beginning of the end.

The meeting was called at short notice. No one was in doubt about its purpose and all would have striven to attend without Kite's forceful inducements. The conference room was full, filled with the still whisper of expectation. For the past month the department had resembled a rumour factory, exhibiting the qualities of the finest tabloid journalists. The lack of tangible work offered the teams nothing to occupy themselves with save lunchtime speculation, beery after work contemplation, daytime day dreaming. Activity on the floor of the department confined to an on-going CRA post mortem, often tied to the latest protagonist being interviewed. The directors warily moved around touting their leadership potential, oblivious to the requisite qualities of leadership. The greater the campaign, the more their chances receded, the more they were mocked behind their backs, or in one or two cases, to their faces.

The most important attribute for leadership success was to win business. Personal skills, important in the political world of Westminster, mattered not one jot in the reality of money making. Staff happiness was not influenced by a pat on the back, a word of encouragement. It was solely dependent on bonuses. The powers that selected Carpenter's successor were all too aware of the need to generate their own bonuses. They needed a born again salesman, not a mummified relic.

It was under this cloud that every member of the department arrived at the Bank, prepared to endorse whatever was thrust upon them. The heat of the room forced the melting snow all too prevalent on shoes and jackets to steam into the atmosphere, helping accentuate the pressure building within the gathering. The pressure for a resolution of their predicament. They were to be partially satisfied.

The Naked Bank

The directors sat leaden faced in the front row. The youngsters at the back remained quiet, their position the weakest in the room with the exception of one or two senior knife throwers who staked everything on leadership success. The middle management, the driving force of department inertia, were more concerned with next year's bonuses following the calamity of CRA. They would leave for another paper tiger institution if unsatisfied. All possessed impressive resumes, which with an accomplished tongue, was enough to secure a job at one of the many City institutions intent on recruiting mediocre talent from their rivals.

Carpenter entered from a side door, bounding onto the stage with an evangelistic enthusiasm which belied his rumoured depression. This was his final speech, the kind of tragic monologue which all great actors secretly crave. For who would not swap the heroism of Bogie's runway farewell for a life of comfortable happiness? Which male is not drawn to the gallant failure, the satisfaction of dignity and composure in the face of defeat? A sacrifice for the greater cause. Carpenter was such a man, the type who sank with his ship. Facing a collection of individuals with no concept of responsibility, remorse or duty, pursuing only their ambition of power and greed.

"Thank you for coming," said a polite Carpenter who for once was certain of his audience's interest. "You will all be aware of the difficulties we have been in over the past month or so. The internal report was completed and reviewed by the senior Bank management yesterday. In light of its findings, I felt it was best for the morale and direction of the department if I stepped down. As of this morning I resigned my position as Head of Department. I am pleased to say that Henry Jacobs had been appointed in my place and I have every confidence in his ability to take the department forward.

"This may be a shock for some of you. I can honestly say that the department has made great strides over the past two years for which I am immensely proud of the contributions of each and everyone of you. Henry is the right man to take that on to the next stage. I see no reason why we...you...cannot become one of the best corporate finance departments in the City. You must continue to believe in yourselves for you have the talent and dedication. It was an honour to serve with you and I shall miss you all. Unfortunately,

while I can share the vision, I can no longer be part of it. God bless
you all."

There was a tear in Carpenter's eye, and many more in
those facing him, with the exception of the first row. A spontaneous
round of applause greeted the end of Carpenter's reign and he
paused, with dignity, to accept it. The clapping lasted a full minute
before he raised his hand,

"Thank you. I am touched by your support."

And then he left, and Henry Jacob whose presence on the
stage was now fully understood, remained alone, exposed to a
department without a say in his accession, a royal appointment from
above. The decision of a smoke filled room. The election of a Pope.

Fergus sat at the back of the room, one of the department's
untouchables. He watched as Jacob, stood to give his own pep talk, to
answer any questioner bold enough to speak. Fergus was a child of
Carpenter. He had been orphaned without explanation. No one was
told the contents of the internal report, only the consequences.
Hayden Forrest was gone. No one knew his true fate, a gas explosion
destroying his country cottage, two bodies but not his. The press
speculated a faked suicide. Fergus suspected something more
sinister.

Jacob pushed forward his modest belly as he spoke, Fergus
half expecting his flamboyant bow tie to revolve as part of a carefully
rehearsed circus act, designed to reassure the restless natives. The
natives were too stunned to absorb his platitudes. Wondering wither
Carpenter?

The meeting ended with a whimper. No one asked a
question and his staff were dismissed with some dissatisfaction by
the new pontiff. The next day fifteen people were made redundant,
each receiving a black bin bag as thanks for their paltry efforts. With
potential dissenters removed, Jacob gained security, the department
lost its heart. And then there was the Claire Snow story.

*****

Huge office. Cigar smoking big wig, the term big wig
doubly correct. Charles Blackwell was a senior member of the Bank,

The Naked Bank

sitting on its Board, and high profile enough to justify his own supply of Havanas. He also sported a big wig. This was not embarrassing rug syndrome, where the wearer opts for a flat shag designed to loosely blend in with its owner's remaining hair, at least until those strands unilaterally turn grey presenting a picture of multi-coloured thatch. This was more similar to the Michael Jackson look. Not the latter day tangled mop, although Blackwell would surely have been happy with such a pseudo-sex god look, a sort of older Antonio Bandaras. No, this hair piece had its roots in the seventies, a cross between Leo Sayer and Crystal Tips and Alastair, The Professionals meets Paul Michael Glasier. A fashion statement abandoned in time.

The rest of his dress was no more modern, perpetually awaiting a seventies revival. Kipper tie, wide lapels and bell bottomed suit might one day return after all the sane people have been taken out and shot. This begs the question as to Blackwell's own sanity. The suit and hair piece date to the day when his wife left him, indignant at the house reeking of tobacco, and her husband's foreign trips to the more notorious night-spots of Europe and the Far East. His suits and ties remained in mourning, fixed in style at that instant, the woman who might replace the wardrobe long gone. Her revenge forever impregnated on the lapel of Blackwell. "Big swinging dick", she snorted to those that would listen. "More like Bite Sized Cocktail Gerkin." There was no chance of reconciliation with a woman who so attacked his corporate machismo.

Claire Snow, despite her two years at the Bank, had never met this man, and had barely heard of him. With Sir Wig and Jonathan Gross choosing to lay low for a while, not wishing to be accused of hypocrisy while the bin bags flew, Blackwell was thrust to the fore. "Time to earn your money, old man," was Sir Wig's encouragement when Blackwell protested. Fortunately, Blackwell was unaware of the full circumstances surrounding his rather unpleasant task, otherwise even his enormous salary would have been insufficient to cover his conscience.

Claire entered the room, which while not quite resembling the giant aeroplane assembly factory at Boeing, was almost as large as her entire department. In fact, it took her some moments to identify Blackwell at the far end of the room, drawn to his presence by the luminous glow of his tie. There was no carpet, Blackwell's pile quotient having been sacrificed to his head. The bare wooden floor gave the long walk to his desk an ominous feel. Claire clicked her way towards his desk, feeling as if she was paying the headmaster a visit. She had no idea of the fate that awaited her and so while nervous was unworried. How threatening could a man with such crazy hair truly be?

As so often happens on formal occasions, she was no more than half way down the road to Blackwell when her bottom began to itch. Now this sounds ridiculous, but itchy bottom syndrome can strike anyone, no matter how dignified, at any time. It is most annoying being impossible to cure. More or less anywhere else can be discreetly scratched. When a violent itch breaks out in the derriere region there is nothing one can do in polite company. The nuisance had the advantage of taking her mind off why she had been summoned to see this strange man, so much so that she increased her pace, soon able to plant her offending appendage on the thankfully hard chair placed in front of Blackwell's desk. Designed to create maximum discomfort for its occupier, in Claire's case, as she pleasurably squirmed on its harsh surface, it had the opposite effect.

"Glad you could come at such short notice," said Blackwell without any sincerity.

Claire nodded, relieved that her itch, at least temporarily, was gone.

"This whole business about the CRA has been very unfortunate, very unfortunate indeed. We are always sad to lose people of the calibre of Ian Carpenter and Hayden Forrest."

"Have you heard anything from Hayden recently?"

"Uh, no. As I was saying, this whole business is very unfortunate. Members of the Board were able to review the internal report yesterday and it makes very sad reading."

"When can I see it?" asked Claire interrupting the great man.

"I'm afraid you cannot. It is not for public consumption."

"But I am surely entitled to see what it says about me?"

"No, it is not Bank policy."

"I see."

The Naked Bank

"However, I can tell you some of what was in the report."

"Good," said Claire who now moved to the edge of the seat.

"It is very critical of you, I'm sorry to say. It seems your conduct in determining the legality of the documents fell short of that expected."

"But..."

"Let me finish young lady. A little contriteness is called for here. Your role in the distribution of these documents, as well as your receipt of a payment from an unidentified offshore source, places severe question marks over your character."

Claire could not believe this.

He continued, "In view of the scandal this placed the Bank in, and our desire to draw a line under the whole affair," Blackwell cleared his throat feeling very much the messenger. "I'm afraid we're going to have to let you go."

"Sorry?"

"Very much so."

"No, I mean did I hear you right? You are sacking me?"

Blackwell hated being put on the spot. "Technically, yes."

"What do you mean technically. You either are or you are not?"

"Well, for both yourself and the Bank it would be better if you resigned."

"I bet it would. Well you can forget it."

"I see." Blackwell was authorised to deal. He had not dealt for twenty years and it excited him. His authority ran to one hundred thousand pounds. "In return for your resignation, and your agreement not to speak to the press, we are prepared to offer you a sizeable cash inducement."

Claire was steaming. "How sizeable?"

"Fifty thousand."

"Forget it." Claire stood to leave, unaware of the effectiveness of her implicit negotiation on the nerves of the old man.

"OK, one hundred thousand. That's the most I can offer."

Claire turned to look at him. She was angry but still possessed her sense of perspective, which was why she was a better

305

banker than Blackwell. She was being fired while he lolled around contemplating how to spend his over-sized pay packet.

"One hundred and fifty and you have a deal."

Blackwell gulped. He was out of his league. "One moment please." He lifted the phone. "You heard that?....OK, fine." Replacing the phone, "You have a deal."

Claire was livid. "Who's been eavesdropping on me? You bastards. That will cost you another hundred thousand, or I go to the press today."

She turned on her heel, gave her bottom a really good scratch, and marched out.

Half an hour later and she was hiding in the toilet. A feature of her life, she had begun to find the cubicled walls of the ladies strangely reassuring. They were looking for her, trying to toss her off the premises. It was her last little laugh to give the security staff the run around. It would not be long before they put two and two together. As far as she was aware, there was no video camera to track her within the pink pampered sanctity of the powder room. As she stretched out as best as possible on the lowered toilet seat, she admired the plush carpet that could only adorn a ladies. There was no carpet in the gents. No range of cosmetics and oils for the enjoyment of the Bank's male's staff. No perfumed hand towels. No hairdryers or wardrobe for the storing of coats and evening wear. No such thing as equal treatment.

A rap on the door told her the game was up. It was Miss Bu Gerrie, her tenaciousness having tracked down the corporate finance fugitive.

"Claire, I know you are in there. Why don't you come out before I have to do something you might regret."

Claire laughed and the personnel woman. "And exactly what can you do to frighten me, you old bat."

"Uh, uh," flustered the preening peahen. "Come out or I'll get security in here."

Claire recognised it was time to end her own childishness, and flushed the toilet for effect. Opening the door she was faced by a triumphant Bu Gerrie. The woman's bony fingers clamped Claire's wrist and there was no hope of escape.

The Naked Bank

"If you will come with me, Miss Snow, I can have the pleasure of despatching you from the premises."

The rest of the department was treated to the sight of Miss Bu Gerrie hauling Claire out of the toilets and to the bank of lifts, where predictably they had to wait several minutes.

Claire felt like bashing the woman, but restrained herself, not wishing to accumulate an assault charge on top of everything else.

"The greatest trick the devil ever pulled was convincing the world he didn't exist," Claire said.

"What?"

"Kevin Spacey, the Usual Suspects, you should see it Miss Buggery."

And then she was in the lift and then on the street.

"Goodness knows why, but the compensation you requested will be deposited in your account today. And good riddance to you Miss Snow. I never did like your sort."

Miss Bu Gerrie turned with a sneer and left Claire, outside, in the cold.

"How can you shoot the Devil in the back? What if you miss?"

*****

A mile away, another office, a similar scene. John Greggor's room was small, with carpet and comfortable chairs. His hair was his own and his suit belonged to this decade. It was Lara's turn to sit in front of her boss's desk, though this time the initiative was hers. She knew the contents of her own report. But once again the power, and the smugness, rested with her male superior.

"First, let me say that me and the Committee were very impressed by the work that clearly went into your report. You uncovered far more than we anticipated when the investigation was launched. The Committee takes your allegations very seriously and feels there is much substance behind them. However, we feel the investigation should not be taken any further."

Lara's surprise was as great as Claire's.

"I'm sorry."

David Murray

"You see there is no proof for a criminal investigation. Think about it. Byron Black, your most credible witness killed himself.....

Lara remembered the evening well. Inspector Jaffe rang her at two in the morning with the news.

"I have some bad news."

Why else would he ring except to tell her Josh had been found? There was a body, the wrong body.

"....there is still no trace of Josh Walker, the man who can validate the source of information. The only witness is Claire Snow who is discredited by her role in the affair. Her alleged source of the material is Hayden Forrest, a man who has also disappeared."

"Don't you find it odd that anyone who can progress the investigation dies, conveniently disappears or is implicated in the plot, no matter how spuriously, and is therefore ruled out as a credible?"

"There does seem to be a series of unfortunate co-incidences."

Snort from Lara.

"We know that some funds were transferred from an off shore company to Swiss Bank accounts. As you know, there is no chance of tracing these funds since we have no jurisdiction to investigate Moscow Chetnik Bank, the alleged source of these funds, though again there is no evidence. Likewise if Icarus's funds originated from off-shore what does that prove?"

"Surely there is enough to continue the investigation. These are serious allegations of money laundering and the proof seems pretty conclusive to me."

"Your report makes that abundantly obvious. There is a very fine line between proof and speculation and your theory swings wildly towards the latter. London has a reputation to maintain as a solid financial centre. If we investigated every alleged money laundering case, half the banks in the City would be involved. And we couldn't have that now, could we? Each takes up huge resources and each is virtually impossible to prove, and potentially damaging to the institution in question. Must I say more?"

"So you are happy to sweep it under the carpet?"

The Naked Bank

"No, not quite. Steps will be taken which may become clear to you in the near future. In the meantime, you are to receive a commendation for the quality of your work. You will not leave empty handed."

"Leave?" Lara was confused. Her report was not to be followed up yet she was to receive a commendation. She received a commendation but was being kicked out? Apparent contradiction layered on contradiction.

Greggor noted her confusion and smiled smugly. He understood the full situation. She never would.

"Yes leave. Your firm has requested your immediate return. We are naturally sorry to see some one of your ability go, but you are, after all, under contract to your firm. There is a permanent job here if you prefer, but I can't say we can match your new remuneration package."

"New?"

"Yes, it seems you are to become a partner."

*****

Lunch at her club. Mac tucking into Roast Lamb carved from the trolley, sipping her fourth Diet Coke. With her second helping rapidly disappearing, she anticipated dessert, as much as you could eat from a selection of fifteen exquisite choices.

Her guest was distracted from his own grilled sole and mineral water, which was fortunate for while healthy, it was not filling. Greggor had been set a goal to lose half a stone to lose by Easter, and his wife was growing impatient at his feeble one pound loss to date. A man under pressure salivated at the sight of Mac's satisfied appetite.

"Perhaps you would like to get to the point before dessert," munched Mac, "I hate to be distracted during the main course of the day."

Greggor, filled with fear that he witnessed only the aperitif, wolfed a mouthful of fish, and gathered his thoughts.

"It was an unexpected surprise to receive your message. For several days we've been mulling over the Bank situation. Something needs to be done to resolve the situation. Your solution has our full

309

support. We are, however, a little worried about the vehicle you intend to use."

"Icarus?"

"Precisely."

"Let me explain." Mac put down her knife and fork. The next few minutes would pay for lunch, for life. "There is a problem with Icarus. It can remain the same, in which case its shares are suspended, a situation that must eventually change. It can be wound up, which given its lack of assets, means a lot of people will lose a lot of money. A difficult situation for the Stock Exchange to explain why the shares were not suspended earlier, and, more to the point, why they were not investigated for unusual share dealing. The liquidator will seek to recover their money by suing everyone left, right and centre. That will include you guys, the Stock Exchange, the auditors, the lawyers and of course the Bank, a scandal which will do little to enhance the Bank's hopefully rejuvenated reputation.

"If Icarus makes the play, all these embarrassments are avoided and the shareholders get their money. The Icarus problem goes away and the Bank has a new owner. Walter Greenhalgh has agreed to sell his stake to Republica Bank, who will inject the necessary capital for Icarus to make the acquisition. Icarus already has Bank of England approval to own a bank, for if you recall you granted it to allow them to buy the CRA's bank. Another good reason for events not to come out into the open, wouldn't you say?"

"That makes sense. And the Bank is taken over, removing the need for us to take confidence sapping measures against its senior management."

"And the alleged money laundering doesn't come into the open, saving your face, and a scandal that really would hurt the City's reputation with the Americans, not to mention hardly impressing our European friends."

"When are you ready to move?"

Mac picked up her knife and fork. "This afternoon." She took another mouthful, but by now it was cold. Pushing her plate to one side, she motioned to the dessert waiter. Always in need of more.

Afternoon tea on the Commons Terrace. Chilly but spectacular, looking across the Thames at the white of London's

The Naked Bank

winter skyline. Neither Mac nor Jack Youngblood MP felt the cold, both ably insulated by a combination of thick coats and all-season blubber. A pair of Blue Whales, floating on a flood of money. The deal would make Mac richer than she could imagine, no longer part of USB she was now in partnership with Walter Greenhalgh, negotiating a deal which made him a lot of money after having mopped up Icarus shares before the deal was announced. Insider dealing at its best. Carter and Republica Bank also owed her a favour, partially repaid by a sizeable deposit in an untraceable bank account in Bermuda (the USB private bank was far too insecure). The CRA had agreed to drop any action against Icarus in return for a few prized assets belonging to the Bank, sold of course by Icarus at a reasonable price. And Youngblood was in the process of being appointed consultant to the new company, in return for his support for the acquisition.

All the bases were covered, as Mac might once have said. As part of her new life she pledged to avoid all baseball metaphors. If cricket was good enough for Greenhalgh then it was certainly sufficient for her.

"Here's to the future," suggested Youngblood as they clinked glasses of well chilled champagne.

"The future," replied Mac.

Youngblood sipped his favourite drink, no longer fearful of being exposed as a champagne socialist. These days it was more dangerous not to be.

"What about Lara Waters? Aren't you afraid she might kick up a fuss?"

"No. She will accept the situation."

"How can you be so sure? She came to see me."

"Really. She is feisty."

"And she gave me a copy of her report and asked me to investigate a cover up."

"And you told her?"

"Why, that naturally I would give it my urgent attention but that it would take several weeks."

"And then?"

"She left, apparently satisfied."

"And you will sit on it?"

311

"Indefinitely. What if she goes to the press?"

"Oh, I don't think she will do that. You see her firm has made her a partner. The same firm that has managed to retain its audit of Icarus with a substantially raised fee. Icarus will be her first client. She will not do anything to damage her new found status. She's a smart girl. A lot smarter than that Hogg Midgely character. Apparently he's been sent packing to Moscow."

"Is that like being sent to Coventry?"

"Yep, but colder."

"He really is going to Moscow?"

"Yes, to head up their mining division. Lots of trips to Siberia I understand. His punishment for a shoddy job on the Dedalus accounts. They had to take some action to keep their regulator happy. He was the fall guy."

"And what of Claire Snow?"

"She's sorted. Enough money to retire. Her family's pretty wealthy. Throw in her Swiss money, which no one has asked for, since no one can prove where it's come from. She's a wealthy woman."

"And Hayden Forrest?"

"I suspect he won't surface again. Best not to ask too many questions, Jack."

"Agreed. How about more champagne?"

*****

The snow covered Hampstead Heath was beautiful. Christine ambled along its edge enjoying the crunch as her boots sank into the virgin whiteness. She wore a head scarf to keep the wind from her ears, sunglasses to protect her eyes from the glare created by a resurgent sun. She was alone.

It was now four weeks since Byron's death. For the first week she had stayed with Claire, unable to cater for herself, stricken with guilt for her lover's death. Claire had been a source of strength, a pillar upon which to spill her soul, her feelings, her wishes. In those days it all came out. Her obsession with work, her desire for success. Her fear of failure, her fear of being alone. Then something happened. It was difficult to say exactly when, but around a week after Byron's death she stopped feeling sorry for herself and turned her pity to Byron. She still did not fully understand why he killed himself. She did see that it was nothing to do with her. He had been lucky to enjoy her company for as long as he did.

Claire told of her own adventure, confiding in a new friend. No matter what Christine experienced, Claire had faced worse. She had lost something which Christine valued more than anything, professional respect. Through no fault of her own, she was stigmatised to save the reputation of her superiors. Bryon had killed himself to save Christine's reputation, or so she believed, and for that she remembered him with fondness.

Attending the funeral, she comforted his wife who was unaware of their affair. One day perhaps she might tell her, but she doubted it. With her secret apparently safe, she became a family friend, in those early days after her recovery often looking after the children. Her penance for the affair, she liked to tell herself, although secretly she enjoyed their company. It even sparked a thought that one day she might have children of her own, a spark quickly extinguished by the human career machine.

Two weeks after the suicide, she returned to her own flat in North London, unaware of the cameras, which had in any case been removed. She did not suspect the tape, which still sat next to the Black's video machine, waiting to be discovered by Julia. That house lay empty and the video lay unwatched, a ticking bomb.

Christine never returned to Gilbert, Wilkins and Horsefly. She was visited at home by the three senior partners, all of whom attempted to persuade her to stay. None of them used the unusual methods employed by the fourth, deceased, senior partner, and none of them were as persuasive.

Her resignation lifted a weight from her mind. A decision which she had dwelt on ever since Byron's death. How could she look at his colleagues after having his brains blown out all over her?

Her wandering brought her to the edge of the park. Looking back her footsteps marked the circular route she walked, bringing her back to the point she entered. There were few cars on the roads and she wandered up the road towards her new office. The snow was wetter here, gritted several times and she concentrated to prevent ending up on her backside. It would not impress to return after lunch on her first day with a wet bottom.

Entering the town house, she waved to the security guard who nodded back. She took the stairs up to the second floor and paused to admire the plaque on her door as she opened it. 'Christine Edgerley, Group Solicitor'. With a rub of the plaque for good luck, she smiled and entered the room, closing the door behind her.

Downstairs the security guard watched on his monitor as she climbed the stairs, flicking to another channel to watch her take her coat off and sit at the desk. She stared out the window at the snowy scene. Bert smiled at the black and white image and whistled. Giles Bonnier knew how to pick them.

*****

Lara looked up as her assistant entered.

"You asked me to remind you about your lunch appointment," said Fifi, still slightly uncomfortable with her new boss.

"Thank you Fifi."

The woman remained in the doorway.

"Is there anything I can do for you?" Lara asked, herself uncomfortable with the position.

"Uh, yes. Is it all right if I leave early today? I have an aqua aerobics class."

"Have you finished your work?"

"No."

"Then I suggest you attend a later class. I take it there is one?"

"Yes," said a sheepish Fifi, "but there's a really hunky guy taking the early class." She appealed to Lara's sense of fair play.

Lara looked at the dipsy girl. She was in a good mood, she was meeting Fergus for lunch. "OK, just this once."

"Thanks," smiled her assistant.

"Oh, and Fifi. I am a reasonable person but I expect more than Hogg."

"Yes, Lara. So do I."

The Naked Bank

It was the same Italian restaurant. It had become their Italian restaurant, meeting every couple of days to discuss the latest events. Today they were the only customers. Anyone else and Luigi would not have opened. Lara and Fergus were his most regular patrons.

"They want me to leave," said Fergus.

"No."

"Made me an offer I couldn't refuse. Seems I don't fit in with the re-established old guard. I won't have to work for a while. I might travel for a while."

"You don't seem the travelling type.

"No...perhaps I'll find another job."

"Thought about returning to accountancy? You could work for us."

"Not really. I quite fancy a job helping people. Maybe in a charity or something. I've had enough corporate intrigue to last a lifetime....You heard the Bank has been bought out. By Icarus."

"Yes, they're my clients now, remember."

"Mmm. They made you an offer you could not refuse."

"I guess...It's only a job," said Lara.

"Sir Wig's to head up the new group. With a pay rise."

"I've heard he's very good."

"You're the only one then. I suppose continuity is important for the Bank's reputation."

"I guess," said Lara still a little embarrassed in Fergus's company by her new role.

They both looked at the menu for several minutes.

"Janet called me today," said Fergus matter of factly.

"Oh, yes. Is that good?" said Lara a little pensively.

"I don't know. She left a message. I haven't decided whether to call her back yet."

Lara looked at him. "Let me know if you don't."

"I might just do that," Fergus said with a glint in his eye.

*****

Daily Herald, February 21
Icarus secures takeover of The Bank

Yesterday The Bank's shareholders approved its takeover by Icarus plc. In one of the most twisted of City deals in recent years, Icarus has bought out the institution which advised it on its ill fated bid for the CRA. Following that fiasco, it was inevitable the Bank would fall prey to another, the surprise was that it was to Icarus, a vehicle set up to buy such undervalued assets. Icarus shares rose £5.50 to close at a new high of £35.

Chairman Sir Wig Forthwright is to stay on at the Bank. While his role is unclear, the protection of his job is likely to have smoothed negotiations between the two parties. In yet another development, Nicola Macintosh, who formerly advised the CRA against Icarus's approaches, was today named as Icarus's primary advisor.

*****

Giles made the long walk to the end of the room with a spring in his step. Mr Vittori bade him sit, a command which he naturally obeyed. Once again the interpreter hovered.

"Mr Vittori wonders whether you have brought the money?"

"I have," said Giles as he handed the briefcase across the desk.

Mr Vittori opened the case and stared inside for a moment, before holding up a set of car keys.

After a swift exchange with his master in Italian, the interpreter asked, "Mr Vittori is unclear as to the significance of the keys. He does not need another car. He would like his money now please."

Giles grinned. "You will find the keys open the van parked outside in the courtyard. I needed something a bit bigger than a briefcase. This time we've done very well. Very well indeed."

THE END